Michael Pye, former S
The Movie Brats (with
King Over the Water. I
between Europe and Ne

ELDORADO

'In Eldorado Michael Pye employs the classic ingredients of the modern best-seller – big money, both old and new, sex in some unusual forms, power, gold, valuting ambition and catastrophe – and somehow stirs them into a mixture that is both original, well-researched and enthralling'
Daily Mail

By the same author

The Movie Brats (with Lynda Myles)
Moguls: Inside the Business of Show Business
The King Over the Water

MICHAEL PYE

Eldorado

PANTHER
Granada Publishing

Panther Books
Granada Publishing Ltd
8 Grafton Street, London W1X 3LA

Published by Panther Books 1985

First published in Great Britain by
Hutchinson & Co. (Publishers) Ltd 1983

ISBN 0-586-06299-8

Printed and bound in Great Britain by
Collins, Glasgow

Set in Times

This book is fiction. The characters, corporations and events are all invented. Only the circumstances are real.

Prologue

He made himself climb the stairs. The bank was shuttered and cold, like a cave. There were tarpaulins over the marble stairs and sawdust where the packers had been. He thought that at least they'd organized the end of the world quite well.

Forty years ago, more, he'd first walked into the bank, a young man joining the quiet, domestic house of Kellerman Unger. It had been a small Dutch bank hunkered down by the Amsterdam canals, managing family money, and lending to the old Dutch empire. He had seen the bank grow and swell and change, seen it butt into London and triumph in New York and then, when it had an awesome power, he had seen Kellerman Unger fail. It had seemed abrupt to outsiders.

It was no longer the failure of one bank. One bank tripped another, and another, in a rush of disaster. The bluff of thirty years was called, and in its wake, money came tumbling down – not just a currency, but the function of money itself. The first day they understood, there had been stolid, honest burghers out on the streets with guns, thinking they could recover the dreams and futures that were irrevocably gone. Outside, he could still hear soft explosions.

Money was dead. There were no more rules. The last legal action with any effect had been the closure order on Kellerman Unger – a formal procedure that started anarchy.

He wanted to remember the great days. He saw the ceremonial portraits, stripped from the wall, now standing at drunken angles on the floor. He wanted a cup of coffee in a china cup. He wanted to be neat and reliable as he always was, and he wanted his strong body and his sharp mind to serve him still. He had to give the last rites to a life that had once been his.

He walked into his office. There were ordinary folders of letters to sign and ordinary legal pads, an ordinary pearl-grey tape recorder. But it no longer added up to the office of the senior executive of a worldwide bank.

He sat down at his desk and took the legal pad and began to write his own name, over and over again. 'Koolhoven, Koolhoven, Koolhoven, Koolhoven . . .'

He had to write a report and explain it all, but his mind circled as a man's mind does in the early morning, asking the same question, seeing the same image over and over. He knew all the obvious points. Banks lent too much money to Third World countries. They depended too much on deposits from the oil kingdoms, and suddenly the oil kingdoms needed their money and the Third World countries couldn't pay. Banks had shuffled out of national laws and into a rarefied world where they policed themselves, sometimes. Banks had started to play wild games that had nothing to do with factories or wealth, everything to do with abstract principles, a gamble on constant confidence. And it went wrong, and that was part of Kellerman Unger's fall.

In New York when he left they were torching the city. There were chemical yellows and reds billowing up from the streets, the tanks ordered out on Fifth Avenue. The City of London was a wasteland, like a long Sunday, and there were barricades in leafy suburban streets; a surprising number of people had guns.

Koolhoven got himself a drink, caught a sight of his face in the cabinet glass and saw, for the first time, an old man. He looked grey and defeated. He remembered a time when he had been young and straight, when the body that hardly dragged him up the stairs seemed capable of anything. He remembered a brilliant beach, a morning in 1950, a day when you could smell the heat rising on the wind.

He was watching children play.

He tried to remember where he had been. It must have been the shade of a line of feathery casuarina's, along the fringe of the beach; their needles were a carpet that stopped the growth of anything else. He had seen gardeners amble across the beach in their wide hats, moving the ink-black seaweed that might mar the sand. He had seen the perfect turquoise water, out to the white line of the reef. And he knew, sitting in his cold bank office and trying to wrestle with figures and generalizations, that the whole awful disaster had begun in this place. The death of money, the cracking of the future, began with a family, a house in the Caribbean, a particular morning.

The children had a game. The boy, Pieter, twelve years old, trickled sand with rapt attention on to the belly of the girl, Marisia, just eight. She squirmed, but neither of them giggled. This was serious play – brother and sister magic. It was the last time they came to the island, the time they finally shut the great house on the beach; but you would hardly guess it.

Through the trees, Koolhoven could see a swirl of silks at the door of the house – the Widow Van Helding, a dazzling woman, a New York model in her time and a star. Koolhoven saw her take the car into town.

The children heard the car pull away and they smiled a little.

Pieter Van Helding, Marisia Van Helding, a girl who was blonde and fine-featured and a boy who was sturdy and graceful, alone on that hot, white beach.

They played until their elder brother Willem appeared, through the arches of shocking red bougainvillaea. He was a gawky boy on great stork legs, waiting for his body to grow round his bones. He liked women as a refuge, a mark of independence. He had memories the other children lacked.

One morning in January 1942, he'd returned from a night at a friend's place and found his father at the door of the great house. Someone had entered during the night, bound the old man and taken him to the door. They set him on the steps, doused him with gasoline and set fire to him, and left him to burn like a candle. Willem saw the blisters and the doctor told him, thoughtlessly, that meant his father had burned alive.

The story had pushed battles off the front pages and the Widow Van Helding returned to the island, Marisia still kicking inside her, for the trial of three black men for murder. In court, the Widow's mind and body were curled around her unborn child, and sometimes she felt a movement, winced a little and smiled. The smiles in the middle of the ugly testimony made people talk.

Marisia knew her father only from a line of photographs in silver frames. She saw him in a felt hat, looking rich in London, looking strong in Kenya, looking ill at ease among black-tie people in Cuernavaca. There was one absurd corporate picture in which he sat, his big body trying to struggle out of formality, while a photographer tried to turn him into what he was: an immensely rich man; a gold prospector who had struck the motherlode; a clever, brusque, sometimes brutal millionaire; a company chairman.

But even Marisia almost remembered what the body had looked like. There were books about the murder, and they showed the old police pictures. People had theories, still: they offered them for money, promising either to publish or hide, and they offered them out of obsessive interest. People always looked twice at the Van Heldings.

When Marisia and Pieter saw Willem, they stopped their game with the sand, dusted themselves down, and walked hand in hand to the open beach. Willem didn't grin; he simply fell in behind them, as though he had been summoned. He looked a great, soft boy.

Koolhoven stirred in his shade. This was wrong, he knew, but he could not guess how. He told himself they were only children, only playing.

Pieter and Marisia sat opposite each other on the sand. Their bodies seemed to match each other as neatly as old lovers; the maids saw that, and were shocked when they walked hand in hand. They were still and perfectly controlled. Both of them had taken from their father one thing: will. Marisia could make things change when she wanted, and Pieter had authority unlike the other white boys on the island, something that came from himself, not from his kin or sex or money.

All this the maids had tried to explain to Koolhoven once. He did not want to understand.

Pieter pulled a red-handled Swiss Army knife from his pocket and laid it on the sand, blades extended in a cross.

Willem stood over them, watching. His face was blown a little by breakfast beer; it looked weak and wanton. He took something from his pocket that was furry and alive, something so small you couldn't see fear on its unformed face.

Marisia made seven indentations in the sand in a perfect circle.

Willem was serious, and, more alarmingly, he seemed to take the younger children's game for granted. He handed the little furry thing – a kitten, perhaps – to Pieter.

The kitten lay quiet in Pieter's hand. He took the knife and impaled it with a single, sharp blow, like a surgeon, and set it on the sand to struggle and kick, turning like the hands of a clock between the seven indentations. The sun stunned the kitten quickly. It wasn't a slow death.

Pieter took up the animal and put it in Willem's big hand. He put a short, sharp blade into its belly and pulled. The guts must have spilled on to Willem but he didn't flinch.

Pieter spoke. In memory Koolhoven supplied the words, but he was almost sure he had not been able to hear the boy's soft voice over the sound of the sea. He couldn't swear that Pieter said: 'It's you.'

Koolhoven couldn't stop them. He wasn't that easy with the Widow Van Helding any more and besides, the children had made their own law on the beach. Willem was brushing back a sheaf of wild hair from his eyes, then he stopped; he accepted, passive and alarming.

Pieter held the knife again.

Willem was big enough for tarts and town and beer and cars, and yet he couldn't stand against the children's will.

Marisia began to chant. Koolhoven could hear her high voice with surprising clarity. She was saying: 'Scaredycat, scaredycat, scaredycat . . .'

Pieter spoke softly. He handed the knife to Willem and Willem licked it clean and then he and Marisia stood as Willem shuffled off the beach. At the margins, Willem retched with the taste of blood.

Marisia and Pieter touched hands.

Suddenly they played again – sprinting down the beach, tumbling into the water among the silver-needlefish, and diving between each other's legs. A starched maid, sweating in the sun, came down the beach to call them out of the water and the sun and take them to lunch.

Koolhoven never mentioned that morning to anyone, but he did ask where Willem had gone, and was told he had taken the great tank of a Buick into town.

At three the police came. They had found Willem buried in a wall in the smashed remains of the Buick. There was a smell of rum. There had been a girl with him from the bar but she had walked away for fear of questions, and he had driven the last mile alone. He had spun the wheel deliberately to hit the wall which was the island's strongest, built to keep blacks from coloured in the 1920's.

It was hard to bury Willem on the island. The coral could not be dug and the coffin had to lie surrounded by stone. The Widow wanted a proper burial, and the priest accepted that Willem died accidentally to humour her. They covered him with a little sparse earth and left him.

Then Koolhoven saw the children.

Pieter and Marisia were side by side, paying their last respects to their beloved, departed elder brother. There were no tears. Pieter was proper in a little dark suit and Marisia was in a sombre dress and they held hands. When earth hit the coffin, they turned to each other and smiled. They were patient, understanding smiles.

Koolhoven stared at them. The idea came to him like needles that Willem had been a sacrifice. Pieter and Marisia were celebrating a victory, quietly.

There had been a black girl wandering in the graveyard, quiet until the Widow went away and then shrieking with pain and sorrow. One of Willem's girls from the town Koolhoven supposed, and for a single, brutal moment he wanted her – wanted the same kind of warm escape that Willem used to find, wanted to wipe away the children's little smile, their sense of ordered malice.

There was nothing he could say that would make sense to outsiders, or even to the Widow. He nursed his secret like a malignancy, and it hurt him every time he tolerated, helped, even stirred the later conspiracies of the Van Helding children. It meant he knew that nothing was beyond them, and he couldn't bring himself to say that, even when the children were grown and they had murdered money, and set loose the anger in the city streets where cold and danger roamed.

He parted the window shutters carefully. One of the old canal pleasure boats was bobbing downstream, bouncing from side to side like a slow pinball, its glass dome crazed with bullet holes. On the deck was a huddle of men and women dressed in black, and they were singing to each other a loud, hopeful hymn from the polders. The Elect were going to salvation, and Koolhoven wished he had their certainties. When the boat passed out of sight the oil on the canal was like dull rainbows. There was an explosion. Koolhoven found himself startled back to his desk and his gin and his job.

He must write down what he knew – not just the dull, obvious points he had rehearsed, but the real story. There was a chain between those children on the beach and the breaking of the city outside. He looked up only once before he began to write, and smelled fresh fire, and saw a cloud of light like a firework on an overcast night. The rain came gently, and washed the air clear for a while.

There were no more excuses. No more images. He would make sense of it all, he promised.

1

The Viscount bounced down at Heathrow and settled on the ground like a tired bird. At least, Koolhoven thought, the turboprops didn't fall out of the sky like the Comets, but they made you feel every mile of the journey. Even Amsterdam to London, his regular trip, began to seem like an adventure through clouds and risk.

And London was overcast, grey and practical. Pieter Van Helding shivered a little as he walked down the steps of the plane. Another long day of bloodless people to watch and study, another day in which he would learn but not achieve anything. He felt hobbled by Koolhoven's kindness, resentful that he had no true independence, and he strode for the terminal trying to leave the older man behind. But Koolhoven was strong and not likely to fall back. They crashed through the terminal doors together and made for passport control.

Koolhoven was the teacher, Van Helding the pupil. Koolhoven did the nursing, steering, prompting, and Van Helding simply listened, rarely volunteering an opinion, never speaking out of turn. He watched people with an intensity Koolhoven did not have time to notice or understand – watched, and drew out which man was lying, which had cards yet to play, which knew he was losing. He could sense the flow and the bones of a meeting, and watch the drama work itself out just as he expected. And most curiously, he felt an anger at his endless waiting for power that he never communicated to Koolhoven. It would only be a matter of months, and Georg Van Helding's will would give him a quarter of Kellerman Unger and Marisia the same. Then he would have power over the people who now

now used him as social secretary, assistant, trainee – and sometimes pimp, for the Americans who arrived in Holland to buy up companies and who needed a little warmth, a little shocking before they returned to their small-town proprieties. When Van Helding had power, he would use it as brazenly as he had waited for it patiently. It suited him that nobody knew that, yet.

Koolhoven tended him like a child. The morning of London meetings was dull and routine; Koolhoven proposed an outing. Since Pieter had never seen the gold vaults, they would visit. It was good for Pieter to see how markets worked, what the physical plant of money looked like; the one lesson Koolhoven taught again and again was that the form and the organization of a market can influence how it behaves. The reason bad news stops trading in a share is that the specialists on the floor of the exchange can't cope with a flood of orders. They can't make a market if many people want to buy or sell. The reason commodity prices sometimes dip or soar dizzily has something to do with the bullpen atmosphere where commodities are traded – the roaring, barking, jumping and shoving of the dealers' floor. And the reason the price of gold in 1960 never moved more than a few cents was the discreet morning meetings of the only dealers big enough to profit from such tiny shifts, and the fact that the London market-makers had to call the Bank of England to find out how much they had to sell. Gold had been taken off the market floor, and treated with special reverence. Van Helding should see that, too.

The last morning meeting was at Kleinwort Benson, and the sharp, slim director who offered them sherry looked almost appraisingly at Pieter. Van Helding was sharp enough to know the reason – a calculation before an invitation, in case the scandal of Georg Van Helding's death would make Pieter an awkward guest. But the director evidently thought such considerations unimportant.

'My son,' he said, 'is getting up a small party for his college's Commem. I don't suppose you'd like to join him?'

Pieter smiled.

'I'm afraid I don't quite understand,' he said.

'Of course,' the director said. 'Commems are the college balls at Oxford – at the end of Trinity Term, in a month. Black tie and too much champagne and Swedish au pairs.'

'That sounds very pleasant,' Pieter grinned.

'Then I'll tell Jasper. We're having about a dozen, including the de Grunwald girl, Katherine. I don't know if you know them?'

'Mr Koolhoven has often mentioned them.'

'They are our Paris correspondents,' Koolhoven said. 'I usually deal with Gilles, when he's there.'

'Indeed,' said the Kleinwort director, who had softened noticeably. 'Perhaps another glass of sherry?'

After lunch, Koolhoven took Van Helding to the roadway before the bullion vaults. There was a grey Austin sedan wedged across the street, a gesture at security while a heavy, squat truck went under steel shutters to deliver its load. There was a guard on the door, settled in a stuffy office that smelled of coal fires.

'Not much magic,' Koolhoven said.

The first office was plastered with coy pin-ups and held pallets on which was some heavy matter shrouded in old, torn sacking, and piles of neat white wood boxes, each sealed with red wax and reinforced with metal strips.

'This is the gold,' said their guide. 'As it arrives, and as it leaves us.'

Koolhoven nodded.

Van Helding was walking with a sort of reverence, like a child at a first communion. He thought what a strange matter gold was. You sold shares in steel companies without bringing the drop forges into the marketplace to show. You sold hog bellies and copper without storing it in the basement. But gold was different – it was security in hard times, wealth under the bed. You had to handle it to understand.

Their guide motioned them into a small room with a great steel pole at its centre. They stood quiet for a moment, and then the floor began to sink beneath them, and the smoky, friendly warmth of the room became chilly and sharp. In the vault, there were rows of old-fashioned safes along the wall, and some of them lay open – showing stacks of parcels wrapped in old newspaper, just like market cabbages, unglamorously covered in yesterday's football and gossip and special offers.

Koolhoven wanted Van Helding to be excited, and Van Helding obliged. He asked to handle the gold bars, and stepped forward to an open safe. At first he misjudged the weight of the bar and almost dropped it, and then he began to unwrap it slowly.

It was sickly, a lifeless yellow when he had it on the table, and its surface had been scratched by knives and nails like a monument where tourists leave their marks. Van Helding set it down.

The guide told him to take out more bars. He did so, and unwrapped them, and as the pile grew a little miracle began. Massed together, the gold had a warm orange glow and the imperfections ceased to matter. There were 400-ounce bars for Dubai and Kuwait, and then who knew where; and ten-tolas for Malaysian bazaars; and kilo bars for the retail market in Zurich; and all those fragments took on a life of their own, as though the glory of gold was there. It wasn't hard to imagine distant trade and intrigue – merchants haggling in a souk, or sheiks stacking up physical, immediate wealth. Instead of entries in an account book, this was tangible and solid.

Van Helding began to wrap up the bars again, in old *Daily Heralds*.

'Lovely stuff,' said the guide. 'Wouldn't mind a bit of that myself.'

Koolhoven watched Van Helding as he handled the bars. There was something off key about his look – not awe as Koolhoven had expected, but understanding. Van Helding didn't just handle or value the gold; he was reading it.

'On that,' Koolhoven said, didactically, 'rests the dollar, and world trade.'

'I can see why it fascinates people,' Van Helding said.

As the floor rose around them, a new and prosaic sight appeared – squat handlers shifting the heavy boxes into a truck, and steel shutters ringing down into place. Van Helding's mind raced. He could see the wonder of gold, why it took people's minds and hearts – like valencies in chemistry he thought, gold has hooks that hold to human beings. But it was also a commodity, and the fascination it held for other people was all the more reason to treat it coldly. Van Helding felt immunized by the sight of the ordinary life of the vaults. He would not surrender himself to the bazaar legends. He'd remember sweat, strong tea, coal fires, and pin-ups with long blond hair and crossed legs.

After all, he didn't want wealth that was tangible. He wanted power – and comfort would follow. In a few months he would be owner of a quarter of a major Dutch bank, no need to claw and scheme simply for the money to buy a canalside house or spend winters in the Caribbean. One of the huge advantages of growing up rich is that you can concentrate on what you really want. You know the sometimes glorious things that go with money will follow, or that you have already had them, and that they are not the point.

And besides, an idea was born in his mind.

'The English astonish me,' Koolhoven said. 'They've had the London gold market open only six years, and already it feels traditional.'

'The Americans didn't want them to reopen, did they?'

'No. They still don't, really. The Americans think of gold as a great pile in Fort Knox that keeps the dollar strong. Europeans tend to think of it as a hedge against troubled times or a commodity – personal property, anyway, not the magic that guarantees money. It's an awkward difference of opinion.'

'And the price?'

'Fixed,' Koolhoven said, 'by the Americans largely, and to support their dollar – $35·08 freight on board at London. Of course the price is higher if you want to deal in small lots, like jewellers do. They have to do that in Zurich; London is strictly for the big boys.'

'But if the dollar wasn't quite so secure – if people started to have doubts about it?'

Koolhoven shrugged. 'The Americans still have the gold to manipulate the markets. And it's still the central banks who control the supply. It's pretty much a fixed price, with the London dealers taking their turn on a few cents' difference each day. It's not a market anyone can play.'

Van Helding looked thoughtful. Sure, there were big governments trying to control the price – and the Russians in the background selling gold when they needed hard currency, and the South Africans. But there was also a limited supply and formidable demand. Anyone who was nervous about money wanted gold. The French slept with it. And those dollars, guaranteed by gold, no longer operated just where the American Federal Reserve Bank could control them. Billions had left home for ever – money used to pay for petrol and gasoline from the Gulf, to buy European companies, to help the shattered, blackened ruins of Europe rebuild after the war. All those dollars were in circulation in Europe. In theory, some

European nation could collect up all the dollars in its territory and go to the Americans and present them, demanding gold. There must be enough dollars loose in Europe to dent, if not ruin, the American reserves. So if there was reason to worry about the dollar, about the American economy, then there might be a sudden demand for gold – the kind that central banks can't afford to dam up. Something would give, and the gold price would break away from its secure-seeming mooring.

It was an interesting theory, Van Helding thought. A pity he could hardly put it into practice. When he had his share of the bank, things would be better; for the moment, he might as well be a poor boy – rich on paper, illiquid in practice. No chance to build up a position in gold in London, for example, against the day when the market broke. He hadn't the cash to go on buying.

Koolhoven butted into his thoughts, goat-like, determined that Van Helding should not be too private.

'I think,' he said, 'you're being launched in British society. If you go to that dance, that is.'

Van Helding grinned.

'I could see him having second thoughts while he spoke,' he said. 'He wondered if people would remember Father.'

'They will,' Koolhoven said. 'They remember him in Holland, after all, and in France, and it hasn't hurt you there.'

'At least people are talking,' Van Helding said.

Koolhoven watched him, startled by the remark. He hadn't guessed that would matter to Van Helding. But then there were signs he had missed until recently of just how serious was Van Helding's ambition. He was beginning to think he didn't know the half of it.

'Dinner,' he said, firmly.

The apartment was a dazzle of chrome and steel and mirrors, and even so Marisia Van Helding glittered. She was dressed, more or less, and a wonder – a girl's fresh face above bare back, firm breasts, a body to be touted and promoted. Marisia knew just what was happening and she loved it. She was learning power.

'. . . thinking about going to one of the Californian universities,' said the Widow Van Helding from the far end of a Lucite dining table. 'But I really don't know which one she should choose, Dr Foster.'

Foster was a decent Orientalist, meshed like a bird on lime. He said he was sure that only his own university could do justice to Miss Van Helding, then he blushed, then he became uncomfortably aware that his cock was making a decision his faculty committees would have to ratify.

'Such a pleasant state, California,' said the Widow. 'I always regret that I can't spend longer there each year.'

Like much else the Widow said it was a lie, but said with such impassioned concentration by the speaker that truth hardly mattered. What fascinated men like Dr Foster, and all the others, was the unspoken message that the Widow thought them worthy of undivided attention. They were mesmerized, excited, and the Widow could work on them at her leisure.

But still, the talk of California was a particularly barefaced lie. The Widow was New York and its suburbs – Nantucket, Paris, Gstaad, and the Caribbean. Even while her husband was alive she had lacked enthusiasm for the smart bits of Maine, the hunting country of Virginia and the second house in Palm Beach. As for the final years of tax exile, she considered her metamorphosis into hostess and housekeeper nothing more than an elaborate joke. That was how she paid for her present freedom, with all the friends who braved the sandflies only once, the dinner partiers offered to dull colonials with a saving grace. She'd paid, and Marisia, she would make damn sure, never would have to pay.

And so she promoted Marisia, at seventeen, which was easy enough in a town like New York where people appreciated a glamour that would have seemed out of place in a more rigid or dowdy city. The Widow could have made Marisia a pudding-faced English girl in lace, ready for marriage, or a good Dutch democrat, or a studious French intellectual, but she had refused. She wanted Marisia to be almost American.

'So out of touch,' murmured the Widow Van Helding, who did not find Dr Foster promising. He blushed and retreated too much. 'What,' she said, loudly down the table to where Marisia was holding court, 'is new?'

The boys said it was fine to go visit the A-queens at the San Remo, or go out to the Fox in Brooklyn to see Murray the K present live artists miming canned music, or attend any temple of what was struggling to be rock 'n' roll. A small Harvard contingent, trapped in that no man's land between childhood and adulthood which in 1960 did not yet have a name and a style, looked blank. The boys also said there was a ramshackle needle factory on the East Side in the 80s, where an artist called Horst worked, and where people on speed and drag queens and poets and rock people assembled, where you could see people staring at their own faces in mirrors or silverfoil or even knives.

Marisia liked that idea. She reckoned it was time for risk, and they'd go to Horst's place to gawk at the oddities. That was the sixties, she said, that was new, and that was – she hesitated for a moment, her English still not perfected – 'groovy'. Then she wondered if you could say that.

Dr Foster resented the Widow's sudden withdrawal of attention. He tried manfully to coopt the expedition. 'Significant images,' he said, 'of the banality but essential energy of pop culture – a view of themselves.' Someone at the foot of the table said Horst did windows for Tiffany's, but then so did Jasper Johns.

'I want to go visit,' Marisia said, firmly. 'Now.'

And poor Dr Foster set down the Armagnac he had taken in preference to the sticky cordials he liked more, and went red-necked and smiling to the door. And the party piled into big yellow taxis and sprawled across each other, giggling, and headed for the end of a street in the high East 80s.

'Nothing here,' said the Widow. 'Nothing. I shall refuse to leave the taxi.'

'Lady, refuse,' said the cab driver. 'Refuse, I beg you.'

'. . . essentially iconic quality . . .' Dr Foster was hugely gratified by the way Marisia seemed to tumble softly against him each time the cab was stopped short by a traffic light. His mind was crisscrossed with silken scarves, naked bodies, the joint ministrations, soft but cruel, of mother and daughter and – '. . . er, fame in our time, that is . . .' Dr Foster was lost in a great mire, between the need to reassert his authority and the need to have Marisia work her fingers very gently '. . . he represents, that is to say, but also abstracts.' He wondered if he had made sense.

'Yes,' said the Widow. 'And is it true he lives with his mother and a drag queen on Lexington?'

The flotilla had halted before a dark building, a steel facsimile of some half-remembered Italian palazzo with windows that were variously boarded, unlit, or backlit with ultraviolet and some that were pierced with huge, lazy, rust-crusted fans.

'Very well,' said the Widow, purposefully. '*Allons-y!*'

There was a freight elevator which pulled itself laboriously up past damp and flaking walls, and when it came to a halt the great iron grille refused to open. The visitors stood self-consciously, unsure what to do next. There was a long, shapeless noise like the drone of a mechanical bagpipe or the cry of some desolate animal, broken by arhythmic bangings. Through the iron gates they could see a man sitting in a sort of yoga position.

But the elevator door stayed locked.

At the end of the corridor the gloom began to stir, and a figure came forward dressed in white that glowed like atom dust in the ultraviolet. It was swathed and menacing, and a full eight feet tall on teetering heels.

It came to the door of the elevator, rattled the gate and said: 'Yes,' in the bass, stentorian tones of an English butler at a baronial door. Marisia knew the game immediately – 1940s movies, Universal.

Dr Foster said, much too loudly, 'We came to see Horst.' And he wished he was back in California with his nice dull wife, had never tried to know artists in New York, had never been to the Cedar Café and never fantasized about scarves and daughters.

'What did you bring?' the figure asked.

'Er,' said Dr Foster, 'we are interested in . . .'

Marisia could see the creature's face now. The eyes were black with kohl and the lips and teeth bore scarlet traces like the remains of some diabolic meal, although really from Woolworth's make-up carelessly applied. The creature set back its head and roared.

Smiling, one of the boys tried: 'We bring love.'

The figure looked faintly interested but said: 'Wrong coast.'

'Did you bring money?' the figure asked, significantly.

'Certainly not,' said the Widow. 'Not to this part of town.'

The figure seemed impressed by the sense.

'Or drugs?' it said, hopefully.

'We want to see Horst,' Marisia said. 'We wanted to see his work.'

'Hell,' said the figure, backing off. 'Tour-ists.' It began to chant the word. 'Tour-ists. Tour-ists.'

A fresh-faced boy who sounded like Harvard came pounding down the corridor. 'Candy,' he said, 'will you for God's sake let the people out of the cage?'

'Life is a cage,' Candy said, sententiously. Still she obliged, tripping a little and losing a high shoe which took with it a full eighteen inches of height.

'I'm sorry about that,' the Harvard boy said to the Widow Van Helding. 'Horst really likes people and he gets these weirdos.'

They walked the ultraviolet corridor into the area that was Horst's studio. It had once been a factory and there were jumbled remains of funnels and vats and sluices crammed up against the walls. There was also a screen of silver foil behind which two men were doing something Marisia could not quite imagine (and she was not naïve), and a lardy woman, fierce-eyed, hoiking her skirt to stick a hypodermic in a pudgy thigh. And a man in stylized black leather – S & M gear was still something rare – who broke away from a neuter-faced line of watchers along the wall and went into a kind of dance which turned without warning into a rushing attack on the sitters, who hardly blinked.

'It's quiet tonight,' the Harvard boy said, with filial devotion to the Widow.

At the heart of it all, like a great white queen settled in the hive, was Horst with his canvas, a box of acrylics, and the calm, uninterested look of a bank teller making change. He seemed no more than an electrical connection between the furies all around him and the picture shaping itself on the canvas.

The Widow Van Helding stepped forward, presented herself and began one of those easy talks that depend on grace and grit in equal proportions.

'Hi,' said Horst. He set down his brush. In almost one breath he added: 'Di-ya-wanna-cum-to-the-Peppermint-Lounge?'

'Certainly,' said the Widow. 'If it's amusing.'

Horst, who had a vein of scrupulous honesty, looked at her sharply and said: 'Not yet. But it will be, in a few months.'

Candy, flanked by a pair of more confectionary drag queens, now addressed herself to Marisia. She stroked the girl's arms and said 'Lovely stuff.'

'Star stuff,' said the other queen.

Marisia looked at them as though they were already friends. She liked the wildness, the relentless energy they pumped by needle into themselves, afraid to sleep in case they missed events, and she liked the plastic sense of culture. Dr Foster was trying to make a speech, and the Harvard boy was listening with mock attention, and it was clear the good doctor was in a panic.

They left for the Peppermint Lounge after Horst had prudently but unmaliciously checked that they had money. They settled to the high-decibel, unsubtle beat of the dance-of-the-week and Horst drank root beer. He stared at Marisia as though she was an omen to be read and he said:

'You'll be a star.'

Candy said she, too, would be a star and Horst said: 'Superstar.'

'We'll all be rich and famous,' Marisia said.

'We'll all be famous,' Horst said, sagely. 'Some of us will make money out of it and some of us won't. That's what matters.'

Then he asked Marisia to be in a film and the Widow decided it was time to show some protective feeling towards a seventeen-year-old daughter, lovely and stylish as she might be.

'What would I have to do?' Marisia asked.

'Sleep,' Horst said. 'I just know you sleep well.'

'Alone?' the Widow asked, suspiciously.

'If you like,' Horst said. 'I don't do the peeps anyway. Not that I have anything against the peeps – in fact if you like, we could go see . . .'

Dr Foster had taken a deep breath and decided to reassert himself. He could barely compete with the noise and wildness around him, so he decided on a quite different tack.

'I would be most happy,' Dr Foster said, 'if Marisia would consider the University of California.'

Marisia giggled at the comeback. Horst regarded her with his affectless concentration, his great blue eyes still and unblinking. Marisia was glad to find she could stare him down and say 'no', but she was even more glad to be propositioned. She liked the idea of being a star.

Candy came up to her and spoke with surprising affection.

'For the sixties, child,' she said, pressing a set of black capsules into Marisia's hand. 'We gonna need all the energy the good CIBA-Geigy can give us.'

'You want to know about the gold price,' O'Higgins said. 'I'll tell you. The atomic weight of gold is 197·2. The atomic number is 79. The price is $35·08 f.o.b. at London. Nothing changes. Nobody will ever make a killing in gold.' He gulped his coffee and said, with a grin: 'I just want to be proved wrong.'

Pieter said: 'It would be more exciting for you, I guess.'

'Right,' O'Higgins said. 'Here I am with the riches of the Orient and the glories of Eldorado and what do I help run? A market, like a suburban grocer's. The speculators all go to Zurich and I can't do business that isn't massive and the business is so damned proper that it hurts.'

Koolhoven had stepped out for the morning, leaving Van Helding in the charge of O'Higgins, a big, rufous Anglo-Irish man with a sharp tongue and a face already bruised by drink. O'Higgins didn't expect to survive very long as a banker, and he let himself talk out anything he felt. Tact was beside the point.

'But you can see the gold fix, if you want to,' O'Higgins said. 'Just remember there won't be a wild rush of action. It is a meeting of gentlemen.'

The lift was old and rickety, used only to go up and forbidden to people coming down; since the lift was in Rothschilds' office, it was usually called quaint. Six members of the London bullion market assembled in its cage each working morning, and went up to a committee room that overlooked a City courtyard. A secretary dialled T-I-M for the speaking clock and held the line until she heard the flat, toneless voice say: 'At the third stroke, it will be ten thirty pre-cisely.' And the fix began.

It was nothing to report, an arcane ritual the guidebooks only sometimes mentioned. At the head of a long, polished table sat the man from Rothschilds', his authority clear and his eyesight dimming. It was his bank that had the right to refine gold at the Royal Mint, and by his green chair there was a telephone with a direct line to the Bank of England. At the other desks around the room each member of the market had a line to his own dealers and a little Union Jack on a stand – a Christmas gift to the Rothschilds long ago which had turned out useful in the fixing room. The ritual was simple enough: if a dealer wanted to stop bidding to consult his office perhaps, he need only raise the little banner and say, 'Flag up.' The fix would wait for him.

Van Helding from his sideline seat saw something impossibly ordered – a sense of propriety that no living market should have. Everyone had a history. The man from Mocotta's knew his firm was older even than the Bank of England; indeed, had tried to put the Bank of England out of business in its early days by buying up its debts and presenting them all for payment on a single day. The man from Johnson Matthey knew his gold bars had special cachet throughout the East, not least because they were best for smuggling through hostile Customs like those of India. Even the junior firm – Samuel Montagu – had a hundred years of dealing under its belt. The men round the table seemed fat with time. And they had a market so structured that prices could slip no lower than $34·90, no higher than $35·15, according to demand and the Bank of England's supply. With such tight margins, the deals had to be huge to support real profits. Outsiders could not hope to play.

It was wrong, Van Helding thought, not meaning any sort of moral judgement but simply watching the way the market conducted itself and considering the passions that gold unleashed in the outside world. The two did not fit. This gold market had mostly to do with money, not with the metal itself, since until recently the price could swing no more than two cents either way when the dollar was especially strong or weak, and the new swings were influenced by exchange rates as well as supply. The older dealers deplored the new volatility. They considered themselves the architects of an orderly market – acting for the South African producers who supplied three quarters of the West's demand, acting against the Russians who had a nasty habit of dumping fifty-tonne lots whenever they needed hard cash in a hurry. It was one of those simple chains that survived the end of the Empire – naturally, the South Africans sold through the Bank of England in London, and naturally London became the centre of gold trading since it controlled most of the supply. Naturally, if you had the conservative cast of mind, such golden ties would continue. It took a Van Helding to see that the machine was not at all natural, had outlived its time.

At ten thirty sharp, the man from Rothschilds opened the meeting. Each dealer round the room declared if he was a net buyer or a net seller. The man from Rothschilds said: 'May we have numbers, please?' and noted what each dealer said. Only then did he pick up his private line to the Bank of England to report the market's appetite that morning – how many 400-ounce bars it wanted, how much it was prepared to pay. And the disembodied voice of the Bank, barely audible in the room, could deal – or it could answer back: 'No gold.'

And then the serious business of dealing began, with each member of the market cradling the telephone which linked him to the dealers who knew just how hot their customers were for gold.

It took minutes. That morning, gold settled at $35.09, a tiny fraction above official parity, mostly because the Swiss were buying moderately. Their indulgent banking laws allowed them to sell gold bars at retail to the world.

The meeting shut down, and O'Higgins followed Van Helding to the door. Rothschilds' man, hands tight on the handrail, was leading the way very slowly down the spiral staircase to the ground. The whole dignified, quiet business had been finished, and Van Helding more than ever thought it strange and almost absurd. Outside, the economic reviews were warning about the American balance of payments, the weakening dollar, the economic troubles of the USA; here, the value of the dollar was made to seem rock solid. Billions of dollars were loose in Europe seeking some new use, trying to establish their own value; here, the value of the dollar was fixed from Washington. It couldn't last; it had to break.

He remembered what Koolhoven said about the form and manners of markets often explaining how they moved. He thought about moving a large sum of money into gold, waiting for the day when the price inevitably exploded. Then he thought that he had no such large sum of money and that he could hardly borow it. Unless, of course, he found a source that couldn't ask questions, might not even miss quite hefty funds. It might not be quite honest, but . . .

At eleven thirty that morning, Van Helding crossed a line.

* * *

The Widow Van Helding led the way out of Bergdorf Goodman and up Fifth Avenue to the Palm Court at the Plaza.

'It is,' she said, 'time that we talked.'

She ordered coffee and watched Marisia refuse the pastries in a proper fashion, and cleared her throat.

'I am going to talk like a mother,' the Widow said. 'I want to know if you really want to go to California and if you really want to read theatre arts.'

'Yes,' Marisia said, 'I think so.'

'And you're sure?'

'As sure as I can be without having done it.'

'Because I have to say,' said the Widow, 'that I think you will find it very difficult after New York. You have been quite a star here, and it will all be different on the West Coast. You'll be a student in a very American town. That is not at all the same thing.'

'I realize.'

'I just want to be sure this is not a whim.'

'I want a career, Mother,' Marisia said. 'Not just for decoration, but because I really want something to do. Besides, it's years and years before I get my share of the bank, and even then I'm not sure I want to get involved in Kellerman Unger.'

'You're not sure? You mean you've thought about it?'

'Of course. After all, I get the same share as Pieter, only later.'

'By which time Pieter will no doubt have taken over the whole business for himself.'

'Maybe. But maybe not, when he knows I am going to be his equal.'

'You have five years to wait. Pieter has hardly one year.'

'Seven and a half months,' Marisia said.

'You have been thinking very hard about the bank.'

'Sometimes. It means I'm going to be rich, I suppose.'

'Naturally,' the Widow said. 'And naturally you will be richer still when I die. The bank is only one instalment, after all; there is also the income from the gold companies.'

'I don't want to talk about money,' Marisia said. 'We don't have to. And I don't understand it enough, yet, to sound sensible. What I think is that I see rich people here who have no sense of direction at all – rich is all they are. They don't do anything, they spend their lives on a social circuit that's as fixed as a prison and I suppose they have a good time, except that they always seem to be looking for something new to break the monotony. I'm simply not like that.'

'It's possible,' the Widow said, carefully, 'you might like to spend some time now in Switzerland.'

'Mother, really . . .'

'Listen to me. You're about to do something very risky, and I will tell you why. You are exotic. I don't mean for the moment that you are bright and pretty and the rest. I'm not paying you a compliment. I'm saying that you are different, and likely to be different wherever you go. You may sound American, even look American, but you're a European child with a European family and European money. You will very soon be rich in your own right, free to do what you want. All of that will make you an outsider, and people may want you to buy your way in.'

'I fit here,' Marisia said, 'I think. I think people take me seriously for what I am. I mean, me, not the money.'

'Probably,' the Widow said. 'But you will always have to be a little careful, a little suspicious. It isn't comfortable to know that, but it's true.'

'I am like everyone else,' Marisia said. 'People don't know who I am.'

'The trouble with being a Van Helding,' the Widow said, 'is that in the end someone always knows who you are. Your father's death was something notorious, you know. People still write books about it, and they still try to make appointments to see me, to tell me "the truth" about it all. You may wake up one morning and find your name is all across some supermarket tabloid – up there with Hudson's divorce and Monroe's love affairs.'

'I know I won't be unknown,' Marisia said. 'But I don't want to be some anonymous little mouse. I like being known.'

'I am simply warning you.'

'You don't need to say all this.'

'For the sake of my conscience,' the Widow said, 'I have to say all this. But please understand me, properly. If you want to go to California and study and become an actress, I am delighted. You'll last longer than I did as a model. You'll have all the choices you want. And you can be what you want, where you want. Just don't forget that the name may also be a burden.'

'I bet nobody else in Equity has the same name.'

'Nobody would take it.'

'I don't believe it,' Marisia said. 'A good press agent . . .'

'Marisia,' said the Widow coldly, 'you sound like a child trying to shock her mother. You should know better.'

'A good press agent could make my name famous. That's all I meant.'

'I do hope so.' The Widow smiled, a warm and summery smile that seemed quite uncontrived. 'And now, perhaps we can stop being serious. I need a bath, and then we can organize lunch.'

Marisia said, so fast and low it was almost inaudible, 'I love you.'

And the Widow Van Helding rose in full and fine sail from the table and said: 'I know. And I'm grateful.'

And together they walked from the Palm Court into the bright, hot city outside.

* * *

Van Helding had the advantage when he walked into the room – a square, big room on the ground floor of a front quadrangle, with big windows on to flowers and grass and trees, and furniture of uncertain age. There were girls in dresses a little too formal for their age, and boys who were well scrubbed and restless inside their dinner jackets. Van Helding made a stir. He was manifestly a man, moving with self-assurance, knowing the outside world, and the boys of his own age were still a little troubled by their sex and strength. The boys, indeed, were loud and drank too much and joked about sex, and the girls seemed herded together. At least two of the girls were called Caroline. Van Helding knew exactly where he was.

Before the Commem began – just after ten, when soft summer dusk had gone purple and trees were great billowing shadows over a perfect lawn – there was light supper. Van Helding looked around. Jasper, son of the Kleinwort director, had direct and brutal designs on his girl, a pale but spirited redhead; Jasper was talking to no one. Of the girls, most seemed uncertain about their role, more comfortable when they did not have a single partner and the awful choice of whether or not to, when the time came.

And there was Katherine de Grunwald. For this evening she was designated Van Helding's partner, and they met almost shyly. She was a soft, gentle, self-effacing girl, but brightly literate like all properly educated French kids of her age. She was tall and dark, and she was dressed in long, light silk. Van Helding thought she was lovely, and he thought who she was was lovely, too.

'I feel very lucky,' he said. It was somehow not a tacky line; he managed to imbue it with meaning.

'And me,' Katherine said. 'I was afraid they had just put the foreigners together.'

'You want some champagne?'

'A little. Did you come from Amsterdam?'

Pieter made a face. 'Did you come from Paris?'

'No,' said Katherine, with dead seriousness. 'From Dublin, actually. I was helping on a dig.'

'For Celtic stones? Or another Book of Kells?'

'For Viking Dublin,' Katherine said. 'It interests me. I like the idea of warrior chieftains and marauding bands. And beards.'

Pieter rubbed his chin, shiny smooth. 'I shall have to wear one.'

'You don't need one,' Katherine said, and she walked to the window, waiting to be followed. 'You don't know anyone, do you?' she said. 'I suppose Jasper's father wanted some fellow bankers here – to make sure all is respectable.'

'Do you think of bankers as so respectable?'

'My family is,' Katherine said, 'except for Uncle Gilles. If you put them all together in a room they become a family portrait at once. Or a board meeting. They have pokers for backs. They don't unbend.'

'You're not like that.'

'Nobody under eighty is like that, except in my family. I'm afraid when I become twenty-one my spine will suddenly lock into place, and I'll stop dancing and I'll be straight for ever and ever and ever.'

'My family . . .'

'I know about your family,' Katherine said. 'I'm not sure my father approves. And I'm sure my mother doesn't. She was once at a party with your mother, and she thought your mother was far too pretty. She came back with some terrible story she'd made up about how your mother had goat-gland injections and drugs from black men.'

Pieter giggled. 'She probably does.'

'I like it here,' Katherine said. 'The English all get loud and silly and we can be private.'

'Not private,' Pieter said. 'Not really private.'

Katherine looked at him and flirted a little. 'Private enough,' she said. 'For the time being.'

At ten the boys and girls began to process slowly from the rooms, out across the Inigo Jones quadrangle at the back and through the arch to the great lawn, where marquees were full of instruments being tuned, and trestle tables being set.

'I wonder about the food,' Katherine said.

It was one of those warm, gentle evenings in England when the smell of night-scented stock comes sweet and full from the garden borders, and the lawns are manicured and the trees lit for spectacle. It seemed too early to join the party, although the others had rushed for the discotheque in a basement, and Pieter and Katherine walked to the shade of a weeping beech that was thick with leaf. They parted the branches that trailed to the ground and discovered a seat by the trunk.

'England is very romantic,' Katherine said. 'It's a pity about the English.'

Pieter said: 'You sound very worldly-wise.'

'I don't think I like things to be romantic,' Katherine said. 'One of my friends at school married for romance and it was terrible. She was bored and she was poor, and she has to live in Sardinia and wash socks all the time.' She shuddered. 'She wrote me one time that she felt like a woman, and the next time that she was looking for a good divorce lawyer. I think her parents went out to save her.'

'I can hear the music.'

'Don't you like to be here?'

'I like it very much.'

'I suppose . . .'

The branches parted and Jasper, with his compliant redhead, bustled in, not at all happy to find a private bench already occupied.

'I say,' Jasper said. 'You two seem jolly friendly.'

'Making polite conversation,' Pieter said. 'Is the band good in the marquee?'

'Very good,' said Jasper, with infinite meaning. 'You'd enjoy it.'

And Pieter and Katherine walked away.

Inside the great marquee, a band was playing a kind of rock 'n' roll – a little too slow, a little too diffuse, but recognizable. Pieter took Katherine to the floor, bowed with great solemnity, grinned, and began a furious jitterbugging dance, a kind of startling burgher's jive. Katherine followed with bright eyes and flushed cheeks, laughing at the tricky turns and sudden acrobatic movements.

She finished the dance looking expectantly at Van Helding. He pretended to ignore the invitation and danced again.

She was impatient. She wanted him to acknowledge her properly. She was not simply a little girl, despite the silky propriety in which her mother had dressed her, and which she and her girlfriend had tried to edit by pulling at the neckline, fooling with the length. She was a woman, an equal; they were banking aristocracy. She thought Van Helding was not a Jew, but then she hardly was, and it did not matter. He was strong, he was forceful, and he was capable of being charming and kind. That would do for the moment.

But he wanted only to dance.

She circled him, and she tried to tease him to catch her, but he danced with great precision, and he controlled her movements. She couldn't quite break away, and she couldn't quite stop following him. She was laughing, glowing and trapped.

Then he wanted to go to the bar.

She put her arm around his waist, and ran her fingers under his cummerbund. She scratched, deliberately. He didn't flinch; he smiled. They took champagne at the bar, and a dish of strawberries that tasted like all of summer and thick, English cream, and they sat, face to face, biting into the big fruit and sucking gently at them.

She said: 'I'm glad you are here.'

Pieter smiled. He hadn't calculated this, but it suited him very well; she was doing the pursuing, and to court her he only had to stand still, to respond in ways the more manic English would not provide. You didn't get a girl like Katherine de Grunwald to bed, of course, although there were expedients that were possible; but then bed was not really the point. Pieter Van Helding sensed the chance of a grand alliance – two banking families, a dynasty.

'They're good strawberries,' Katherine said. 'My mother had the gardeners grow a patch in the country, but they were never like these. It's something . . .,' her expression, smug with Pieter's attention, patronized everyone else in the room, '. . . that the English do really well.'

She liked his strength, his will. She wanted someone like that: someone who was as substantial as a de Grunwald, and such people were rare.

And he for his part thought she was a pretty girl, but very young, and rather mild. He also thought the de Grunwalds were the perfect alliance. Their homing pigeons had arrived hours before those of the Rothschilds after Waterloo, something they did not boast about for fear of embarrassing the junior bank; they had staked the Barings for the Louisiana Purchase, discreetly; and with the same discretion they had run the overdrafts of a half-dozen of the more indulgent European royal families in the past century. Their business was essentially private. When the Nazis came to dispossess them, they had never quite managed to trace the full extent of the pictures and property and shares that were tainted – as the SS said – by de Grunwald ownership. The net was too wide, and too complex, for even the SS to unravel.

'Do you mind your name?' Katherine asked, suddenly.

'No. Do you?'

'Sometimes. They publish books about us, too. I found one on the railway station today. It had awful stories.'

'They weren't true?'

'Oh, some of them were. But they always make things up and miss the real scandals – don't you find that? From outside it must all look so very different.'

'I expect people are jealous.'

'People want to pity us,' Katherine said. 'They want to pity you because of your father. They like that.'

'I don't see why,' Pieter said.

'People always want to find the flaws,' Katherine said, 'and they're always there, and then they're happy – it makes us just like them.'

'But we're not like them,' Pieter said, flatly.

'You don't even sound as though you're boasting.'

He lifted her to her feet, and said: 'Not boasting. Telling the truth.'

They went to the more sedate of the marquees, where several starched dons were circling with their angular, ribby wives.

'Let's go back to the tree,' Pieter said.

In the weeping beech, there was nobody now, and the sounds suggested that dance and music and food and drink would hold all the others at bay for a while. Katherine leaned across to Pieter and kissed him.

'I didn't want to wait,' she said.

Pieter said nothing. He leaned back against the trunk of the tree, and loosened his tie. She had a sense of doing what she was supposed to do, but there was no simple moment in which she met his eyes or felt his will.

'Kiss me,' she said.

Pieter said: 'We have a room at three,' and then, looking at his watch, 'for just thirty minutes – a sitting room. I expect we'll be tired by then.'

'Kiss me,' she said.

'You're very impatient.' He looked up at the stars, only to find the upper branches of the weeping beech kept them from view. He heard a rustling and when he looked down again she had taken off her dress and was unhooking her bra.

'No, no,' he said. 'Not like that.'

She looked ashamed, as though she had admitted something, confessed without checking to see that her confessor was worth trusting. She was caught in the awkward play of the hooks behind her back, and yet she blushed and crossed her hands across her breasts. She had made a mistake, and she was not sure how or why, and he was staring at her. He knew things she couldn't guess at, was waiting for moments she had not planned or dreamed.

'It's all right,' he said, and took her in his arms. 'It's all right.'

He was a prize that would not simply surrender, he was saying, and even a de Grunwald would have to ask, not demand. He was defying her. Or else, she was attempting to face him down, and he was prepared to take an interest only on his own terms. Or else – she was utterly confused.

That summer Marisia went to Malibu and panicked. She wondered for the first time if she would be happy with all the mindless Californian physicality. She made friends with Angela, daughter of an old-established English couple, movie producer and professional wife, whose cynicism bothered her; Los Angeles, they kept saying, was where the frontier ran out and there was no more West to go, and people lost hope.

And the people of her age were so manifestly boys and girls. Even the sharper, more sophisticated ones had read very little, still lived in blue denim and windbreakers, scuffed their way to the wide, white beaches and motored their way back. She loved the beach, but not for long. She couldn't quite adjust to a civilization where the car was even part of courtship, a form of display as well as a way to travel. She missed yellow cabs, Swiss mountains, Caribbean peace, and even the dull, flat Dutch lands for which she had developed an unreasoning, late adolescent passion.

David Grant was a welcome arrival. She had rarely been more vulnerable, and he was exactly right: English, in his early twenties, already a reporter for one of the London Sunday papers, big, brown, and intelligent. They met at the film producer's house in Beverly Hills, which was all greenery and glass and views of careful woods; and they talked furiously. And Marisia also listened. She did not expect to star for the moment, only to discover what Grant had to say, and since he had things to say about places she didn't know, she was fascinated. It was the old thrall of travellers' tales. Besides, he fitted her image of a hero – strong, direct, kind. And he listened to her when she described what he did not know, like Horst's studio, and the present state of the Peppermint Lounge, and Murray the K's shows in Brooklyn; they exchanged notes on alien cultures. They went down to Barney's Beanery while it was still an artists' hangout, and David Grant taught Marisia to play bad pool; and they liked the collapsing, decadent and unfinished look of Venice, then only a failed housing development around canals. They drove at night to look at neon, and they wondered at the grandiose style of the *nouveaux riches* of the 1920s Hollywood, and the Beverly Hills mansions that seemed to have been built like hot-air balloons and then inflated beyond a natural size. And they talked, as Marisia could not talk with the Californians.

Then David Grant left after three weeks, quite suddenly, on some assignment in South America for his paper. Self-deprecatingly, he'd explained himself: an ambitious vicar's son, determined to work in Fleet Street, willing to go to Latin America, in which the British had little interest. The continent fascinated him – the ways in which old bravados, transplanted from Europe, survived intact on such alien ground while at home they had faded or been bombed away. He said he found Argentina, for example, almost nostalgic – old forms of fascism, and gentry, and Italian machismo (if such a phrase was proper) that at home would not be tolerable, but which on the wide pampas had become a way of life. Marisia had just made herself interested (Can democracy survive in Uruguay? Will the 1960s be the decade of the military? What is Stroessner really doing in Paraguay?) when the man disappeared.

'He's cute,' one of her girlfriends said. 'But he's very British. And they're all queer.'

Marisia smiled. 'Yes,' she said.

'You mean he is queer?'

'I mean he's cute.'

But she regretted the word as soon as she had produced it. She had the most curious feeling that she had met a partner, an ally, and it infuriated her that he should disappear so casually.

For a long day, she badgered airline offices and travel agents about trips to Asunción, or Buenos Aires, or anywhere she might casually run into the man again. But what she felt was not some grand, consuming passion; she was sure of that. It was simply that a friend had got away.

She felt isolated again in Los Angeles, where she could walk out into the gardens of her friends' houses and have no sense of other people – not close, not distant, not any sense at all. In any big European house there was always the knowledge that where the woods and lawns ended, another community began, one to which the big house was linked; but here, each house had its perfectly closed world, gated and guarded, and there might as well have been nothing else. Travel between those capsules was just as closed.

'What this is,' Marisia said to herself, swinging in a great canvas swing between tall shade trees, 'is self-pity.'

Her control was phenomenal for someone hardly more than a child, and so was her will. She had decided on California; she would make it work. She would not waste time moping after other ways of life; she would throw herself into this one.

She bought herself sneakers, jeans, the uniform of the beach, and one of those curiously over-generous bikinis that seemed so outrageous in the early 1960s. She petitioned her mother for a Thunderbird, which was excessive but desirable. She took to the beach and took possession of it with her walk and her eyes and her sense of glory.

And she waited, in case David Grant might write to her.

The house was high and huge, a façade embroidered with stone faces and curlicues, a mass of brown stone looming from a Paris boulevard. Up its pompous stone steps Katherine de Grunwald went skipping. She rang the bell, a clasic old retainer groaned to the door and half-resentfully admitted her, and she went running through the hall to her uncle's study.

She threw open the door and she said: 'I'm getting married.'

Gilles de Grunwald turned to her, awkwardly because he had been deep in conversation and his wheelchair would not easily shift.

'Damn it,' he said, 'you send cards for that sort of thing.'

'I wanted to tell you first,' Katherine said. 'Before Mummy and Daddy.'

The Baron Gilles de Grunwald twisted himself, felt an inner pain and winced. He was a great cantankerous globe of a man, whose body had gone gross since the legs were killed in the war by a bullet that fragmented his spine. He glared at Katherine and said: 'Congratulations. You will forgive me if I finish this conversation? Then I shall organize some champagne.'

'Yes,' Katherine said. 'Yes – but I thought you'd be happy.'

'Happy and busy,' Gilles snapped.

Katherine found herself brushed outside the door, and she realized she could not have identified the man with whom Gilles was talking. His face somehow lacked any distinctive features. His colouration was mousy, his anonymity complete.

'Forgive me, Gregory,' Gilles said. 'These things do happen. Marriages and so forth.'

'Please,' said Mr Gregory. 'Think nothing of it.'

'I've organized a bank draft for you. You're going to need some new bank to handle some of the payments, you know – for the sake of security.'

Mr Gregory nodded. Even his suit, although nicely cut, was unremarkable, and his eyes seemed a mere cosmetic front for the operations of a busy mind.

'It is none of my business what you do with the money,' Gilles said. 'But I imagine there are times when you need to move cash without anyone knowing quite where it goes or where it comes from. For those times, you need a bank that isn't Grunwald Frères.'

'We had thought of that,' Gregory said. 'For example in the Meyr business . . .'

'Indeed,' Gilles said. 'You must tell me about the Meyr business. You know that he handled a couple of Grunwald pictures at the end of the war – pictures that somehow slipped out of the SS stores. A Uccello, quite fine, and a Duccio. Not at all the usual romantic crap.'

'He handled a lot that the SS once had in their vaults,' Gregory said. 'We think we now have the case against him finished.'

'You got him on the pictures – or the rest?'

'The pictures,' Gregory said. 'The Dutch police are

convinced by that evidence. They don't seem quite so willing to accept that the respectable Mr Meyr could have denounced various Jews to get the pictures. And, of course, we hardly have written proof – as we do for the pictures. Sometimes people hate to believe the truth.'

'Usually,' Gilles said. 'Half of Europe has something to hide from the last war. More than half of France, if you ask me. They don't like people poking around.'

'That is why we have to do it.'

'Of course,' Gilles said. Some bone and nerve grated in his lower back and he began to sweat a little, trying to show no sign of the pain. 'Will they – damn, damn.' He closed his eyes for a moment, trying to will away the nervous pain. 'I mean, will they make an arrest?'

'Oh yes,' Gregory said.

'And what then?'

'We start chasing the money machine.'

Gilles glared. 'That's a good phrase for headline writers, but what the hell do you mean by it?'

'During the last war, as you know, there were illegal channels for shifting money. Some of it was Jewish money out of Germany, and not all of it went where it was supposed to. Some of it was Nazi money out of Europe, and it's still missing. Some of it was the currency that the Nazis grabbed from European banks – and which they had to cash in America to get hard currency for buying ballbearings and tungsten and things from neutral countries. Quite a merry-go-round.'

'A nice thought,' Gilles said. 'I was just a puppy with a rifle at the time. I doubt if I would have understood the papers if I'd seen them.'

'Some very respectable names were involved,' Gregory said.

'You think you can get arrests on that sort of thing?'

'I doubt it,' Gregory said. 'I don't think there's a police force that really knows how to prosecute fraud, let alone fraud in wartime. But we can make sure nobody profits. We can find some of that Jewish money and bring it back. We need the money, as you know.'

'I give you what I can.'

'You do. Edouard doesn't.'

'He's given up being a Jew. Assimilated. People make the usual remarks behind his back and he doesn't even have the consolation of knowing who he is. He gave it up.'

'We have a list of banks we think we can prove were involved – from the US files. There's been no difficulty in getting the papers.'

'Why should they bother?'

'Consider,' Gregory said. 'You're a Dutch banker. You were involved in some – let us say, slippery business during the Second World War, and you want it all forgotten. Intelligence files turn up which could spoil your reputation and remind you of a lot of unpleasant things. They turn up, what's more, when the Meyr case is on every front page, and everyone is asking how a Nazi crook like Meyr could have been protected for so long, and lived out his life so peacefully. All of a sudden, just for a while, people find it shocking that such things were concealed. You'd probably cooperate to save yourself, I think.'

'It's clever,' Gilles said. 'Probably immoral.'

'It's an advantage we didn't expect from the Meyr business, but which we might as well exploit.'

Katherine, waiting in the drawing room, had become impatient, and wandered out to the corridors. She wondered whether to knock again at Gilles's door. She would have to go home soon and tell her parents and wait for that inevitable moment when they judged her, judged what she said and what she planned. They judged everything, according to some fixed table of proper thoughts and actions. She thought their minds were starched. She thought, at least Uncle Gilles would respond like a human being.

'Do you have names?' Gilles asked. 'Of the banks involved?'

'Do you really want to know?'

'I do. Otherwise I wouldn't say so, damn it, would I?'

Mr Gregory opened a discreet attache case and produced a typewritten list. It was headed 'Banking Contacts'.

Gilles scanned the list. 'There's one of our correspondent banks here,' he said, handing it back. 'Kellermen Unger in Amsterdamn. Old Jan Unger. Looks like a stick insect.'

Gregory said: 'Up to his neck.'

'Don't believe it,' Gilles said. 'He wouldn't have had the courage. Too dried out.'

'Maybe it didn't take courage,' Gregory said. 'Maybe the German High Command held a gun to his head.'

'We'll see. I wouldn't let that list out of your sight, mind you.'

Mr Gregory smiled his humourless, grim little smile.

'Don't worry,' he said.

And he prepared to leave with a discretion that was almost theatrical.

When Katherine finally came into Gilles's study, she was troubled and subdued.

Gilles said: 'I rang for Tourchon.'

'Uncle Gilles,' Katherine said, now feeling as though she had to nerve herself to tell him her news just as much as she would have to prepare herself to confront her parents, 'I am going to get married.'

Gilles grinned. It was as though this was the first time he had heard the words, and he seemed delighted. The delight faded fast as the old cracked spine spoiled his power to smile, but for a brief moment he seemed warm like a sun. And Katherine was glad she had brought the news to him.

'Tell me,' Gilles said. 'And make sense, for God's sake. People in love usually talk the most infernal tosh.'

'He's Pieter Van Helding,' Katherine said. 'He will own

a quarter of Kellerman Unger in a few months. He's going to be very successful.'

'Kellerman Unger.' Gilles said, and with a straight face added, 'We hear so much about them.'

'Have you ever met Pieter?'

'I don't think so. Perhaps with Koolhoven on one of his Paris visits – quite a striking boy, about twenty?'

'Yes,' Katherine said. 'That's right.'

'Isn't he a little young?'

'I don't know what you mean.'

Tourchon waddled into the room with a tray and dry biscuits and glasses and a bottle with the awkward metal clasp that marks a cramant.

'I'm sure your parents will say that,' Gilles said. 'I won't make you rehearse your answer. Have some wine.'

Katherine smiled, hectic cheeks all white and red. She seemed to radiate happiness.

'Good luck,' Gilles said. Silently, he reflected that they did indeed hear a lot about Kellerman Unger – perhaps more than was good for the peace of mind of the Baron Edouard and the Countess Seraphine as they contemplated the marriage of their only daughter. But that was not Gilles's affair. He kept his distance from the rest of the family and their weak-kneed, decorous ways, and if they chose to be shocked, that was their business. His business was to enjoy the wine.

'Uncle Gilles,' said Katherine, 'it is all right, isn't it?'

At the end of the working day Pieter Van Helding made a last call to London.

'I heard a story,' he said, 'about gold.'

His friend at Samuel Montagu said: 'Go on. Tell me. All I know is there's a terrific fuss because the British actually want their gold in London, for a change. They say they're sick of having it stacked in a vault in New York with only the labels changed when it's bought and sold, and they want to be able to tell the politicians the Bank of England is overflowing with the stuff. Of course, it won't be. I have it on good authority the floors aren't strong enough to carry all the gold we're owed.'

'People cashing in their dollars for gold?'

'I guess so. Enough dollars floating around Europe, God knows.'

'And the price never changes?'

'I told you before. It's like the atomic weight. Oh, it shot up to $35·11 today, did I tell you? A whole three cents.'

'Thanks,' Van Helding said.

He waited until the offices around him had emptied and various colleagues had said good night after asking if he wanted a drink. When he sensed that he was almost alone in the great bank building, he began to make calculations.

They – the college of economists and financial columnists and wise men – kept saying the dollar was overvalued. People settled big debts with gold, because it had a fixed dollar value, and when the dollar went up and you already held gold, it became a cheaper way to pay your creditors than trying to buy dollars in the open exchange markets. That was clear enough. Everybody seemed to think the American dollar cost too much. And they were nervous, distinctly so, about the next elections. They sensed a new style in the Democrat Kennedy, and although his chances of election were clearly minimal against the experience of Richard Milhous Nixon, he might shake things up. Bankers hate things to be shaken. Kennedy might defend the dollar to the death, or do nothing of the sort; he might go off on some wildcat expedition and alarm the world; or he might prove too liberal and generous and soft. Kennedy, and the new style, made the old men very anxious.

Van Helding could rehearse all that, and the fundamental arguments that meant the price of gold had to break loose, and still the price did not shift. All those old-established, decorous names around the table at the gold fix would not allow drama to enter their meticulous market. They'd rein in, tamp down, pull back for as long as they could.

And Van Helding, just for a moment, wondered if he had made a mistake. It had all seemed so logical, even inevitable. And he had checked to see which accounts were run on a discretionary basis, and which were run for people who could not in law know what was done for them – Americans hiding assets overseas, occasional persons who needed discretion in the management of great, even regal, fortunes and others who simply would not involve themselves with the Dutch part of their wealth. Those people often allowed the bank to make its own investment decisions, and Van Helding had made such a decision – to transfer funds, to set up an account in a nominee name and buy gold in London. The amount, so far, was US $6 million. The account was filed among Pieter Van Helding's personal holdings.

Of course it was all right. If the price didn't move, then Van Helding had simply moved clients into gold to protect them against currency fluctuations, now the dollar was riding so high. They'd accept that. If the price of gold moved, there'd be a profit, he'd pay back the accounts he had stripped and give them a bonus, and everyone would be happy.

But he planned something else. He couldn't yet use the bank's money, or even make his own decisions. He needed cash. And he had planned to take – what should he call it? an informal commission, perhaps – at least, a share of the profits on gold. And he'd use that money well, the basis of his own fortune.

It wasn't happening. And if it didn't happen soon – now it was September – there would be audits and checks and people would ask how a junior bank officer could move $6 million undetected. Jan Unger would ask. Koolhoven would ask. Pieter Van Helding would be caught.

He looked at the figures on his desk, and he realized they didn't mean a thing. You could add and multiply and calculate for hours, but the fact was that markets didn't move by logic. You had to understand the feel, the sentiment.

Pieter Van Helding was close to admitting he had got it wrong.

'You are not going to believe this,' Marisia's girlfriend said. 'There was a reporter from the *National Enquirer*. I didn't think they had reporters, only finks.'

'What did he want?'

'Pictures of you.'

'I'm flattered,' Marisia said. She put down a letter from David Grant in Rio; she needed to concentrate.

'They're doing some story about how – how your father died.'

'You can say it out loud,' Marisia said. 'It happened before I was born, remember. My father was murdered, and I know it.'

'You don't talk about it.'

'There is nothing to say. It just happened. I never knew him, so I don't know if I would even have liked him.'

'The reporter asked if it haunted you.'

'I don't forget it, if that's what he meant. I don't live it out every day, either.'

'People talk about things like that out here,' the girlfriend said. 'People always seem to be confessing . . .'

'I don't have that much to confess,' Marisia said. And then she grinned, 'Yet.'

'I mean, it must upset you?'

Marisia took a deep breath. 'What did you tell the reporter?'

'I didn't tell him anything – I mean, hardly anything. I

said you thought about it. I said you maybe talked about it in your sleep.'

'That's something I couldn't deny, I suppose.'

'If you want to know,' the girl said, 'he said he would write about you anyway, whatever I said, and he gave me some money and my parents haven't given me this month's allowance yet and . . .'

Marisia looked at the girl, pitying, angry, disgusted all at once. 'Did you make the story good?'

'He seemed to think you had been in a movie. With Horst. He said you must be in Los Angeles to become a star – and to forget. He said all that and I suppose I nodded and he gave me money.'

'Where do I get the *National Enquirer*?'

'They sell it in the supermarkets – where they have the chocolate and the gum, by the checkout.'

'The reporter didn't want to speak to me?'

'He said he would like to speak to you. But I said you didn't speak to anyone.'

'How much did he give you?'

'It doesn't matter.'

'This might as well be businesslike,' Marisia said. 'More than a hundred?'

'A hundred.'

'Have you got his number?'

'He said he was a stringer. He said he was their man in Los Angeles, although he didn't have an office number to call, so perhaps he isn't the top man. He had a number, though.'

'Call him,' Marisia said. 'Call him and tell him I'll talk.'

'You don't mean it?'

'Of course I do. Get him to give you another hundred. We could go down to Mexico for a few days – live it up.'

'I thought you'd be angry.'

'I'm angry,' Marisia said. 'But I'd like to meet this man.'

Two days later, the man who claimed he was from the *Enquirer* called.

'I'm glad you understand,' he said, 'how much better it is to cooperate with the Press.'

'Oh yes,' Marisia said.

'We might come to your apartment?'

'I think,' Marisia said, 'that might be a bad idea. But I'm sure we could meet somewhere else – somewhere mutually convenient.'

'But we could take pictures . . .'

'Very well,' Marisia said.

When she put down the phone, Marisia turned to her girlfriend who said: 'I think you're taking all this very well.'

'Yes,' Marisia said. 'I am.'

'But do you think it's wise to have him over here – I mean, he could be almost anyone, couldn't he?'

'Yes,' Marisia said. 'He could, couldn't he?'

'I didn't mean to give him this address,' the girl said. 'I must have just let it slip.'

'He was paying,' Marisia said. 'He was entitled to a few slips.'

'I think you're being horrid.'

'Do you happen to have your father's office number?'

'Of course.'

'Then I have a call to make.'

Marisia dialled Henry Fowler, who at four was contemplating the comfort of his chair and desk and bar and wondering if he should take scripts home that night or simply drift to the bars.

'Mr Fowler,' Marisia said, 'I have a problem, and since my mother isn't on the Coast, I have nobody else to turn to.'

'My dear,' said Henry Fowler.

'Your daughter has given my address, and an interview as well, to a man who claims to be from the *National*

Enquirer. It seems they are writing yet another piece about the death of my father, and I'm to be the new angle.'

'I can't believe Angela would do such a thing.'

'I don't think she quite realized all the implications,' Marisia said sweetly, looking directly at Angela's startled face. 'Besides, the man gave her a hundred dollars. In cash.'

'And she took it?' said Henry Fowler, vaguely.

'Oh yes,' Marisia said.

'Can I talk to her for a moment? Is she there?'

'I wouldn't say such things if she was not,' Marisia said. She handed Angela the phone and Angela took it with a marked reluctance, as though it might be hot. There was a brief interrogation followed by a minor explosion at the other end of the line.

'You didn't have to do that,' Angela said. And she began to cry.

Marisia took the receiver. 'I'm sure there are lots of people at the studio who know how to handle this sort of situation – unwanted publicity and so on. I wondered if perhaps there was someone who could help me. I don't know American law and I don't really know too much about newspapers and this whole business is very upsetting.' Just enough emotional throttle, she thought, to ensure that he feels this is an emergency and, in some obscure way, his fault.

Henry Fowler fell immediately. He deputed a studio lawyer and a couple of studio heavies – occasional stunt men with spectacular muscles who looked inflated in clothes – to help out Marisia. It was agreed that they would be on the premises when the reporter arrived, and they would intervene if necessary. The stunt men were immediately taken with Marisia, as though she were an amiable, friendly toy, and they watched her with serious, unbroken attention. There was a copy of Aristotle's *Ethics* by the bed that worried them but they decided it was a foreign book. Besides, the girl was so pretty and so kind, and no bastard reporter was going to take advantage of her just because her Daddy died suddenly.

The lawyer was more precise.

'I'm not here,' he said, 'except to make trouble for this man – and the best way to make trouble is very simple. How old are you, Miss Van Helding?'

'Seventeen,' Marisia said.

The stunt men clucked appreciatively.

'At seventeen, Miss Van Helding, American law makes it very difficult for a girl. But it makes it even worse for a man who lays a finger on her. Under eighteen, it's statutory rape.'

Marisia shuddered a little and said: 'That sounds a little drastic.'

'When he sees the studio heavies, he might back off anyway. You're very young, and you're not in the motion picture business, and yet you've got moguls looking after you – and those whom the moguls look after usually get peace and quiet.'

Marisia said: 'He didn't sound that sort of man.'

'There was a time,' the lawyer said, 'when the studio lawyers pretty much ran this town – if your star was in trouble with some girl, and the girl saw the police, you got the charges dropped and the girl buried. Anything worse, you got the case run out of town. I'm sure we can do something for you. Just enough to scare him off, make him feel he daren't write a word, and then enough to make him spread the word that anyone who messes with you has got to face the whole studio machine.'

Marisia smiled gratitude and her mind tried feverishly to process the chances and the risks. She was listening to a lawyer, and hadn't her mother always told her that lawyers said they could do everything and did nothing, that they boasted more than they delivered? That you went to talk to them because you had no choice, and you went with no expectations? She had never dealt so directly with a lawyer before, and he seemed a man who wanted to deliver so badly she did not know whether to trust him. She didn't know how this worked, or how to judge the man. She only knew that in a few minutes, there would be a man who said he was a reporter that she'd invited to the apartment, and it was her responsibility.

It would be better to say nothing, to be invisible, she thought. If she said nothing, they'd write nothing worse that they'd write in any case. Maybe they'd photograph her in the street, say she was fleeing the past, and so what? She thought the *National Enquirer* didn't last more than a week. She'd hurt for a moment and then be forgotten in a rush of divorces and scams.

The doorbell rang. The lawyer and the heavies went to wait in the next room.

The reporter was younger than Marisia expected. He ought to have been heavy-set, jowly, in a stained raincoat and a slouch hat, like the movies, and he was actually dressed in a perfectly proper suit. He looked almost too formal and frail for California.

'This is,' he said, 'a very nice apartment.'

'I don't know quite what you want to ask me,' Marisia said. 'Maybe you could tell me.'

'The paper is planning to write – about your family, and the bank, and why you're in California. We're writing about Europeans in California.'

No, you're not, Marisia thought; none of your questions to Angela were about Europeans in California. It was all about a night in 1942 when a man was burned to death like a candle on his own doorstep.

She had never seen the image so clearly before.

'I am very ordinary,' Marisia said. 'I'm going to UCLA because it's a good university – school, you say, don't you? It's very good for theatre arts. And I like the climate. I don't know what else to say.'

'You want to be an actress?'

'Maybe. I think about it.'

'That's why you like Los Angeles?'

'I like the beach, too. I'm seventeen.'

'You don't think your name might be a problem?'

'I don't understand.'

He was embarrassed. He never thought he would have to spell out his question. Marisia looked hard at him and tried to judge if he was alarmed and she felt sick in her stomach and scared. She had to get this right, or there'd be years of pursuit by other papers; she understood that. If she wasn't careful, she would be a story, a press clipping, no longer a person but the sum total of what had been written about her. David Grant had told her about all that. She wished he was there to guide her answers now, a warm presence and not just a distant correspondent.

'I mean, people still remember your father's death . . .'

'I don't talk about that.'

'You mean you won't talk about that? You refuse to talk?'

'No,' said Marisia. 'It's something people have forgotten.'

'I don't think so,' said the reporter, trying to be avuncular. He slid a little toward Marisia along the couch, confidentially. 'I know it's very difficult for you, but . . .'

'It's not difficult. It's just the past.'

'But you're so far away from home . . .'

'No further than a lot of people in my class this year, I don't suppose.'

'It's as though you didn't want to be where your father died.'

Marisia felt anger for the first time – cold, clear anger. That was simply a damn fool question, and she would let him know it.

'We sold the house in the Caribbean years ago. It was good for wartime, but it didn't suit us any more.'

'Your whole family ran away.'

'It was one of our houses,' Marisia said. 'We spent a few months there each year, and then we went on to different places. Don't you understand?'

'I understand very well. You don't have to be brave for me. I'm your friend.'

He was already withering under her glare. She wanted to be treated like an adult, and he was trying to fool her. It was so obvious.

'There's a new book,' the reporter said, 'about your father's death. I'm sure you'd like to know what's in it.'

'No,' said Marisia. 'No, thank you. We've heard a lot of theories, of course, and I'm just not very interested any more.'

'But you should be interested. After all . . .'

He put out a hand and touched her arm, and she shouted. The heavies came bundling into the room, great balloon arms out, and the lawyer followed.

'Are you all right?' the lawyer asked.

'Of course I'm all right,' Marisia said.

'You realize,' the lawyer said, 'the penalties for assaulting a minor?'

The reporter said he was there on invitation.

'Is it likely a girl would invite a man presenting himself as a reporter to her apartment alone?'

'That's what she did.'

'You think a court would believe it?'

The reporter looked blank-eyed around him, wondering what had happened, wondering what had gone wrong with a technique that calmed widows, made UFO victims tell all, brought confidences from the onetime maids of quite famous people.

'I'm warning you to stay away from this girl,' the lawyer

said, and the heavies, amiably, moved to either side of the reporter.

'You lay a hand on me . . .' said the reporter, but the heavies had already gently lifted him from the sofa and were propelling him to the door. They set him down on the threshold and quickly searched him. He had a camera, and they took out the film and let it dangle in the sunshine. He had a small tape recorder and they took the tape.

'That's theft,' the reporter said.

'That's statutory rape,' the lawyer said, 'when it comes to court. I don't think the judge will mind a little defence of a teenage girl alone.'

'Who the hell are you anyway?'

The lawyer named a mogul and a telephone number. 'My God,' the reporter said. 'You really are muscle. Not just the India-rubber men here.' The stunt men looked unhappy, like dogs that have been sharply rebuked, and they also looked a little menacing.

'I'm going,' the reporter said. 'Lousy story, anyway.'

'By the way,' the lawyer said, 'we've called the *Enquirer* just to tell them what you were doing.'

'You called them? I'm not sure they all know I'm working on this.'

'They don't. But you might pass the word among your freelance friends that Miss Van Helding just isn't worth the trouble. You write about her, you don't work again. Not in this town. Say goodbye to your studio pass and your commissary meals and all of your access. Goodbye for ever. And get back to Peoria and write the gossip there.'

The heavies assembled like a Victorian sculpture at the top of the stairs and, with a slight nudge and a boot, encouraged the reporter to get quickly to his car. They flexed and beamed.

'That seems to be that,' the lawyer said.

'Yes,' Marisia said. 'I didn't know I was so famous.'

The heavies grinned.

'Would any of you like a beer?'

'At seventeen?' said a heavy. 'Well, I suppose if you're expecting company . . .'

After the beers and the thanks, the party left and Marisia heard tyres screaming on what was otherwise a quiet Westwood street. She looked around the room, and it felt unfamiliar, violated by that last scene. She didn't fit here any more. She couldn't call Angela in the circumstances; she might not see Angela again. She regretted that, in a way, although she had needed to protect herself. A friend was a big price to pay.

But most of all, it made her angry that she had had to bother to defend herself – against that sad, weak, tired-looking little man who wanted to trick her into one single sentence he could sell. And to mount a defence, she had put herself in the role of grateful little girl.

She heard the telephone ring and she went to it slowly.

'This is Amsterdam calling Miss Van Helding,' she heard. 'Please hold.'

There was a moment's electronic babble, and then she heard Pieter. It made her heart stir, and it troubled her breath for a moment. She hadn't heard his voice since she came to California, and in this moment when she felt particularly alone and isolated, it was the voice she most wanted to hear.

'Sis,' Pieter said.

'I hate that name.'

'Don't all the Americans call you that?'

'I only have one brother.'

'I have news,' Pieter said. 'Marisia, I'm getting married – to a Grunwald.'

'You're marrying a bank?'

'Katherine de Grunwald. She's not as pretty as you, but she's going to be richer.'

'Married,' Marisia said. It was a heart stopper, she

realized; it sounded final. 'Married to a Grunwald.' She was clenching her fist until the long nails cut into her palms. 'You'll be too grand to talk to us.'

'When you're a movie star, you can snub us.'

'I wouldn't want to.'

'You wait. We're getting married at the Grunwald chateau, we think.'

'What do you mean you think?'

'Katherine has only just told her parents. And I have to pass a sort of family inspection.'

'It'll be like getting a visa here,' Marisia said. 'Doctors, I expect, to make sure you can breed.'

'I thought you'd be excited.'

'I'm too surprised,' Marisia said. 'When will the wedding be?'

'We want it to be in September or early October. You'll come?'

'But with term starting and . . .'

'Make them hold classes until you get back. You can do it.'

'I think it's – stunning,' Marisia said. 'I really do. I'm longing to meet her.'

'Come to France in a couple of months,' Pieter said. 'Or we could all meet up in Maine, if Mother is still there.'

'Yes,' said Marisia. 'Yes, we could. It might be nice to get out of the tropics for a bit.'

'I love you, sis.'

'I hate being called that.'

'I always will.'

'Me, too,' Marisia said, and she settled back on the sofa, but she sensed the warmth where the reporter had sat; she shifted herself.

He was very young to marry. Proper people don't marry, if they're men, until thirty. He must be marrying for a reason. Of course, he might love Katherine de Grunwald. She sounded very grand, a kind of *ancien régime* personified, old money dressed in lace. She sounded a little too grand for Marisia's stomach.

Marisia started to cry.

'Don't give your money to the Grunwald's,' the Baron Gilles was saying, very straight in his wheelchair. 'I don't. Prefer to keep things separate. I keep my little vineyard, and I keep my investments.' The Baron Gilles had appointed himself host to the meeting between family and Pieter Van Helding, apparently out of kindness to the boy; and since he liked to talk, he was talking now, as much to shut out pain as to tell stories. 'Proper little vineyard. No fancy labels, but proper Burgundy.'

'You'd only put your name on a bottle that was *premier cru*?'

'Not my name, certainly not. Damned arrogance, changing some name that's been known for a century just for the sake of the family. This family, too. Bloody nonsense. It would be like doing it for Edouard.'

'I was always told the growers settled all that last century – and now they won't let anyone else join the club even if the wine is wonderful.'

'That's as may be,' said the Baron Gilles. 'It is possible,' he said, reflectively, 'you read altogether too much. Edouard thinks you are illiterate.'

'The Baron knows I did not complete my studies.'

'The Baron thinks you never started. Still, Edouard's a fool.'

'It's very kind of you to invite me here. Before the inquisition, as it were.'

'Kindness. Nothing of the sort. I think you're a pimp, if you want to know. One of those clever young men who sell our companies to the Americans and take a commission. All those damn dollars floating in Europe because they earn more money here than at home, and buying up companies. *Le défi Americain*. I tell you, we should collect all those dollars and send them to Washington and say – take your damn paper. We want your gold. Our gold. We're bankers to America at the moment, whether we like it or not.'

'Perhaps the General . . .'

'Don't talk about de Gaulle. Just don't raise the subject. Edouard in his heart of hearts thinks it's a sin to give away Algeria, although he'll never say so in public. He's proud of France and proud of de Gaulle and he hates the whole damn thing. Typical of Edouard – all mind and no sense. Do you want some more whisky?'

'I'd better not.'

'You'd better. Face this damn portrait gallery with a clear head and you'll run. Much better see them drunk.'

'They can't be that bad, sir.'

'They can. I shall be happy to retire very soon and leave them all. I shall be settled in my vineyard and I shall drink all the wine when it is of age and eat pâté made from the thrushes that live on the grapes. No more money, and no more pimps like you – and no more damn family duty. By the way, there is one thing you should know before you go in.'

Pieter nodded.

'Edouard doesn't much like the idea of you. Oh, he'll be civil and so will Seraphine, as well as she ever can, but he isn't happy. He'll agree to things because you're a coming man, you'll soon have a quarter of a respectable bank, and anyway it's what Katherine wants and he's never been able to refuse her anything she's set her heart on. But he doesn't like you. He doesn't like the business with your father, in the war, the way he died, and Seraphine doesn't much like your mother – too pretty, she thinks, and too wild. He'll welcome you to the family, if he must, but he won't welcome you to the bank.' A knife of pain began moving with terrible slowness along Gilles's spine, and he fought to get words out. 'Don't count on anything, young man. Anything.'

There were sounds of others arriving at the door, and the Baron Gilles pushed himself forward to greet them. They maintained an elaborate fiction that Pieter Van Helding had not yet arrived, and the family arranged themselves in Gilles's overstuffed library, in the warm air by the bare hearth as though they needed to huddle by a fire.

After a due pause and a few drinks, Pieter was discreetly summoned. The great doors of the library were ceremonially swung open, his name bellowed by Tourchon, and he walked in.

The group was male, and the social grace of women would have helped them. Something about the formal room and the learning, little touched but impeccably boxed in leather, and the culture, philosophy, and history of France coopted to the Grunwalds' greater glory by being bound in buckram and stamped in gold, and the other parts of French culture presented in cases behind glass, all made the family group seem even more stiff and Edwardian and pompous. The huge and eccentric landscape above the fireplace was a whim of Gilles's, an allegory of the Muses cavorting among glens, libraries, crows and pigs, theatre curtains and dancers and sheep and horses and towns. Generations of Grunwald children had known the picture as 'Naked Ladies go to the zoo'.

The room, as Pieter Van Helding saw at once, was Gilles's joke, and the family was using it as an embassy.

'Messieurs,' Pieter said.

There was a grumble of acknowledgement around the room.

Gilles had equipped himself with his habitual glass of champagne and manifest short temper at a family reunion; a cousin, Hugh, was stiff in a Louis XV chair designed for a man half his size, consumed with a schoolboy anxiety lest he be introduced by his proper name, Heubertise; there was a vague, fey figure introduced as Alain, who might have been Hugh's son; and there was the paterfamilias Edouard, posed by the fireplace, legs crossed at the ankle like the upright effigy of some mediaeval knight mysteriously wearing evening clothes. There were a half dozen others, scattered in pools of light around the room, who could neither be excluded decently nor included fully.

'It is my great pleasure, Pieter,' said Edouard, 'to introduce you to the Grunwald family, and to welcome you.'

Much too young, Edouard was thinking, but self-possessed enough; a bright boy, but not at all a gentleman. His dinner suit, for example, was all too well cut. Gentlemen's dinner suits should acquire a baggy familiarity with age, not lie sharply along the lines of the body. Probably, Edouard thought, new.

'I should introduce you,' Edouard said.

The Grunwalds' family sadness was that, unlike the Rothschilds, they lacked a London branch and a clever branch. The French family disposed of an empire – for there was much more than the bank – whose roots were obstinately French. There was a hotel company, a silver mining enterprise which was a source of constant woe, the dead remains of railways in Peru where for once the British had been outbid, the plastics company in the South of France which had brought Bakelite to Europe, sizeable interests in the South Pacific, and most of all the name – to most Europeans synonymous with money. The bank was essentially Edouard's territory, although Gilles was acknowledged to be what creative spark the institution now possessed. The rest was divided among the family, and required rather little attention. Edouard and Gilles were the powers in it all.

'Imagine this will interest you,' Gilles said. 'You seem to take an interest in the business.'

'I didn't think you of all people considered money vulgar,' Edouard said stuffily.

'Not vulgar,' Gilles said. 'Dull, since I had enough of it. First you work and struggle and care and then you inherit and then you live life to the full – as a cripple. God's plan.'

'Gilles,' said Edouard with a world of meaning.

'I'll behave,' Gilles said.

'Gentlemen,' Edouard said, 'I propose a toast to Pieter Van Helding and to his marriage with Katherine. Welcome to our home.'

There was a clinking of glasses.

'And welcome to the family too,' said young Alain. 'My uncle forgot to say that.'

Gilles harrumphed from his corner: 'I notice he didn't welcome you to the bank, either.'

Edouard looked at Gilles as a matron might inspect a rat. But the damn man had the right of veto on bank decisions and he must be courted, even at his most petulant and impossible.

'He means you won't inherit,' Gilles said. 'All entailed.'

'I am a little young,' Pieter said, 'and he is a little young for that to be a serious question. I am honoured to be associated with the House of Grunwald. I don't have ambitions to take it over.'

Too glib, Gilles thought, and too old. Koolhoven had trained him well.

'We thought it might interest you, since you are to be a member of the family . . .' Edouard cleared his throat '. . . to see a little of the memorabilia.'

Cases were brought down on loan agreements exchanged with assorted royal persons, and ancient ledgers, and letters (perhpas not entirely genuine) exchanged with the London bullion dealers when they were trying to ruin and shut the Bank of England in the 1690s. All the impedimenta of old money, brought out to impress.

Van Helding was polite, but in his mind he reviewed the

documents of his own father's past. A bastard's birth certificate, a Dutch girl stranded in America, an invented name; the undocumented, endless walk to the Yukon, and the map of the miracle lode he had discovered there; some yellowing press cuttings and a couple of sensational paperbacks, all tending to show that those who crossed Georg Van Helding met curious and convenient deaths – one mauled by a bear, one drowned, one said by the more credulous press to be a rare case of a man gored to death by a walrus. Then there would be the images of Georg Van Helding with wife and family in a new and social role, looking uncomfortable at proper events, held there only by ambition. And from the war years, whatever papers showed how the Van Helding fortune had been salted away from inconveniences like exchange control and tax and law; and the headlines about the murder. It was a gaudy story, even by the Grunwalds' standards.

'. . . books we never allow anyone else to see,' Edouard was saying. 'This might amuse you . . . the overdraft of an English king. The Rothschilds thought they were the only ones obliging him, and to tell the truth, so did we.'

'We were never repaid,' said Hugh, gloomily.

'Bad banking,' Gilles said. 'Tell him about Uncle Marcel.'

'I hardly think . . .'

'Inherited the collection of the Duke of Parma,' Gilles said. 'And you'll never guess what that was. No? Then I'll tell you. Pornographic watches.'

Pieter said: 'I don't quite . . .'

'Pornographic watches,' Gilles said. 'Every time the movement moved . . .'

'Quite so,' said Edouard.

They were such a crochety, lifeless lot, Gilles excepted; no blood between them. They were bored with being who they were and what they were and reluctant to have anyone join them on their old and certain eminence. Van

Holding felt sorry for them, as young men often feel for the older ones. He had his ambition, he had his plan for gold, and he had time.

'Gentlemen,' Tourchon said from the door, 'dinner is served.'

'Just doing you a favour,' Noam Gregory said. The Baron Gilles was preoccupied with plans and Gregory looked more anonymous than ever. He had a middle-aged face with no marks to distinguish it from any other except for its stillness, its economy of mood and gesture. You couldn't tell if Noam Gregory was on your side or not, except that this day he was on the side of the Baron Gilles.

'You've looked around?' Gilles asked.

'I don't much like it,' Gregory said. 'The place isn't defensible, not unless you put a cordon five miles round the chateau.'

'We need your ideas.'

'You're sharp at this yourself.'

'You're better,' Gilles said. 'That's the point.'

In the late afternoon sun, tall vines and palms in the conservatory took out the view of placid green around the chateau. Gregory sat like a civil servant charged with death and justice, a bureaucrat moralist, and he chain-smoked cheap cigarettes – South African, not French. The smell was rough and pungent, like a soldiers' bar. He made notes on a pad, and he reviewed them one by one – roadblocks, observers, snipers, likely forms of trouble.

'I don't have much special knowledge,' he said. 'It's the wedding of the year, it's *le tout Paris,* it's *le tout Europe* for all I know. So it's a target, that's obvious. We don't know too much about the FLN except they've got plastic explosives and they use them. I guess blowing out the wedding of the year would be a coup for them. It's a big, fancy Establishment affair after all.'

'I don't think Algeria was worth it,' Gilles said.

'Better not say that too loudly. You'll get both sides bombing you and the army moving in.'

'Seraphine keeps telling me about the day she married Edouard. All the tenants came up from the farms looking rustic, bringing gifts.'

'It's 1960,' Gregory said. 'If you want to do that, bodysearch them.'

'I can't get used to that, you know. Not for an event like this – something that should be *aimable*. Too much like war again.'

'It'll be war,' Gregory said. 'Give it time. It's only just starting now. In a few years, bombs will be commonplace and you'll live behind walls, if you know what's good for you. No more ostentation.'

'God help us.'

'I suppose you can account for everyone who's invited, and everyone who's going to be here as a guard or a servant?'

'I can't account for what happens in their hearts,' Gilles said. 'They may be secret FLN for all I know. But I can identify them, yes, if that's what you mean.'

'That isn't good enough for safety.'

Gregory sucked on his raw cigarettes, and the Baron Gilles looked up at the delicate, glossy fronds of the palm trees. Each man was thinking coldly and professionally. Neither was finding easy answers.

'There are a couple of people I might recognize,' Gregory said. 'It's not my usual line of business, but I'm good at faces.'

'You could look around?'

'I suppose. And I could have a second look at the patrols. You have radios and guns – regular checks?'

'We'll have to.'

'Keep the perimeter as tight as you can. That way the guards can be thorough and out of sight. I don't imagine the Grunwalds want it known they've got a rifle trained on every distinguished guest, just in case.'

'I suppose we just hope,' Gilles said. 'And keep our eyes skinned.'

'As always,' Gregory said. 'You know they're going in after Meyr tomorrow?'

'I didn't know.'

'I'll tell you the story later. When we've got through the wedding.'

'Everything in good time,' Gilles said.

A single bell rang out across the fields of lavender and a cool river and the neat, formal bushes and lawns of a classical, slide-rule French garden. The air was still and unnaturally clear, as though the Mistral had passed. The world had a sense of sweet order, and the chateau an almost theatrical splendour.

Koolhoven moved there uneasily. He always said the trouble started that day.

The Grunwalds' castle bustled with starch and lace, and bare-chested labourers digging the charcoal pits for the *méchoui*. Inside, the Countess Seraphine marshalled her family like a dowager drill sergeant and kept back the memories of her own wedding – flowers massed in the chapel until the poor nuns were sneezing, the pathetic procession of peasants up from the farms with little gifts, the castle open so that anyone could come and drink *vin gris* in celebration. This time, there were guards and warnings and the peasants would need passes if they cared to come. If only that General de Gaulle, newly returned, could massage the army into compliance, persuade them that Algeria did not matter. It was really, the Countess Seraphine thought, so far from Paris and so far from all their concerns and so inconvenient.

'I remember all the tenants,' Seraphine said, 'when we were married.'

'Poor devils,' Gilles said. 'Forced march to the chateau with their presents.'

'I don't like having guards,' Seraphine said. 'I don't see why we should go behind walls.'

'Ask Van Helding,' Gilles said. 'Think what happened to his father.'

'That is a terrible thing to say.' Seraphine had stiffened herself into Queen Mary and become imperious. 'Please try to keep a civil tongue today.'

But Gilles was licensed by his wheelchair captivity and the pain of his legs and body, and he took the licence just as far as he could.

'Never did find the killer, did they?'

'I am sure,' Seraphine said, deadly serious, 'they hanged somebody suitable.'

'Burned to death, too. Filthy business.'

'I am going to tie your cravat,' Seraphine said. As she did so, she allowed no interruption but when she had finished, and her fast, bony fingers were at rest, Gilles started again. He liked to see cousin Seraphine riled.

'Said there was a woman there, jumped from the balcony to get away – got gangrene because she couldn't see a doctor and explain how she broke her leg.'

With his fat fingers he loosened the overtight knot that Seraphine had prepared.

Strung like grey pearls along the pathway the guests in frock coats advanced towards the shrill sound of the bell. There was a gleam of tall, burnished hats and a fury of feathers. The only detail shocking to some nineteenth-century ghost would have been the glorious glass in the chapel windows – ecstatic, leaping figures in red and blue, transfigurations by Matisse.

The Grunwalds, except for Edouard, were in place. There were spinster cousins and long-faced men with vacuous faces and the Baron Gilles at the end of the row, using the position forced on him by his wheelchair to keep a steady watch on everyone, as in his Resistance days. At least his eyes had not betrayed him.

He watched the Widow Van Helding in particular, and the good, grey Koolhoven at her side. She was fresh and lovely, eyes dark and bright, ageless as though the natural order had been suspended for her particular benefit; the Countess Seraphine, secure in her corsets, disapproved. Koolhoven sat a shade too close to the Widow, Gilles thought. He was only some damned accountant, after all.

The single bell ceased tolling, and Koolhoven looked around. He was proud of Pieter – collected, elegant, triumphant at the altar, perfectly controlled and presented. He was like a strong man who moved with delicacy to avoid breaking things.

There was a bustle in the aisle and Marisia arrived, with the Englishman David Grant in tow. She was breathless and she looked cross, and the other guests at first disapproved of her untimely entrance and then were fascinated. Beside her mother they could see the same intelligence, the same beauty, the same economy of movement and gesture, and they could also see the young, white skin and the sense of life. She had dressed severely, but she tugged at the eye, and she did so with no self-consciouness.

Pieter Van Helding was aware that she had come, looked back. Marisia looked solemn, crossed herself; Pieter smiled; and then the grand conventional pomps threw the eyes to Katherine's entrance.

On Edouard's arm she looked happy, but also determined, and her air of romantic pallor somehow made the speed of wedding seem decent again – a matter of enthusiasm, not necessity.

And the ceremony began.

The foreign bankers had not quite grasped the rules of a *méchoui*. When the sheep, brown and succulent, were lifted from the charcoal pits, the Englishmen tried to carve them as though at Sunday lunch in Surrey, instead of tearing and gobbling. Their politeness was stiffened by the presence of the Widow Van Helding, a star in dull company, and by the fact that her ever present escort Koolhoven had slipped away for a moment.

Koolhoven had serious business. It involved intercepting Pieter and somehow divorcing him, only for the moment, from Katherine as they passed together over the neat lawns and through the guests, like aircraft looking for a landing. On one pass Koolhoven managed to take Pieter away, while Katherine dealt with a particularly bossy Grunwald aunt.

'Unger called,' Koolhoven said, beaming to left and right while talking with deadly seriousness. 'He's making trouble.'

'He has a great sense of timing,' Pieter said.

'He's not a tactful man. Nobody ever said he was. But he's still head of Kellerman Unger and he's not inclined to let anyone forget it.'

'Especially since in a few months he won't be trustee of a quarter of the shares and I will be their owner.'

'Waste of time talking like that,' Koolhoven said. 'He wants me back in Amsterdam within twenty-four hours.'

'Did he say why?'

'Something to do with you. And something to do with gold. He didn't elaborate.'

'Why does he want you?'

'I assume,' Koolhoven said, 'he has something to do that he wants settled while you're out of the way. And a honeymoon is almost bound to distract you.'

Somebody asked if that was Pieter Van Helding's father; somebody else, eager to tell old gossip to a willing audience, explained.

'Did he say anything in particular about me – I mean, anything except gold?'

'Not directly.' Koolhoven was enmeshed enough in the conversation to greet a gaggle of Paris slickers who had never seen him before; they tittered among themselves.

'You ought to cover your back,' Koolhoven said. 'Unger is up to something, and he's still got the bank, you know. He's powerful. Anything he's got on you, he'll use if he can.'

'You think I've been – indiscreet?' Pieter looked amused. 'The trouble is – Katherine and I are supposed to leave late tonight for Amsterdam and then for Kenya. Once all this eating is over everybody puts on another layer and there's a black-and-white ball. I suppose we could elope, but we're guests of honour.'

'You might want to stick around a day or two,' Koolhoven said. 'Find an excuse – Katherine's a bit sick, overexcited – the plane's delayed or something. That would give me time to find out what's on Unger's mind.'

'People don't postpone honeymoons,' Pieter said. 'It looks bad.'

'Depends on what Unger knows,' Koolhoven said. He came to a dead halt and looked very directly at Pieter, a big, bluff, friendly man trying to show his concern. 'Is there anything I should know? Anything Unger might have uncovered at the bank that could be embarrassing?'

'Certainly not.'

'I'm your friend, Pieter.'

'And we're both Jan Unger's employees. For the moment.'

'He said something about gold. Someone going long on gold.'

'Does that sound likely? It's a fixed price – has been for ever. It'd be like betting against the sunrise.'

'Somebody might have an idea,' Koolhoven said. 'And they might have found it difficult to put the idea into practice – for lack of money.'

'People always have ideas,' Pieter said, and he began a

new progress across the lawn, back to where Katherine was waiting. He was tickled with congratulations in assorted tongues – the broad-sounding Languedoc French of the tenants, the occasional German of newly restored industrialists who thought the Dutch understood them (or at least would no longer object) and a faint English bray from girls with small breasts and long skirts and no hopes between school and marriage.

Van Helding looked abstracted and concerned. He was thinking of excuses and they would not come. And he could see, across the lawn, walking by her Englishman, Marisia Van Helding. She looked very sensual, glowing with youth and the late afternoon sun.

'You've been leaving your own party,' she said. 'I saw you making phone calls.'

'That doesn't count,' Pieter said. 'I didn't get through.'

'I'm not surprised. They have three different phone systems in this country and not one of them works.'

'You sound very American. Besides, I'm allowed to make phone calls.'

'Not on your wedding day. People watch.'

'It was business. Not that you'd know anything about that.'

'I know a lot of things,' Marisia said, 'about a lot of things, which is more than you can say for the people here. They're boring. Mummy is starting to make anti-French remarks.'

'You can't say they're boring. I just married them.'

'Well, I didn't,' Marisia said, tartly. 'And there's a fat man in a wheelchair who keeps trying to pinch my breasts.'

'Le Baron Gilles de Grunwald.'

'He pinches them quite hard. I bruise easily.'

'He's allowed to do that. He's a hero.'

'I think tonight will be grisly. I'm going to come as Camille – all tragic and dying. And bereaved and in black. I miss you.'

'You have to come in black. It's a black-and-white ball.'

'I could come in virginal white.'

'Nobody would believe you.'

'It's true,' Marisia said. 'They're very slow in California.'

'I'm glad.'

'I bet Katherine will.'

'Wear white, you mean?'

'Believe me,' Marisia said, and she danced away among the long shadows.

'I'm going to be away years and years and years,' Pieter called.

'See if I care,' Marisia said, and she passed by a last, gaunt Lyons banker tearing at cold, salt mutton, a knot of ladies tied by resentment that the feast was over, and a handful of the guards who were now quite visible as the lawn thinned out.

Pieter Van Helding and his bride made their formal exit from the lawns. Katherine briefly intercepted a kind of glare from Marisia which she didn't want to understand.

And the Baron Gilles was upon them again, cornering David Grant this time, which had the effect of trapping Marisia.

'Work for a newspaper? At your age?'

'I'm going to Paraguay for them.'

'Why?'

It was not a polite conversational challenge; it was a declaration of war.

'It seems interesting just now,' said Grant. 'Sir.'

'You should go to Africa. Africa's interesting. Look at Algeria – can't even give it away. Civil war here, and people with bombs and black feet storming into France wanting bungalows. Army hates to give up anything. Everybody wants bungalows.'

Marisia hugged David, ostentatiously, and relished the sour look that Gilles did not bother to hide.

'You with him?' Gilles asked.

'Yes,' Marisia said.

'Pity,' Gilles said, and occupied his hands with the wheels of his chair. He rolled a little way away, and turned. He barked: 'You a spy, Grant?'

'What an odd idea,' David Grant said.

'I thought most of you young men in foreign parts were spies – that's how you make your money. Nothing much in lineage on faraway places for the London Press. And your father – in the diplomatic, I suppose, or the Army.'

'The Army once, sir.'

'Haha,' Gilles said. 'Never trust him, my girl. He'll disappear for months on end, never write a word and never send you cables because of security. Don't trust him.'

And the Baron rolled triumphantly away.

'He's an original,' David Grant said, thoughtfully.

'He's awful. He couldn't keep his hands off me. He's embarrassing.'

'I don't suppose he means much harm.'

'You're so innocent,' Marisia said. 'So English. He means deep harm. You only have to look into those eyes – wells of resentment. He hates anyone who can walk and dance and . . .'

'And . . .' said David, grinning, leaving the unspoken word to trail on the air.

'I said goodbye to Pieter. I expect he'll be too busy at the ball this evening.'

'We could go for a walk,' David said. 'It's cooler down by the lake and there's hardly anyone left.'

Marisia saw her mother sweeping back to the chateau, attended by a little adoring court which was predominantly heterosexual, unlike the cliques around other startling women of her age. She was more earthy than grand; she made people hope, not just admire. And it took her time to shed them all, one by one, and return to her dressing room and the phial of vitamins to restore her eyes and her long, ritual bath.

But the Countess Seraphine blocked her way.

'Such a lovely dress,' she said, frigidly.

'And yours,' the Widow Van Helding beamed.

The Countess spoke highly of Dior. The Widow said his death had been so sad. And now there was talk that clever young Yves Saint Laurent would open a salon of his own. Beatnik clothes, said the Countess frostily, were not for her. Perhaps not, said the Widow with cold appraisal. They stared each other down. If the Baron Edouard had shown the slightest public partiality for the Widow, there would now have been awful social war.

Not that the Countess did not try.

'How is that amusing place,' she asked, 'that you have in the Caribbean?'

'Such trouble with the staff now,' the Widow said. 'And the house does not hold pleasant memories.'

'Ah yes,' said the Countess and swept away, sure she had spoiled the peace and success of the wretched Widow.

And the Widow gave a little crooked smile and straightened herself and walked to the terrace, not much amused by the spectacle of such desperation.

'Heaven,' Katherine de Grunwald said. 'Just us and the elephants.'

Pieter said: 'It might be better – if we didn't go at once. There's trouble there.'

'There aren't that many planes,' Katherine said. 'We might have to spend a week in London. In October.'

'There's something in Amsterdam. Business.'

'It's got to wait, Pieter.' She sat down heavily on the sofa. 'You promised when we'd done the wedding and the party and the ball, we'd be off and alone together. You said we'd be private, get to know each other better. We've hardly ever had time alone.'

'We won't lose a day, I promise. We just – wait a little, that's all.'

She shrugged her shoulders and threw off the fine silk robe she was wearing – proper for a wedding night – and she stretched out naked on the sofa. He came to her and traced a subtle line with his forefinger down her body.

'I love you,' he said.

'That isn't necessary,' Katherine said.

'But I love you. I do.'

'And I love you. But I want to go on the safari.'

'You could have your bath. I could join you.'

'Come now.'

'I have one more phone call to make.'

She flounced to her feet. 'I always have to seduce you,' she said. 'I hope it won't always be like this. I'm supposed to be innocent and you're supposed to be worldly.'

'I am worldly,' Pieter said. 'And nervous. And when we're away from this house, and alone, I'm going to love you until you can't breathe.'

Katherine said: 'One phone call. Only one.'

'Tyrant,' Pieter said. He put out a hand and smacked against her firm buttocks. She went to the bathroom with a smile.

And he went back to the telephone, intent.

The great hall of the chateau had become a dazzle of black and white. There were diamonds and starch and trailing gowns and footmen in wigs and candelabra full of flames which shivered in the night breeze, and great operatic steps for guests to climb before their names were rung down into the crowd by a stentorian butler and they passed along the receiving line.

And the evening's star was Marisia. She appeared at the head of the stairs, blazing with life and cut stones, her decorous, sober, reasonable white gown slit as though accidentally up the thigh. She was a scandal in motion, a model of propriety if she chose to stand still. Katherine, with only ordinary happiness, looked almost drab beside her.

'*Enchantée*,' Marisia said along the line; to Pieter she made an ironic curtsy.

The Widow Van Helding said quietly: 'Are you quite sure you haven't overdone it a little, darling? Or underdone it?'

'It'll brighten things up,' Marisia said, and went to dance with David Grant.

Around the marble floor, Katherine and Pieter waltzed impeccably, the model couple; and in the corner, Marisia's presence stirred a little wind of gossip. Gilles, close to the bar, watched her with real interest. He had seen the fantasy child that afternoon, pretty like a maid, a kind of doll for dreams, and now he saw the woman. She was strong and disconcerting, and coming into the power of her sexuality as surely as her brother had settled himself close to the heart of money.

There were Grunwald cousins to dress the walls – some from great blue and white jasmine-scented houses at Carthage, some from tax-exile apartments in Monaco (Edouard affected to disapprove), one from an opulent estate in Virginia where single-handedly she was wrecking her husband's aspirations to the US Senate, one from jail (grievous bodily harm had been the charge, in Manchester). The word 'suitable' was on many lips, as in whether Van Helding was 'not suitable' by reason of his father's death or 'suitable' by reason of his bank.

'Let's go out for some air,' Marisia said to David Grant. 'I can't stand these people any more.'

They escaped down gravel paths from the wide windows, and they noticed that in the shadows men moved with great discretion – perhaps footmen, perhaps guards.

'It's like the *ancien régime*,' Marisia said. She had nearly read history in Europe.

'Except they don't show much sign of falling,' David said.

'Regimes never do when they're at their weakest.'

'I don't hear the peasantry baying at their doors. And besides, they don't pee on the stairs. I always thought that was what brought down the French monarchy.'

'They don't have loos either,' Marisia said. 'Not enough.' She scampered ahead of him for a moment, and struck a pose – floodlight from the chateau catching a glint of leg. 'Mummy says Europe is full of Communists. Are you really a spy, David?'

'Very minor,' David said. 'I get to steal minor secrets.'

The pathways were lit with flambeaux, cloths soaked in pitch and flaring up, until they came to the shadow of the trees.

'I have a right to know,' Marisia said. 'It isn't a joke.'

'If I said I was you wouldn't believe me because spies never admit it, and if I said I wasn't you wouldn't believe me because spies never admit it. So it wouldn't matter what I said, would it? You wouldn't know what to believe.'

Marisia had finished being skittish. She came up to him and stood pressed against him for a moment, running her fingers along his thigh. He shifted, pleasurably. She settled for a moment into the warmth of his arms and then took him by the hand, through the low hedges of box to the high and wild grass down by the lakeside.

They stood and looked out at a single great fountain, ringed with stone dolphins, that rose in the centre of the lake, and they moved to the thicker grass, a private hollow between tall stems.

Marisia teased a little. She slipped down her dress to show her breasts – warm, rounded, with wide, brown nipples – and she led David's hand to her nipples, and then pulled him closer, his tongue washing and tickling her. She sensed the rise of her nipples in answer to his tongue, and she helped as he pulled off his dinner jacket, his cummerbund, his shirt.

She bent down and ran her fingernails across his back, and she worked meticulously to loosen all the studs and the buttons. Their bodies came together, naked to the waist, and she felt infinitely older than anything she could do, here and now, with this man. She felt ready for something fierce and consuming, something to take her away from the ordinary business of her life.

Mama was in the castle, putting on glamour, and Pieter was married, and the evening was only slightly chill. Out of the breeze, it was still kind and warm, and Marisia admitted David Grant's tongue to her mouth, put her arms around him and felt the pressure of his hard maleness against her.

She slipped off her dress and her stockings and heaped them on the damp grass, and David Grant was naked, too, except for one absurd black sock, and they came together with a violence that was brusque and needy. He bit at her breasts, and seemed almost about to apologize until Marisia shut his mouth and moved it down to work into the triangle of her sex, first past lips of flesh, then opening the hood of her clitoris, teasing, playing, working.

Marisia shivered, from the breeze, from the motion of the tongue, and she twisted down to the ground to take his hard cock into her mouth, playing and fooling with it, allowing it to press into her.

It was easier than she had imagined, a question of simple physical principles. She felt pleased with herself.

And then she wanted everything, and also she wanted the first time to be over. She slithered up from him, and turned and allowed his cock to rub purposefully against breasts and belly and then to work into her, urgently, and at first with difficulty, and then quite suddenly he was in her and she was full of the sensation. He thrust with a brute enthusiasm which matched her own greatest pleasure, and she felt herself contract and pulse and rise out of her body into a distant, white forest, and she felt him spurt and spurt, and they moulded to each other.

So lovely Pieter was married, then; and Mama was so self-composed in places where Marisia was bored; and now she had her revenge. Two young, perfect bodies, entwined in the wet, hair slick, limbs flushed, the blood on her thighs a badge of triumph.

Her triumph, she thought; a triumph to be shared.

'Let's go back to the ballroom,' she said.

'I have to dress – I can't . . .'

She tweaked a tuft of hair above his buttocks, golden hair, and he frowned.

'I want to go now. While I feel like this. While – '

There was a shuffling noise.

'*Merde*,' said the guard.

He must have been there for minutes. As they tried to disentangle from each other, they saw him, piece by piece – a solid pair of gardener's boots, a paramilitary uniform, a rifle, a farmer's moustache, a red-brown beret. Marisia rolled over and tugged her dress to cover her, and she saw poor, scarlet David Grant, desperately stuffing himself into trousers.

'We had orders,' the guard said, 'to cover this part of the lake. I thought I heard something – '

'That will be all,' Marisia said.

'You wouldn't tell the Countess – or the Barons?'

'I wouldn't dare,' Marisia said. 'You were doing your job.'

And as she regained her composure, and dressed herself again, she thought the whole thing had been sweet and pointless – not the painful initiation she had feared, and not the glory either. She felt contented, as though after a good meal. David Grant, she noticed, seemed to feel he had been honoured. Marisia had given her body and that must mean something. That odd idea would haunt her in later life. She always wondered why women's surrender was supposed to be full of meaning, and men's was merely opportunism. Men didn't give their bodies; they fucked.

The guard went off by a tactful route, sloshing into the lakeside mud.

'I didn't know there were so many guards,' David said.

'There are always guards,' Marisia said. 'There are lots of people with plastic bombs.'

'*Plastiques*,' David said. 'Plastic explosives, not plastic bombs.'

Marisia gathered her dress about her, tidied herself a little and stood up.

'God,' she said to David Grant, 'you can be boring.'

But, she told herself, useful, too.

The Baron Gilles was manhandled down the ramp and then pushed by a formal footman down the paths. He was tired of the evening and the grand event – and the great risk it represented. He was tired of his pain and the fact that its persistent knifings left him irascible and odd. The pain was real and constant, yet its outer signs were eccentricity. He could never be sure to control how he talked or shouted or grimaced in public, try as he would, and when he was no longer sure, he begged for privacy. Out here, where the evening air held a hint of autumn damp, he felt more alive. He did not need to pretend.

The Baron Gilles was on a tour of inspection. Against the lights he looked bizarre – a round man in a chair, formally dressed, pushed by a footman in knee breeches and periwig.

'Any trouble?' Gilles asked a footman on the path.

'Nothing yet, sir,' said the footman. He had a gun at his hip, and a rank in the riot police.

The Baron passed on, into the cover of the great trees. Edouard and Hugh had thought all this security melodramatic, and agreed to it only as an indulgence to poor Gilles. But Gilles had a sense that there was a new threat abroad, an arbitrary terror that fed as much on publicity as on military actions. Some would be for specific purposes – the plastic explosives in Paris mailboxes designed to keep Algeria French. There would still be incidents like, for example, the Reichstag fire, when the men with torches knew exactly what they wanted to achieve, and whom they wanted to frame. But there would also be random, horrible, unsettling moments designed to rock the system, diminish people's sense of an ordered life and turn them to panic. Only one thing was predictable: the targets of the new terrorists would come from the headlines. And the Grunwald ball, tonight, was a headline.

Inside the great hall, the chatter and the music swelled. They were talking about the weakness of the dollar, the health of Chanel, the question of whether St Tropez would be possible again next year; there was a small group of intrepid adventurers who had just discovered Fire Island and had no intention of putting the word around just yet. It looked like such wonderful order, where patient servants went on their quiet duties between the animated, gaudy crowd.

Katherine Van Helding suffered for her new name. People talked about the Van Helding murder, she discovered, and still fell silent when she came near. She would have to live with that memory. She wanted marriage, children, escape from the machine of her family, and she wanted an identity of her own – but she did not want the name. She wanted Pieter to comfort her, but he was talking, again, with the dull grey Koolhoven.

'Within forty-eight hours,' Koolhoven was saying. 'If you're not back in Amsterdam by then, I can't hope to hold Unger. Whatever he's planning.'

And Pieter went thoughtfully back to Katherine, composed himself, and made ready for the grand ceremonial ending to the evening – when the young couple would be toasted, when the company would watch a fury of fireworks and then cheer the new Van Heldings off to bed.

On the great lawns and among the woods, figures with rifles moved silently, like night animals. The keepers were best; they knew the ground, and they could step around the tear of a bramble or the crackle of a twig. A nightjar sounded above them, hoarse and strident, but did not fly away.

The Baron Gilles stopped by a great tree. 'We should have a guard here,' he said.

'We have men all round the house, M. le Baron.'

'But we haven't been challenged. There's nobody here.'

The footman threw the brakes on the wheelchair and went to search the low grasses by the side of the path. Gilles felt his skin rise and prickle, the raw, sharp certainty of danger. He always said his helplessness made him more strongly aware.

The path led to a folly in the English manner, a summerhouse of twisted woods; it was just out of sight from the chateau and screened against the summer mosquitoes from the lake.

Marisia and David could see it through the trees as they picked their way back to the ball. Worse, they could see the Baron Gilles, his unmistakable silhouette.

'It's the old man in the wheelchair,' David hissed.

'Shit,' Marisia said.

The Baron Gilles seemed to sniff the air like a hunting dog. In the Maquis, his name made him too conspicuous and he was never taken seriously; so he had to be good, better than the others, always. He knew something had happened.

'The man's gone,' said the footman, returning from the undergrowth.

'Maybe he went for a drink.'

'They have strict orders not to leave their posts. And he was a military man.'

'Military men have mixed loyalties just now,' said the Baron Gilles. 'That's half the trouble.'

'He knew his duty.'

'Then find the bugger,' said Baron Gilles.

The footman, stiff and bewigged, rolled the wheelchair close to the summerhouse. Gilles played a powerful flashlight along the borders of the path, searching. Marisia and David saw the beam of light, the curious little procession – joined now by two other guards who had heard the alarm – and began to crawl carefully away, staining their clothes with the bleeding green of the grass.

'You'll have to take the grass out of your hair,' David said.

'Do you think they have special redressing rooms?' Marisia said. 'A wing for illicit lovers?'

'If they did, nobody would go and frolic in the grass.'

Marisia said: 'You have no imagination.'

They both heard the footman's shout. 'Over here!'

In tall grass, where the passage of bodies had beaten a corridor, the footman had found the missing guard. Someone had taken a length of barbed wire and twisted it around his neck, gouging and strangling at once.

After the shout, there was a flurry in the little summerhouse. A man jumped from the door into the low bushes. The guards gave chase. The man had the forceful, blind stride of a runner, but the bushes caught at him, snagged his skin, and finally set a snare of roots to bring him down. The guards caught up with him and dragged him back to the Baron Gilles.

The Baron saw a young man, struggling until one of the guards clipped him behind the ear, and he sagged a little.

'What have you done?' Gilles said. 'I don't give a fuck who you are, I want to know what you've done.'

The man was silent.

'Use your boot,' Gilles said. A guard obliged. 'And search the summerhouse. He must have stacked stuff there.'

The guards separated, some to search and some to hold the prisoner.

'He had a knife,' a guard reported. 'He didn't have a gun.'

Gilles tried to move himself forward to confront the prisoner but the grass held him back. He had to motion to the footman to move him up.

'Not very professional, was it?' he said. 'You don't leave bodies so close to pathways. Hide them.'

The prisoner looked blank.

'And you may as well say what you're here to do.'

Silence.

'Very well. Then we'll go back and look more closely at the summerhouse.'

The prisoner jerked a little in the grasp of the guards.

'You don't seem to like that idea,' Gilles said, and he ordered the footman to go forward. 'Something dangerous there? Something you're afraid of?'

The prisoner hung his head in what could have been defiance or submission.

The little group had climbed the steps to the summerhouse – the Baron Gilles lifted laboriously as though he, too, was a prisoner – when the guards who had been searching appeared triumphant. There was a bundle, tied like a parcel, that should not have been in a gentleman's summer retreat. It had been hidden, but quickly hidden. When Gilles saw it, he made the guards put it down, stop their triumph at finding it, and he said to the prisoner: 'Is that it? Is that what you brought?'

The prisoner said nothing.

'We can leave you here with that parcel,' Gilles said. 'Would you mind that?'

The prisoner scanned the floor.

'Tie him up,' Gilles said. The guards took the prisoner and some raw wire and bound his arms and legs. They made a noose and forced his head through it, then tied the noose to the strong crosstimbers of the summerhouse. If the man moved, he died.

'We are going to leave you here,' Gilles said. 'Do you understand that? Do you understand French?'

The man's slight nod brought the tender flesh of his throat against the wire. 'I understand,' he said. 'It is the people's cause.'

Gilles moved forward, slapped the man. 'I don't want anyone to die,' he said. 'Tell me what that parcel is and tell me why you're here. Are you the only one?'

The prisoner gave Gilles a knowing look as though amused at the older man's nervousness.

'Then let's clear out,' Gilles said.

Guards reluctantly left the man alone, and followed the footman and the wheelchair down the little rustic path. For a moment, the sky filled up behind them with a fire that was like the sheet lightning of a tropical night. Marisia and David, pelting for the chateau, thought it was the start of a summer storm. In the chateau, only a few genteel commotions – a drunk, a malicious remark – disturbed the civilized calm. Then the fire caught the resin of the summerhouse and took it high. It was a mass of flame.

Gilles reached down for the walkie-talkie that he carried with him for emergencies. 'Start the fireworks,' he said. 'Get them started now.'

Abruptly, a rocket rose above the chateau and opened in great streams of metallic light.

'Early,' said the Countess Seraphine.

'Perhaps they are worried about the weather,' said the Widow Van Helding.

The Countess shivered a little. She was annoyed to find herself so close to the Widow, and even more distressed that she could hardly move now. They would watch the fireworks together. An amplified baroque band began to fill the gardens with harpsichord and strings and obvious Bach competed with firewheels spinning in white and crimson on a high frame, with flares and flashes, reds and greens and silver.

The Countess looked at the Widow. Glands, she thought, or something bought from black men, or the knife; something must explain the perfect maintenance of a perfect beauty. But however closely the Countess looked, she could find no telltale signs.

The sky filled with a swell of cascading light and fire, with the dry, violent sound of firecrackers and the balls and rivulets and falls of gaudy light. It obscured the resin torch of the folly except to Edouard, who looked as usual in the wrong direction.

'Looks like the summerhouse is on fire,' he said. 'Gilles playing fireworks again, I wouldn't be surprised. Silly bugger.'

Gilles summoned firehoses from the lake, and the summerhouse died down. Fireworks glittered their last over Purcell – 'Come, Come Ye Sons of Art' – now playing within the ballroom with the singers massed at one end.

'To cel-e-brate to cel-e-brate our tri-i-um-phant day . . .'

Outside, the Baron Gilles, sooty and stained, was giving orders. The footman, periwig lost in the bushes, came pelting down from the summerhouse and announced that the body was there. Gilles said he had no doubts. A charred mess of flesh hung on wires, and Gilles ordered the men to bury the body in one of the pits where the sheep for the *méchoui* had been cooked.

He had no intention of admitting anything about this night. Nobody should know. His family, his place must be completely secure – or else there would be other attacks for other reasons, other attempts to conjure fear from random guns and bombs. Nothing had happened; that was official. If the rich were known to be so close to risk, the rules of the game would change beyond recognition, and Gilles would not tolerate that. Better there was a secret war; he knew how to fight those.

'Tell the police in the morning. And tell them to keep their mouths shut.'

The ring of soiled, bedraggled guards, lungs full of smoke and resin, coughed a little and agreed.

'None of this matters,' said the Baron Gilles. 'None of it.'

He looked back to the chateau and thanked God for its security, and had the footman roll him to a servants' door.

2

On the D-train to Amsterdam, Katherine turned fractious.

'It will be cold in Amsterdam,' she said. And then: 'Nobody will understand why we're putting off the honeymoon. People don't do that. They'll think something is wrong.' And then: 'I can understand a bank, you know. If something is wrong, you could tell me.'

Van Helding would not talk. He had newspapers spread around their compartment and at each stop he checked for some other, local paper that might have different stories. There were headlines about Princess Margaret and Anthony Armstrong-Jones (THE QUEEN CRIES AT NIGHT: WHY DID MARGARET DO IT?) and a piece on the TV debates between Nixon and Kennedy (KILLED BY A SHAVE: NIXON AND KENNEDY IN IMAGE BATTLE) and sinister rumblings of an Algerian war with its tentacles in suburban Paris.

There was also a story of a man called Ernst Meyr, an elderly recluse famous for his art collection. The stories grew larger closer to the Dutch border. He was an old man, to judge by his photographs, delicate and almost kindly looking except for his cold, grey eyes. Now he had been arrested, a frail little figure between hulking cops, and it seemed he had been a major Nazi collaborator who marked down Jews for slaughter and took what Rembrandts and Rubenses (and decadent Mondrians) did not fit Nazi taste. He was charged with murder, being an accessory to murder and grand larceny, and the figures in the charges were like all the figures of the holocaust – too large to have any meaning and yet too important to deny. One of the Jewish Nazi-hunting groups had pinned Meyr down. The Dutch authorities had been unwilling to rake old coals, it seemed, but newspaper pressure had finally forced them into action. There must, Van Helding thought, be some very nervous people in Holland, people with things to hide, facing the possibility that their past was edging to the surface, day by day.

What Pieter Van Helding could not find was any substantial story about gold. He hadn't expected the gold fix to be reported – it was too esoteric. But he needed some event, some reason why on a particular day the pressures in the gold market might blow the cap on the price.

He read an essay on John F. Kennedy. It was sceptical of Kennedy's chances in the November elections, but it said he represented a new strain, a new generation taking power.

'You could tell me,' Katherine said. It had become a kind of test; if he would not tell her now, he would never tell her. It was like the first person you see on New Year or the child's game of opening eyes suddenly on an emblem of the future. And it must be something bad to bring him back; appearances, she knew, were vital to a banker.

Maybe he would trust her in time.

The family returned to Paris, and the Baron Gilles remained to dig the body from the charcoal pit and deliver it to the local police. Official reports showed that a man had died tragically and accidentally during the firework display. The police were understanding; they had no wish to admit a failure of security in their own territory. And they naturally understood the unfortunate delay in discovering the body, and the faint, sweet smell that hung around the ground-black features.

And when the Baron Gilles had completed his chores he took himself to Paris, to a small Burgundian restaurant down by the École Militaire which was much frequented by UNESCO bureaucrats. And after a while, Noam Gregory joined him.

Gilles had settled himself over a *petit pot des gris*, like a cat over prey.

'I'm sorry we didn't do better last night,' Gregory said. 'At least it wasn't big trouble.'

Gilles shrugged. 'One body at a party is easy to explain.'

'Don't joke,' Gregory said. 'I never understand jokes.'

'You have to learn,' Gilles said. 'You're a diplomat.'

'Only on my second passport,' Gregory said.

'When I carried an English passport I wanted to be described as "gentleman". But the passport office didn't think a foreigner could be a gentleman. Have a drink.'

'No, thank you. You forget that while your mother was deferring to your father on the great Bordeaux, mine was buying chocolate-flavoured Manis chewitz.'

'You can rise above your origins,' Gilles said.

'Sometimes too far,' Gregory said. He didn't mean it kindly. He disliked the Grunwalds' meticulous assimilation, product of money and influence for a century or so. Even after the Nazi onslaught, Edouard de Grunwald remained obstinately settled in the way his Christian, European colleagues did things, and showed no spark of interest in the Zionism that helped fire Gregory. Yet Edouard, like Gilles, would sometimes express a fervour that was quite unexpected, and which helped raise cash for special business, special expeditions. Gregory valued the support, but he might have valued more a willingness by the gilded Barons to shut their offices on Friday afternoons and consider God. Not that Gregory took the Sabbath too literally; in his line of work it was a luxury.

'We've finished in Holland,' he said. 'Prosecutors have the case. We made sure the papers knew it was watertight.'

'It will stick?'

Gregory ate a little salad. 'Enough,' he said. 'We had

the Berlin files. They might throw them out, but the story is pretty clear. He named Jews. He named hiding places. And he did it for art.'

'Nobody ever saw the pictures, though,' Gilles said. 'Just a dry old man surrounded by the pictures. I suppose he didn't plan to sell?'

'He couldn't very well. Pathetic, really.'

'Praise God the Abwehr's files are more open than the FBI's.'

Gregory said: 'We'll know who the FBI protected one day. And that's another story.' He drank water. 'We're lucky Meyr is inside at all. I assumed he'd have a doctor who'd swear he had a heart condition and then he'd whistle up bail. You know he lived in a fortress – couldn't even entertain friends.'

'He'd be alone now,' Gilles said, very thoughtfully. 'In solitary confinement, the papers said.'

'No,' Gregory said. 'We wouldn't do that. It's better we remind people in a courtroom.'

Pheasants arrived, truffled, pot-roasted and settled on crisp squares of bread fried in butter. Gilles felt a pinch in his shoulder become an ache, and ache roar along its own firepath through shoulder and spine. He turned a little pale, a little angry.

'Waiter,' he bellowed. 'Waiter, damn it. Never here when you need them. Waiter.' A boy came running. 'I want another bottle of the Ermitage. Now, damn it.'

Gregory looked at him, appraisingly. He wondered what were the risks that one day this angry pain might betray him in a public place. He had known the Baron in the Maquis and admired him, but that was before the bullet and the wheelchair.

'Ermitage,' said Gilles, back on a more even keel. 'The alchemy of the three soils. You knew that, of course? Clay and the granite and the alluvial. You need all three soils to make the wine.'

'God provides,' Gregory said. 'You said you had something to discuss.'

'We had a wedding in the family, as you know.'

'I don't know anything against Pieter Van Helding,' Gregory said. 'If that's what you want.'

'He works for Kellerman Unger. And Unger . . .'

'We don't have quite enough to make the case.'

'And if you did?'

'People are angry enough to listen,' Gregory said, 'after Meyr. It's been a useful reminder.'

'I suppose I have the story,' Gilles said. 'Unger and old man Van Helding were moving currency and gold out of British Empire territory during the war, right? And Unger was the one who got a lot of people's money out of occupied Europe . . . some of it Nazi money.'

'That's the story,' Gregory said. 'It isn't clean, at all. Some of it was Nazi money they needed to get back to America for hard currency. It didn't buy them bombs, but it bought them ballbearings. Some of it was cash from the vaults of various banks – across the Atlantic by U-boat, bank it in Recife, send it by courier up to the USA, and cash it in New York. Old man Van Helding just seemed to use the service. He had gold and cash and he didn't like being told his patriotic duty.'

'You're sure old man Van Helding was involved?'

'He had a yacht, he had money problems, he had a partner who set up deals. It's circumstantial.'

'If you went after Unger,' Gilles said carefully, 'I suppose the murder of Georg Van Helding would come up again?'

'I suppose so. It's a good story. Besides, Van Helding had a lot of money, and a lot of money isn't ever neutral. It's on one side or the other.'

'That might embarrass us,' Gilles said. 'That is, if you ever did decide to move against Jan Unger.'

'We might all be embarrassed,' Gregory said. 'But there

are more ways to use our information than telling a prosecutor.'

'Is that a promise?'

'How can I promise? Things change all the time. But with Pieter Van Helding married to a Grunwald, and the Baron Gilles so generous to our activities – '

'Understand,' Gilles said, 'that I don't give a damn about Jan Unger. He can take what's coming to him.'

'He will,' Gregory said. 'He will.'

At eight, Van Helding left his office. He wanted to be away from the telephone, from Katherine nagging to know when he would return, from Unger checking on his junior's movements, from Koolhoven's kindly but unhelpful talk. He had been calculating for hours, it seemed, without finding answers. He had lists of figures, statements of account. He had set out the code names of the accounts in order, and written down exactly how much he had 'borrowed' from each for his plunge into gold. He then checked the audit date, when the bank inspectors would next appear, when customers might next ask after the health of their money. He already knew the scale of his risk; now he had to know its due date, when he would be caught.

US $6 million. Of course, he could always sell on a good day and get back the money, lose a little on commissions of a quarter per mill, but that would be defeat. Besides, a private seller of that volume of gold would be bound to attract attention. At best, a sharp-nosed market would reckon that Van Helding was $6 million in trouble.

And there was another problem: whom precisely had he involved in buying gold? He knew the names on accounts that he himself had brought to the bank – mostly Americans who had come to buy companies in Europe, had been entertained by Van Helding, had left behind money where the prying eyes of the Internal Revenue Service could not reach. He had discretion over much of that money. For a start, many things – like holding gold – were illegal for residents of Britain and America, and would make official protest difficult for Van Helding's clients. Yet Pieter did not feel secure. These were men (and some women) whose power had intricate connections. They would not need law to punish Van Helding for his policies. And the bank inspectors did not normally concern themselves with the exact identity of foreigners with accounts. They would look only at the figures and the figures looked terrible.

Van Helding needed the index to the real names – the people who held the coded accounts that Jan Unger administered. He had taken funds from them, too. In the pool of gold-grey light on his desktop, the papers, names, and numbers seemed to dance. He needed respite.

It seemed likely there would be an index in Koolhoven's office. Koolhoven had his own clients but they tended, like the Widow Van Helding, to be people who enjoyed rather than needed discretion. Koolhoven was bound to know as much as Jan Unger would tell anyone about the bank's business.

Van Helding walked the half-lit marble corridors to the mezzanine, a cold and bombastic place which clients and staff alike were inclined to avoid. His footfalls clicked on the floor. He whistled, to show where he was; he must not seem to be doing anything secret.

A night watchman called out 'Good evening' and Van Helding said: 'I haven't finished yet.'

On a landing the ticker tapes still ran, sporadically. This late, there were New York prices and New York news. There was also information, hidden in a scroll of commodity prices, the the London gold fixing was at $33·15. The British were still demanding physical shipment of gold they were owed. They wanted actual metal in the vaults, a solid sign of national reserves. Even that unsettling in the market could not move the old men's price to the point of profit.

Van Helding came to Koolhoven's door. The bay for his secretary was unlit, and beyond that the door to the office itself was open a little. Streetlights caught the glass over a Mondrian that hung at the mantelshelf. Van Helding entered.

Like a thief, he felt a moment of almost sexual excitement as he crossed the threshold. The risks, the $6 million, the obstinate flatness of the gold market were no longer dull or terrifying to him: they were electric.

If any night watchman happened to pass, or if anyone else was working late, he would need some kind of alibi. He would take a drink. They would understand that. He went to Koolhoven's bar and pulled out a bottle of jonge jenever, proper Dutch gin. But he did not put on the lights. The worst they could say was that he had become a secret drinker.

He sipped the drink, and he looked out over the canal waters, slick and dark. He walked to Koolhoven's desk, set the glass on its edge and then worried that it might mark papers or leather. He pulled at drawers, but they were locked. He looked up at the Mondrian – beaming sodium-yellow from the streetlamps below. Light flashed from the polished, shiny surfaces of the room, from a brass lamp with an onyx shade taken from the Shanghai branch of the Hong Kong and Shanghai Bank; pens in a neat row; the metal of a telephone dial. Koolhoven was orderly and conventional, and the convention on the bank's security plans was for a safe to lie behind a painting. Van Helding looked at the crisscross intricacies of the Mondrian. He looked, and wondered.

Suddenly, the half-light and shadow turned into a glare. Someone tapped Van Helding on the shoulder.

'I presume you need this,' Koolhoven said.

He pushed a pile of photostats into Van Helding's hand.

'You should have had the key to the accounts some time ago, I suppose, but Unger didn't like the idea. Besides, I didn't think you'd be such a damn fool. Tampering with Unger's accounts was asking for trouble.'

Van Helding said: 'You know?'

'Of course I know,' Koolhoven said. 'I knew at least half the story in France, and I knew the rest when I got back here. I couldn't see why you should be so alarmed if your deals depended only on your accounts. Of course, if you'd tapped into Unger's clients, and Unger knew, then you'd have good reason for flat panic.'

Van Helding's face was blank.

'What are you going to do?' Koolhoven asked. 'Do you reckon you can unload six million in gold before the bank inspectors catch you – or Unger does?'

'Something will happen.'

'Let me tell you a golden rule,' Koolhoven said. 'Gamble money on an investment idea. Gamble other people's money, for preference. But never gamble your life.'

Koolhoven took his own seat behind his desk and lay back. 'How do you expect me to react to all this?' he asked.

'I don't know,' Van Helding said, and it was the truth.

'You've got an idea. That's already more than half the bankers in this town. They want to pour money into Indonesia because it's what they always did when we had an empire. They don't even notice they've been expropriated. The only territory they care about is mapped and sold a thousand times already. At least you're thinking.' Koolhoven took out a small, cheap cigar and lit it. 'On the other hand, if you go to jail at twenty-four, we none of us look good.'

Van Helding gulped his gin.

'Very well,' Koolhoven said. 'I'm glad you don't have a glib answer. It means you know how serious the problem is. If you look at the lists I gave you – and they're complete, by the way – you'll find the three Unger accounts you tapped. And you may see why there is some problem.'

Van Helding began running a finger down the lines – the code name, the code number, and the real identity of the account holder.

'I can save you the time,' Koolhoven said. 'You made all the transfers for gold at retail to Zurich banks under one of three names, and since all three names were romantic composers, and I know your taste in music . . .'

'My God,' Van Helding said. He had reached the first of Unger's accounts, and he now knew who really held it.

'You weren't stupid,' Koolhoven said. 'You got the accounts over which we have almost total discretion, which was wise. And you got the big accounts, the ones where your sort of take wouldn't be visible for a while. But you might have thought . . .'

'R-5 is Unger himself.'

'That's how he knew in the first place. It's his mad money.'

'Which he naturally watches very closely?'

'Which he looks at, every so often. R-5 is for long-term ideas.'

'Gold,' said Van Helding, ruefully, 'looks like a long-term idea. Do I need to know the other two?'

'Yes,' said Koolhoven.

'T-22 is – Christ!'

'You exaggerate,' said Koolhoven, 'but you have the right idea. She's had to handle some tricky business stuff for her husband to get him out of trouble and she likes to keep a reserve account in case of trouble. She's always being examined publicly and she hates it. She uses this bank, like she uses dozens of others, for things her loyal subjects might not approve.'

'And G-150?'

'When the Allies were cleaning up after the war, they needed help – people who could nail collaborators and Nazis. Jan Unger didn't have a clean war but he had a wonderfully active peace. And he made friends, for whom he still does favours. G-150, if we ever sent them a bank statement, would live at PO Box 500, Queen Anne's Gate, London.'

'Which is – '

'British Intelligence. I don't know exactly which branch. The point is that Unger buys his safety by keeping these accounts efficient, safe and intact. They are truly secret. And that is why, Van Helding, you have to understand that Jan Unger is going to try to destroy you. He doesn't have very long before you can start voting your own shares in Kellerman Unger. He has to move fast. He watches everything, and you've made some mistakes.'

'But,' Van Helding said, as cunning stirred like a snake in leaves, 'he can't admit what has happened to clients' accounts, can he? He wouldn't dare make it public.'

'What makes you think he would need to? If you went on trial for embezzlement, nobody would be happy. But if Unger simply let you go, exercised some mercy, your future career wouldn't exist. Every bank in Europe would know there was a problem with Pieter Van Helding and they're sentimental creatures – they'd remember your father's murder and they'd start talking about bad blood. You're too young to have a track record and not rich enough yet to do without one. People know you've panicked, because you married a Grunwald and stalled the honeymoon. All Unger has to talk about is a little problem at the bank and how he thought it was kinder to let you find your own way. And that would be it.'

'Why are you bothering with all this – with helping me?'

Koolhoven puffed at his cigar. 'You think straight. You have courage. But you don't have skill yet. This is the first time I've seen you under pressure, and I don't want to see you wilt.'

'I can look after myself,' Van Helding said.

Koolhoven took back the list of names.

'Really?' he said. 'I don't reckon your clients are going to complain. All those American corporate giants you used to take down to the bars and find women for – friends of yours, as you said. They don't want it known where they keep money abroad or what their money does when it's not at home. And they don't want it known they got spanked by a tart in Amsterdam on a wet Thursday . . .'

'If that had been all they wanted,' said Van Helding. 'Mostly, they wanted to do the beating.'

'So the clients aren't a problem. Except the ones who are so powerful they don't need to make excuses. They'll just withdraw their business, put it about that you can't trust Kellerman Unger any more.'

'You mean Unger can't do anything without spoiling the bank?'

'I wish I did,' Koolhoven said. 'Unger spent years as your father's partner. He reckoned a gold prospector got his fortune easily and then bought what he wanted – titles and position and women. Unger had to go on working, drying up like a stick insect, taking the risks in Europe during the war, trying to keep things afloat while your father was a tax exile on a Caribbean island. Unger hated your father, and because of that, he hates you.'

'He wants me out,' Van Helding said. 'That's not news.'

'He's damn nearly got you out,' Koolhoven said. 'Either you move the price of gold, or you unload six million dollars worth, or you square Unger – or you get ready to go off on honeymoon and come back without a reputation.

'And shut the lights off when you leave.'

* * *

Jan Unger had business with the Grunwalds. It wasn't quite fortuitous, but it wasn't quite contrived, either. They had property – grand, barrack-like hotels in the wrong places – and Unger had a buyer, a firm that was planning to fill the once opulent railway hotels with a stack of eager, hopeful tourists going abroad for the first time. Planeloads from Manchester, Unger told Gilles de Grunwald, shipped to seaside glory. Gilles de Grunwald understood.

But it wasn't what Jan Unger had to say, not the meat of his conversation. That was still to come. Gilles de Grunwald thought how like a stick-man he was, with a thin, brittle body and claw-like hands, and a pinched face. Other Dutch bankers of his generation might spread to buttery proportions, but he seemed to wither with time. You could tell when he felt happy or satisfied; little muscles worked under the thin skin; he twitched with glee.

By the sherbert, Jan Unger felt he could broach the real issue. And Gilles de Grunwald gave him a cue.

'I think we can deal,' Gilles said. 'Of course, now our banks are virtually married, I suppose we'll have to make sure it all looks good. Make sure the outside shareholders are happy; there are still a few. Make sure the government doesn't produce any damn nonsense about control passing outside France. That sort of thing.'

'I am really most flattered,' Unger said, in his high, tense voice. 'A liaison with the Grunwald bank would be more than we usually aspire to.' He sighed and laid down his spoon. 'We owe a great deal to Master Pieter's charm.'

'Family likes him,' Gilles said. 'Family never likes outsiders.'

'I think I can say he is a most talented young man.'

'Bright,' Gilles said.

'But young, of course. Young and sometimes unfortunately impetuous.'

'Seems sound enough to me.'

'He is sometimes a little less sound – on the rules, if I can put it that way. Yes, on the rules.'

'He steals?'

Unger sighed and looked away. That was precisely the message he wished to convey, but by indirection and suggestion. Crime and scandal always sounded more magnificent when it came coded in hints.

'He may be a little enthusiastic about the use of funds,' Unger said.

'Thank God,' Gilles said. 'I'm tired of old men doing little deals. We're not honest like priests, any of us – we all have things to confess. We might as well be spectacular with it. It's the mean little tricks I hate.'

Unger said: 'But of course we all work within certain conventions, do we not? We are reliable in our dealings. We can be trusted. I fear that is the system which Master Pieter does not yet quite seem to grasp.'

'Damn it,' Gilles said. 'Do you want the hotels or do you want to tell stories about young Van Helding? He's only a boy. No time for any stories worth the telling.'

'I am afraid Master Pieter has rather advanced himself,' Unger said. 'There are stories that would worry you about a man twice his age.'

'Be specific,' Gilles said, 'or be quiet.'

'Really,' said Jan Unger. 'I hardly know if it is proper for me to share the affairs of the bank with even such a distinguished outsider.'

Peck at the words, Gilles thought, like some long-legged bird; peck and hint.

'However,' Unger said, 'I suppose you will have to know in due course, since the matter is unlikely to remain private. It seems young Van Helding has been shifting clients' funds to his own purposes. Six million dollars' worth.'

Gilles began to cough, and the cough jarred the nerves

in his back and made them burn. Unger watched him, alarmed and offended all at once. A waiter came up and tried to support Gilles's back, but he thrashed out with the pain. It took minutes for the attack to subside and when it did Gilles was embarrassed at his body's betrayal and furious at anyone who had seen it.

'Don't like that kind of talk,' he said. 'Easy to say. Difficult to prove. Tell the police if you're so sure. Get him out.'

'I would not like the world to think that Kellerman Unger is at all careless with the funds of clients,' Unger said.

I bet not, Gilles thought; the stick-man is punctilious.

'But you don't mind if I know?' Gilles pushed himself heavily back from the table, and he sent a red carnation in a crystal vase crashing to the floor. 'Very odd. You can send me the details of your client's offer in writing. I don't think we need talk again in person.'

Gilles de Grunwald, despite the flurry that his wheel-chair exit caused, seemed to be gone in seconds leaving Jan Unger to scan the bill.

The Baron was shuffled into his car and back to his office, and up in the elevator to his grand space in the Beaux Arts building which put a screen of marble and allegoric figures round the workings of Grunwald Frères.

He did something that he would usually have considered indiscreet. He called Noam Gregory and he said that he wanted the Unger file. He said it was time to use it.

October 17. Van Helding had taken to counting the days and so, more awkwardly, had Katherine. Nothing had changed in the gold markets and Pieter's hope of a profit – something respectable to offer the clients – was dwindling. Katherine said the weather would be bad in Kenya, her friends thought the marriage was over before it started and the Countess Seraphine was making calls full of maddening pity and understanding. 'People keep ringing,' she told Pieter, 'and they don't understand. They don't see why we're not off hunting elephant in Kenya. It's something like a crossword puzzle – real gossip for them to puzzle out for hours.'

'I don't see why they care,' Pieter said. But he did.

There had been a memo on his desk that morning, a summons from Jan Unger. It was marked confidential. Since Unger only had to lift a phone to summon Pieter the meaning of the memo was obvious. He had settled on tomorrow as the day of reckoning.

Van Helding wondered what he ought to feel. He'd manipulated people before, but in a clerkly way; gold was his first grand scheme. He was clever at making people do what he wanted. But now he wasn't sure what he most needed, or who owed him enough to provide it. Time, perhaps, for his father's will to give him the unanswerable advantage of a major shareholding. Gold to soar in price, just for a day – long enough to sell out and settle. Ammunition, something to use against the stick-man Unger and put him in his place.

Only nobody was giving him those things and he had searched for them for ten days. Koolhoven wasn't providing solutions, as he usually did. Van Helding was on his own.

Yet he didn't feel dread. He understood that fear is the unconstructive emotion, the one that blocks out rational thought. He and Katherine would have friends for dinner that evening, people slightly older than themselves, and they would eat a solid *hazepepr* and drink a solid Burgundy and feel autumnal – avoiding the questions everyone wanted to ask. It would be a very middle-aged affair and Van Helding would show no signs of alarm or worry. Let the friends think the delayed honeymoon was caused by – what? Perhaps a medical problem Katherine didn't like to discuss, or a family matter, or anxiety about the situation in

Kenya, which would have been reasonable enough. It was all right, he told himself, all right.

He wandered in from his dressing room. Katherine was in satin that clung to her long, elegant haunches as she leaned forward to settle an eyelash by the dressing mirror. Pieter stood at the doorway and watched her. She was lovely, and she knew that he was watching; she moved herself sensually, slowly, and nothing about her was casual. She loved him to watch. She was eager.

'Good evening, Mrs Van Helding,' Pieter said.

He came up behind her, first cupped and fondled her breasts, then abruptly pulled up her satin shift. She stared into the mirror, eyes bright with anticipation. He held her facing the mirror, while his hands settled down her belly to the lips of her sex. She wriggled out of her pants, and she watched herself being undressed.

'Like this, like this,' she said.

Van Helding plunged into her from behind as she leaned over the gilt and glimmers of the dressing table, and she stared into her own face, her own wide eyes, her own parted, wet lips, into the very workings of her own sexuality. They forced against each other as though fighting, and she began to come violently, and he responded by suddenly shouting out as he came.

And she looked into the mirror, seeing the formal face she had begun, all proper shadowed eyes and red lips, now full and flushed and gleaming.

She thought they would always calm arguments this way.

Dinner was just as dull and fustian as she had feared. She had never known this kind of middle-management affair; Grunwalds were not in that position. Nor, she thought, should Pieter Van Helding be. He would never talk about the gap between his holdings of bank shares, carefully shielded from him by banks and trustees, and his present, rather lowly position. Jan Unger said he was learning the business. The Baron Gilles had suggested Unger did not trust Van Helding. Either way, he was a manager who almost owned control of the business, caught between two roles, stranded.

Only for a moment did the talk catch fire. One man talked a little of Eldorado, and Pieter seemed to quicken.

'They thought it was a city somewhere,' the man said, 'a place of limitless riches, where the buildings and the wagons were gold. And they went after it on grand expeditions – the Spanish who were told to bring back gold at any cost, and Walter Raleigh trying to win his Queen's approval, and all the rest of them – all seeking the place just beyond the savannahs, just across the forest. Except . . .' The man drained his glass, waiting for it to be refilled before he would continue. '. . . Eldorado never was a place. El Dorado was a man. Once a year, the priest would be covered from head to foot in gold leaf, and he would be taken out to the centre of a great, black lake, and he would be thrown over the side – a sacrifice to the lake gods, for good fishing.'

Van Helding thought gold was pursuing him – dreams of it, stories of it, cities filled with it, sacrifices made to honour nameless dark forces with sufficient gold to win approval. The talk of gold made him briefly short-tempered. There was no more history or rhetoric that night.

When the guests went, and Katherine had curled herself in bed like a child, wanting protection from the day, Van Helding was still too restless to sleep. He had gone past being tired, to that state where ideas recur again and again and the mind circles on itself. He sat downstairs, by the fire, with a glass of gin, still in black tie.

The telephone rang at eleven thirty-five.

'If you're thinking of going for a walk,' said a voice, 'come down towards Leidesplein.' He named a bar. 'We have something you want.'

Van Helding had the natural paranoia of a man who knows he is not quite in command of his circumstances.

'I don't understand,' he said.

'We have something you want,' the voice repeated, 'and Unger won't wait much longer. You'd better come and talk.'

Pieter's mind, disturbed from its settled and obsessive course, went whirling. It could be Unger: perhaps the old man was devising some mantrap for Van Helding, to finish him utterly. It could be – but how many people knew enough about his troubles with Unger to call him this late and expect compliance with an apparently absurd request?

'I have to change,' Van Helding said. 'I can't come down to Leidesplein in full evening dress.' He wanted the voice to respond, to show some clue to identity.

'You have half an hour. At midnight we leave.'

'How will I know you?'

'You won't. We know you.'

Van Helding put down the phone before the blank line and the return of the dialling tone could tease him. This, at least, was something different from his usual clerkly risks. And Unger's peremptory demand to see him was for tomorrow morning.

A full, red-gold harvest moon confronted him each time he turned a corner of street or canal. The leaves, now scarce and scattered, were russets and reds, and even the sodium glare of the streetlights seemed a kind of debased, anaemic, chemical gold. He thought how odd it was that a whole city could tune itself to his special obsession.

The bar was a small brown bar, beery and friendly, and half full. There were a few couples in booths along a wall, but mostly the drinkers lined the bar counter. Van Helding calculated he might as well make it easy for his caller to find him. He stood back from the bar and leaned against an ancient Wurlitzer, all stained glass and changing coloured lights. The music was mostly oom-pah-pah Dutch, but there were a couple of singles, marked with different coloured cards, of early Bill Haley. The crowd did not look like a Bill Haley crowd. Van Helding dropped his coins into the ma- chine, chose 'Rock Around the Clock', and waited for trouble.

It came almost immediately. Drinkers at the bar turned in protest. The barman cut the power to the jukebox. Music seemed to drain out of it as the record slowed to a stop.

Van Helding stood back with his beer and a sense of satisfaction. He was not anonymous any more.

He looked around. Any one of these drinkers could be the voice on the phone. Perhaps it was a bellyful of drink that led to the phone call, and a bellyful of drink on Van Helding's part that made him take it seriously. Van Helding put aside such thoughts.

The man was burly and nondescript, but in the cosy bar, with its thick leather seats and its thick curtains at the door, he seemed cold and foreign. He offered Van Helding a beer and said: 'Haven't seen you for a couple of years, Pieter. Not since the Farrago deal.'

Van Helding was sure he did not know the man, but he did know the Farrago name. It was an American conglomerate in the making and Van Helding had helped it buy a Dutch steel mill. This man, though, he did not remember at all. The voice sounded vaguely, but not exactly, American. The face was unfamiliar. Yet he certainly acted and dressed like a lonely Yankee businessman on the loose in a strange town.

So the cover story was good. Van Helding felt at once relieved and terrified that he was dealing with professionals.

'There's some papers,' the man said. 'You might like to have a look at them. Why don't we go back to my hotel for a nightcap?'

They left the bar like old business acquaintances, allies,

not intimate, both marooned in Amsterdam and grateful for a familiar face.

Around the corner, Van Helding was bundled into a car. He was not pushed, but he was made aware that his own will did not count. It was neat and quick.

'I don't need to identify myself,' the burly man said. 'Call me Noam.'

'Pieter Van Helding,' Pieter found himself saying, with formality.

The car pulled away from the canal area, and turned towards the suburbs of the city. Van Helding noticed his companion wore a gun.

'You have a problem with a man called Unger,' Noam said. 'So do we. Just for the moment, you don't need to know who we are. But there's a file on Mr Unger at the State Department in Washington, and another one in Berlin from the de-Nazification commissions. They're not very flattering. We thought you'd like to see them.'

'What's in this for you?'

'Let's just say that we have an interest in keeping people like Mr Unger on the run. The Allies forgave them at the end of the war. There wasn't any reason for us to forgive.'

'And you? Who are you?'

'Read the papers,' Noam said. He snapped on a pale reading light at the back of the car and pushed a folder to Van Helding.

There had never been so much detail; that was Van Helding's first thought. There were stories from gossips, FBI informants so carefully anonymous it was impossible to say who had told what to whom. There were circumstantial accounts of a whole life, varying in detail and credibility, and a sheaf of bank statements. It was those that caught Van Helding's eye.

'You're the banker,' Noam said. 'What do you think they prove?'

Van Helding read them through.

'Very little,' he said. 'They look like private files – what was actually there. I guess I'm meant to look at the dates.'

'In 1942, money was moving. That's what you need to know.'

'Moving where?'

'We think Mexico.'

'But my father seemed almost spent out when we settled the accounts at the end of the war – I mean, when the bank did. He had his bank holdings and he had his gold shares – but not all of them any more.'

'I said they were moving to Mexico. I didn't say they got there.'

'How would they move physical assets, anyway? Weren't there submarines all along the Atlantic coast?'

'They used the submarines,' Noam said. 'The U-boats. And yachts, and once they used a banana freighter. Anything that moved either safely under the water or inconspicuously above it.'

'Unger collaborated?'

'He sent the Nazis' gold – and the notes they'd taken from the banks in occupied Europe. Your father kind of hitched a lift. I don't think he realized the risks.'

'He thought it was Unger's plan?'

'Presumably. The Nazis got hard currency and bought their metals and ballbearings for their guns. The people like your father got their money out of the British Empire where it was supposed to be trapped for the duration. There were even a few Jewish fortunes that managed to get away.'

'If the FBI knew all this – all Unger had done – why didn't they prosecute?'

'Usual reasons,' Noam Gregory said. 'Unger made himself useful and they used their discretion. At least we guess that's what happened. We don't have access to those records, yet.'

'So you're not the Americans?'

'I told you not to worry who we are. It's beside the point.'

'Can I use this material – I mean, can I take it away?'

The car had just gone beyond the streetlamps, out into the flat polder land where water seemed to lap the sky.

'My hunch is you don't need it,' Noam said. 'You just need the cover sheets from the files. If Unger sees copies of those, he'll understand. Someone somewhere knows his story and is ready to use it.'

'I take these sheets?'

'Right,' said Noam. 'And you get out here.'

The car came to a sudden halt. The great red-gold hunter's moon had slipped behind passing clouds and turned sallow. Then it was eclipsed. A numb, damp cold nudged at the men by the roadside. Noam made his farewell, shaking hands, and Van Helding thanked him. As the car drove off, he wondered why he had been grateful.

It was one in the morning under an intermittent, unreliable moon, the wind picking up and cutting keenly across the damp, flat lands, the first drops of a cold ice-rain clattering around him. He pulled up the collar of his dinner jacket. He began walking back in the direction he had come, thinking it was the only thing to do, but also realizing they had driven a full three quarters of an hour from Amsterdam.

The damp cut into him. His walk seemed likely to be lonely. He began to run a little, but his steps clattered on the icy road, and seemed absurd in the empty silence all around him. Running was not the answer.

He thought he heard an engine, but decent Dutch Calvinist country folk don't come out to meet the Devil on a bone-hurting autumn night. He dismissed the thought.

The engine noise seemed to come closer, to roar in his ears.

He turned, finally, and saw a brightly-lit taxicab pelting towards him. All its interior lights were blazing, and its headlights full on. Its sign said it was for hire. It was so absurd, so comforting a vision that Van Helding almost dismissed it as some night-time mirage. But it stopped when he waved.

Inside, a screen separated him from the driver. He tried to open the doors, but found they were locked shut. It was warm, but not at all comforting, in this small, moving prison. At least, he thought, as he began his blind journey back to the city, the man Noam knew how to organize. The half-dozen sheets he held on his lap gave him time and an advantage. If gold would not move, if the clients' accounts could not simply be replenished, then at least he had friends against Jan Unger.

And warm and happy as he was in the thought, he was also sharp. He was sharp enough not to trust his new friends at all.

Unger called for sweet coffee which arrived immediately. It had cost him real, physical effort, to arrive late at the bank, after a habit of years. But he wanted Van Helding to wait and ponder. He wanted Van Helding to suffer.

Since it was almost ten o'clock, he presumed Van Helding would be in the outer office by now. He checked on the neat little note of calls which his ample secretary had left for him. He would handle the calls before the paperwork that morning, he thought. It was his reward for the triumph of the day. His stick-thin body thrummed with the thought of removing Van Helding, once and for all, and exiling him from the possibility of return.

It was Van Helding's father who had brought Unger to such difficulties with his overambitious plans, abandoned Unger in wartime Europe while continuing from tax exile his peremptory demands. It was Van Helding's father who had left young Pieter such stock that the Van Helding family had become an obstacle to what Unger wanted. He wanted the bank of Kellerman Unger to remain what it properly had been – his fiefdom, his castle, the place where he had fought and bled.

If Van Helding was indeed in the outer office – he must be by now; he was only a boy; he would be scared – then he would have to wait. Three calls concerned Unger before his domestic, disciplinary duty.

At the end of the first call, he ignored the little buzzing of the intercom. Let the man wait. He made his second call, an exchange of courtesies with a Munich correspondent. The third, more tricky, involved an afternoon call to an American client who had been disappointed in a first attempt at a European takeover and now needed a new deal – more for fashion's sake than for business. Unger wanted to offer either the Grunwald hotels or a bright new tourist airline. The first was solid, the second might not be quite as sound as it seemed – maybe too risky for the temper of the Americans. At the same time, he must do nothing to upset either the Grunwalds, who hated to look fools, or the airline people, who were sure they were the wave of the future.

The call was a wonder of diplomacy, one of those exchanges modulated like music. When it was finished Unger looked at the desk clock and at the high church steeple visible from his window.

It was ten thirty, and he buzzed for his secretary.

'Yes, Mr Unger?'

'Is Van Helding there?'

'No, Mr Unger.'

'Has he left already?'

'He hasn't been here this morning at all, Mr Unger. Were you expecting him?'

'Call his office. I particularly asked him to be here at ten.'

'Yes, Mr Unger.' The brisk, metallic voice clicked off.

Unger had his first moment of doubt. Divine providence was not wholly reliable 'Mr Van Helding is not in his office, sir,' said the intercom – disembodied, and therefore curiously authoritative.

'Find him,' said Unger.

He turned at last to the pile of papers on his desk. There were some internal memoranda which did not seem urgent – his business with Van Helding had far more weight – and some personal letters which could be answered briskly, and a set of accounts. There was also an envelope with a compliments slip stuck to it casually with Scotch tape – from Pieter Van Helding, Kellerman Unger Bank.

He tore open the envelope. The taut, nervous body that had shivered with anticipation all morning was suddenly still like a river stopped with ice.

He had seen so many of these files before. He had even helped to compile them in 1945 and 1946; perhaps he knew their strengths and limitations better than anyone. They were only a record of rumour, after all, written at a time when proof was something hard to come by.

But someone, outside his own tight circle, had seen the file they had written on him. Pieter Van Helding had seen it.

There was nothing on the envelope, or with the photostats, to hint at what Van Helding intended to do with his new knowledge. With the whole scandal of Meyr – his art, his friends, his arrangements, his protectors – a file like this could be extremely damaging. Worse, Unger did not exactly know what the file contained, and Van Helding had cleverly left him guessing. The envelopes held only the cover sheets of the files and a copy of some damning index cards from Washington and Berlin: 'Unger, Jan: subversive activities of'.

One thing he could see. On the front cover there were codes for informant. He had never cracked those codes, but alongside were boxes to rate the information as reliable or not. Whoever filed the history of Jan Unger had checked the box for 'reliable'. They thought they had the truth.

It was absurd of him to panic. He had a crime against Van Helding – embezzlement perhaps, irresponsible misuse of clients' funds at least. Van Helding had only a mass of intelligence information, files that could never stand the test of a court of law and might never be published – files Van Helding could not legally hold. The Americans would never tell the whole story – too many respected American citizens had, like Jan Unger, bought their way back from disgrace at the end of the war with information, cooperation, the right moves. But then, if the files were to be generally known, not in the newspapers but among bankers, and while the Meyr scandal was alive . . .

Jan Unger had one of those rare, devastating moments when he did not take for granted one single axis of his settled, respectable life. It was all in doubt.

Van Helding could stall the meeting no longer, but he went to see Unger with no sense of victory. He had played his cards; there had been no reaction. He knew the strength of Unger's case.

But there was a last thing he could do.

He called a man he had known at Mocottas – the senior London bullion dealers. He could not raise the man. 'He's in at the fix,' they said.

Then he called friends in Zurich. If London was the wholesale gold market, controlling South African and often Soviet sales, Zurich was the retail store.

Van Helding asked a Zurich banker to investigate if he could pick up a vast amount of gold – vast by Zurich standards, although London dealers thought it faintly effete to think in quantities below a tonne. He timed his request so that it would reach the London dealers at the fix.

And then he went in to see Unger. The meeting was as

formal as if lawyers had been present. Unger had even thought of tape recording the talk, but he thought again. It was 1960; such things were not yet fashionable.

'Van Helding,' Unger said. His desk was clear, somehow especially clear of that plain brown envelope full of facts which had so terrified him the day before.

'I have some rather disturbing information. It has been brought to my attention that sums of money are missing from clients' accounts, and these sums have been chanelled to correspondents in London and Zurich – not in the bank's name and not in the clients' names. In your name. My information is that the money has been used for sizeable purchases of gold.'

'There are client accounts,' said Pieter, 'that I manage at my discretion. Naturally, we have occasion to move the money, sometimes discreetly – to buy metals, or stocks, or bonds. That is our business.'

'These transactions are not properly recorded.'

'I've meant to talk with you about book-keeping arrangements for some time,' Van Helding said. 'We have a system that is so old-fashioned.'

'I mean, Pieter, that the money has been diverted for your own use.'

'I can't understand how you would get that impression. I have simply covered the track of some clients who can't legally be in gold. Quite simple.'

'We are not Swiss,' Unger said. 'We have laws here to obey. One of them forbids embezzlement.'

'I will talk to the accountant,' Van Helding said. 'We can't have misunderstandings like this.'

Unger sat back in his chair as Van Helding left. Very well, he would not break and confess. Unger had not expected that. It would take time to hook him, time to gaff him, time to see him beached and bloody and finished. But Unger would see it happen, be sure of that.

* * *

It was 20 October. The long, hard wait for the gold price to move was telling on Pieter Van Helding. If it would only go above – say – $35.20, he would be able to escape with honour. He would have a profit for the clients' accounts, an explanation for everything. It would almost count as victory.

At ten, an American client rang to ask about his account – a refuge for money where the ever-inquisitive authorities in Washington could not quite reach it. He seemed troubled.

Ordinary behaviour, Van Helding told himself. It was ordinary for a man to be concerned with the fate of his money. This was a man who thought nothing of calls at four in the morning to check on the state of affairs. Yet Van Helding, in his jangled, tense way, allowed himself for a moment to think that stories must have reached America.

He told himself to stop it. There was another meeting that morning – routine: Unger, Koolhoven, Van Helding – and he went in fear of it. Unger must have some second line beyond the personal accusation, some course of action considered and planned out. This morning, perhaps they would know it.

Unger was as brisk, almost pedantic, as usual. He had expected an alliance – Koolhoven and Van Helding, mentor and pupil – and he found one. He dealt with ordinary business and then he let them wait out a long minute's silence before he turned to the inevitable subject.

'I've only hinted to you, Koolhoven,' he said, 'of a little trouble we have here in the bank.' He cleared his throat. 'It is a question of the management of client accounts – accounts that Pieter handles, and some that you and I thought we were in charge of. There's six million dollars missing. I think it's in gold, in London and Zurich, and I think Pieter Van Helding put it there. For himself.'

Van Helding had to answer, now the allegation was public. It hardly mattered if Koolhoven was sympathetic to his case or not. It mattered more that the story had been told to witnesses, as fact.

'I presume,' Koolhoven said, 'there is evidence.'

'As accountant, you should know better than anybody.'

'I do know money from discretionary accounts sometimes goes in surprising directions at surprising times. I don't consider that my business, provided we don't break the law and the books balance at the end of the year.'

'These deals,' Unger said flatly, 'are not within the law.'

'I think this is all a misunderstanding,' Van Helding put in. Anything to defuse the situation, to play out time.

'Nevertheless,' Unger said, 'I feel obliged to take action. I have brought forward the date of this year's bank audit.'

'Isn't that rather an expensive trick?' Van Helding asked.

'I am not given to tricks,' Unger said. 'It is a precaution. If the audit shows something wrong, then I shall expect resignations. Even the banks that vote the Van Helding trust would expect resignations, I'm sure.'

'The money is not missing,' Van Helding said stubbornly.

'Then the audit will simply help us sort out affairs earlier in the year,' Unger said. He was bland and utterly self-confident, so it seemed. The papers he had cleaned from his desk – those plain, buff files – would speak against Van Helding's father, against the bank which was the foundation of Van Helding's little fortune. He could hardly use them. They amounted to the stories of unknown, unnamed men, talking in a bar somewhere, reported with more or less care by some FBI man with an interest in making his reports good reading.

Yet Van Helding mentioned them, obliquely.

'The files I sent you some days ago – '

'Not relevant,' Unger said. 'But thank you for letting me see them.'

Outside the room, Van Helding turned to Koolhoven and showed his nervousness. 'What do I do?' he asked.

Koolhoven shrugged, and walked away.

Van Helding walked out of the building, although it was not yet midday. He wanted a raw steak sandwich. He did not know if he had appointments; he was holding himself together by will and nerve. He picked up a morning paper he had already read, and stood by the edge of the canal, watching the wintry rainbow of its oily sheen. He was cold and lost. He should have brought a coat, anything rather than shivering out here in the inhospitable October damp.

Those papers, given him that night, should have been magic; yet they failed him. He was losing his battle – to stay in the bank, to win the bank, to be a power within Europe and America, a money captain.

Desolate, but with his face stilled so that he could smile if it was socially required, he returned to the office.

His secretary had left a note.

'Gone to lunch. Gold at $39·75.'

He had spent so many weeks waiting for just this information that, when it came, it barely registered. Of course the American dollar was weakening and the price of gold rising. Of course Europeans, anxious about currencies, wanted to buy gold. Of course some little deal – like his own artificial flurry of interest in a big Zurich purchase – might swing things. But the Bank of England, he had come to think, would never lose control of the London market – could not be allowed to lose control.

But, marvellously, it had. The official gold fix was up above the $35·08 figure that had so long seemed immutable.

What Van Helding had to second-guess now was: for how long?

He called O'Higgins, expecting not superior knowledge

or information, but rather a sounding board for his own opinions.

'I think you can say,' O'Higgins said, 'The fix isn't fixed. Price going every which way. I've seen trades as high as $40. Got anyone who wants to sell?'

'Can it last?'

'Not a hope, old boy. The central banks will have to get control. It's not just some metal, after all, it's the basis of money and exchange and world trade and a good bit of Bretton Woods.'

'Political, you mean – they'll have to bring the price down?'

'Can't think what made them lose control,' O'Higgins said.

Van Helding thought of the Americans, the rebuilders of Europe, the opponents of the London gold market in the first place – and now the Kennedys, pledged to support the price of the dollar, which in turn meant keeping down the price of gold. Yet if they held the price of gold down, in dollars, it would pay more than ever to use dollars to buy gold and to sell the gold in other currencies.

Van Helding called Zurich. His Bahnofstrasse contact said he could sell almost 200,000 ounces. There was suddenly that much speculative interest. Van Helding said his own big buyer – the one he had produced days before – was now not interested, but he might have sellers. He had 171,000 ounces of gold in accounts, nursed now for nine agonizing months. He could sell what he had, when he wanted.

But not today.

He thought: what if the Americans act overnight, and simply crumple the market, as they have done before? The time gap was against Van Helding; Washington could act until ten o'clock on an Amsterdam evening without keeping a single secretary over her appointed hours.

But it's going to go higher, Van Helding thought. Not much, but higher. They'll have to consult, long and shamefacedly, before they can settle the price again. He felt an exhilaration that his long-odds gamble was working, and looked set to work even better. If he could just hold on, he would have made himself.

Overnight he was sleepless, until he rose at dawn to a cold shower, strong coffee, and a morning dash to the office. He brought together all the files of all the accounts he had – adjusted – for his coup.

At eleven that morning, after the London fix, he was a net seller of gold – between $40.25 and $41.50. On that hysterical day, the kind of vulgar day the gold market had hoped never to see, he sold at the top. The very sight of disturbance in so august an institution as the London fix – the impact on South America, on Europe's nervous countries – had sent the price bounding.

By two in the afternoon, he had unloaded everything. The last ten-tola bar was sold. Some went to Malaysia, some to Bahrein and Kuwait (a legal way out of the otherwise tightly guarded sterling area), and some to buyers whose exact location and exact nationality and residence it would have been unkind to ask. At two he gave instructions to cable the proceeds of the sales back to Amsterdam, divided between the accounts he had depleted. Each received what had been laid out plus ten per cent – a reasonable return in the early 1960s, and one that implied that Van Helding had sold out at a conservative level.

The profit was almost a million dollars. When the ten per cent was paid, Van Helding kept the balance in Switzerland. It would be safe there, and unobtrusive.

On 20 October, he thought, he had been about to resign in disgrace from Kellerman Unger.

On 21 October, by the grace of God, the Bank of England, and the US Treasury (with the help of their acolytes, the Rothschilds), he had made the books ready and respectable for the auditors, pocketed $370,000 in cash, and made Unger look a fool.

That night Katherine and Pieter Van Helding shared a magnum of Lanson '47 and danced in the cold, wet garden.

Jan Unger was quiet at his morning meeting with Koolhoven. He was perfectly still, and his long, thin face was without expression.

'Pieter and Katherine send their greetings,' Koolhoven reported. 'From Kenya.'

'Yes,' Unger said.

'I'm glad the business of the gold resolved itself.'

'Yes,' Unger said again, and then: 'I'm sure Pieter Van Helding has a brilliant future.' He looked out at the grey morning clouds and the bare trees. 'Brilliant,' he said. 'God help us all.'

3

Jan Unger was cold – cold enough to wear a heavy topcoat on a brilliant summer morning, to go walking with a face that was solemn and blue-white even in the sun. He walked without pleasure, measuring miles obsessively. He wanted to be out of the city and away from the machinery of his life and yet it pursued him here.

He shouldn't have come to walk near Meyr's house. That was a mistake. He remembered the day when Meyr was arrested and taken out before a firing squad of photographers, and he remembered the day Pieter Van Helding had left some papers on his desk which threatened him, Jan Unger, with the same fate. That was three years back, long, losing years.

Worse things would happen now. Marisia was almost twenty-one, almost old enough to take over her shares in Kellerman Unger. Of course she was young, and a girl, and abroad; probably she would be happy to leave the proxy votes where they lay, in Unger's hands. But the situation would be unpredictable with the Van Heldings in secure possession of more than 45 per cent of the bank. And of course if the lovely, the glorious Widow Van Helding should fall from a horse or run under a cab, the situation would be even worse for Unger. She had a life interest in 10 per cent of the bank, which was nicely controlled by dull trust lawyers in New York. If she died, the shares went to the Van Helding children. They would have the bank.

Unger turned a corner, and came to the gates of Meyr's estates. They were padlocked, and the driveway looked as though nobody had passed that way for months. Grass was taking back the road, and the bushes had grown wild.

Unger stood at the gates, staring. It was a cold, terrible future, to be thrown out of what comfort you had made yourself because of some new moral order. Meyr had only done what other men had done, except that he had been caught. Jan Unger had done good things for Jews and for goyim alike, as well as for some higher ranking Nazis. They hadn't had a choice. They couldn't have said no. And besides, there was nobody to tell them it was wrong to cooperate. The immediate, pressing, gun-holding power was German and Nazi; you could not simply pretend it did not exist, and use the shield of morality to protect yourself. Jan Unger wanted someone to tell him he wasn't wrong, he hadn't been wrong; that he'd paid his dues.

Out of the shrubbery stepped a man in a grey uniform, neat and with a gun. He spotted Unger and marched to the gate.

'This is private property,' the guard said.

'I know,' Unger said. 'But nobody lives here any more.'

'Not now.'

'A man called Meyr lived here. Didn't he?'

'Once. He was a Nazi. They caught him and put him away.'

'Oh yes,' Unger said. 'I remember.'

'Move on,' said the guard. 'You don't have business here.'

And Unger turned, his narrow shoulders stooped and hopeless.

A little way down the road, he was passed by a large black Mercedes which stopped suddenly and reversed a little.

The window wound down.

'Jan Unger?' said a voice from the back of the car.

Unger paused for a moment as though he wanted to admit nothing, and then grudgingly said: 'Yes.'

'Can I give you a lift? I'm heading back to Amsterdam.'

'I don't think I know you.'

'You do,' said the man in the car. 'From Berlin in 1945 and Amsterdam before that. Koch. I was with the industrial boys.'

'I don't keep in touch,' Unger said.

'You should,' Koch said. 'In case you ever need anything.'

'It's a little late for that, isn't it?'

Koch came to the window, a steel-grey man with heavy jowls.

'I don't think so. We haven't all disappeared, you know. Some of us have companies and some of us have – banks. If Germany wants senior bankers, there aren't any who didn't get some experience during the bad years.'

'The bad years,' Unger said.

'That's what they call them. Personally . . .'

'I'd rather walk,' Unger said.

'We must have dinner. I'll call you.'

Kock wound up the window of the limousine and sped away, leaving Unger standing puzzled by the roadside. There wasn't anything he wanted except the end of Pieter Van Helding's power over him, and that wasn't something a gaggle of old German friends, acting on sufferance from the new moral order, could possibly deliver.

He began to walk, like a clockwork soldier wound into action.

Koolhoven waited in the drawing room. He had business with Van Helding, but more than that, he wanted to see little Georg – now almost two. He doted on the child, watched all the processes of talk and teeth and walking with a sentimental, grandfatherly fascination. His face brightened when the child was close; when the child went away to the nursery he seemed sad. Koolhoven had seemed too big, too rational a man to be vulnerable until Pieter saw him with the baby.

'He has to sleep now,' the nurse said.

'Just a minute longer,' Koolhoven said.

'I really think nurse knows best,' Katherine said, signalling with an eyebrow that the baby be taken away. 'Would you like a drink?'

And the baby was removed in long, woollen shawls and Koolhoven looked disappointed.

'We have to keep feed times and bath times and bedtimes regular,' Katherine said. 'Nurse insists.'

'I expect so,' Koolhoven said. He wondered if she really liked his interest in the child. She seemed suspicious and almost jealous. Since Koolhoven was the one who brought treats and presents, he was the one who brought out the smiles and grins. He seemed to be loved.

'Pieter will be down in a minute,' Katherine said. 'I expect you two have business to discuss.'

'I'm afraid so.'

'I'll leave you, then.'

It was as though she had wanted to police his time with the child and now she felt he could be left alone.

Van Helding was late and newly showered and boyish.

'Business,' Koolhoven said flatly. 'I had a brief talk with Unger this afternoon – this and that. He's adamant about the Warburg prospectus. He doesn't want anything to do with it.'

'Then he's a fool,' Pieter said. 'Can't we outvote him?'

'It's a management issue, but he could always say it had to be decided at board level. And he has the votes there, still. He has his own shares, and he still votes Marisia's.'

'So we get left behind by history? Thank God that can't go on for long.'

Koolhoven said: 'You're sure about the deal yourself, I suppose.'

'You don't mean you have doubts?'

'It simply looks odd. It's the first time anyone has put

together a deal in Eurodollars and it's for building roads in Italy. You can't say that is orthodox.'

'That's the whole point. There are millions of dollars in circulation outside America. Nobody's known how to use them. This deal uses them properly – and it gives people a chance to raise money outside the usual rules of capital markets.'

'No rules, big risk,' Koolhoven said.

'Not necessarily,' Pieter said. 'Or do you assume that every government rule makes the world a better place?'

'I assume nothing. I only know there's another Dutch underwriter, and the names on the prospectus look respectable even by Unger's standards. It's worth a try.'

'That's exactly what Unger won't see,' Pieter said. 'All his life he's worked by the rule book and now he's got a chance to write the rules himself, he panics. He's got the morals of a policeman.'

'Not necessarily bad,' Koolhoven said.

Van Helding sneered. 'And not very profitable, either.'

Koolhoven said: 'There do have to be rules.'

'I know,' Van Helding said. 'And I want a share in writing them.'

'Georg looks very well, little Georg.'

'Yes, he does.'

'You're building something for him.'

'Oh no. I build for myself. You know that.'

'Yes,' Koolhoven said. 'I suppose I do.'

'And now, if you'll forgive me, we have people coming to dinner – not very proper people, I'm afraid. Young and dumb.'

'You need to take some time for yourself.'

'I do. There's really nothing I do that doesn't amuse me, somehow. I don't have time for other things.'

Koolhoven rose and said: 'Give my love to Katherine.'

And he left Pieter in the drawing room, with its stripped pine from London and its colour-field painting, a shimmering red mass, over the mantelshelf, and its utterly unfamiliar style. Koolhoven could hear music as he climbed into his car, and he didn't know it.

Pieter Van Helding was beginning to seem quite alien – not the boy he'd helped to train, but a force with his own laws and dynamic working, in a different world. Koolhoven wondered for a moment how long he would be able to keep up.

The music he hadn't recognized was the first Beatles album. Katherine liked the tight, formal shapes and the precision and she played it loud.

In his room, Georg Van Helding turned in his cot. The big, soft English nanny came to watch him and she noticed that he was bruised on the arms. She had seen him rubbing himself earlier in the day and thought nothing of it. Now she thought furiously.

Downstairs the guests had finished dinner, and a couple were dancing – demonstrating for a laughing crowd. Georg Van Helding blinked awake, and stared up at shadows playing on the ceiling of his room. He called out. He could hear, but not understand, the gale of laughter far below him.

The nurse looked more closely at her charge. From his mouth there ran a scrawl of blood, down the side of his unformed face.

Before she went downstairs, she called the doctor.

Marisia Van Helding lay on what looked through the viewfinder like the wide marble floor of a great hall. She showed as much flesh as late-night TV could tolerate, and she writhed a little as an adenoidal boy from Modesto poured artificial blood over her. Two men with solid, carved beards encouraged him. Then the boy took a sword and put it firmly on her stomach, and she thought the cold steel tickled.

'That's enough blood,' said one of the bearded men,

Marty Genovese. Through the camera Marisia appeared dead, cut through with the prop sword. There was blood in grotesque excess, like crimson snow.

'Right,' said Marty. 'Get the big klieg over a little to the left and we're ready.'

There was a volley of hammering and sawing and a sudden splintering. Marty looked anxious.

'And please get the carpenters to keep quiet. We're all on the same side, God knows, not to mention the same payroll.'

His colleague, called Alan, went off to negotiate with the workers. There was a murmur, a cross cry of 'We're paid to strike this fucking set, not keep it up for a bunch of kids', a brief silence, and Marty called: 'Action.'

Marisia writhed on the painted marble, struggled up vengefully, fell back defeated – a lady vampire breathing her earthly last. She could feel the prop sword slipping as she rolled her eyes, pouted demoniacally and rasped her eyes.

'Cut,' said Marty. 'That's a print.'

'Of course it's a print,' the cameraman said, belligerently. 'What makes you think we have the stock to shoot it again?'

The hammering started again. A huge flat, tall as the light bars that formed a kind of net above the soundstage, began to fall slowly down. It had seemed to be a timeless wall of a great castle, its period inexact but its solidity and evil beyond question. Now it lay flat, struts visible, ancient stone visible where the canvas had torn. Lights for a lightning effect came into view.

'We'll have to change angles for the close-up,' the cameraman said. 'We're getting the light from the other half of the studio now.' He paused, and fiddled with a lens. 'Or we could do it like *Vampyr* – remember that? All superimpositions, go in close?'

Marty nodded, sagely. He sometimes seemed to know

the repertoire of all shots used by all other directors in all possible circumstances, and he was never reluctant to reproduce them, in an emergency. Marisia decided there was no point in moving, and she stayed patiently close to the ground while the crew manhandled camera and dolly into position, and trained their neat, exact vision on her face. The adenoidal boy added some extra blood.

'I could be subtle,' he said, 'if we had colour.'

Marisia pouted, rolled her eyes and fell back, once more.

'Foam?' said the boy, hopefully. 'I could make her foam.'

'She's turning to dust,' Marty said.

The boy nodded.

'And how exactly are we going to do the special effect?' the cameraman asked. 'I mean, I don't want to say anything but if they've taken down the castle, they'll want the floor pretty soon. Lunch breaks don't last for ever.'

'We steal the floor,' Marty said. 'Anyone got some twenties? Right, then give them to the head carpenter. We only need enough floor to match backgrounds – six feet by six will do.'

Marisia sat up. The sword fell off her belly and she wiped away some of the blood – a tasteless confection known, in homage to its main English users, as Kensington Gore.

'Is that all?' she said.

From high in the steel girders above the sound stage a great chandelier, full of effects candles of everlasting wax, came spluttering down to the ground, close to Marisia's last position. She scampered for the side.

'How many days did Corman give you?' she asked.

'Three. That's to shoot it. I had two extra days to do the script.'

Marisia watched a terrible wall, damp, crawling, stones jutting and full of crevices and plague-bumps, reduced to plywood and moulded plastic.

'Does he always make films like this?'

'Always,' Marty said. 'He's paid for the sets, after all, so he gets as much as he can out of them. Sometimes he makes the second film himself, and sometimes – well, he gives someone like me a chance.'

'I didn't expect to be a vampire,' Marisia said, 'when I enrolled at UCLA.'

'I didn't expect you to be a vampire,' said Marty, briskly. 'Not until Corman said there wasn't enough blood in the last reel.'

The crew emerged, one by one, from the remains of the sets, each one with a brilliant angle on some so far undestroyed vista. They settled in the diner across the road, a kind of prototype Ma Maison for graduate film school students, to do their deals and exercise their fantasies.

'There's the chase to do,' Marty said.

'There's a great shot in *The Third Man*,' the cameraman said, 'in the sewers – where the whole frame is full of water, and all you can see is the stick figures. We could do that sort of thing – shoot wild and cut it together.'

'Venice,' Marty said. 'That's it. We go down to Venice tonight and shoot there. Listen, if Orson Welles could make Venice into the Mexican border, we can make it Transylvania.'

Marisia appeared, startling in a skimpy peasant outfit and obstinately clinging blood.

'I'm going to write a thesis,' she said, 'on low-budget film-making as art and hygiene. Isn't there anywhere I can shower?'

'We need the blood,' Marty said.

Out of a gym bag the adenoidal boy produced a rubber skull. He liked not to announce such effects, but Marisia looked at it with simple, professional interest. There was an alarming eye in one socket and a shred of hair attached to the skull.

'Gross,' said Marty. 'Absolutely gross.'

'Thank you,' said the boy, humbly.

Marisia said: 'My mother always did worry about my bone structure.' Nobody seemed inclined to laugh.

They ate hamburgers while the skull sat, shiny and foul, between them.

'Do we get an extra day's shooting if we agree to shoot at night?'

'I doubt it,' Marty said. He was a stocky, bearded man, prepared to play his Italian-ness to the very hilt if he could get his way. 'And I don't care. We have the camera, we have the stock, let's make a movie.'

'I know,' said the cameraman, bugging his eyes, fixing a radiant smile on normally grumpy features, 'I-have-a-great-idea-kids-why-don't-we-put-on-a-show . . .'

And someone started to hum 'Babes in Arms'.

Marisia contemplated the good-natured chaos about her and drank her coffee slowly. She had bumped into Marty first at a campus cafeteria, and he had actually said 'I can make you a star.' The line was so startling Marisia had no time to prepare her resistance and she listened to his plan. He was a graduate film student. He was working, with no union card and for almost no money, as an assistant on a horror picture – an almost cultural horror picture which hoped to do for Gogol what Vincent Price had already done for Edgar Allan Poe. Gogol's main attraction seemed to be that he was out of copyright.

Marty had been given the remains of that film – a day's work left on the star's contract, the run of the sets until they came down, film stock, and a gang of helpers. His enthusiasm, his obsession, convinced Marisia almost immediately. He said when he was eight he opened his first movie theatre, in Pasadena, in his house. He said he had spent his adolescence entirely in movie theatres; he had seen the works of John Ford from the front row. He said he had always made films, even when he didn't have a camera, stock or lights; he would draw flicker books on the edges of anything with pages. Once, he was beaten for animating Spiderman down the sides of the family Bible.

And Marisia anticipated play. It was only a few days, after all, and she would strike some glorious romantic poses, say 'doom' a great deal, and alternately run in blind terror and glow seductively. However, play at midnight in cold, damp Venice did not appeal to her.

But Marty did not consider it play.

'If we get the chase,' he said, 'I think we may have a plot line.' His frankness was disarming. He had inherited a jumbled story about a sculptor who boils his victims in wax to make a show on the faces of terror (which would make a title, Corman agreed) but he had been told to turn the sculptor into a vampire. Marisia was his solution.

'We'd better get going,' the adenoidal boy said. 'The effects stage.'

'The effects stage,' said Marisia, wonderingly, as they piled into a pair of Chevy pick-ups and roared out into the decent great recesses of Westwood. At the back of a neat suburban home was a neat suburban shed, where the stolen floor from the studio had already been laid.

First, Marisia writhed for a close-up. Then the adenoidal boy, shaking the plastic bottle sadly, put more blood on her and said it was almost the last he had. Then he put a fright-wig on her to represent the start of rot and decay. Then the artificial eye was put over one of her eyes. Then the eye was replaced in the socket of the skull with an awful little suction sound, and the skull replaced the living Marisia on the marble floor. The skull itself was peeled of rubbery flesh, and then the grinning, naked bone was taken away and dust replaced it. The boy took a vacuum cleaner on reverse, scattered a few dry, painted leaves, and allowed the dust and leaves to blow gently away.

'Poetic,' he said. 'I got it from the Terence Fisher *Dracula*.'

Marisia watched with fascination. She knew a little

about the mechanics of film, enough to realize the wonderful speed with which this group was working. Under 'proper' conditions, there would have been studio days with a choice of flirting, playing poker, or reading books. But under 'proper' conditions, she could not have worked in a film. She was only a theatre arts major at UCLA.

Her problem was Marty. He had made a pass at her, as she had expected, and she had refused, as he had expected. Yet the camera gave him a power over her that would never have been present in any mere sexual encounter – a power to intrude, possess, and manipulate. Besides, Marisia did not take this film seriously enough for Marty. She knew it would go out with some other shocker to play before entangled teenage audiences in drive-in theatres, full of Cokes and fries and plans for sexual experiments.

Marty thought differently. This would be his first real credit – his name as director on a proper movie. He had shot a couple of nudie pictures before, occasions contrived to allow nipples to dangle before an ogling camera, but those did not count. He wanted never again to be a second assistant director and dialogue coach. To Marisia's alarm, he began to talk about this movie's style, about himself as its auteur.

She curled in the corner of the suburban house, still made up in case they needed to reshoot, still dressed in her gypsy shift. She looked oddly homely and innocent as she slept. She had worried until she dozed what the owners of the house would think when they returned to find it full of blood and wild women.

In her dreams, she seemed to be asking herself if this business of pretence and projection was what she wanted. Softly, she began to dream of being a movie star.

The white corridors were bleak and relentless, until the doors to the doctors' offices. Once through the doors, there were leather chairs and kind lighting. Yet Katherine did not find the gentler, more amiable rooms a comfort. Georg's survival would depend on science, exactness, on a clinical and sterile skill. Kindness was not what she needed.

'There really is no reason to be alarmed,' the doctor said.

Katherine wondered if he would later call Pieter aside and tell the truth. She hated the doctor for his kindly lies, and yet she knew she could not challenge them. It was all one convention – challenging the lies, and she must also challenge the authority that could cure baby Georg.

'I won't lie to you,' the doctor said, smiling. Katherine thought: he wants to pat my knee to reassure me. 'The blood tests show a very high white cell count, and leukaemia is one possible diagnosis. But there are others. We shan't know until all our tests are complete.'

'We hoped . . .' Katherine began. 'That is, I had hoped you would have an answer for us already.'

'Not a certain one. We may have to keep Georg here for another day, perhaps two. He'll be home after that.'

'We can see him?'

'Just for a moment. He's very scared with all the new faces around him. It's often better not to disturb children when they're in hospital.'

Katherine said, hopelessly: 'We could bring him toys – familiar things. We could talk to him and make him less scared.'

'I don't think so,' said the doctor, smiling his avuncular, authoritarian smile. 'Just for the moment what matters are the tests. Let us get on with them, and you'll have him back very soon.'

Pieter sat back from the exchange, trying to read what the doctor really meant. It was obvious the doctor thought of fear as a communicable disease, an infection which could be kept away if parents could be kept away. He meant a mother was no way to calm a child; a needle was better, more reliable, not given to hysteria. Van Helding saw Georg, very clearly, in a bright, white, featureless room, in a sterile cot, in the middle of machines.

And it was like that in the ward, where Georg scuffled under the bedclothes that lay lightly over him, his arms bruised from blood tests and illness. Katherine sensed the monstrous little change, a mere shift in the balance of the blood, that had turned the child's own body against him and left him pale and weak from the mutiny.

'He's asleep, Mrs Van Helding,' said the nurse.

Katherine longed to hold him. Pieter was preoccupied with other matters, he looked again and again at his watch. He had done his duty, and it was time to move on.

'I have to go,' he said. 'Management meeting.'

'But they won't say what's wrong with him. They want us to stay.'

'That's not possible,' Pieter said.

'Pieter, please stay. I can't be in this place all by myself – in those corridors, waiting.'

'I'll send a car later.'

'Please,' said the nurse. 'The baby is trying to sleep now. You're disturbing him.'

Pieter was already at the door, and he strode for the car and the town like an impatient man.

Katherine in the corridor again seemed to be the only emotion, open and bloody, in the whole sterile place. The doors never opened, and nobody passed through these waiting chambers. The crises hidden away in special places where chrome and steel and sluices made it possible to dispose of fear, if necessary. Katherine thought the place was alive with pain, behind the unlabelled doors.

And she was alone, and Pieter had gone, and she would have to be strong.

Koolhoven sensed Van Helding's rush at the afternoon meeting and asked what was wrong.

'Nothing,' Van Helding said. 'Georg has a problem. Katherine's handling it.'

'He's sick?'

'The hospital is handling it.'

'The hospital?' Koolhoven was genuinely concerned and he wanted to know more.

'This isn't the time to discuss such things,' Van Helding said.

'But I'm concerned.'

'Katherine will deal with it.'

Jan Unger creaked into the room on stiff, reluctant joints and settled at the table.

'Gentlemen,' he said. 'There is some detailed business to consider, but the prime matter is I think the annual report.'

Van Helding coughed. 'And the Autostrade bond issue, surely – Warburg's Eurodollar business?'

'Possibly,' Unger said. He was still chairman of the bank, still the senior man. He could veto actions by Van Helding and sometimes make the veto stick. True, he was painfully aware of how little time he might have left, but that was all the more reason to hold the bank within narrow limits and make it work as he wanted.

And besides, he was to have dinner with Koch that night and some friends of Koch's. He felt better among his own generation, with people who shared his own – mistakes.

'It is vitally important,' Pieter said. 'that we participate in the Autostrade deal. It's the first, I think, of many such deals. If we keep out, we deny ourselves the privilege of banking anywhere in the world – breaking out of the petty national restrictions. We also deny ourselves access to a billion-dollar market which is going to get stronger and stronger.'

'For the annual meeting . . .' Unger began.

'That doesn't matter,' Pieter said.

'. . . I propose to make the chairman's address on the

subject of dangerous developments in international finance. I thought I would call it "gypsy money" – a good phrase, don't you think?'

Van Helding looked dangerous.

'What exactly do you mean by gypsy money?'

'Deals,' said Unger, twitching a little with pleasurable anticipation, 'very much like the Autostrade bond issue on which you're so keen – deals where banks don't have to follow national law, and the money is dollars that have nothing to do with America, and nobody is ever quite sure who guarantees a bond.'

'Read the prospectus,' Pieter said. 'It's a perfectly proper dollar bond for a perfectly proper outfit.'

'I think my theme will be generally appreciated.'

'It will make us all look damn fools – reactionary beyond belief.'

'I don't think,' Unger said, gathering papers, 'we need discuss much more today, do you? Nothing that can't wait for tomorrow morning.'

And he went stiffly from the room, his old, thin body shaking with delight.

Pieter sat glaring after him, and Koolhoven tried to calm him, but unsuccessfully.

'Damned idiot,' Pieter managed to say.

'He is chairman. Let him have his say.'

'He is chairman,' Pieter said grimly. 'But not for long.'

In his own office – promoted now to a space on the executive corridor – he sat fuming. Out there was a world where the frontiers of money were at last coming down after Depression, a war, and a painful recovery, and Unger stood betweeen him and controlling that new empire. Unger was the one. When Marisia had her share of the bank she would hardly oppose Pieter; she loved him too well. When their mother died, the majority of bank shares would belong to him and to Marisia. And Kellerman Unger would not be one of the old, imperial banks, with no idea where to put their cash now Indonesia had gone red, and Surinam seemed insignificant. Van Helding would not join the old men grumbling into their gin.

Van Helding had a last appointment at five. He had taken a call earlier that day from someone called Noam Gregory. The name was half-familiar. Gregory hinted at information given, favours done, and favours now required. Van Helding agreed to see him.

He knew the man at once – the stocky melodramatic figure who had taken him out to the polder to tell him the truth about Jan Unger, or as much of it as Van Helding could use. Noam Gregory's anonymity was perfect camouflage; his business suit seemed to talk for him.

'I will come to the point,' he said. 'I wish to open an account and make some payments.'

'I'm sure there is no difficulty there.'

Gregory smiled. 'Payments in a confidential manner.'

'You're sure you don't want Zurich?'

'I am a great admirer of the Swiss,' Gregory said, 'but no, I do not need another account in Zurich. The transactions I have in mind need to be routed very carefully. A payment from Switzerland is too obvious. An account in Switzerland isn't always the easiest thing. We like – to cover our traces, sometimes.'

'You realize Dutch law and Swiss law are very different?'

'Of course. The account will be in my name. I simply ask that my name does not go to the Bank of the Netherlands.'

'That's tricky to organize.'

'But perfectly possible,' Gregory said, 'for such friends.'

Van Helding nodded.

'At various times, in my business, I need to move large amounts of money – but no more than millions of US dollars. It is also possible that the money will sometimes not arrive in time for the transfer, if you understand me. Sometimes we have to take advantage of a business opportunity while we can.'

'You want a line of credit, in other words.'

'No more than two million US. But no less, either.'

'And your principal? Who is your principal?'

'I am,' Gregory said.

'What do I know about your credit rating? I am still a banker, after all.'

'I am a good risk.'

'I don't mean to doubt you, but my problem is the auditors here. I would need some sort of collateral for the credit line.'

'Aren't the papers enough? The papers on your colleague?'

'I would prefer assets. Anything that can go on the books and not be too conspicuous. I'm sure you don't want to be too conspicuous.'

'We do not have assets,' Gregory said.

'Then perhaps – paper?' Van Helding gestured to Gregory's briefcase. He presumed other deals like this one had been struck with other banks who also had to convince their auditors. There must be some phantasmal paper that could be produced. He waited while Gregory reached into his briefcase and pulled out a weary pile of documents, which he pushed across the desk.

'I had hoped,' Gregory said, 'this would not be necessary.'

The pile was full of gaudy marks on vellum, Gothic printing signifying nothing. It was like an autumnal rollcall for old empires. There were Czarist bonds, fixed in gold and now worthless since the Revolution; and shares in lost railways that had once climbed the Andes in someone's dreams; and speculations from the 1920s in outlying plains in Argentina, or in Colombian coffee or New York patents (one could almost have been the precursor of satellites, but was not); and the remains of London companies that once grew the finest Assam tea, or brought back rubber from Malaysia, or owned the civic cemetery in Dundee. Such companies are left as paper ghosts around the healthiest of stock markets, and Gregory had collected their paper systematically.

'I don't suppose,' Van Helding said, 'any one of these is still an active quoted company anywhere?'

'I don't think so.'

'Then we can set our own value on these shares – for the auditors?'

Gregory grinned. 'It is a pleasure,' he said, 'to do business with a gentleman.'

'And will you be making a deposit today?'

Gregory produced one last document from his briefcase – less grand but more prepossessing than the others. It was a letter of credit on Grunwald Frères for a quarter of a million dollars US.

Van Helding paused. He was surprised by the Grunwald connection, and he wondered again precisely what Gregory did, what he wanted, why and how he traded in information. He was something of a blackmailer, clearly, and something more than a simple broker of information, for that would hardly be business. And the reason he came to Van Helding, Van Helding supposed, was that one of the Grunwalds saw a chink in the coming man's armour, a weakness that could be exploited. They needed him; that was clear.

Gregory watched Van Helding's silence intently, trying to calculate and fathom it. He worried for a moment if Van Helding had the power to deliver the proper protection, but he assumed he did. He wondered if Van Helding needed slight jogging.

'The earlier material,' Gregory said, 'which I'm sure you remember. We have someone interested in publishing now – a serious work, of course, nothing sensational. It is difficult to refuse such an offer. Such things should be known.'

Subtle, Van Helding thought. He knows I am so meshed with this bank – not least as part owner – that I won't want scandal around its name. Unger remains the senior spokesman. If Unger is discredited, the bank suffers.

'There may be some difficulties about the publication, of course,' Gregory said. 'Legal matters and so forth.'

Van Helding calculated quickly. Unger discredited, the bank would suffer. But if Unger were finally discredited, his opposition to matters like the Eurodollar dealers would be put aside for ever. And Van Helding would have no more rivals at home.

'You know how these things are,' Gregory said.

The final point came to Van Helding, who had a cold eye for the exact position he occupied. He was too young. If he emerged as chairman of Kellerman Unger in his twenties, and if the old management seemed to have fallen away, it would be pure luck if his authority could carry the bank and keep it credible. He needed an old man at the top, and that old man was Unger.

He rose, shook hands and said: 'Let me have a note of the details.'

'I shall need to move money to Oslo,' Gregory said. 'Very soon.'

Van Helding raised an eyebrow.

'You won't want to know why,' Gregory said. 'You'll understand soon enough.'

For a moment, Van Helding saw headlines in crimson.

Katherine called and called from the hospital; she did not reach Pieter until Gregory had been shown from the building.

'They do think it's leukaemia,' she said.

'I know,' Pieter said. 'The blood and the bruising. The doctors said that.'

'They want to keep Georg overnight.'

'Then come home. He'll be fine.'

'I can't leave my baby here. It's so – sterile. He'll be terrified.'

'Then they'll give him a sedative.'

'He is your child, too.'

Pieter said: 'Katherine, we have a dinner engagement this evening and it matters. You'll come home.'

'We can't just go out to dinner. Georg is in hospital.'

'I'll send the car,' Pieter said.

As he walked down the main marble stairs, he saw Unger at the door, more than ever like some emaciated cartoon banker, a fleshless, predator bird. Unger was in fine feathers, ready for an evening out – something businesslike, Pieter assumed, and practical, just like his own plans.

'Good evening,' he said courteously.

Unger looked at him with something close to contempt. 'Good evening,' he said.

The two men caught each other's eyes in a brisk duel of wills, and Unger looked down first. Van Helding wondered what possible dinner invitation could have made the man so smug and certain.

The car reached the canalside house a full three quarters of an hour later, and Katherine was in tears. She sat on the sofa with eyes gone weak and lifeless, rubbing at her face like an animal in distress.

'I can't do it,' she said.

'You will do it,' Pieter said. 'It's something we have to do.'

'You have to do it. I don't.'

'You have to do it. That's part of the rules.'

'But with Georg . . .'

'We are not going to mention that damn child,' Pieter said.

He left the room briefly and returned with a small box which he laid, reverently, on a side table.

'Candy,' he said.

'No, Pieter,' Katherine said. 'I want to stay here.'

He took out the tiny spoon, put powder on a mirror and divided it carefully.

'Candy,' he said, looking at her with enough warmth to make her briefly feel reassured, but with a will that was not going to accept disobedience. She felt cold and alone. Candy would be a nice way out. She didn't have too many other choices.

She sniffed the powder and waited for the crystal high – red-eyed, wet-cheeked, and then, quite suddenly, smiling.

Pieter nodded. 'Now we can go,' he said, 'when you repair your face.'

She went like a child, humming.

The house had once been a hunting lodge, but a hunting lodge somewhere else – in another time, in another country. Its dark panelled walls carried trophies – buck, stags, a few great snarling heads of tiger and lion. There was a faint smell of must and time, as though the air had not been stirred around these admirable, mounted dead for months.

Jan Unger had his undertaker's look, dull and sombre. He waited in the hallway to be announced. He felt mildly nervous and alert, surprised at himself; this was only to be a meeting of old friends, and that was nothing to fear. Koch in his black Mercedes had only come to Amsterdam to see old friends.

But what old friends! When Unger walked into the main, high hall of the hunting lodge and looked around, Koch greeted him and introduced him. Big, buttery men in evening dress were all around him, a formal, black-and-white parade. They talked intently, but in low tones, as though they had a lifetime of fearing to be overheard.

A man was presented whose face at one time had been hideously burned. One eye had the skin pulled from around it, like some anatomist's drawing. Kock presented one of the leading economic advisers to Adolf Hitler. Unger was unsure how to respond to the man. Others like him were already, he knew, soaring in the new hierarchy of Western Germany because they were the only ones who knew about the running of a national economy first hand. They were indispensable, and occasionally denounced. This man, they said, had an interest in I. Farben when that firm built labour camps at Auschwitz.

'Good to see you again,' he said to Unger, and Unger wondered if he would have recognized the whole face.

There was a large, blustering Swedish man with huge, bulging blue eyes, a cartoon Nordic figure. He had been an industrialist with substantial interests in Bofors Gun. He had also been a friend of Goebbels and a mediator in the early months of the war and an economic freeway for money and goods later.

'*Enchanté*,' he said, surprisingly.

Unger looked again around the room and wondered if anyone there felt, or was, as innocent as he was. He had not been at the heart of things, able to see what the whole Nazi machine meant and intended. He had been ignorant. He had tried to help clients, whether Jews or not, whether Nazis or not. He had done banking business, nothing with treason or guns or gas. Somebody had to keep the wheels turning, even in wartime.

But Unger realized that the others in the hall took him to be one of them – the same politics, the same morals. He was just another of the brotherhood.

One man said quietly: 'It's unfortunate you've had to be so involved with the Americans. I can't help feeling that Jewish capital – '

'I'm sorry,' Unger said, and he broke away for another drink, leaving his companion startled.

This was a nightmare. He had worked throughout the war to preserve, not destroy, and perhaps as it happened he had helped what was by 1945 the wrong side. But he did not belong here. Yet they all thought that he did, assumed he shared common interests, expected him to be sympathetic and to come to them for help.

'Quite unnecessary attention,' said one man, as Unger passed. 'All of that is over now. A few radicals want to drag it up again, and to what purpose? To further the cause of Bolshevism. That's all. We are the backbone of Europe's economy, and they want to hurt us because that way they hurt the West.'

'It's an old alliance,' said the Swede.

Unger felt meshed by eyes. His long, thin body froze with alarm. It wasn't only the exposed nerves of the first man's torn face, or the extraordinary exophthalmic monster of a Swede; it was the self-righteousness of the people around him, and the calmness of their stare that he could not meet. It was a mistake to have come. They had enrolled him, simply by his presence.

And then he began to feel the friendly tug of their welcome. He had nothing to be ashamed of. Perhaps they, too, were innocent, misjudged and misrepresented by a hostile world.

'Heartless,' said the economic adviser to Hitler. 'To go after poor Meyr after all these years, and simply because he did his duty in the war. Most unfair. If I could find the people who finance that kind of action, I would . . .'

'Yes?' Unger said.

'I would take action. Or rather, I would see that action was taken. I am not exactly a soldier any more.'

'But I imagine they cover their tracks?'

'We know some of the main contributors, but not where they put their money, or how it gets out – there's a screen as you would expect. They don't want anything known.'

Nor do we, Unger thought. We think it unreasonable that the great, stolid continuity of ourselves be interrupted by anything as ephemeral as a war, a few million dead, a period of insanity. We have the same job we always had. And in many ways, we regret the past, as well.

He sat down heavily at the dinner table. This was no time to have a moral crisis, not when he was in the midst of such powerful and untroubled people. He couldn't choose sides; only one side wanted him.

They were so wonderfully ordinary, plain and pudgy, in their starch and patent-leather pumps. It could have been any brotherhood, any mutual organization, perhaps simply a reunion of men who had been together at college or school.

Jan Unger heard himself say: 'Most unfortunate about Meyr.'

Marisia lay on the Malibu beach, bored and blank. Above her wheeled high gulls, and before her the Pacific roared and rustled into shore, and the surfers rode the glass rolls of water. She closed her eyes. She could hear the birds and the sea and the surfers' shouts. She opened her eyes. It was the same damn sea, the same damn birds, the same damn surfers. Something had to change.

After the movie, there was only the campus and the classes and occasional parties – Bel Air and Beverly Hills, some student parties at suburban homes, some dormitory parties. It was, she supposed, fun if you had known nothing else. But Marisia was discovering her ominously low threshold of boredom, and waiting for a new adventure. To be on camera, dodging the cops around rain-slick locations in Venice, had been exciting; but now the billboards and big screens seemed to have nothing to do with her. She had played out her dream, and she had to wait for the next chance.

That was going to take time. There had been murmurations from her Dean that perhaps a little more concentration on school work would be welcome, just before finals.

She was concentrating now, she thought, concentrating on forgetting it all. Damn coefficients, valencies, social classes on the Rose scale, the style of Thomas Hardy, and Strindberg: Man and Dramatist. Damn it all.

The others, led by her director Marty Genovese, hadn't wanted to tell her at first; that was clear. They weren't sure how a European girl would react and what she might think if they mentioned the problem with money. As Marty put it, when finally he cranked himself to reveal the plans: 'You're different.' And then, after a moment. 'I mean that as a compliment.'

The entire matter had become so oblique, and so loudly rumoured in all the others' gossip, that Marisia finally asked directly.

'It's a matter of business,' Marty said. 'Whether we could act as a sort of a – courier.'

'Explain.'

'There's some stuff to be picked up in Mexico and brought back. And it might be difficult at the border – so someone asked us if we'd do it. Because, you see, they wouldn't worry too much about a gaggle of college kids.'

'Stuff? You mean drugs?'

Marty said: 'Yes.'

'It sounds like one of your plot lines.'

'No, I swear it, it's true. We take the money down and bring the stuff back and we get a commission.'

'You've got the details?'

'We get them tonight.'

'You get how much commission?'

'We take ten thousand dollars down. We get a thousand to split – plus gas.'

'And you didn't want to tell me?'

'You're rich. And you're European. And we didn't know what you thought about drugs. It's only cocaine – nothing bad.'

'I want to come,' Marisia said.

Marty blustered off across the beach as though he was relaying some imperial whim. When he came back, he looked crestfallen.

'It's off,' he said. 'They can't get the money.'

'Drug dealers who can't raise ten thousand dollars?' Marisia said. 'What kind of amateur organization is that?'

'I guess more amateur that I thought.'

'How old are these people?'

'They're on campus, too.'

'You know where they buy?'

'I know the name of the place.'

Marisia was up and sparkling. 'We'll go anyway,' she said. 'I'll stake it.'

'You haven't got ten thousand dollars,' Marty said. 'You're always telling us how rich and liquid aren't the same thing.'

'I'll get it,' Marisia said. 'Can we go next weekend?'

'I don't know. I have to check.'

'Check,' Marisia said.

Pieter Van Helding no longer rushed home. There was a lifelessness there which disturbed him – made up equally of Georg's sickness and Katherine's unhappiness. He wasted time running over the newspapers again in the office, even the crime pages, and he noticed one photograph – a man in a heavy coat sprawled on a snowy street, black blood around him against the antiseptic white of the ground. There had been a shooting in Oslo, just after Mr Gregory had paid out almost all his credit, and just as suddenly replaced the funds. The victim was a Lebanese, and when his home was searched for clues, the police had found a sizeable cache of arms. Nobody was quite sure what to make of it.

None of Van Helding's business, he thought to himself, and none of the bank's. Money was neutral, its transmission even more so, and its uses something far outside his competence to judge.

Time to leave the office, tease out the lights, one by one, half hope the telephone would ring to delay him, wait to call for the car until the last possible moment.

He closed the inner door of his office when the phone began to ring.

'It's me,' Marisia said, and for a moment he had no idea who was calling. Then he realized, and he felt a flush of excitement, and he was hard.

'I need some money,' Marisia said.

'You don't beat about the bush.'

'I need ten thousand dollars.'

'Ask your trustees for it.'

'I know they won't give it. And Mother never lets me have anything over my allowance. I've got a business proposition, though.'

'For me?'

'For me. And I don't have the cash.'

'You'll have to tell me about it.'

'I can't do that.'

'What are you doing – smuggling?'

'Don't be silly. I just don't want to explain it all on the phone. It's too complicated.'

'I couldn't lend you the money without knowing . . .'

'You're not my banker. You're my brother. Remember?'

'You're not in any kind of trouble? It's not an emergency you can't tell Mother about?'

'I told you. It's business.'

'I can't do it, sis.'

'But it's no money at all to you. And I'll have my share of the bank very soon anyway. It's just a matter of getting an advance.'

'You can't just take money out of Kellerman Unger when you want to,' Pieter said, stuffily.

Marisia slammed down the phone.

But she wasn't going to give up. She had a regular allowance; perhaps she could borrow against that. And she had almost a quarter of a reputable bank that would be her personal property in a birthday and a bit. That had to be worth something, somewhere. After all, they had only to dash into Mexico, buy (if all went well; some residual caution made her put that in), and dash back again. The market in Los Angeles couldn't be complicated to tap. And it was something to relieve the passive tedium of term time. It was also a question of saving face; she would not admit to the others that she had to back down from her plan, because they would think she had lost her nerve. She did not lose her nerve, and she would not let anyone think it.

At home, the baby Georg Van Helding lay full of hospital chemicals and white like paper. He sometimes seemed to fade and sometimes to rally, but he lacked the sense of life he once had abundantly. Katherine went to his room and cried, but she found it hard at times to remember he was her beloved child. She'd come to depend on his warmth against her, his responses, his laughs. She was half afraid to let Pieter know how much she needed her husband, body and soul, now that her child was sick.

The Van Heldings sequestered the child and the tragedy, and they maintained their social life. Formality was a way of escape; it dammed up bitterness and anxiety for a while and gave an illusion of control. Dinner parties, friends said, must be such an intolerable chore, and it was wonderful how Katherine coped. In reality, she couldn't have coped without them.

'I don't know what to do,' Katherine said that night, since they were dining alone. 'I don't know what consolations I should claim. I just feel stranded, Pieter. We're Jews, but we converted too well, we can't wail any more, and we're Christians, but if I light a candle or pray to a saint it doesn't mean enough. Gilles never did convert, and he still talks about Zionism, even if he looks like an elderly French gentleman with gout, which he is. And Edouard and Seraphine and the rest of them – they half made the change, only half. They don't get bothered much by God or cherubim of any persuasion.'

Pieter looked at her, part encouraging, part indifferent.

'You don't know what I mean, do you?' she said.

'I worry about Georg, too.'

'You think there's always a powder or a pill to solve the problem.'

'I don't see the point in an excess of emotion.'

'I want to pray about Georg,' Katherine said. 'Pray to . . .'

The telephone, distinctly, rang.

'I think,' Pieter said, 'I heard the telephone. I asked the servants to interrupt dinner if it sounded important.'

'How are they to know?'

But the servants had already heard, and the large, dark parlour maid, uncertain on her feet like a stuffed toy in motion, bumbled into the dining room to say that the master was wanted.

'Does it matter, Helga?' Katherine said.

The big, dark woman nodded, strongly.

'Don't go, Pieter,' Katherine said. 'Don't go, if you love me. It'll be business, I know it, and you won't talk to me any more.'

Pieter left the room, and big Helga said: 'It was California, ma'am. It must have been important.'

In the hallway, he took the call.

'You are sure, Pieter? A lot hangs on this,' Marisia said.

'I am sure. I am sorry. No money,' Pieter said.

'Damn you,' Marisia said.

It was still only one in the afternoon in California and she looked through her little red address book. The number of Angela's father seemed to stand out. Fowler. Studio fix-it and factotum, somewhere between power and the butler's pantry like many senior Hollywood men. He would surely know someone who would help.

It was almost a nineteenth-century idea, but Marisia had seen the advertisements and knew that it persisted: raising money against expectations of an inheritance. Her own bankers in New York flatly refused, citing the Widow Van Helding's special instructions – and that left outside banks and understanding people. People like brokers in reversionary interests.

Perhaps Fowler would know such people.

'Have you seen Angela recently?' he asked by way of social chat.

'Not often,' Marisia admitted.

'I'm not surprised,' Fowler said. 'She's taken herself up North to some farm settlement where they all sit around in dirty clothes and talk about their previous lives.'

Marisia stated her business.

'Well,' Fowler said, 'I know who would help you – and you'd much better not get involved with any of those newspaper shysters. You go and see my friend Henry Klein. Klein, Gosman Associates. He's a financial adviser, lots of high-powered clients, and he'd know exactly how to organize this. After all, it's not that much money.'

Fowler called Klein. It was a call less casual than might have been expected. He explained who Marisia Van Helding was, what she would inherit, and what Kellerman Unger was, in so far as he knew. And Klein at the end of their talk said: 'Thank you very much,' which seemed a curious response for someone being tapped by an adolescent for ten grand. Marisia was the kind of person he had been waiting for.

Klein's office was in a white-painted colonial fake on Santa Monica, through a door of classic Californian

Formica, in an atmosphere of air-conditioned chill. Marisia felt undressed at once.

'How,' Klein said, 'can I help you?'

He was a short, well-made miniature of a man, California-healthy but in a dark, formal suit from the East. He was not ingratiating, but he was, like the better sort of doctor, understanding.

Marisia explained that she needed $10,000. She could secure the loan on expectations of allowance or expectations of inheritance – within a very short time. She could not say what the loan was for.

Klein sparkled a little, and smiled, 'If you could,' he said, 'presumably you would go elsewhere for the money.'

Marisia nodded.

'Very well,' Klein said. 'If you need the money in a hurry, it's yours, cash or cheque. You're very well introduced by Henry Fowler. And it's really not such a large sum of money. But you'll forgive me if, just to protect myself, I make some inquiries – about Kellerman Unger and the rest?'

Marisia made no objection.

Henry Klein thought the paper she signed, giving him authority to make reasonable checks on Kellerman Unger, was well worth the $10,000 he had paid for it. Indeed, she might even pay back. She was a spectacular girl, and she talked very sensibly – nothing circumstantial, no evasions, just the point. He liked her style.

He liked carte blanche to peer into the workings of a European bank – just the sort of European bank he'd suggested to his principals earlier – even more than he liked the girl. God favoured the industrious with great luck.

Marisia took cash.

Katherine's daydreams had churches full of golden candlelight and flowers and frescoes, the rainbow panoply that compensated for pain. She prayed in those daydreams and lit candles, and saw crowds of blessed martyrs. The whole exotic ornament of the Church danced in her mind.

She tried not to think about Pieter, or about herself; she kept her mind for Georg. Besides, Pieter was brutal and unconcerned and still excited her. It wasn't right that such masochism should go with passion. If he had been more humane, she might have loved him less. And for that, she despised herself. She was a Grunwald, a woman of great family and fortune, an heir to one of the great European families; and she had given it up, easily, to Pieter Van Helding.

There was a commotion on the stairs, as though someone had slipped in a hurry, and Pieter almost fell through the door.

'Shit,' he said. 'Katherine, I have to go to Switzerland.'

Katherine looked up.

'You don't understand. My mother died.'

'In Gstaad?' said Katherine, wondering.

'Her heart just stopped. She had a house up in the mountains, in the canton she came from – she never told us exactly where. She grew up there and she went back there each year for a month or so, without fail, since my father died. It was her place.'

Katherine said, with real sympathy, but still afraid to show it too clearly before she knew how Pieter was feeling for himself: 'You'll go at once?'

'There will be things to clear up. She wanted to be buried there, I know. We once had a very businesslike talk about it, sitting at a desk – where the money went, what the wills said, where she wanted to be buried.' Pieter was overcalm. 'We never even considered she might die at home. Somehow we always thought – a plane crash, or an accident on Fifth Avenue, or just old age.' He sat down, bracing his back against the chair. 'But not sickness. Not that.'

'Perhaps the place made her feel peaceful,' Katherine said. 'Peace enough to die.'

'It was sudden,' Pieter said.

'Poor Pieter.'

'I don't know why you're supposed to be thankful if death is sudden. It leaves so much unfinished business – things to say.'

Katherine went to the drinks cupboard. 'You know I can't come with you – not now, not with Georg still sick. And you'll have family business to settle.'

'Yes,' Pieter said. 'She was very young.'

He hated the sense of vulnerability – of such glorious vivacity brought to a sudden end, just as the liveliness of his son had been drained away by illness.

He also had to calculate. His share in the bank, Marisia's share in the bank, what they inherited when his mother died – it was damn nearly a majority of Kellerman Unger stock. They only had to be able to outvote Unger, after all, and the spare shares in trust for heirs of Marisia and Pieter didn't only reduce the family holding; they also reduced Unger's and the number the Van Heldings needed to outvote him. If Marisia would only cooperate, then he had all the power he could want in the bank. A new world opened.

Jan Unger never understood a man who failed to answer his telephone. He had always faced things down, tried never to evade matters; and now he was calling and calling, hearing that absurd frog croak of a tone, and Koolhoven was refusing to answer.

Unger would not lose his temper. He had crawled through a war protected by a carapace of insensitivity and he had no intention of losing his grip now – especially not now.

He needed Koolhoven. If it was true that Mrs Van Helding had died suddenly, he remembered something ominous: that Marisia would inherit her share of Kellerman Unger immediately, and that the Widow's life interest in the bank would be divided between the children. That meant the Van Heldings could outvote him constantly, unless – unless Marisia and Pieter were not quite so much a team as he assumed. He needed to know from Koolhoven what she was like, this Californian girl with whom he now had to contend, this little film star. Surely she would be open to persuasion.

But Koolhoven did not answer. The line seemed to creak with the ringing tone.

It had been so easy up to now – the conservative bank trustees giving Unger their proxies, voting in line with him, allowing him to set policy even when Pieter Van Helding inherited a shareholding almost as large as Unger's own 30 per cent. He always controlled the ultimate weapon: if Van Helding wanted to throw him out, or change the board, or make his policies stick by threatening management changes, he could not do it. He did not have the votes. Until now.

Answer, damn it, answer.

But then if Koolhoven did answer, there was no guarantee he would want to help Unger. He always took Van Helding's side. He had all the more reason to take it now that Van Helding also had the stock.

He dialled Koolhoven's number one last time and waited, and there was no answer. The moment he put the phone down, it rang.

A country voice, strong and guttural, said he was speaking from the police station by the Leidesplein. There was a Mr Koolhoven there. The voice was sorry to trouble Mr Unger, but Mr Koolhoven had mentioned his – that was, Mr Unger's – name, and this was Mr Unger of the bank?

'He asked for you, sir,' the policeman said. 'He doesn't seem to have anyone else who can help. It's a matter of identification and – er – bail.'

'Bail,' said Unger, genuinely startled.

'Bail, sir, I'm sorry to say. Mr Koolhoven seems to have been in a fight. And he has had a drink or two.'

Unger called a taxi and went out into a rain-slick night. In the police station, he was acutely conscious of being on foreign territory. Bankers did not come here, only criminals and people outside the law and the people appointed to deal with them. He cloaked his tall, meagre body in a raincoat, and he almost seemed to pull his umbrella low to mask his face. He came to the desk as anonymously as he could.

'I came to see Mr Koolhoven?'

'You'll be the lawyer?' The country voice had come from a barrel-chested beer drinker.

'I'm a colleague.' Unger leant across the station desk and gave his name.

'Oh, yes, sir. Thank you. And if I might have a word with you . . .'

In a side room Unger was stiff as a dressed broom, wondering what the rules of the place were. He smelled human smells – sweat, urine, fear – that offended his fastidiousness. And he wondered whether to mention names, offer money. The one thing that never occurred to him was that the Leidesplein police were actually embarrassed by having a middle-aged banking gentleman in their cells.

'I don't think your Mr Koolhoven has the habit of the gin,' said the policeman. 'I suppose you can confirm he is with Kellerman Unger?'

'Oh, yes. He's our financial man – the secretary.'

'Sounds very grand,' said the policeman. 'He doesn't by any chance have a bit of a drinking problem?'

'Certainly not,' said Unger. He would always defend his class against rude suggestions from the lower orders.

'I'm glad. He's a bit of a mess, though. You'll see.'

Koolhoven looked like a big, muscular boy, all wet with

rain and gin, his body slumped forward and his eyes watery and remote. The man of organization and planning had simply folded up, under the force of some nasty blows which had left his head bloodied. He was a powerful physical presence, like an animal resigned to its captivity.

'You came,' Koolhoven said. 'You bloody would.'

'I really don't understand,' Unger said. 'Were you attacked?'

'I was sad. So I drank. I got into a fight and the policeman had to bring me here.'

The policeman said, quietly: 'No question of assault on the police, sir.'

'He needs a doctor,' Unger said.

Koolhoven shook his head. "The policemen cleaned me up. I owe them an apology.'

Unger became officious. 'And are there charges against this man?'

'That depends,' said the policeman.

Koolhoven groaned and asked to be left in the peace of the cell; Unger wondered whether the time had come to produce his wallet.

'It depends on whether I can release him into your custody. I have to check his record, but from what you say I'm sure it will be clean. Then if that's all right, we can let him go and think no more about it. No harm done, except to your Mr Koolhoven. He's a big man, but he doesn't know how to put his weight behind a punch, thank goodness.'

'I should hope not,' Unger said. He looked at Koolhoven's matted bloody hair and darkening eye and was glad he had proved inefficient at something.

'If you could get him home, sir . . .'

In the car, Unger had become even more bright and exact, and Koolhoven more battered and woolly. 'I really think I should know what happened,' Unger said.

'So should I,' said Koolhoven ruefully.

'Extraordinary,' Unger said. He rubbed together his spindly fingers, making a triumphant steeple from them.

'I was depressed,' Koolhoven said.

'People don't just throw away fifty respectable years to get drunk on the Leidesplein because they're depressed.'

Koolhoven looked at Unger with contempt, and he opened his wide shoulders almost menacingly. 'What the hell would you know, Jan Unger?' he said, and fell back against the car seat. 'I lost something. Someone. What does it matter?'

'You lost someone?'

'They bury her and I won't be there. Not even there. No reason to go.'

'You mean Mrs Van Helding?'

'Cold, cold, cold, cold,' said Koolhoven. 'You wouldn't understand.'

An anxious housekeeper took Koolhoven in hand on the doorstep. She had worried about the break in his habits. Usually – well, gentlemen had their little needs to take care of, but Mr Koolhoven did all that on a Thursday, and sometimes he took dinner in town at his club, but not without telling her first.

Now he came up the stairs all blood and stains like a painted martyr. She wanted to comfort him and he refused, and thin, brittle Unger helped push him upstairs to a bath and bed.

Unger wondered if he should ask questions now. A little kindness might persuade Koolhoven to be helpful.

'I wanted to ask you about Marisia Van Helding.'

'Ah yes,' Koolhoven said, stretching bruised limbs. 'Your new boss.'

Unger glared at him.

'She's tough and she's Pieter's friend. That is all you need to know, I think.'

Unger said: 'Good night, Koolhoven. We must talk tomorrow.'

But Koolhoven, tired and full of gin, had fallen back on the pillows and was snoring vividly.

Unger walked in the street for a while, despite the rain. He felt as though, in an evening, he had been expelled from the Elect – taken from God's chosen and put down with the rest. There was no more certain privilege. He was about to cede power to a child, wilful and brutal and blackmailing, whose ideas of doing business offended Unger's sense of propriety. He could taste the risk in something like the Autostrade bonds, and the whole idea of the Eurodollar market, and he was appalled; and his bank, Kellerman Unger, was going to enter those areas now. There was nothing more he could do to stop it.

There was a telephone kiosk, brightly lit, just ahead; it beamed through the steady, sodden rain.

There was a number at the hunting lodge, a faint suggestion that if Unger ever found himself in trouble, the friends at the hunting lodge would find some way to help him. Absurd, of course; short of a well-aimed bullet, it was hard to see how they could take power from Pieter Van Helding now.

He could call.

He didn't know Koch and the others too well. He knew their records, of course. They wouldn't be gentle or scrupulous because they could not afford to be. They wanted to enforce forgetfulness on Europe, a smothering failure of memory which would save them from judgement.

Unger thought of calling the hunting lodge – and saying what was true – that Van Helding had documentss and was trying to blackmail Unger, and besides Van Helding was married to a Grunwald.

He couldn't do that. He'd never been one of those who'd just waited for the chance to take out his spite on the Jews. He'd tried to be scrupulously neutral, to do nobody any harm.

But Van Helding would do him harm, would do him down and end his power.

He walked to the telephone kiosk. He was trying to calculate what to say. If there were things he wouldn't say, yet there were things that perhaps they had to hear at the hunting lodge before they took action.

'Herr Koch?' he said.

'Two cars,' the border cop said, stretching himself luxuriously. 'Two cars full of kids from some fancy school up north, all having a good, good time. All going to Tijuana.' He let his chair fall forward and he slammed his fists on the table. 'Only you didn't go there, did you? You had a meeting with some Tex-Mex trash and you bought a lot of white powder and you try to bring it back because you think everyone on the border is such a damn fool. Not smart like you kids from some fancy school up north.'

Marisia said: 'I don't understand. We went to Tijuana, we met the other kids there. I don't know them. I'm a foreign student at UCLA, you see, and . . .'

The cop said: 'Bullshit. Don't give me that fancy-talking bullshit.' He was a young man, big-bellied, waiting to grow into the full glory of his bullydom, but getting there fast. 'You knew all about it. You went down there to score, didn't you? I tell you, it makes me sick. You go to fancy schools and all you can think of doing is running a little coke across the border just like a bunch of dumb Chicanos. You're not telling me you need the money. I bet you're loaded.'

Marisia said: 'I don't have money.'

'Dumb cunt,' the cop said. 'Dumb, dumb, dumb. You wait till we search through that car and we find everything – every last thing – and you won't see the ground you'll be on a plane back home so fast. You see.'

'But you haven't found anything,' Marisia said.

'We're going to take that car apart. Strip the fenders off

and take the transmission apart and check out the fuel tanks. We got the authority.'

'Officer,' Marisia said. 'I know you have the authority – it's just that I don't understand why you picked on us. We went down to Mexico for the weekend and we did nothing wrong, as far as I know. We just had fun.'

'I wish I could afford that kind of fun.'

'And now you're holding us and I have to be back in school tomorrow morning. I'm afraid I won't make it.'

The cop pushed his head forward like a turtle, and leered eye to eye at Marisia, a smell of tired breath and beer around him.

'You go nowhere until I say.'

'Yes, sir.'

'You say that again,' the cop said. 'It sounds good coming from you, with your pretty face. Say it again.'

'Yes, sir.' Marisia said.

'That is good,' the cop said. His wide, flaccid face was animated by a fierce stare and the start of a grin.

'You stand up.' the cop said. 'Stand up now, over there.'

Marisia obeyed.

'Now you tell me the truth or else I may just have to forget I'm a gentleman.' He laid on the table, in slow and ritualistic fashion, his gun, his night stick and his handcuffs. He was wanting Marisia to anticipate, and watching her carefully, and she had to hide her careful thinking under a mask of alarm. He wanted the alarm; she would give it to him. She had screamed on cue for Marty's vampire, and she could certainly manage it here. She bowed her head a little, that was what he wanted, signs of submission; and she said:

'I don't know about the others, of course.'

The cop looked interested.

Very well, then that was the way out she would take. They had gone down to Mexico as a party, they had bought cocaine from the contact organized by friends, and clearly the sheer oddity of scoring cocaine in a country that doesn't produce it had tipped off some police informer. But say Marisia pushed the cop's attention to the other car – just that. Say she said she couldn't account for where the others had been. Then perhaps the cops would concentrate elsewhere, and let her go, and if she and Marty got through the border, they still had more than enough of the white magic hidden – about their persons and in the side-panels of the car – to make a decent profit.

And she could give the cop what he wanted. She knew that.

'I know we didn't buy anything. I don't know where the others went.'

'You can remember, can't you? Stand up straight.' She obeyed. 'Turn around and spread your legs and your arms. Now listen to me.'

She did as she was told. She could no longer see him, but she could hear his faint, fat snufflings of excitement.

'I could get one of the women to search you. A real body search. Strip-search.'

'They went off by themselves for a day. I don't know where they went.'

'Your friends – they use drugs?'

'I don't know, sir.'

'That's good. You don't know and you're such buddies?'

'We only met them down there. I don't know anything about it – it's the first time I've been in Mexico.'

'I checked the books. The immigration books.'

'Then you know that's true.'

She felt uncomfortably stretched and vulnerable, and she wished the charade would end. But she also knew something simple: this man could be led, manipulated, very simply, by the act of obeying him. It excited him too obviously.

'You make me sick, you kids. You got everything. You do things like this.'

'I did nothing, officer, except spend a weekend in Mexico. I didn't know what to expect, I'm not even American, I don't know my way around this country too well. I'm not the sort of person who could fix up a drug deal in Mexico and pull it off.'

'Maybe,' said the officer. 'Maybe not. Maybe you're very clever.'

She tried to relax and turn herself a little to face him.

'You stop that,' the cop said. 'You stop that now or I'll have to handcuff you.'

There was a buzz of activity outside the door. Marisia was terribly afraid that Marty Genovese would be talking about his civil rights, and registering the kind of protest that shows up on the Richter scale. She listened hard. But what she heard was her own name.

And: 'You mean she's right here?'

The door of the interrogation room blasted open and a senior policeman entered, and saw Marisia spread-eagled, and the cop walking beside her, face red and bloated.

'You,' the senior man said to the cop. 'You stop what the hell game you're playing now. You stop it, you hear?'

Marisia turned round. She wanted to relax and knew it would be dangerous.

'Miss,' said the senior man, 'are you Marisia Van Helding?'

'Yes,' Marisia said.

'Then I'm afraid I have some news for you.'

'News?'

'Maybe you should sit down.' The senior man kicked the other cop very hard on the shin and motioned him to get out. 'This is news from home,' the senior man said. 'UCLA tried to contact you and your lawyer tried and some studio friends – but all they knew was that you were down in Mexico and coming back. So they left a message with us at the border. I'm sorry we didn't get to you before.'

'Please tell me what the news is.'

'Miss Van Helding,' the senior man said, wringing his hands in embarrassment, 'I am afraid to tell you that your Ma . . . passed away.'

Marisia stared ahead. She heard the words and she considered her situation and her only feeling was that they would let her go now.

'We've made arrangements,' the cop said, 'to have you escorted to San Diego. There will be tickets waiting for you there.'

Marisia realized she did not know where the tickets would be for. She asked, and the cop said: 'Switzerland.' He seemed surprised that she didn't know.

'I'll send your friend in,' he said.

Outside the door she could hear the cop telling his senior officer. 'That's the kind of stunt they all pull. How do we know her mother's really dead? Huh?' And the senior cop saying: 'You don't know who that girl is. If you want to know, neither do I. But I know who called me, and I ain't taking chances. She goes free to San Diego.' The cop said: 'But the other kids – she said the ones in the other car . . .' The senior cop said: 'Burn 'em. Just get her and her friend out of here. Fast.'

Marty looked shaken when he arrived. He was openly amazed at Marisia.

'How did you do it?' he asked. 'Why are they letting us go?'

'I sacrificed my mother,' Marisia said.

'You're joking.'

Marisia said: 'My mother died. It's that simple. They only just got the message through to me. I have to get the plane from San Diego.'

'I'm so sorry . . .'

'I don't want anyone being sorry,' Marisia said. She was

shocked cold inside, as though the fulcrum of her life had been taken away. The world lacked balance.

'I mean . . .' Marty said. 'If there's anything I can do . . .'

They drove furiously from the border to San Diego with a police escort. After a few miles, Marisia started to laugh. Marty's first thought was that she had become hysterical, but then he looked at her again.

'You realize,' she said, 'the California Highway Patrol is escorting twenty-five thousand dollars in cocaine from the border? And you have safe passage to Los Angeles, thanks to them.'

'Don't laugh,' Marty said, checking the rear mirror. 'You're in mourning.'

Marisia said: 'You know what to do in LA?'

'I don't know what to do with the money . . .'

'Hold it. Anywhere. Till I get back. I'm coming back rich and that should make it easier to hide.'

'Rich,' Marty said, thoughtfully.

The village lay at the end of a cold lake, a mere scrawl of houses bound in blue shadow and closed against the winter. There was a church with an onion dome, civic buildings that in summer would be bright with geraniums, snow that blurred the houses and weighted trees and sparkled in the sun. The air was perversely clear; distant mountains seemed close, movement on a field across the valley was almost tangible. The wind called föhn had come from Italy and crept into the valley and made people and landscapes as sharp as they could bear and maybe more so.

The Widow Van Helding's grave was in a few inches of frost. In the churchyard the smell of incense and cattle mixed. Pieter and Marisia Van Helding heard the ice-earth drum on the coffin lid, the single bell ring out across the valley, and thanked the priest and the unexpected half-dozen mourners. In the lane, the breath of cattle came like smoke.

Marisia spoke first. 'I didn't expect this.'

'It was her place. She never let us come here.'

'I didn't know her, you realize. All those years, and I never guessed she came back each year to somewhere like this.'

They walked cautiously over the iced snow, back to the main square of the little town. Villagers had watched the Widow grow here, expecting her to marry and breed the sons essential to a hillside farm, to feed a man his seven meals a day against the cold and the cruel labour. But the Widow was special, even then, and she could not be suited to the steady, old routines. Even the nuns thought she might go to school in Geneva for a while, and from Geneva she had made her way to Paris, and from Paris to New York. She was a wonder to the people of the valley – their daughter, returning home each year, but a phenomenon. They never resented her or wanted her to fail; they liked her too well. She knew where she came from and liked the fact.

Such a simple principle was not what the star Marisia and the banker Pieter wanted to hear. They knew their mother's gloss and sophistication, her contrivance. In the valley, by the grave, they had to contend with her private world, full of unreasoned emotions and loyalties. It was as though she had shifted shape before them at the moment they were putting her into the earth.

'I got the lawyers working in Amsterdam,' Pieter said, 'and in New York. It'll take a month or so to work out exactly where we stand.'

'There aren't any surprises?'

'Not that they could see. Each of us has twenty-two per cent of Kellerman Unger, as of the day Mother died. Plus Mother's lifetime interests in six per cent of the bank, which we now share.'

'Partners,' said Marisia, doubtfully.

Pieter's car, brought from Zurich, trailed them along the road almost silently, the spikes on its snow tyres pricking the snow into curious patterns. The great stillness of the mountains, and the awful, unavoidable clarity of the air made the Van Heldings feel constrained, as though the movements of eyes or lips, the thoughts behind words, would be visible across the valley.

'She died alone?' Marisia said.

'I think so.'

They took car and driver up to a high road which angled back and forth along the flank of an Alp. Pieter gave instructions to find the house, but they had to ask at a restaurant in the high village, and when they arrived, the place was shocking.

It was ordinary – a wood farmhouse, grandparents' house at the back, ornate shutters, and a smell of apples and cheese. Someone was paid to keep it as though it was lived in – to store things, warm things, keep a sense of life in the corridors. In the kitchen there was still the high, tiled wall of an oven, a spectacle of blue and white which heated the house against the outside cold. And the house, Marisia noticed, had its little resonances – quavers, murmurs, sometimes wood shifting – against the silence of the snows. The mountains only rustled sometimes when the soft, warm winds of the föhn started high snows into little falls.

'There must be someone here,' Pieter said. He shouted, and a solid, apple-dumpling woman came to greet them. She had a few words of French, but mostly she spoke Swiss German, and they talked by pointing as much as speaking.

'I want to see Mother's room,' Marisia said.

The apple-dumpling woman led the way to an unpretentious room, wood walls, new starched sheets, and drawers to hide the paraphernalia of the Widow's looks –

the vitamins, creams and powders. It was warm, almost stuffy, and it looked out on unbroken snow.

It was a place that needed animation, or it would stifle you, Marisia thought. She realized how strong her mother must have been to spend time here. And she remembered, when she was ten, thinking in false sophistication that Mother must go away that long month to see some lover in the Swiss mountains. Now she realized that she came here to meet herself. Marisia wasn't sure she was ready for such a confrontation.

She thought of Marty, bubbling and operatic and she thought of straight, kind, brown David Grant, and she thought of the second carload of kids abandoned at the border to their fate, and she realized that in this warm, womb-like place, you couldn't bring in memory or incidentals of the past. You had to be in this moment, and only in this moment. It was funny how people always assumed you'd remember and ponder in tranquillity. In fact, that wouldn't do at all.

She went down the wood stairs to the main corridor. The apple-dumpling woman was putting on a hefty coat and preparing to leave.

'*Le souper*,' she said, '*dans la four*.'

'Thank you,' Marisia said.

'*Je reviens demain matin à dix*.'

They said good nights and Marisia went back to the kitchen, where Pieter had curled himself around a bottle of Glenmorangie he had brought with him.

'Have you seen the loos?' he said. 'There's one which is just a chute down to the cellar – and it's full of ice crystals.'

'I suppose it works,' Marisia said. 'Our supper is in the oven. Do you want to stay here overnight? We could always go back to the village.'

'Is it getting to you already?'

'What do you mean?'

'The quiet.'

'I like it,' Marisia said. 'It's just not the easiest place to be after a funeral.'

'You want to talk?'

'I don't even know what I want,' Marisia said. 'Whisky, I think.'

They settled in the clutter of the living room, a jumbled place with wooden furniture and little carvings and sets of pewter and silver all around. It was as far removed from the Widow Van Helding's severe New York chic as Marisia could imagine. It was her past, frozen and waiting to be lived. Outside, a heavy moon had slipped out of the valley and hung over blue-white snow.

'We haven't seen each other much,' Pieter said.

'Not for a long time. You were a bastard not to give me that money.'

'I couldn't do it, really.'

'You could have done, you simply didn't want to. Don't you want to know why I needed it?'

'No,' Pieter said. 'You'd want me to disapprove and then I'd disappoint you.'

There were no flames or shadows from the stove's ceramic wall. Marisia had jet lag, the whisky warmed her stomach, and she felt great sorrow.

'Things seem very simple here,' Pieter said. He was looking at Marisia more warmly than she liked – looking at her long, fine legs which were a swimmer's legs, and shaping her breasts with his mind. And she knew that despite her tiredness, she was also looking – looking at her mesmerizing brother as a man.

'I don't think they're simple at all,' Marisia said. 'Except that this place doesn't fit into either of our lives – it's somewhere apart.'

She held out her glass for more whisky.

'You're feeling all right?' Pieter asked. 'You're drinking more than you used to.'

'I didn't drink at all,' Marisia said, 'when I was thirteen, for God's sake. It's a difficult night and I want a drink.'

She didn't seem tired; she seemed strong and disconcerting and alive, a face that couldn't hide thoughts, a cascade of long hair.

'You know,' Marisia said, 'I remember holding your hand at Willem's funeral. I dream about it sometimes. It was like today – do you remember they couldn't open a grave properly because of the coral, like they couldn't dig deep today because of the frost? And that black girl who started screaming that he hadn't been buried properly – that he'd come back.'

'You're raising ghosts.'

'It's just you and me now,' Marisia said. 'And Katherine. And Georg – how is Georg?'

'Sick,' Pieter said, 'and full of hospital chemicals. That's why Katherine couldn't come today.'

Marisia said, flatly: 'Do you care about Georg?'

'Yes,' Pieter said, 'in my way.'

'You don't have to lie to me. I know you too well.'

'I said,' Pieter repeated, 'in my way.'

Marisia stood up and walked to the window, and looked up the long, sleek range of snow that was faintly iridescent under the moon.

'Do you still scare people?'

'I don't know what you mean.'

'You scared Willem. And you liked doing it, too. Most boys might take the wings off a fly to see what happened, or leave a fish out of water by accident, but you seemed to want to scare Willem. You wanted to make him go underwater and then you held him down.'

'You do sound morbid.'

There were streetlamps down in the valley that Marisia could just see, and in places the snow bore vague ridged tracks. Pieter was looking at her legs, she knew.

'I didn't realize Mother came from this,' she said. 'If

you just say Switzerland, it doesn't sound like this place. It sounds like parties and Gstaad and the piste.'

'This is a toy,' Pieter said. 'Our mother never bled a pig.'

'Killing pigs is man's work.'

Pieter shrugged. 'We'll see,' he said.

Koolhoven was full of aspirin and bismuth and remorse. The Widow had meant more than a bottle and a half of gin on a wet night and a brawl, and he wished his secretary would not look so damned judgemental at his first visible sign of humanity in twenty years. The dragon at the door spared him the jarring sound of a phone bell but she was also particularly prim. 'That nice Mr Koolhoven,' he could hear her saying at a coffee break. 'You wouldn't believe it.'

One call did get through that morning. Even the dragon lady could not deter Noam Gregory.

'It is very urgent that I reach Pieter Van Helding,' Gregory said. 'He said that if I ever needed him you would know.'

'Van Helding is at a family funeral. In Switzerland. I don't think we have a number for him.'

'I do mean this is urgent.'

'If it's bank business, perhaps I can help.'

'It's personal.'

'He's at a house his mother had in Switzerland – canton Obwalden, somewhere. Or he could be at a hotel there.' Koolhoven shouted to his secretary, who found no number in her Roladex or in her book.

'This personal business,' Koolhoven said, 'if I get through to Van Helding, or if he calls, is there a message I can pass?'

'I say this once and once only.' Gregory said, 'and you have to believe I know what I'm talking about. Somebody – some of the old guard, if you get my meaning – has put out a contract on Pieter Van Helding.'

'A contract?' said Koolhoven. He read Raymond Chandler; more recent gangster talk was foreign to him.

'He's going to be killed.'

'Christ,' Koolhoven said. 'You're sure . . .'

'I wouldn't waste time on calls like this if I wasn't sure,' Gregory said.

Koolhoven had something else to say – anything to keep the strange voice on the line and demand an explanation. But he only had time to ask for a name, to be told 'Noam Gregory' and hear a dial tone return as the phone was slammed down at the other end.

'Very interesting,' said the Baron Gilles de Grunwald to Noam Gregory. 'Would you mind very much telling me what this is all about?'

'Networks,' Gregory said. 'Old boys from the Second World War who don't like questions asked. Fellow travellers with the Nazis who reckon they have scores to settle. People who call each other up and take action that nobody actually orders. People who kill because that seems like the easy way to solve a problem.'

'Someone like Jan Unger?'

'He wouldn't have known what he was doing. He probably just said Van Helding knew too much and wasn't he a bloody nuisance and could they help? I doubt if he knows what's been done on his behalf. That's how the networks survive after all – things happen as though by coincidence. People do each other's crimes.'

'You think it was Unger?'

'It may have been. Or it may have been the Oslo business. Things leak,' Gregory said.

'Especially when things happen close to Unger's nose?'

'Maybe.'

'Oslo must have been quite remarkable business.'

'Oh yes,' said Noam Gregory, grimly.

* * *

'I could fly down the mountain,' Marisia said. 'Like a bird – over all those cliffs and crags and drifts. I'd be free.'

'You're not free?'

It wasn't what she meant, not really. She was alarmed by the warmth, by Pieter's eyes, by the sense of remoteness and safety even for extremes.

'I suppose,' she said, 'that's why I spend so much time being someone else. Being Californian. Even being an actress.'

'You never told me about your film. Except it was called Blood Something.'

'They had to call it blood, because that sells movies. Then they took five months to think up the other word. It hadn't got anything to do with the story, of course.'

'Tell me about the story.' Pieter looked expectant.

'I'm a vampire. I take the souls of men. And I get nailed in the last reel. The man who made it is very good – or he's going to be. Marty Genovese. He'll take over Hollywood some day.'

'Maybe I'll invest in him.'

Marisia smiled. 'Maybe I will. You forget we're equals, now.'

'In a way,' Pieter said. 'Except that you don't seem to want to come into the bank and be serious.'

'How could I? The first sight of an actress in the boardroom and your lot would panic. Think of nice old Jan Unger and all the nice old men like him – dry as sticks. They'd feel threatened. They might get excited and crumble.'

'Do you want the bank?'

'I'm not giving it up, Pieter. I want things out of it – not just money either. Maybe power one day. I don't know yet.'

'I wanted to ask – if you'd give me the proxies on your shares, until you've decided what to do. So we can vote together.'

'Really,' Marisia said. 'I almost thought of giving them to Jan Unger. He's so cautious he couldn't possibly make any difference until I decide what I want to do. It would be like freezing them.'

'You wouldn't do that?'

'I wanted to fly,' Marisia said. 'Let's at least go for a walk. Now. Look at the snow and the ice and the mountains. And the moon.'

'Look at the thermometer,' Pieter said. 'Just because it was clear and dry today . . .'

'I bet you've got thermal underwear,' Marisia said. 'You were always sensible. You'd come to a funeral ready to ski, if you got the chance.'

'You want to go night skiing? Nobody does that. It's too dangerous.'

'Scaredycat,' Marisia said, 'scaredycat. Scaredycat.'

'I like a risk,' Pieter said. 'But I'm not suicidal.'

She knelt suddenly and kissed his hands.

'Please, big brother, please . . .'

Koolhoven had a list and he had the telephone and he was getting nowhere. The priest from the funeral was out giving rites to some exhausted *Älpler*, and his housekeeper didn't speak anything but Swiss German. Credit Suisse gave the number of their banker in the village, but he didn't answer; after nine, the mountains are silent, and even taking a bath is a social offence. Telephone calls were simply ignored.

Electronic bloody wonders, Koolhoven thought, and the buggers just don't answer and that's it. Finished.

He had wondered about Mr Gregory's account after the phone call. There was a $2 million line of credit with no credible collateral, and that was odd, as though Mr Gregory was secured on some invisible credit; and while Koolhoven couldn't read such an arrangement as clearly as a soldier reads a map, he did know it meant trouble. Trust worth 2 million is also worth killing for.

He thought of a telegram. He tried his very few words of Swiss German on the distant operator.

'*Es tut mir leid*,' she said. 'Really sorry. They deliver tomorrow. Everything's shut. It's a small village.'

'We could send it to a phone number . . .'

'There is no phone for that name or that address. Listed or unlisted.' She lost patience and the line went dead.

He tried the village hotel – he should have done so first, in all logic, but he did not really think Pieter would stay there. The police wouldn't do anything because he couldn't convince them that it was a life and death emergency. Nobody wanted to understand him; it was the time of the föhn winds, people were short-tempered, the snow would be tricky after a day of slight thaw, and the road to the Van Helding house was difficult at the best of times, a ladder of sharp angles.

Koolhoven's housekeeper brought him chocolate for his nerves. She hated to see him shaken from his routine in this way. He was such a kind man and now he looked sick from the night before, nauseous and pale.

The church didn't answer now. The village was shuttered until dawn, soft and secure.

And he knew it, suddenly, in his bones: Pieter Van Helding really was in danger. Something had gone out of control.

'Not Pieter,' he said, out loud. His housekeeper, retreating down the stairs, thought she heard him say something and thought she had better ignore it. He was not a well man. He might say wrong things.

A last chance, absurd as it seemed. He could ask Jan Unger. There was really no reason why the stick-man should know more of the address and number of the Widow Van Helding than he, Koolhoven, did, but perhaps Pieter had left some message or been in contact.

'Unger?' he said. 'Do you happen to know where I can reach Pieter?'

'Somewhere in Switzerland,' Unger said. 'This is really a rather untimely call, don't you think? Has young Van Helding been found out in some new peculation?'

'He may be in danger.'

'Danger? Who on earth says that?' Unger sounded impatient, but it might also have been unease if Koolhoven had been listening for unease.

'I can't go into all that. It's simply urgent that I reach Pieter, and I thought you might have some clues . . .'

'I could tell you the address,' Unger said. 'He did leave that. There was no telephone, I believe. It's an isolated place in the mountains. Canton Obwalden.'

'I know that,' Koolhoven said. 'Those addresses are worse than useless unless you can find someone to go up the mountain to deliver messages. And the Swiss are all sound asleep in bed by now.'

'Then it will have to wait until morning,' Unger said. 'I don't suppose young Van Helding is in any real danger.'

The two men were both thoughtful when they put down their phones. Koolhoven thought he had now exhausted every line he could think of. Unger wondered if they were going to scare Van Helding, or if Koolhoven's melodramatic message was true . . .

They wouldn't harm Van Helding, of course.

They wouldn't harm Van Helding, would they?

He wondered if there might be anyone at the hunting lodge, but the number they'd given him for emergencies didn't answer.

'They're civilized men,' Unger thought, and he realized he was drumming his fingertips on the table. He didn't know if that was worry or a sense of satisfaction.

Snow draped the mountains like silk – ruffled in gullies, shifting with sounds like a fall of dust, sometimes piled into still drifts and sometimes shaped and twisted by the winds and currents that had a separate, violent life above the almost unbroken circle of the mountain peaks.

'Nobody walks at night,' Pieter said.

'Shh,' Marisia said. 'Listen to the wind.'

It was still, but it was also uneasy, a breathless place waiting for some trial. Cold came down on them as they walked from the house like a stone. They saw strange shapes in the snow, made from drifts and moonlight. Long, languorous blue-grey shadows stretched away to sudden whirls of snow.

The walk was almost easy. Only occasional ice snatched at their feet. The cold seemed to settle into their flesh despite their hefty down coats. The roadway led up the mountain a little from the house towards what in summer was a Swiss Army camp. No night birds stirred because no prey stirred, and even the deer had come down the mountains to steal the cattle food

High up in the bowl of rocky peaks there was a movement. It might have been snow settling again after a day of sun, shifting in a tiny avalanche.

'Look,' Marisia said, 'deer.'

The movement was in the lee of a scrubby, low wood, where the snow was botched by little trees.

'They couldn't be up there,' Pieter said. He whispered, out of odd respect for the night. 'Maybe goats, not deer. They'd die.'

He felt sharp-eyed, alert, his senses stirred. Up in the blue-white snows there was a susurration like skirts in summer grass, faint and out of place. Pieter Van Helding did not even strictly hear it. He saw the movement, sensed a change. They were being watched. They were out on an exposed wall, iced into slow movement, and a lone skier was coming down towards them.

'Listen,' Pieter said. He knew he needn't whisper; he

remembered the wind and the skirring of snow that you hear on skis.

'It's the deer,' Marisia said.

Then Pieter was sure. The figure had crossed out of shadow and it was coming down fast.

'Run,' he said on sudden instinct. 'Run like hell.'

He pulled Marisia into the lee of the drifts the snow-ploughs had left along the track. They skidded and tussled their way back towards the house. Their footfall was silent, except when it rasped on ice. For those few moments, Piter Van Helding was sure any sound would rise into the stillness of the Alps and linger, a kind of signpost to their slow progress back to the house. Even their breathing, he thought.

The man on skis must know he too had to be cautious. Or did he expect to be a calamitous surprise, arriving out of the silent dark?

Up high, there seemed to be a silence, and even the little scuffles of snow had stopped. The moon and the clear air after föhn showed what might be tracks. And the tracks seemed to stop by the little wood, where Marisia had thought she saw deer, and Pieter thought he could see the shape of a man, oddly twisted.

Nobody carried a load on skis, not now; perhaps in some nineteenth-century Englishman's dream, but not in an age of snow tyres and tractors and snowmobiles. The lone skier could have no legitimate business in the shuttered village, and there was no telephone in the house, Pieter remembered. His mother's retreat was made to be proof against intrusion from the outside world.

Only the house could protect them. And such a long descent at night – where had the man come from? – must mean attack, and the only likely target was Pieter.

The man was moving again. Pieter pushed Marisia through the door, threw the latches, took down the heavy skeleton key to drag the cogs of the ancient iron lock into place. Night, cold as the traitors' place in hell, was shut out.

Now: defence. This place was meant to be a living place, as though the Widow was always here; that was part of her fantasy. It followed there must be a rifle in working order for the militia. There was nothing by the boots and the door, where a man might think to keep a shotgun. Maybe it was hidden in a closet where the wife wouldn't find it. Around them the whole house seemed to sigh and sing in the rising wind, settling on its deep cellars. It seemed alive and vulnerable.

Marisia scrambled through kitchen cupboards. The rifle must be somewhere, but it needn't be easy to find or get. The theory was not that an enemy might come across the hill at any time, but that a man must be ready when the call came. Pieter tried stair cupboards, and the first floor. The house seemed full of the echoes of their search and its own, noisy business. Pieter thought of the tool cupboard in the outer hallway; Marisia tried the basement door which would not budge; Marisia hurried into the living room.

'It's here,' she shouted. There was a closet by the window which should have held only linen, but there was also a Karabiner 7.5mm and ammunition. Van Helding felt the weight; it was a serious, balanced weapon. It would do.

Then the lights died.

Piter Van Helding stood by the door – the front, the main door – and Marisia said, very seriously and calmly: 'Did someone do that? Did we do that?'

'I don't know.'

Now the snows outside, glittering and pale, were easier to read than the shadows of the house, and he thought he could see the man, coming in fast, bringing himself to a halt, pausing, and moving on cautiously.

He pushed the rifle to Marisia. 'Can you use it?'

'To kill pigeons.'

'I'm going to get to the car. We need light.'

'I'll go,' Marisia said. 'We need a good shot.'

She undid the latches, opened the lock and moved cautiously in the lee of the house, bounding the last yards to the car. It was facing uphill, thank God. She waited. Light now would give away their positions. She half feared a sudden scratching on the window, a smashed glass, sudden movement just outside her range of vision. Someone was out there, coming in, twisted by a weight that could be a gun.

'Now,' Pieter shouted.

She turned on the headlamps and flooded yellow quartz light across the snow. In the beams was a trim-bodied figure, a bare hundred yards from the house, with something bulky across his shoulders which he was pulling down.

Van Helding stepped forward, into the car lights.

'Halt,' he said. 'Put down that gun.'

The man still scuffled with his weapon. He could hardly move cross-country with a loaded shotgun. He needed to load.

'I will shoot,' Pieter shouted.

His voice seemed to loosen powder snow in the high mountains, and the sound echoed from rock to rock. It was as though he was stamping his will on the lifeless snow.

The man looked up. His eyes caught the car headlights' beam; he must have put down his goggles to handle the gun. He began to raise the gun to his shoulder.

Van Helding fired twice. The man dived, awkwardly, legs tangled with his skis, the weight of gun and pack pulling him slowly downhill. His skis splayed apart, making a brief fountain of the diamond-hard glitter, and after an ungainly moment he came to a halt.

Marisia came from the car and walked forward. Van

Helding was storming up the mountain, rolling from side to side as he tried to rush without proper snowshoes. He fired once more, apparently into the air, and he startled new life out of the night. Some village lights flickered, and a car droning along the valley road far below seemed to accelerate in fear. Deer in the trees below started to flee. There was a sense of something wild that was loose in this most ordered of places.

Pieter reached the man in the snow. The man tried to raise his upper body, but not in supplication. He looked very directly at Van Helding, and his hand was still twitching open and shut, open and shut, scrabbling at the snow to find his gun.

Marisia stood at Pieter's side.

He looked at her; she seemed to nod. He raised the man's head. He pulled the trigger of the rifle once, and again, and the very matter of the man's head seemed to fall bloodily apart.

He set the body back, gun hot, blood on his neat gloves, and Marisia nodded again. She looked at him with a collaborator's respect and with a lover's glitter.

'Pieter Van Helding,' she said.

They went hand in hand to the house, very briskly, and once through the doorway they fell onto the cold, old stone flags of the hallway and tore at each other's clothes, taking off the down and thermal barriers, their senses stolen away by the smell of blood and fear. Pieter Van Helding rushed into Marisia, and Marisia welcomed him in her like furies, and the stillness of the night was ruined by the feverish noises of their lovemaking.

And the high snows fell silent again.

4

Van Helding passed through the moonscape just before Culver City where oil pumps peck at the land like birds. He wanted to think business: his client, Helios SA, an uncomfortable mixture of movies and office equipment, needed to have its life saved. He could only think of Marisia. They hadn't met for almost two years, except briefly once at the Schiphol airport, once at Biblios in St Tropez (she was with David Grant; the noise was too much to talk), and one brisk drink at the Plaza in New York. They had said nothing of consequence; they had tacitly agreed to be in different towns – until today.

He remembered the night in the mountains. He remembered the next morning when the faint warm breath of föhn had shifted the snow, and the man's body was gone. His tracks down the mountainside had melted and blown away. When Pieter and Marisia disentangled in a sticky, ruined bed, they found that the night before had been erased – except for the Karabiner rifle that lay dirty in the hall.

They were quiet and sober in the morning, not denying or discussing, and unwilling to ask each other what could be next. The only certainty was that there must be a body out there in the snow. They could hide it, hope that it would not drift to the surface until the spring and then go unexplained, but they would have to know that it was securely buried, not a scant few inches below the surface. And they probably had to tell the police something. In a clockwork place like this valley, those shots would have been heard. There would be men in uniform asking for explanations.

Marisia went outside and looked across the snow. She fell to her knees, and began scrabbling at it with her hands. Pieter fetched shovels. They tried anywhere within the beam of the car headlights, anywhere something poked up through the glittering ice-crust of the snow and suggested a ski or a pack or a gun.

They heard the sound of an engine on the road, and it was round the bend and in sight of them before they straightenend up from digging. It was a police car, moving cautiously over the snow.

They looked at each other. They'd have to explain. They dropped their shovels and went to acknowledge their official visitors.

There were polite good mornings and the senior policeman warned he had something to say. They went inside to the warmth of the *Kachelofen* wall.

'You're Pieter Van Helding? And this is your . . .'

'Sister,' Marisia said.

Pieter wondered if they would search the house.

'We had a message from Zurich, sir,' the policeman said, 'a rather curious one. It seems a Mr Koolhoven was trying to contact you last night. He wanted to tell you – well, that you were in danger.'

'We were here for our mother's funeral,' Pieter said.

'I do realize, sir,' said the policeman. 'I don't want to make this any more upsetting than I have to. But the message seemed to suggest there might even be an attempt on your life. Now of course, nothing like that has happened, has it?'

Marisia thought: They'll have to believe us. She said: 'Yes. It has.'

'Ma'am?'

'Someone came down to the house last night on skis – Pieter challenged him and he wouldn't stop so Pieter shot him – there was a rifle here. And this morning, we were looking – looking to see if he was still here.'

'Sir?'

'That's true,' Pieter said. 'I thought you'd come up to ask about the shots. They must have been heard clear across the valley.'

The senior policeman looked worried. 'You don't think, sir, the delay in delivering the message had anything to do with this . . . I mean, we weren't to know . . .'

'It's good to have notice of unexpected visitors,' Pieter said. 'Especially when they carry shotguns.'

'And the body, sir? Just where . . .'

'A shotgun, inspector. Something to kill with.'

'We don't know where the body is,' Marisia said, 'or even if there is a body. He was very close to the house, but the snow must have shifted during the night.'

'Föhn,' the inspector said. 'The wind from Italy.'

'I expect so. We looked and looked . . .'

'This is very unfortunate,' the inspector said.

Outside, the snow looked uncommonly settled, as though its contours would not change until the thaw. The inspector wanted to test the car headlights again, and dig again, and they turned the snow to find nothing.

'Of course,' Pieter said, 'he may have got away. I'm not a brilliant shot.'

They found nothing, until the police car was set to drive off. It reversed, and then went forward, and the spikes on the tyres found the body and brought up little gobbets of nylon and flesh from below the snow. The spikes went twice across the man's body from feet to face, leaving a little track of red-brown blood.

Marisia turned away, and Pieter stopped the car by shouting, and the junior policeman stood aside to retch and cry.

'He didn't get away then, sir,' the inspector said.

They recorded a death in self-defence, since the body was too badly mangled for a proper forensic analysis of how close the shot had been. They closed the file.

Marisia looked at the body, made herself look. The consequences of their meeting, she thought. You have to be able to face the consequences.

In the car back to Zurich, they had hardly talked. Pieter remembered only that Marisia had said she was going back to California. She'd written later that UCLA had gently suggested she and they might part company, and she had started to act, built a reputation as a fatal lady in the Z-films. She was a kind of pop icon, according to one magazine piece she'd sent to him: a strange, lovely woman standing with fierce eyes at the mouth of a cave, or the turning of a road, with great wolfhounds on a leash, like a steel engraving from a Gothic novel.

It's only a party, Pieter thought to himself.

'I'm going back to California,' Marisia had said. 'And that's it.' She thought he understood she wanted to be separate from him now. The idea that you surrender to a grand passion was absurd, she thought; you keep it as a fantasy, but you do not indulge it. There are other things to do.

She'd worked, furiously. She'd built herself a portfolio comprising equal parts of capital and a professional reputation, an ability to pull a particular younger audience into the movie houses. And as the Corman boys slipped away from making movies about wasp women and vampires and battles beyond the sun, and into the mainstream of the industry, Marisia followed. They knew her; they understood her; she made the same jokes, did the same drugs, and although she was rich, she seemed like one of them. Marty Genovese even forgave her when Magnum Studios gave him his first $20 million picture, forgave her for rescuing him on their cocaine rush from Mexico to LA (which is not what good women do). Genovese cast her.

It was Marty's wrap party, at the end of the movie. At the end of the last morning, cast and crew headed across town to MGM at Culver City. Marty himself was late, buzzing with drink, the end of shooting, and a jab of amphetamine administered by his underage girlfriend in the trailer.

'If they don't give me a movie at MGM,' he said, 'they can give me a party. Me, the boy from America. Glendale, Queens, and 42nd Street – all of them – son of Arthur Freed, John Ford, Raoul Walsh. You know, I saw the world in New York theatres and never got propositioned once.' He rampaged, like a puppet clown with red-blown checks. 'And what do I get now? I slave, I learn, I love the movies. And I get $20 million worth of stinking shit.'

'You're the director,' Marisia said. 'You said it.'

'And do you know why? Let me tell you why. Look around. You know this is the very railway station where Fred Astaire arrived in *The Bandwagon* and Greta Garbo in *Ninotchka*.And over there, that great pile of rotting wood is the European square from *David Copperfield*. And that house . . . It's Ashley's house from *Gone With the Wind*, they brought it over from RKO . . . and those rhododendrons, they're part of Tarzan's jungle. And that's the house from *Philadelphia Story*. And do you know why it's falling apart and rotting like monuments in a wilderness?'

Marisia did, but Marty would tell her anyway.

'Because of money. Those bastards in the MGM building – they want to sell this place and build a hypermarket. A hypermarket, for God's sake. Culver City doesn't want it. The hypermarkets around here don't want it. But the studio boys, they'd rather build a bastard hypermarket than love the things they've got.'

A fey publicist said to Marisia, quietly: 'I just don't understand that kind of talk. I thought he was such a movie buff, and when I offered to share my very special collection of Miss Stanwyck, why . . .'

'Money,' Marty said, 'the bottom fucking line. That's

all they understand. The idea that it might be risky and difficult and emotional out here doesn't occur to them. They don't know the stars, they don't know stories, they don't know talent – they don't know shit.'

Marisia beamed, feeling responsibility for Marty even in his present state, but she said, under her breath, 'Could you get Lolita to give you something to bring you down? Or at least a blow job to take down the energy level. You're fucking up. The money's coming, this time, and they all want to pat you on the back and write you cheques. You don't want to put them off, do you?'

'One day,' Genovese said, 'I'll have a studio of my own. You'd back me, wouldn't you, Marisia? You could be my star.'

'Like Marion Davies was to Randolph Hearst,' Marisia said, dismissively. 'There's a brilliant actress who didn't work because she had money in the firm.'

'You'd back me?'

'Stuff it, Marty. Get some downers.'

David Grant made his way through the crowd to Marisia's side.

'I'm glad you're here,' Marisia said. 'Henry Klein's here. You remember – the sort of banker who helped me out once?'

'I thought he helped you out more than once.'

'First time he lent me money, second time he gave me advice. Investment advice. Mostly good, I have to say.'

'I'll be nice to him.'

'And he has something to do with the money behind this picture. Some Palm Springs people, he says.'

'Nice. I'll be worshipful.'

'Don't be sarcastic.'

'Marisia, I love you and I'm happy to be here, and if I hear any more movie talk – don't these people talk about anything else?'

'Do newspaper people talk about anything else when they're together?'

Henry Klein came over and beamed. She thought again what a neat, small man he was – taut and exact. Either a mass of repressions or a force of self-control; she wasn't interested enough to find out which.

'I have a surprise for you,' he said. 'I think you'll like it.'

'Tell me,' Marisia said. 'If it's a penny stock in Denver . . .'

'Nothing like that. I've been doing some business this week with someone you know. Someone you know very well. He's in Los Angeles trying to salvage some European mess called Helios SA.'

'And who's that?'

'You'll see.'

'Don't keep me in suspense. I hate suspense.'

'He should be here very soon. I sent a car to pick him up.'

'Klein, I'll throttle you . . .'

'Never menace an investor,' said Henry Klein. 'First rule of Hollywood life.'

Marty Genovese, whisky piled on amphetamines, came roaring back, his girl trying to steer him by an arm that wouldn't quite go round his growing belly.

'The Money,' Marty said. 'All Hail The Money.' He staged an elaborate, satirical bow.

'I'm very pleased to meet you,' Klein said.

'You don't know who I am, do you?'

Klein smiled. 'Of course I do.'

'Then name me,' Marty said, dangerously.

'Martin Genovese. The director.'

'Bang right,' Marty said. 'I thought for a moment I was going to have to lay you out.'

Klein smiled again. Marisia noticed that the tension she'd felt in him could also be something to do with solid muscles.

'I hear stories about you,' Genovese said. 'I hear our great and wonderful studio Magnum is about to be bought. The stuff of history on the auction block – sad, even if it is run by two old farts with less brain than come, which at their age is not a compliment. Magnum, the Dream Machine . . .' Marty allowed his voice to rise in an operatic crescendo '. . . crucified by the banks.'

'That's an interesting story, Mr Genovese.'

'Interesting? It's the end of a goddam era, that's what it is. I remember when I left UCLA and I went to this little tiny company that wanted to own scripts and develop projects – you remember that, Mr Klein? Tiny little business and all of a sudden it had lots of money. Never did know where the money came from, quite. So I sat down and I worked. Tore the guts out of some very decent Southern dyke's novella and they touted it around and it didn't sell – tax loss. Let me make a movie, they did, very kind, and they couldn't sell it – tax loss. Just when they were sure I was going to stay cheap they do a deal with Magnum and suddenly I've got $20 million to salvage a musical they wouldn't make at Fox, even after *Sound of Mucus*. I think I've made the big time. They think I'm cheap at the price, which I am. And now what do I find? I find Magnum Studios, the big M, is being bought out by that itsy-bitsy scriptwriting corporation that used to pay my wages. Never did work out where the money came from, even now.'

'Money's complicated,' Henry Klein said. 'It doesn't always come with a family tree.'

'In this town,' Marty Genovese said, 'you don't even want to know where it comes from.'

'Then don't ask,' Henry Klein said, with an odd flash of deep seriousness. 'I'd hate to see your conscience troubled.'

And Klein looked out past the shaded area of the party to where the last straggling limousines were arriving. One of them, he assumed, would contain Pieter Van Helding.

'It's good to work with the young,' Klein said. 'Half the people in this town are too tired to think, let alone invent things. Worn out.' Marisia knew he meant worn out at thirty-five (he was thirty-two) and would mean worn out at forty-five when he was forty-two; and she also knew he was deadly serious. People over thirty-five, sagging, wrinkled, dyspeptic people who needed eyeglasses or bridgework, were anathema. They were time-expired, date-stamped, useless. That was why older studio executives struggled with weights and wore gold chains around carefully lifted and tucked necks and called people 'baby' and chased girls (or boys) to give them back a sense of youth. That was also what added a few thousand dollars to Marisia's pay cheques; she wasn't sure she disapproved.

David Grant said: 'I wish I was back in Providencia.'

Marisia said: 'Just be patient.'

A last limousine pulled on to Lot Two and edged down the narrow road between crumbling sets. Chrome and black sparkled under the high California sun, and the car's tinted windows seemed to hold secrets, not just disguise the passengers. The car stopped, Marisia looked over with vague curiosity, and then she saw Pieter.

'Christ,' she said to Henry Klein, 'you could have told me,' but Klein was already bounding over to Van Helding's side. With him was Katherine; Marisia could see she was pregnant again. She took David Grant's hand, and pulled back a little into the crowd, and waited.

Henry Klein waved and beamed, and pressed through the party like a little tug triumphantly bringing a great liner to port.

'We haven't seen each other,' Pieter said, 'for so long.'

It was a restrained and brotherly greeting, but Marisia's stomach turned over. In books, people always feel simple emotions, she thought, but the fact is that you feel what your guts say and later you discover if it is fear, lust, anger, or distress.

'Katherine,' Marisia said, 'darling, you look so well.'

'I'm David Grant.'

'Of course,' Pieter said. 'I remember.'

And they were stalemated.

Whatever Henry Klein expected from the meeting, Marisia thought, he must be disappointed. But there she was wrong. Klein was not expecting some warm, sentimental moment, but rather a disruption, an upset. Klein liked upsets. The pieces tended to fall back to earth in much more interesting, more revealing patterns.

'Is this a good party?' Pieter asked. 'I keep being told there's an A-list and a B-list out here and I can't tell which is which.'

'If Jules and Doris Stein are there, it's A-list.'

'And are they here?'

'At a wrap party? God, no. This is strictly for the workers. Nobody here owns a studio – except possibly Henry Klein, and he's mysterious as usual.'

'It's odd we both know Henry Klein.'

'He's good. Naturally we both know him.'

'Is it a good film?'

'No,' Marisia said, 'but Marty might save it when he's editing. You make a musical in the cutting room, anyway.' She asked politely after Georg's health, not really wanting to be told, and was assured he was much better, and resting now at the hotel. She then said to Pieter: 'What are you doing here?'

'Nothing,' Pieter said, 'beyond my usual plans for world domination.'

At least Klein and Van Helding had a language in common – money. David Grant and Katherine were lost in the shallows of polite chitchat – how fine were Los Angeles orange juice and neon, how odd the houses in

Beverly Hills, and how little men in the Polo Lounge kept being called to the phone and then saying nothing.

'You've seen the sights,' David Grant said.

Around them the crew was exorcizing the movie. The grips and carpenters were telling outrageous stories and drinking hard, and the very few studio executives and the other two bankers (not important bankers, only here to impress their secretaries with their knowledge of the stars) were out of place. One of the secretaries disappeared to the old Tarzan's jungle with a big, blond carpenter, which snuffed the motel dreams her boss had been nursing for days.

Something or someone was missing.

'Do you know,' asked Marty, passing like a comet on one of his regular orbits of the party, 'where our fucking star is?'

And then, out of the crowd, a middle-aged woman began jostling her way towards the band. She was sharp-featured, plain, dressed more dowdily than Californian taste and climate allow. She was in black bombazine.

By the band, the woman stood up uncertainly on a table and pulled out a clown's giant powder puff.

'I am,' she said, and her voice carried as though by loudspeakers, 'cleaning away all of this shit.'

And the dull woman stripped off a fragment of plastic nose, wiped away the pallor that was painted over her Californian tan, set aside her fright-wig, let her own hair fall free, and took out the teeth that disguised the whole shape of her face.

'Sally!' Marty Genovese shouted. 'Wow!'

For it was indeed the star of *The Music Makers*, the well known, not yet commercial star of Broadway, Sally Giles. And she threw up her arms in the classic stripper's pose, the band began to vamp, and she edged off her implausible gloves. She wriggled slowly down, leaving the bombazine standing by itself. She stood aside from her character, bumping and grinding.

'I thought she was so prim,' Henry Klein said.

'You haven't seen her earliest movies,' Marisia said. 'You won't in theatres, either.'

And Sally Giles, down to a swimsuit, did a set of furious high kicks, turned and let her backside move as though with its own life, then did an acrobat's tumble down to the ground and bowed to the wild applause of the crew.

'More, more,' they shouted.

'She's good,' Marisia said. 'In fact she's the only reason this whole fiasco will be seen by more than a dozen consenting adults in Santa Barbara.'

'Except for you,' David Grant said, loyally.

'It was very well market researched,' Henry Klein said.

And Pieter said: 'We must all have dinner.'

Marisia noticed that, try as they would, they couldn't shake Henry Klein.

It was as though Pieter and David, severally, had decided they had enough of movie talk, domestic talk, and anything except for the range of subjects you find on a dull page of the *Wall Street Journal*. Since serious things were their only common interests, and since they had decided to talk to each other – Marisia regarded that development as mildly alarming – dinner had a distinctly old-fashioned air. Men talked to men, women to women, and everyone was proper, and bored.

'You spend most of your time in South America?' Pieter asked, with a little flash of malice.

'And Los Angeles,' David Grant said. 'Alien cultures.'

'You went to Providencia for the revolution, I gather. That must have been a curious experience.'

'It was a CIA revolution,' Grant said, 'so the American press were faffing and demanding rights and storming around. There was a decent, Marxist East Indian labour leader, who obviously wouldn't do at all, not after Castro, and a black lawyer called Arthur Miller. The CIA decided better the devil they don't know, which is curious logic. They got Miller in, rigged the elections, and his first move was to nationalize the sugar business. They are said to be unhappy in Washington.'

'And I suppose after making such a fuss about democracy and electing Miller, they can't very well overturn him.'

'They've spent the budget.'

They had, as a kind of gag, settled in the Polo Lounge, which is green and trellised, and they were drinking dry Martinis except for Katherine who caused a scene – this was the mid-sixties – by asking for Perrier.

'You should invest in Providencia,' David Grant said. 'I don't mean that it's stable or secure or expanding or any of those things. But the CIA guarantees the government, so they can't let it go bust. And the International Monetary Fund wouldn't dare let it go, because we all know who pays the bills there. They'd repay if Providencia couldn't. But of course, there isn't a wild dash to lend – so they'd have to pay high interest. It'd be like lending to Uncle Sam at the interest rates you could get as a loan shark.'

'But nobody knows who's the banker of last resort, if anything did go wrong,' Pieter said. He was more thoughtful than a casual idea seemed to warrant.

'It doesn't matter,' David said. 'Politics is your banker of last resort.'

'Dangerous idea,' Pieter said. 'Very attractive.'

David Grant wanted Pieter to approve; unselfconsciously, he preened. He hoped Marisia was suitably impressed.

'We could,' Marisia said, shifting in her chair, 'have dinner.'

Van Helding went to the men's room, but a porter, very courteously, barred the way.

'Temporarily closed, sir,' he said. 'I'm sorry.'

'What do you mean, temporarily closed?'

An extremely famous leading man, thin and romantic, sauntered from the men's room. He tripped a little.

'There,' said the porter. 'I think it's all right now.'

Van Helding raised his eyebrows.

'Anything goes up there,' Marisia was saying. 'People sleep on the streets and they smoke marijuana and they talk about free love and some of them may even be doing it. I give it about a year. It's an adventure playground for adolescents, San Francisco, and when they're tired of being free they'll turn wild because freedom doesn't change anything. And they'll gun us down from their nice old beat-up Chevys.'

'Sometimes,' Katherine said, 'I had rather talk about shops. It is less depressing.'

'We're the last ones,' Pieter said, 'for a while, at least – the last ones who wear tweed jackets and take power seriously and write our languages properly. And it works for us, and the kids will find out it doesn't work for them, their freedom.'

'There seems to be a family front on that,' David Grant said. 'You think as one.'

'Don't be silly,' Marisia said. 'It's just that these kids are the first from the middle class to have money and cars and who don't have to worry each day about the future. They're secure. So they start to play games. Pieter and I – we all have enough money. We can play games, too. We've always been able to. It isn't interesting any more.'

'I wish you sounded just a little bit excited,' David Grant said. 'It is a kind of revolution.'

'You can't have revolutions that overthrow nothing, that just withdraw into a kind of daze. Revolutions have to change the established order – break it down to build it up. The children don't bother me.'

'I want to write about them,' David Grant said. 'I want to know where they're headed.'

'Neurosurgery,' Marisia said, 'the amount of mescaline they do.'

David Grant sat back.

'You think your own forms of materialism are enough? That there's no area of spirituality – doubt, questions, faith?'

Pieter Van Helding said: 'Those are words I don't deal in. Your kids in Haight-Ashbury are surplus to requirements, that's the truth. If they worked, if they engaged in productive activity, the economy would go into overload. That's why we have hippies – because we can afford them, and because we can't afford to bring them into the workplace. That's why we have our university intellectuals, talking to themselves, making mysteries out of everything. In the sixties, you write a thesis. In the thirties the government paid you to dig a ditch. It's no different.'

'Learning is at least about something,' David Grant said.

'So is money,' Van Helding said.

'You sound like a Marxist.'

'No reason why not,' Van Helding said. 'It's a pity about all those Slovaks and bureaucrats who got to Marx, but that doesn't mean he was wrong on everything. You wouldn't deny that the reason we have television now isn't just that the miraculous box was invented – it's that the economy started spilling out money that could only be mopped up in marketing and advertising. So people were ready to pay for TV. It dealt with the surplus money.'

'You make it all sound quite certain,' Marisia said. 'But also quite insecure – as though all those dons would find themselves out of work if the economy turned sour.'

'Perhaps,' Van Helding said. 'At least they'd know what hit them. And they'd know they couldn't duck.'

'I think this is boring,' Katherine said, but the other three had become intense. And Katherine herself was even better qualified to talk than the others. It was just that at the moment, with Georg lying sick upstairs and a new baby kicking in her belly, polite conversation was all she could handle.

'You'll be talking about crises of capitalism,' David Grant said. 'And banking as a way to absorb surplus value.'

'Maybe so,' Pieter said. 'Capitalism does have crises. And banking is just the business of faith – it's all about paper that people trust or don't trust, value or don't value. It's not about the real world at all; it's about how the real world is seen. And how it changes, remember. You couldn't get old man Vanderbilt back to make a new fortune building railways in New York State, or fund a new Carnegie Foundation on a steel business. Even a latter-day Henry Ford couldn't expect to make a new fortune in cars, if he started today. Yet bankers are the constant – they judge what people will buy any day, what they believe. People used to believe in Vanderbilt and Carnegie and Ford, and now they don't.'

'And the latter-day Vanderbilts and Carnegies and Fords don't starve,' Katherine said. 'I think all this talk is silly. We still do not have plans for this weekend. Perhaps you know some amusing places – '

'Amusing,' Marisia said. 'I don't know if amusing is the word, and I waited until the third bottle to bring this up, but Henry Klein was very keen that all four of us should go to Palm Springs this weekend. Five, I mean. I think he meant you more than us actually.'

'Georg might like it,' David Grant said.

'You know,' Katherine said, 'probably he is dying.'

That broke the conventions and the peace of the evening. All four of them, round their polite table, felt as if the sea was closing over them.

Their salvation was Marty Genovese, drunk, bearlike round his girlfriend who was trying to steer him, again, away from other people – back up the Canyons for a little drugs and a little sex, if Marty could manage.

'My God,' Marty said. 'Dinner with the Money.' He intoned the word.

'You forget,' Marisia said sweetly, 'we all have money, Marty. It isn't so interesting for us.'

And Lolita steered him away. She sometimes regretted the big, incompetent football player to whom she'd lost her virginity. He was grateful. He never blamed her. He was so much less work than a grown-up. She could feel herself growing up, a decade every dinnertime.

Pieter said to David Grant: 'You're ambitious, too. You're not pure like the children in Haight-Ashbury.'

Grant shrugged. 'I want to do my job. I have to struggle a bit to get the assignments I want. I suppose that's true.'

'I'm ambitious, too,' Pieter said. 'To have power. Real power. And I have another ambition – out of children's books, the sort of ambition you can write about because it doesn't sound as indecent as simply wanting wealth or influence.'

'Tell me,' Grant said.

'I want to find Eldorado.'

'It wasn't a place. It was a man – a priest who covered himself in gold and threw himself in the lake to placate the gods.'

'It was a place,' Van Helding said. His voice dropped and he sounded sincere. 'It was a place in my childhood. I read about Walter Raleigh sailing up the Orinoco, into the forest, along a kind of red-brown little trail that ran all across the maps in the book. I read about the Indians who fled from the Spaniards – all the men, women, children, animals, gold, all crossing the mountains, the forests, to find somewhere to be at peace. Somewhere to be at peace with gold – where other people's appetites wouldn't find them.'

'Through the jungle to peace?' Grant said. 'To death, more likely. Have you ever been along one of those rivers?'

'There's something else. I want to risk my life. I can risk my bank, my money, my capital . . .'

'Better not risk the bank, brother,' Marisia said. 'It is our bank, remember.'

'But I can't risk my life. It isn't exciting enough, yet.'

Katherine said: 'You people talk like boys.'

And Marisia looked thoughtfully at Pieter. Eldorado was an old dream, not exact but playful, something to embroider on a sleepless night or nurture on a summery day. She'd heard it all before, and she'd never known what it meant. Pieter's dreams were meant to be more immediate and manageable.

Henry Klein talked briskly to his principals in Palm Springs, nothing more than a reminder that he'd cleverly arranged to get the papers on Kellerman Unger years back, and they should be grateful. Henry Klein thought they were rather inclined to take him for granted. If his hunch about the Van Heldings was right, they would suit his principal's plans admirably.

Meanwhile, it was a question of landing the pair.

Marisia had once owed him money, but only briefly. She'd repaid him with interest even before her legacy was through; he'd checked that. What had Marisia done for money, once at least, that needed $10,000 in capital and paid $12,000 in a week? It wasn't a difficult question, not in Southern California, close to the border. But he didn't have the kind of proof you can shake at an uncooperative victim, or take to the LAPD. In fact, he had only an assumption. She might have gone to Vegas and played the blackjack tables and seduced a crooked croupier – but she wouldn't, would she? She wanted real risk – like her brother. They were adventurers.

And Pieter Van Helding; he riffled through his notes and the file. He knew about Kellerman Unger – too small for Van Helding's ambition, too silted up with companies like these deadbeat Helios SA people, the ones Pieter had come to Los Angeles to salvage. And Pieter Van Helding still had a boss – Jan Unger. The arithmetic there was simple. Unger still held more of the bank than either Marisia or Pieter separately; only together were they a power.

Henry Klein asked himself how together they really were. He didn't get the right answer.

Marisia called and said she was passing by and could she drop in for a moment? That was not like her; Klein's office was, tenuously, between Bel Air and the Magnum lot, but the film had wrapped and Marisia was rarely a casual caller.

She must want something. Very well, so did Klein. He wanted to know who held the proxies on her shares. Somebody must.

Marisia had learned to like the freeways, the clockwork way the traffic seemed to pull you along a predetermined course. She also knew – these matters became, in her mind, like Russian dolls that fit one inside the other – that people don't make casual calls across half LA. Never mind. Klein had been happy to hear from her, so he must also want something. And she needed information: exactly what Henry Klein was planning with Pieter Van Helding.

It followed that the meeting, casual over coffee in the comforable chairs, was as taut as a cop trying to question his chief's mother.

'We'll see you at the weekend, I hope,' Marisia said. 'At the Rolfe Place?'

'It's very fine. Pieter and Katherine and Georg are coming.'

'I've never been there – not to the Rolfe place. I can't imagine we're going to talk business this weekend?'

'More a get-acquainted meeting,' Klein said. 'And, of course, just to have fun.'

So it was business, Marisia thought.

'Dr Rolfe never comes to Los Angeles,' Marisia said. 'He's such a famous figure and I don't think I've ever seen a photograph of him.'

'Financiers have a way of being quite private.'

'He made his money in the talent agency business?'

'Originally,' Klein said. 'He was a surgeon, you know – and a stockbroker, and a real estate man. A financier, really.'

'They say he is richer than . . .'

'I think you can take it he's richer than almost anyone.'

'How comforting,' Marisia said.

'It must be, for him and his friends. I call them the Palm Springs gentry.'

'We'll all call them that.'

'You and Pieter must be glad to see each other after all this time. Business to discuss, I imagine?'

'A little,' Marisia said. 'I only cash the dividend cheques from Kellerman Unger, of course. And if they're not large enough I go straight to Jan Unger and complain. The gold companies were too important for Daddy to let the family have a say in running them.'

'You like Jan Unger?'

'He's a dry, old man. But he has run the place for ever and it wouldn't be polite to talk to anyone else.'

'But Pieter's really in charge now. Everyone says so.'

'In charge of his shares and his departments, yes. In fact he's called managing director. But he's not chairman of the board yet. He may never be; I may take a fancy to the job.'

'You?' Klein said, and realizing he had been ill-mannered, he added: 'But with your Hollywood career . . .'

'The power interests me,' Marisia said, 'we Van Heldings like power.'

'You should be a producer.'

'I'd rather be a financier. Like Dr Rolfe. I must ask him for lessons this weekend.'

'He would be a great teacher – if he wanted.'

Henry Klein thought: don't press the point. Pieter Van Helding doesn't control her shares. This whole operation has just become more than a little complicated.

The smell was sour and light – fear, disinfectant, sprays to keep away more fundamental stenches. Hospital air, Pieter Van Helding thought, was breathed four times before it reached you, and then pumped out through machines.

Georg had gone off happily for new tests. It was like this in any city they visited: Katherine would insist on finding new doctors, new cures, and there would be tests, brief hope, and finally disillusion. When he could find no excuse, Pieter went with her on these desolate little expeditions; his patience with his failing, battered son was dying. In Van Helding's life the child had become a factor that broke the boundaries of time and attention allocated to it, and if that sounded harsh, Van Helding was past caring. He saw the child's suffering, and he saw the child smiling as he went off for his new attention from the doctors, and he saw a masochist being born.

He wanted fresh air. He wanted to get out of the city, and it's unbreathable varnish of smog – to the mountains, to the beach.

He called Marisia and got her answering machine. He left a message and she rang the hospital an hour later. Pieter claimed that business called and he took a cab back to the Beverly Hills Hotel.

Marisia came into the lobby in a skirl of colours, a little whirlwind of scent, eyes, legs. She got appreciative stares, and she used them, as she always did: taking their power, ignoring their challenge. And Pieter joined her, quickly.

'Henry Klein lent me an Aston Martin,' Pieter said. He seemed boyishly pleased with his toy.

'He must want your business,' Marisia said. 'One way or another.'

'Let's get out of town.'

The car was sleek and silver and wasted on the California urban roads.

'We should go down to the beach,' Marisia said. 'Malibu, maybe.'

'I've seen Malibu on postcards.'

'Then Venice,' Marisia said. 'I always feel safe in Venice.'

The distant hills that ring Los Angeles were only partly visible, and from the freeway they never seemed to change. The suburban clumps of housing seemed all the same. Los Angeles looked more like a town that had been diluted and spread apart by distance – too thin to have a character of its own.

'Henry Klein says Dr Rolfe wants to talk to you,' Marisia said. 'Maybe he wants to get you involved in some huge deal.'

'I'd like that.'

'Nobody seems to know very much about Rolfe,' Marisia said. 'But they tell some interesting stories about his money.'

'Mob money?'

'How did you know?'

'That's what they always say when they can't see how to make the same fortune over again. I expect they'll say it about me.'

The little houses sped by, a frieze on the endles wall of the freeway.

'There are some things going on,' Marisia said. 'Henry Klein drops hints about them.'

'Anything I should know?'

'If we're partners, Pieter.'

'Partners.'

'Very well. Marty Genovese used to work for a script

outfit called Seed – they used to be a mining company in Dakota, and suddenly they turned up in Los Angeles packaging movies and taking a cut of the profits and a hefty fee. Marty wrote for them, but I don't think any of the scripts got made; and he made a movie for them – very sensitive, very personal, very *nouvelle vague*. Very cheap. And very lost.'

'Seed,' Pieter said, veering to avoid an articulated serpent of a Mac truck which had come up faster than he had expected. 'At least they weren't Magnum or Paramount or Universal – all those bombastic names.'

'Seed,' Marisia said. 'Now as far as I could see, Seed wasn't exactly coining money. Yet suddenly, they want to take over a studio – Magnum.'

'I heard about this,' Pieter said.

'No, you didn't,' Marisia said. 'You might have heard about Seven Arts taking Warner Brothers, but that's much more straightforward – Allen and Company from Wall Street and Ray Stark. You can see the money. The curious thing about the Seed deal is that, even by Hollywood standards, their money is weird.'

'You reckon they're fronting for someone?'

'Maybe. You never know in this town. You're making one movie and twenty people sit down round a table to put up the money, and they don't know each other and the money's coming from twenty different places for twenty different reasons. It could be anything.'

'Is Henry Klein involved?'

'Marty thinks so, and he's got a good nose for politics in the business. He always says if you understand the money here you understand everything.'

'He doesn't seem to know what to do with the information.'

'That's his tragedy,' Marisia said. 'I just thought you might want to know a bit of background before Palm Springs.'

'Can we drive past Magnum? I'd like to see it. Maybe there's some obvious reason why outsiders should want the back lot or something.'

'Later,' Marisia said. 'You take the next left.'

They came down into Venice. The palm-trees glittered, the beach was wide and the breakers were high. It was a playground. Girls, sun-brown, wandered as though happily dazed, or sat on the grass in yoga positions. Past the roller-skaters on the boardwalk, a boy juggled Indian clubs with meticulous skill. Quite suddenly his attention failed, the clubs fell around him, his hands went limp, and his smile never faltered. He stood happily in the ruins of his act.

'This place,' Marisia said, 'is more Californian that California.'

In the doorway of a corrupt building, they bought loose joints and they watched the great Pacific clouds, sails of an ocean, through a beatific haze of smoke. Nothing seemed to move except for the children, the muscular children, at their games.

Marisia giggled. 'You must never tell anyone you had a whole day without a meeting. You'll never work again. If you only have one, you can still kill half a day driving to it.'

'You're nervous,' Pieter said.

'Hungry,' Marisia said. 'Dope always makes me hungry.'

She was not so much high as rosy, in a friendly, warm world which somehow ran parallel to reality. She edited out threats.

Piter looked ideal in that afternoon light. He looked powerful and graceful at once, and his eyes had the power to fascinate. It's going to be the first time he seduces me, Marisia thought.

The Aston Martin was against a false adobe wall, and someone had taken a spray can and draped a pair of outline nudes – sexually exact – across its shiny, silver surface.

'Oh my God,' Marisia giggled. 'Someone just expressed himself.'

'They didn't break anything,' Pieter said, with a sense of wonder. 'I guess this will show how much Henry Klein wants to know me – if we're still talking, he wants me bad.'

And they clambered into the Aston Martin, now coopted against its haughty nature to the people's art.

The joints, the sun, the wilful people circling Venice in a dream of strong bodies and simple games, the sense of a town at play made them reluctant to leave. Then, on the freeway, the thought of returning to the wastes of Beverly Hills ceased to seem attractive. David Grant was away at LAX on his way to London: Marisia had no desire to hurry home. Katherine Van Helding would be back from the clinic by now with some new but temporary formula for hope; Pieter did not want to face her. It was easy to stop for coffee, and after coffee to wander up steps and take a motel room for the afternoon, past the kidney-shaped pool and into a big, wide bed.

The desk clerk beamed as he left them.

It was a procession, Marisia thought, like a state occasion or a rich man's funeral. Limousines lined up to crawl the last few miles to the Rolfe estate, and then were waved grandly through the electronic gates. An immaculate driveway led across a greensward, laid on desert with great care, to a long, low mansion which seemed to trail away in every direction.

It was not going to be an easy weekend. She had already decided to leave early – Magnum was starting work on dubbing her movie on Monday – and she regretted coming. That afternoon in a motel bed had changed her sense of herself a little, and she was not quite sure yet how. She had undressed for Pieter, played for Pieter, enjoyed the near-mirror image of their two heads lying like legend on a pillow. In Switzerland sex had been a rush of blood; in the motel room, it was a perverse game. If she'd stayed away from Pieter after Switzerland for fear of passion, she wanted to kill him now, to stop herself from a foolish and messy indulgence.

And she didn't want to be around if Henry Klein and Dr Rolfe were planning to take her brother to glory this weekend. If Pieter's power were fixed, then she would have no choices, and she needed choices.

When it came to it, she and Katherine were packed off for a reluctant round of golf by the awful force of Palm Springs gentility. What a lady does is more circumscribed and ruled there than in any Victorian household. Frocks, golf, flowers, and guest lists were the proper province of women, and since there was no longer a Mrs Rolfe, Katherine and Marisia virtually had the province to themselves.

Van Helding was left, like a witness to a wedding, sitting in the midst of a group of seven men in Lacostes and plaids around a grand pool with a waterfall. The seven looked like power – unselfconscious, unforced authority. If you sat at the Grunwalds' table, you felt the aristocratic version of the same habit of command; here it was the habit of dominance, more brutal and streetwise.

Henry Klein did the talking.

'We represent a diversified concern,' he was saying. 'Real estate, some minor manufacturing, meat-packing, consumer goods, an interest in motion pictures. We have effective control of five major companies on the New York Stock Exchange, and, of course, Dr Rolfe has his seat on the Exchange. And there is an investment portfolio.' Klein paced up and down with his hands behind his back – clearly the junior man deputed to make a presentation, nervous of his superiors' response.

'But we have a problem,' he said. 'We have a sizeable cash flow from our retail enterprises and we need to use it. We would like to move into banking.'

It was direct, breathtakingly so. Van Helding only wondered what retail enterprises created such splendid cashflows. He could guess, of course: in 1945 it would have been ethical drugs into Europe, in 1965 it would be illegal drugs into America. That and girls, numbers, dirty books. He looked around the seven senior men and wondered which one of them controlled which operation, and how directly. It occurred to him to try to read their faces and see which ones had killed in their line of business.

'International transactions often concern us,' Klein continued. 'They must be done discreetly, of course; like any other businessman we resent unnecessary questions.'

'I often forget to ask questions,' Van Helding offered, waiting for and receiving smiles of polite approval.

There was one man he couldn't imagine on the streets, ever. That was the Doctor, as they called him, Dr Rolfe. His fine hands suggested he had once been a surgeon; he had. He was almost delicate-featured, with extraordinary blue eyes which never seemed to blink. A casual glance would suggest weakness in the man, but a moment in his presence would dispel that idea; he was as still and sharp as a knife. He was like a doll animated by a devil; you could never forget that the smiling face was a mask for the Doctor's true feelings and intentions.

'I think Henry has made our case,' the Doctor said. 'He makes it obliquely, but he makes it well.'

A bodyguard sat at his feet, never moving unless told to; a vastly muscled, vastly subservient kid called Joe. Joe made a polite laugh.

'I will tell you what we want. We want a bright man to back. We'd invest, take equity, and leave him proxies on our shares, for as long as he delivered. He'd be there for as long as we liked the dividends. In return, we'd like a little help at times, handling what I like to call homeless money. If a few battered suitcases cross the Atlantic with orphan dollars, we'd like them to find a home in Kellerman Unger, and we'd like a letter of credit from you in return. We like to be able to find a home for money. And we hate to call it "washing".'

The doctor had a high-pitched laugh, and when he laughed, so did the big-shouldered boy at his feet. 'Joe finds that amusing,' the Doctor said. Joe stopped at once.

Van Helding looked around the group. They talked of the need for trust, mutual respect. They talked figures that were like dreams – capital enough to fund expansion into London, maybe into New York. They would relieve him of the need to wait, give him the power that otherwise might take years to assemble. They were giving him the world.

But could he handle them? That man at the end, by the waterfall, with the gold chains and the barrel chest and the look of a Brooklyn greengrocer come into money; how would he cope with such a man? And the Doctor, a cold cherub with big, blue eyes and a voice like an East Coast preacher; what would happen if Van Helding ever let him down?

And the other fear: now he had been offered so much by these men, and at least by implication told so much, did he any longer have the right to choose whether or not to take their offer? Hadn't their frankness trapped him into saying 'yes'?

'Naturally,' the Doctor was saying, 'we shall arrange that the source of your new funds is discreet – through Vaduz, I think, and known names rather than Panama. We want you to look good. And when you come to America in due course, we want your background to be impeccable. Some people in the government here harbour quite irrational suspicions of my friends and myself. We wouldn't want that to complicate your life.'

'And we think you're ready for London,' Henry Klein said.

'You seem very well informed about my business.'

'We always have a dossier,' the Doctor said. 'A matter of simple prudence.'

'And what about the capital structure of Kellerman Unger? Do you consider the equity base should expand immediately? Do you want to buy out existing shareholders? What?'

'You need more capital,' the Doctor said. 'We expect big things of you, and you are not a big bank. You find us the sellers and we'll buy.'

Van Helding was struck by his stillness, like a coiled snake that is ready to strike waiting its moment; and by his grey-haired innocence. He was like a child, and like a cobra.

'Henry,' the Doctor said, 'will be calling on you for some advice soon. We would like to think of that as an audition, as it were.'

'As it were,' Henry Klein said.

Van Helding rose, and the men around the pool dissolved a formal meeting into an afternoon of beer and talk, simply by slight movements, changing chairs.

'Welcome,' Henry Klein said. He was eager, it seemed, for the poolside men to discuss Van Helding without Van Helding hearing. Pieter found himself steered to the golf course and in the company of Marisia and Katherine before he could make any serious protest.

'Thank God,' Marisia said. 'I thought we'd been exiled until dinner.'

'I think I've been exiled, too,' Pieter said.

'I want to go back to Los Angeles,' Marisia said. 'I can't stand being a lady like this. I'm not Nancy Reagan. I'm not Betsy Bloomingdale. I haven't given up yet.'

Katherine said: 'This is very dull, Pieter. It is nice to talk with Marisia, but there is nothing else to do. We don't seem to have any company.'

'This place,' Marisia said, 'is an armed camp. Electronic surveillance everywhere. You can't make a move without someone knowing.'

'Very secure,' Pieter said.

'I don't think I like being that secure.'

Marisia set down her golf clubs, waved away the Mexican caddies, and said: 'I know this weekend matters to you, Pieter, but I'm going. Now.'

'What will you tell them – as a matter of interest?'

'Work,' Marisia said. 'I'll tell them the dubbing is starting a day early.'

'They'll fly you back tomorrow morning,' Pieter said.

'I'm leaving now,' Marisia said.

Katherine looked up, sadly. 'I wish you wouldn't,' she said. 'Think of Pieter.'

Marisia glared, and made her way off across the golf course. She asked the studio to call her, faked the message when the call arrived, and left a note. She summoned her car and drove briskly off to the airport.

'You haven't seen Marisia?' Henry Klein asked Pieter, a little too casually.

'I think she had to go back to Los Angeles.'

'Oh dear,' Henry Klein said. 'Dr Rolfe did so want to talk with her.'

'Dr Rolfe is a fan?'

'Dr Rolfe wanted to talk business,' Henry Klein said. 'I imagine.'

And Dr Rolfe, behind his unlined, ice-still face, calculated. He wasn't sure if Marisia's sudden exit put the price of her stock in Kellerman Unger up or down. He would have to think about it.

Once Katherine was back in the bedroom, she lost her calm façade and began to pace, back and forth over the wide, carpeted floor, her satin robe flying out behind her, nervous and angry all at once.

'Marisia told me about them,' she said. 'Gangsters, they are. Déclassés. Hoods.' But the word came out lopsided, as "oods.'

'We don't talk about our hosts. My partners.'

'You mustn't deal with them. You mustn't.'

'Don't be bad,' Pieter said, with a great show of kindly patience. 'Please be calm. There's only one more day.'

'I am serious,' Katherine said. 'Just because I'm your wife doesn't mean that every word I say is hysterical. You have to tell me what they're offering you, what they want.'

Pieter's kindness faded. 'Are you going to match the offer?' he asked. He took her by the shoulders and held her, a little too hard, hands marking flesh. 'They are offering me the world, and all they want is a return on their capital.'

'In my family . . .'

'In your family it's enough to be a de Grunwald. That's power and prestige and money right there. Well, it isn't enough to be a Van Helding. To get what I want I need backers. And time. And luck. They're giving me all of that.'

'Why do you want so much? Why?'

Pieter let Katherine go, and she crumpled on to the bed, curling herself around the baby she could feel stirring inside her.

'I want everything,' Pieter said. 'I'm ready to risk everything. In fact if I thought I ever would fail, I would bring the whole damn structure down. That's the power that I want. I want to be so strong I can bet the world against my own success.'

'God,' Katherine said, in supplication.

Pieter was on his knees now, hand on her thigh, smiling, the storm of censure passed as quickly as it had come. 'Come and swim,' he said. 'Come and help Georg swim. He likes it.'

'Maybe,' Katherine said, looking up through tears that had been narrowly prevented, 'maybe Dr Rolfe knows someone or somewhere . . .'

'Come and talk,' Pieter said.

But when he closed the bedroom door, leaving Katherine to prepare herself, he was grateful. He liked a life in compartments, where the doors shut neatly. He wandered off into the house, which was grand enough and low enough to harbour pockets of sound that had travelled apparently by accident. But Van Helding suspected that nothing was careless or casual in this place. He was meant to hear what he heard.

Dr Rolfe was talking, in his precise, neat way.

'. . . very disappointed with Mr Ferrara and I think we should let him know, really quite directly. We had an agreement between gentlemen, and I expect those agreements to be honoured. Besides, he can hardly rebuild Wilshire Boulevard by himself. He needs us.' There was a murmur from the Doctor's companion, and then the Doctor again: 'Don't worry for yourself. We are sophisticated people. We never kill the messenger who brings bad news.'

And the conversation drifted away.

Pieter Van Helding knew he should look out for Mr Ferrara's name in the papers.

Marisia stomped the apartment in a sour temper, bored, alone, and fractious. She had tried driving up into the Canyons to see Marty Genovese, but Lolita was lying stark naked by the pool and Marty was tonguing her, and when they broke apart, their only topic of conversation was Lolita's baby. Marty seemed to think she should have it and so did Lolita, but they were both full of a childlike impatience to have the whole process over. Meanwhile,

Marisia noticed Lolita was hitting the Bourbon, which at seventeen was not brilliant for the system, and Marty was getting restless at the restriction of sex and drugs involved in Lolita's condition. Besides, he was cutting a movie, and he didn't need, didn't want people for the time being. Maybe Lolita could go off and do her mammalian reproduction number on her own.

Marisia didn't like the talk, or the situation, and she couldn't get sense out of Marty. At home, there was a message from Pieter again, asking for a meeting somewhere discreet. She called the Beverly Hills and left a message for him – two could play at indirection – saying she was going to the studio next morning, and why didn't he come? She would pick him up at the hotel.

They had almost nothing to say to each other. They drove into Magnum, through the long, narrow lanes between barnlike sound stages and the rolling real estate (newly sold to a British consortium who took its one oil well seriously). 'Hollywood Crude,' said Marisia. 'It produces even less than the one at Twentieth Century.'

Pieter said nothing of substance until they were parking in the lane by the dubbing stage.

'Marisia,' he said, when the car had stopped. 'Please sell your shares in Kellerman Unger.'

'Don't be silly,' Marisia said, and she went to open her door.

'I mean it,' Pieter said. 'It would make my life much easier.'

'And why the hell should I care about that? Since when have you put yourself out to do me favours?'

'You don't understand. You'd get a very good price from the people who want to buy. You could put the money anywhere you wanted – and you wouldn't be dependent on whatever Jan Unger decided to dole out, year by year. He is rather conservative.'

'He's a miser,' Marisia said. 'But I don't need the money that badly. I have a career.'

'If you sell now, there's a ready buyer. If you don't, the market will dry up.'

'Dr Rolfe wants a bank to play with, does he? He has such a nice smile for a barracuda.'

'That's childish.'

'I assume you made a plan over the weekend and I'm meant to sell to Rolfe – for big brother's sake?'

'And your sake.'

'I like having my share of Kellerman Unger. It isn't something I talk about here; I am simply from some exotic European family with money. All that matters here is your last movie – people invent their own backgrounds as they go along. But I like the link with father and with the idea of the family, and the dividends are fine, and it suits me to have money in Holland.'

Pieter said: 'You wouldn't want David to know about us.'

'Nor you Katherine, I imagine. Do a lot of good to your international reputation – divorced by your Grunwald wife who cites your sister. Are you sure you're big enough yet to survive that kind of scandal?'

'Henry Klein tells me that you pledged part of your holdings to him once when you needed money in a hurry. That was how he knew so much about KU. We wondered why you needed the cash and got it back so quickly.'

'That's a long time ago and the pledge is redeemed.'

'Was it drugs, I wonder?'

'Pieter, you can't blackmail me. I am not that kind of person. People know what's weak about me, and I don't care if they do.'

'You won't sell even at Rolfe's price? You realize if I sell, we can bring in new capital and expand the bank and your shares won't be a fifth, they'll be one per cent of the equity?'

'If Jan Unger and I both vote with you, yes. But if we don't, I doubt if you'll get far. You're outvoted at any shareholders' meeting for a start, and you'd need a meeting to change the capital structure.'

'You know a lot for a movie starlet.'

'Star,' said Marisia tartly. 'And now I have to go to work.'

'Think about it, please,' Pieter said, the coldness now gone from his voice. He ran his hand along Marisia's thigh, and she was stiff with annoyance, yet she didn't remove his hand. 'We could go back to the motel and think about it,' Pieter said. She felt exposed and awkward, in a studio parking lot where anyone might come, yet hot and wet and breathless. 'The idea of you in that motel room, undressing for me, coming out of the shower naked, lowering yourself on to me . . .'

'It's a movie. Shut up for God's sake.'

'. . . and working down until I am filling you up and . . .'

Pieter's hands were at her breasts, and her dress tumbled away; his mouth came down, open, around a nipple, and teased it hard and upright, and tormented it very gently while his hand worked down and stroked between the lips of her sex. She wanted his cock, she wanted his hand or his mouth to play with her clitoris, she wanted . . . something more, here and now, even in the parking lot.

'Don't stop me,' Pieter said.

She lay back. She felt him pause and begin to tug down her stockings until her thighs were naked against the cool, supple leather of the seats that clung a little. She began to spread her legs, and she thought she was being licked and tickled and softly bitten into another place and time and dream. She was ready. She wanted him to go away. She wanted to fuck with him. She wanted never to see him again.

She turned on the front seat, skirt riding high, belly flat and bare, and he brought his mouth down on her clitoris and teased it, bit it, turned it between his teeth. She began to arch up from the seat in a state of passion.

And he stopped.

'You will sell, won't you?' he said.

She crashed in a second from some high place. She felt she hated him. She said, 'Shit' and it came like a long, fever cry. And she tried to bring down her own fingers to relieve the ache and the need, but he held her arms.

'It's not like that,' she said. 'I can live through that. I can wait.'

He was startled. She was straddled, half naked, on the car seats, all pink and brown and flushed in the violent sunshine, all hips and sex and nipples hot with arousal and she hated him.

She pulled down her skirt, checked the rear mirror in case anyone was about, came back to her senses and began to tame her hair.

'You realize,' she said, 'I may be your lover sometimes. But I am your enemy. Always.'

She pushed open the door and he half fell, half jumped from the car, like a frog.

She prepared for her day's work.

'We want Magnum,' Henry Klein said. 'That's decided. But we need a little help – your audition, as we said. Magnum has made some disasters. Bombs. Clunkers. Terrible movies with no hope at all – including, I'm afraid, your sister's last picture, *The Music Makers*.'

'It isn't even cut yet.'

'It might be better to save the money. With movies like that Magnum doesn't look too good – but we want it to look good. And solid. We have a buyer for a movie studio when our little company Seed has taken it over. We want the buyer's business and he'll hand it over for Magnum stock. We get into data processing, he gets into the starlet's pants, he hopes.'

'The problem is assets, not income?'

'In New York, they know movies is a cyclical business. They understand. What they like to see is real estate, a film library, all those things – and no problems. We pay off the old farts at the studio, we make the business look good for a couple of years, and we can buy anything with those shares.'

Van Helding looked at an office full of neat antiques, each labelled and numbered. Somewhere there must be a master catalogue. Everything was an investment, an asset.

'I'd like to know of some deals you have going at present,' Van Helding said. 'Real estate, particularly.'

'I'm not giving you a list,' Klein said.

'And how much you need to cover?'

'*Music Makers* alone,' Klein said, looking at papers on his desk, 'is twenty million dollars negative cost, and say another eight million dollars prints and publicity. That's all loss, they tell me.'

'How much more would you lay out to be able to say the movie was a hit?'

'To make a hit?'

'I didn't say that. I said to make it look like a hit?'

'You have ten million, if you can do it.'

'And the list of properties?'

'OK,' said Klein. 'But you've got to work fast.'

'Give me five weeks,' Van Helding said, 'and it'll be magic. Magnum will be the hottest studio in town.'

'Well, well,' Klein said. 'I do hope it works.'

Van Helding walked down the steps of the white-fronted colonial mansion that served Klein for offices – a blatant imitation of MCA up the boulevard – and he stopped for a moment at the newspaper box. The evening *Herald Examiner* had a banner headline, vivid and high: TIE BODY IN TRUNK TO MOB VENGEANCE.

Van Helding bought a paper. He wanted a drink while he thought out the hiding of a $20 million fiasco and a paper would allow him to drink in decent isolation.

There was a wide picture of a T-bird parked in the lot of a West Hollywood supermarket. Five days the car had stood there before security guards began to take note of a pervasive, charnel stink. The police had come, crowbarred open the trunk, and found the remains – blasted by a shotgun – of a man called Ferrara. He had been a property developer.

Of course, Van Helding knew the name.

The nurse said: 'There'll be nowhere to take Master Georg for his walk. And I feel too hot in the uniform.'

'Do what you want,' Katherine said.

'It's not what I want,' the nurse said, primly.

Katherine looked down at Georg, whose skin, still pale, now had some life from the desert sun.

'I see him, I know he's dying, and I wonder if it was worth all the pain of bringing him into the world,' she said.

'Of course it was, dear. And the next one.'

'I wonder about it all. I could still be a Grunwald, I suppose, in a chateau.'

'This is a perfectly nice hotel. You have a perfectly nice bungalow.'

'Pieter wants to stay here a little.'

'It'd be damp in Amsterdam,' the nurse said. She hated confessions. They always came out with things you'd rather nor hear, especially when you were all away from home, and then they resented you because they'd said things out of turn – as though being polite was a trick to make people talk.

'I hate it here,' Katherine said. 'I liked it at first, but not to stay.'

'A man has to do his job,' the nurse said, and tried to excuse herself.

Katherine paced the room and picked up a hefty ashtray, pseudo-Lalique, from the side table. She weighed it.

'You need your job,' Katherine said.

'Yes, dear. Also, I love the babies. You'd be surprised. I don't like to hear you saying Master Georg will be bad. It might harm him.'

'I'm so bored,' Katherine said.

The nurse swept through the door. Katherine took up the ashtray in the flat of her hand and pitched it clean through the window.

The nurse reappeared with a tight smile.

'Had an accident, did we, dear?'

Katherine dissolved in tears on the sofa.

'My client,' said Pieter Van Helding, 'or perhaps I should say, my other client?' Klein nodded. 'Is Helios SA. They used to be one of the great European studios in the 1920s, then they went into office machines, now they need cash – quickly. They also like to think of themselves as a movie company, still. They release films. They even make them from time to time.'

'So?'

'So,' Van Helding said. 'You are going to pay Helios ten million dollars cash to "buy" *The Music Makers* from you. And Helios is going to transfer its own stock to you in payment – face value or directors' valuation, whichever suits you best. Ten million dollars in stock to cover the cash, plus twenty million dollars to cover production costs plus eight million dollars prints and publicity. Then instead of a dud movie costing $28 million, Magnum has an asset in European stock worth $38 million. And a brand new asset when you make your bid.'

'Forgive me for asking an obvious question,' Klein said, 'but if Helios needs cash so badly now, and you're the banker and you won't give it to them, what are the chances that the Helios stock will be worth more than a bent nickel in a year?'

'It'll be worth what you say it's worth,' Van Helding said. 'They're not a quoted company.'

'You're clever,' Klein said. 'Of course you do have two clients. That doesn't always make us happy.'

'The worst movie ever made could be on Magnum's books this way and look good. And of course you can keep its TV value as an asset, if you want to. Helios only wants the cash.'

'It sounds good,' Klein said. 'Do it. If you can, and if it's safe.'

Both men had images dancing in their head. Klein saw a stylish figure fronting for his principals – this side of the law but not always scrupulous.

Van Helding saw Ferrara's head, full of pus, in the trunk of his T-bird awaiting the last judgement in the parking lot of a Hollywood Safeway.

'I said, trust me.' Van Helding almost seemed to plead.

'I don't care about the games any more,' Marisia said. 'I am not selling. N-o.' She cradled the phone like a weapon.

'I'm not going to talk about revealing things, or any nonsense like that,' Van Helding said. 'I just want to talk career.'

'Call my agent.'

'You just made a movie the whole of Hollywood thinks is a disaster. They're laughing at it out in Malibu. Listen to them! It was market researched for more than most movies cost, based on a red-hot Broadway property, stuffed full of stars – and it can't get out of the editing room after three months. The people who've seen it say it stinks. It could bring a whole studio down around it.'

'Thank you,' Marisia said. 'But that was a long time ago for me. I'm starting a new picture next week. With George Cukor.'

'Your movie,' Pieter said, 'has to be a smash hit just to get off the ground. Just to fly – not even to get anywhere. If you do your sums . . .'

'I know about the multiplier,' Marisia said. 'A movie must make twenty-seven times its negative cost to show profit.'

'You're all CPAs out here.'

'We all read *Variety*.'

'Then you know what a disaster you've made. Now listen to me. You made that movie for Magnum and friends of mine are buying Magnum. It would be easy for them to say Marisia Van Helding doesn't work any more – spread stories, say you're on some David Ogilvy list of box office poison.'

'Go on.'

'If they did put the word out, everyone would agree. You know this town. There's your face up on *The Music Makers* billboards all along Sunset to remind people just how much money you cost Magnum.'

'Pieter, I don't know if your friends have that much power.'

'They'll kill you.'

'That,' Marisia said, 'I would believe.'

'Kill your career, I mean. You'll have your shares in KU, but they won't mean much when my friends have bought in. We'll probably pass on dividends for a while. That could get awfully hungry. I don't think David could support you both.'

'I will not sell my Kellerman Unger shares – at least, not to your friends. That is final.'

'Nobody else will want to buy. We won't have high earnings, because we'll be paying out high salaries and putting profit back into the bank. We won't pay dividends for a while. And everyone will know the strategic holdings belong to someone else. There will be no market.'

'It sounds so simple.'

'It is. You sell, or you stop working. You sell – or you try your hand at being a hippie for a while.'

'Or your chums come and kneecap me.'

'They don't believe in unnecessary effort,' Pieter said. 'Think about it, won't you?'

Koolhoven fretted while Pieter Van Helding was away. Even his occasional dashes back to Amsterdam, the showers of memoranda, the snap decisions, were no consolation. Koolhoven needed Pieter to steer and nurture; he found to his surprise that he didn't much like power for himself.

Besides, Unger had become insufferable. The reed of a man now looked broken. Since the night of the attempt on Pieter Van Helding's nerves or life, whichever it had been, Jan Unger had behaved as though he had received a terrible shock. Something had happened he couldn't control. Koolhoven was still puzzling over precisely what had caused the change.

And he was worrying about control. Koolhoven had kept Van Helding within bounds, gently; it was easy while the bank was relatively small and needed its respectability. From the sketchy papers Pieter had left behind in Amsterdam, he gathered Kellerman Unger was about to change in size and in ethos.

The American invasion was something Koolhoven couldn't resist openly, since it offered Pieter so much he both needed and wanted, but it was something he would much rather did not happen.

He didn't expect to see Jan Unger but the old man seemed to need to talk. He had turned as brittle as a dry grass. He stooped more, and he whistled a little between his teeth.

'I am a little concerned,' Unger said, 'about the length of Van Helding's absence. There are some matters he really must clear up.'

'We'll telex him.'

'He should be here.'

'He makes his own decisions. Besides, you know he's hunting new investors – people with big money. It would be foolish to bring him back before he's either failed or succeeded.'

'It's not a question of bringing him back any more,' Unger said rather petulantly. 'It's a question of whether he will deign to come back. My authority . . .'

'He is managing director,' Koolhoven said. 'He takes charge of most policy. I suppose it's his policy to stay in the sun for a while.'

Unger pounced. 'Exactly. I'm glad to hear that you have the same doubts I do. I cannot think it is responsible to remain away from Holland in this way. I know nothing of these people with whom he is dealing. A doctor, it seems. I can't make head or tail of the papers.'

'A Dr Rolfe,' Koolhoven said. 'I gather he is one of those rich men about whom you don't ask questions.' He couldn't resist a dig. 'You must know lots of those, Unger. With your career.'

Unger glared, but his heart was not in it.

'When we have the proposals, I shall certainly oppose them.'

'Without even knowing what they are?'

'I know quite enough. I have an instinct in these matters.'

'If it's what Pieter wants, it's what the bank needs. Not because he's infallible but because the bank needs Pieter.'

'Perhaps,' Jan Unger said. 'I am a little tired of the way in which people conveniently forget the actual disposition of the shares. I am a much larger shareholder than Pieter Van Helding.'

'Indeed,' Koolhoven said. 'We are rarely allowed to forget.'

'I don't throw my authority around. Nobody could accuse me of that.'

'No,' Koolhoven said. He had found his pipe among papers on his desk, and he cleaned it carefully. 'You don't even challenge Pieter, do you? You come to me afterwards and complain.'

'You have his ear.'

'On some things. I still wonder why the major shareholder and chairman of the board doesn't confront his junior if he feels like it. You have nothing to lose.'

'I dislike confrontation. I dislike dealing with Mr Van Helding's schemes. I have my own areas to look after.'

'You sometimes seem afraid to confront him. As though there was something from your past with Georg Van Helding, the old man, that bothered you – some reason why you mistrust Van Heldings as a tribe.'

'Nonsense,' Unger said. 'Although I hear people saying they do not always trust Pieter. My old friends worry about these young men. Impetuous, not at all careful or dutiful. We don't know where they'll carry us, or what they'll tell the world.'

'We all have secrets,' Koolhoven said.

Something curious was nagging at his mind, just below the margins of his thinking. The night Pieter Van Helding was attacked in Switzerland very few people knew where to find him. Fewer still knew where in canton Obwalden lay the Widow Van Helding's house. Unger seemed better informed than most, and Unger had been feuding with Pieter, something he was bad at doing in public. Someone must have told the skier where to find the Van Heldings.

Suppose it was Jan Unger.

It didn't make sense. The old man wanted Pieter out of the way, but not to the point of murder. Unless, of course, Pieter knew something from the war years that Unger was determined to hide. In that case Unger, and no doubt dozens of the others involved, might have an interest in keeping him quiet. Pieter didn't share his secrets; they would presumably have gone with him to his grave.

It was only an intuition, fleeting enough, but it settled with Koolhoven. He said, on a chance: 'We all have secrets. Someone, for example, sent that man to kill Pieter in Switzerland. Someone must have that secret.'

Unger didn't blink. He made a steeple of his long, thin fingers and looked down.

'Somebody,' he said.

'It must weigh very hard on the conscience.'

'I imagine that it must do.'

'It would require some repayment, I imagine. Some favour.'

Jan Unger said: 'I have been afraid of that.'

Katherine, the nurse, and Georg sat in a wan little line against a white clinic wall, waiting. Katherine wouldn't see the doctor until Pieter arrived, and a whole social order crumbled. Doctors are always the ones who are late.

'It's a nice place,' the nurse said.

Georg began to cry.

Once Pieter arrived, the doctors paused, continued their bluff of busyness for a minute or two, and then admitted the Van Heldings.

'We are an experimental institute,' the older doctor said, 'and you must understand there is an element of doubt and chance in what we do. First, we only take on children with a chance. We're taking on Georg because we think we can help. Frankly, our programme was full, but Dr Rolfe . . .'

'Rolfe?' Pieter asked, startled.

'Our most generous benefactor,' the older doctor said. 'We thought of calling this place the Rolfe Clinic, but sadly he was far too modest to allow that.'

'I hadn't realized he was so closely connected here.'

The older doctor swept on with his explanation. They would try many treatments – drugs, blood transfusions, more drugs. There would be corticosteroid drugs in massive doses, for example.

'I will tell you what that means,' he said. 'Steroids depress a patient's immune system – make him susceptible to infections of any sort. Georg may have to be isolated for a while. And the effects of the drugs can be a little drastic in some cases. You have to be prepared.'

Katherine spoke softly, almost in a whimper: 'Can you tell us how good his chances are? Or how bad?'

'I can't promise anything. I can say we have managed very long remissions with many children and in this business long remissions are already a kind of miracle. We may be doing better than we think – the remissions may be a cure. We don't understand the mechanisms yet.'

'You're very honest,' Pieter said.

'We don't have magic,' the doctor said. 'I tell some parents that we do, but that's for their sake.'

'You use radiation?' Katherine asked; she was especially fearful of radiation.

'To the minimum. And I presume Georg can stay today?'

'Can Nurse stay with him?' Katherine asked.

'No,' the doctor said. 'Outsiders can't help and our staff have a twenty-four hour job as it is.'

'Very well,' Katherine said. She was paler than Pieter had seen her for some time, and her features quivered a little in premonition of tears.

At the door of a sterile ward they kissed Georg goodbye. He toddled, very seriously, toward the bed and climbed into it fully dressed. Katherine thought it was terrible to see how familiar he was with hospitals, with tubes for taking blood in and out of bodies and bags of saline drip and needles for injections and all the rest. He took it for granted.

In the car, driving back to the hotel, Katherine said to Pieter: 'You look worried.'

'I'm worried about Georg.'

'And there's something else, isn't there?'

Pieter sighed. 'It doesn't matter.'

'Tell me. I come from a banking family. I do understand.'

'It's Rolfe. And the Palm Springs gentry. I did a deal for them – got a dud movie off their hands, gave them stock in a European company they could put on the books at anything they liked instead of a terrible movie they couldn't afford. It was a clever idea.'

'What's the problem?'

'I gave them stock in Helios SA. It's filing for bankruptcy tomorrow.'

'Does it matter? They must have known they were taking a chance.'

'You don't understand. It was my audition. If I got it right, they were going to pour money into Kellerman Unger – take us into London, New York, Eurodollars – everything.'

'But what have they ever done for you – so far?'

'They got Georg into that clinic. Henry Klein did that. They seemed like such good friends.'

Katherine sat up suddenly in her chair. 'Pieter,' she said, 'you mean you've disappointed those people in Palm Springs – and we just left Georg with them?'

'Don't be melodramatic,' Pieter said. 'I knew you wouldn't understand.'

'I do understand. I want Georg back . . . now. I know what those people are . . . 'oods.'

'They'll have started the treatment. They start right away. If we went back now, we'd just alert them to the fact that something is wrong.'

'But Georg . . .'

She could see him now sitting on his bed, among the tubes and needles, in his little city suit, a tiny figure swinging his thin legs from side to side, smiling.

* * *

Since Marisia got to know lawyers better, she got to like them less. She was being patronized at her own, considerable expense by a Florida tan in a Bill Blass suit, a middle-aged partner who longed to be suitable young. She had been allocated the main conference room – works on torts, a kind of maze of words in which to get lost – and she was taken as seriously as the fees allowed. But the tan wouldn't take her seriously, at all.

'You could always sell,' he said.

'I don't want to. And I don't want my shareholding diluted.'

'You can vote what shares you have. But if you're outvoted . . .'

'The question is simply whether I can block the issue of new shares.'

'Mr Cromwell,' said a fresh-faced associate, 'we can't advise on Dutch law, but there is one point.'

The Florida tan looked impatient.

'Netherlands Central Bank is quite tough on shareholdings – they like to know who owns what. Everything is written down. And the Bank would have to OK the deal, and the buyers would have to have K accounts in Holland for dealing in shares. So if you could persuade the Bank that the new owners aren't in Kellerman Unger's best interests . . .'

'As my associate said,' the tan beamed, 'we are not able to advise on Dutch law. Although if you really wish to pursue the matter . . .'

'I do,' Marisia said.

'I really think your personal reasons, whatever they are, shouldn't outweigh the considered opinion of the bank management.'

'The wonderful thing about being quite rich,' Marisia said, 'is that you are entitled to be arbitrary. Besides, the buyers have allowed certain threats to be made against me, and I don't want them to win.'

'Threats? Miss Van Helding, that is a most serious thing to say. You are quite sure you are not allowing your . . . dramatic instinct . . .'

'At your rates, I can't afford to waste time being dramatic. Elizabeth Taylor got less an hour on *Cleopatra*.'

'As you say, Miss Van Helding. You would know.'

'I want you to tell me what I can do.'

'You have as much power as you have shares. And I gather your brother can match you share for share in any case. What that leaves is very simple: if other shareholders come along with you, you win. If they go with him, he wins. I do not think they will hesitate.'

Marisia got up and rehearsed in her mind a pretty speech about his condescension to a mere woman, a mere actress at that. But she knew she was too angry for it to come out right.

'My wife and I are so much looking forward to seeing *The Music Makers*,' the tan said. 'We do hope to see you at the première.'

Marisia made a graceful smile, nodded acknowledgements, and stormed from the room, ignoring questions about where the bill should be sent.

Since it was not yet one o'clock in New York, there was a chance that there would still be people at Kellerman Unger in Amsterdam.

She thought, briskly. She would not allow Pieter to get away with his crude threats and his basic manipulation. He must not win. But she was cool enough to realize the lawyer was right: she needed an ally. And the only possible ally was Jan Unger – the only man with enough shares.

She called his office.

'So very pleasant to hear from you, so very unexpected.'

Marisia said: 'May we talk frankly?'

'My dear, of course.'

'I am very concerned about Pieter's plans for Kellerman

Unger. I would like to think we might both vote in the same way – against a massive expansion, against the new American capital.'

'Oh yes, yes, yes. I would very much like to think that, too.'

'Then I can count on you? Can I give you my proxies when the matter comes to a vote?'

'Ah,' Unger said. 'Please don't rely on me, not at all. It wouldn't be wise. You see, I think I know what I should do, but I don't think I can do it.'

He sounded tired, unlike the sharp, clerkly figure Marisia remembered.

'I do wish . . .'

The line went dead, one of the maddening cable faults that sometimes cut America off from the world, or the world from America, as you prefer.

'We shouldn't be in New York,' Katherine said. 'They won't let us see Georg at the clinic, we don't know how he is, we shouldn't be out of town. They sent me home from the clinic, Pieter. They sent me home.'

'Yes,' Pieter said. 'I do realize.'

'Maybe they won't even start treating him until Dr Rolfe is happy with you. And maybe . . .'

'You imagine too much.'

'We shouldn't be here, not just for a movie première. It isn't appropriate or right.'

'It's Marisia's film. It was made by Magnum, and it belongs to Helios – if Helios still exists in America in law, I'm not quite sure. We have to be here.'

'I keep thinking about little Georg.'

Pieter went to his window and looked down on Fifith Avenue for a moment. He thought how clever the Palm Springs gentry were, how they could raise the demons in any person's mind, the special, unanswerable demons with whom there is no negotiating.

And he went to dress.

For Marty Genovese had achieved a miracle. For three months he had sat before the Steenbeck editing table (he and the Europeans liked them) and produced a print for the studio to see, and they had panicked; it looked like an art movie. He excised a character, who had been expensive, and invented a whole musical number in the cutting. The studio gave him a new editor. Just when it seemed he might be barred from the lot, a sleepless, tousled cabal of friends assembled to argue and fight and make up Marty's mind before the studio did it for him. Then, to the studio's fury, out of chaos appeared a movie and the executives had to bite their tongues. Marty's miracle was simply that he wasn't fired.

By the time of the première, ownership of the film had passed to Pieter Van Helding's clients, Helios. But since Magnum would still release the film (and still pocket 30 per cent of the take from the theatres as their distribution fee, a point Van Helding had also made to Klein) it was Magnum who worked on making the film look less bad. In the event, they saddled Helios with the bills for a massive New York opening – tuxedos, red carpet, Radio City Music Hall, floodlights and arc lights and personal appearances. The stars made their way to the great marbled wasteland of the Music Hall by way of Sixth Avenue, gritted their teeth against the public indifference (New Yorkers can smell a bomb, and do not care to be seen with one even in the crowd shots on TV news), and waved to anyone prepared to cheer.

Inside, some of the better seats were empty. Not everyone with free tickets could be bothered to come. The producer thought this disloyal and ungrateful. The cast thought it was realistic.

Henry Klein was there, apparently on his own, neat and unsmiling.

Pieter Van Helding and Katherine were there,

Katherine big-bellied like a swan with her second child, Pieter now planning his announcement of Kellerman Unger's great step into the wider world.

And Marisia was acting like a star, a princess telling the doorstepping reporters how happy she was to be in New York, how wonderful it had been to work with Marty Genovese, how much she gloried in the glamour of the evening.

Magnum had conceived the idea of filming the première as a short feature which would precede *The Music Makèrs* round the country – a kind of oblique trailer for the movie. 'Like the bell they used to make lepers carry,' Marisia hissed to David Grant.

Pieter Van Helding had only one problem at the première: the all too obvious presence of Henry Klein.

'This doesn't seem the right time to talk business,' Van Helding said.

'Any time is good,' Klein said. 'We don't have much to say.'

'My wife is waiting for me,' Van Helding said. 'I don't think a theatre lobby is the place to discuss business matters.'

'Anywhere is good,' Klein said. 'You know Helios SA is bust? And we have thirty million dollars in Helios stocks on Magnum's books? And we are about to refinance the gentleman who landed us in that shit?'

Katherine edged forward, smiling to Henry, interrupting almost innocently. 'We should go in, Pieter.'

'I'll be a minute,' Pieter said. 'I'll join you inside.'

Pieter dived into the Art Deco splendours of the men's room, more shrine than lavatory with it's mother-of-pearl and white porcelain.

Klein followed. So did two other, large men. One checked the stalls carefully and, certain that there was nobody there, nodded to Klein. A neat man was washing his hands, and when he had finished drying them in the hot-air machine and left the room, the second large man sealed off the door. He warned anyone else away, saying the room was out of order.

'You wanted to piss,' Klein said. 'Go ahead.'

Van Helding thought the moment was like a parody of all those quick exchanges of gossip or deals after lunch.

'We're not afraid to embarrass people,' Klein said. 'That's one of our strengths.'

Van Helding zipped his fly and turned. 'Am I supposed to feel threatened?'

Klein smiled. 'Yes,' he said.

'Everything is under control,' Van Helding said.

'I want a little more detail than that,' Klein said. 'You've let us down. There's a great mess on the books of Magnum Studios, and you promised to clean them up for us.'

'It will be fine,' Van Helding said.

The muscle at the door stepped forward a little.

'Very well,' Van Helding said. 'I did some phone calls. You won't lose anything on the books, and the money you've spent on *Music Makers* you've lost anyway. Helios is paying tonight's bills.'

'The cheques won't bounce?'

'I don't know,' Van Helding said. 'I don't clear their cheques. Just listen to me. You have real estate deals going through Magnum. I know it. All we're going to do is shift the Helios stock to the Magnum real estate company. Then the stock goes out when you buy a property. There's a shopping mall in Georgia where they've agreed to take the Helios stock, plus the cash, and there's a site in Florida where they'll do the same. The point is, you can then write the property into the books at it's cost – which is cash plus the old value of the Helios stock. By the time you come to develop the sites, the profit will be so large a mere thirty million dollars can be lost. And the loss on *The Music Makers* turns magically into property assets in the South.'

Klein said: 'I don't suppose this deal could go wrong?'

The muscle at the door offered help. Klein refused.

'You're doing these deals anyway. It's simply a matter of writing up the price and getting the Helios stock off your hands. Don't think it's the first time a Hollywood company has done it.'

Klein walked up and down, flicking the door to each stall as he passed it. They could hear the music rising outside, the movie's overture. Van Helding held his breath. If Klein would simply say yes, then all his dreams were intact, there was no problem with the new finance; the world would open to Kellerman Unger. If Klein said no, then the muscle were ready.

'I like it,' Klein said. 'I like the legality of it. And I like the shape of it. We need the assets in Magnum and I'd rather have almost anything than celluloid.'

Van Helding went to wash his hands, looking back at Klein in the mirror. 'There'll be a finder's fee, of course,' he said.

Klein said: 'I suppose so. I am glad that we're still doing business. For a moment, I thought something might happen to you – and with Georg in the hospital . . .'

'I'd be a damned fool not to sort out your problems,' Van Helding said, 'when you're giving me the world.'

Pieter went out to join the party, a good half hour into the slack and lifeless movie on the screen.

Katherine asked Marisia: 'And when do you come on?'

Marisia said: 'Too soon.'

The curtains finally closed to anaemic applause, in which the effects of a scatter of flaks to start the house cheering were all too obviously staged.

On the streets outside, newly-washed by sudden rain, the red carpet leading to the New York Hilton had been soaked. Stars and consorts came from the Music Hall under the flood of light, and marched up Sixth Avenue to drinks. They went in tuxedos and gowns, forging their gossamer way to the inappropriate champagne.

'Smile,' Marisia said to her brother, who walked beside her. 'There will be photographers.'

There were soft explosions of flashlight and a handful of rubbernecking tourists, curious rather than impressed, staring at a different life. Pieter and Marisia presented themselves magnificently – unmarked by time or ambition, it seemed – while Katherine walked behind heavy and pale and David Grant was newly back from assignment and battered by time zones. The Van Heldings glittered on the avenue, turned to a *film noir* set by the sharp light and shadows, the cops ostentatiously protecting the procession, hands on guns.

Out there on the street, Marisia said to Pieter: 'Keep smiling – we have an audience.' And then she said: 'I'm not selling. I'm keeping my shares and I'm fighting you. I think we can beat you in the end.'

'Think of the future,' Pieter said.

'I'm thinking. I have an offer in Europe – after all, Magnum's gossip doesn't reach there.'

'Why can't you help me? You love me.'

'In my fashion,' Marisia said. 'And I'll tell you something else. You try to wreck things for me and I will put the story of your new backers over every front page in the nation.'

'Unemployed Actress Speaks Out: Rumours I Have Heard.'

'Don't be smug. The business pages love a pretty face. They get so few.'

'And if the face wasn't so perfect . . .'

'You're not Dr Rolfe and his friends. For God's sake stick to your class.'

'We ought to make polite conversation,' Pieter said.

'One last thing. For all the time you work in Kellerman Unger I want you never to feel secure. Never. If you get out of line, I will make a scandal.'

'Do we have to be enemies?'

'It's one link the law can't dissolve brother and sister. I'm sticking with you. I'm haunting you.'

'You're getting me hot.'

'Don't fool yourself. This time, I'm cold. Like steel.'

And at the door of the Hilton the paparazzi lights hit them like a physical barrier, dazzling. The morning pictures caught all the glitter in the fascinated, angry eyes of the Van Heldings.

'You make a handsome pair,' David Grant said to Marisia at breakfast. Like everyone else around the Van Heldings, he was trying to make a whole picture out of jigsaw-puzzle fragments, and he was mystified.

'Yes,' Marisia said. 'Yes, we do.'

She turned her attention to an unladylike plate of corned beef hash.

5

The shareholders' meeting was a formality, in the end. Jan Unger was there, thin and taut, and Pieter Van Helding. Marisia arrived a little early and was waiting when the board walked in. There were fifteen or twenty other people, some lawyers, some shareholders, scattered around the room on little gilt chairs.

'Ladies and gentlemen,' Jan Unger said. 'The issue is very simple today and I hope it will not occupy too much of your time. We have a proposal – you have all seen it – to expand the capital base of Kellerman Unger five times, to issue new shares to a consortium of American shareholders. You will also have seen the notes which explain why this is considered . . .'

Pieter Van Helding and Koolhoven both looked at him sharply.

'. . . why I consider,' Unger corrected himself, 'that this change will allow us an expansion which is . . . which is desirable.'

He looked desperately from side to side.

'Which I consider desirable.'

Marisia was furious, but she knew there was no profit in showing her feelings. She sat, and she waited. At the appointed time, Jan Unger and Pieter Van Helding cast their votes for the expansion; Marisia, alone of all the shareholders, abstained.

She talked to nobody as she left and in her hotel room she called David Grant.

'I lost,' she said. 'Let's get married.'

'That's a non sequitur. But the answer's yes.'

'I'll be back in LA tomorrow, if I can. I don't want to stay here any longer – it feels clammy.'

'But I have to go to Washington.'

'Then I'll come to Washington. Don't be difficult.'

'I'll be working in the Archives all day. We have some Freedom of Information Act requests in for the paper and for a book. I need to chase the material.'

'I don't mind,' Marisia said. 'I can always see people in New York during the day.' She paused, and wrung out of herself a confession: 'I just want to be with you.' She had needed to say it; she felt she would want to say it often.

'That's what I want,' David Grant said.

The queue had formed by half past eight at the National Archives – a broad polyestered man from New York with a doctorate to finish; two Mid-western ladies, there for the genealogy, they said; and David Grant. He loved the Archives, the sense of discovery, almost more than the melodrama and tedium of a reporter in the field. There was no need to tolerate the whims of information officers, drink through a skein of contacts to reach one dubiously useful source, hunt in a pack of fellow newsmen at the designated bar.

At a quarter to nine the big, black woman guard stopped missing the eyes of the queue, opened the gate, and there was a rush for the elevators.

Grant had material waiting in the Central Research Room but he planned to spend much of the day among the indexes. Unlike London, Washington has such things: paper slips in long, steel filing cabinets, cards and check lists and catalogues. Sometimes cat-eyed ladies, surrounded by begonias, guard the cabinets; sometimes they are locked behind hefty doors, in the charge of men with solemn faces. Subject only to the whim of the starchy officer from the FBI, they were mostly open and available. Racks and trolley-loads could go down to the

Reading Room. You could trawl for facts, take chances. Every rumour was written down. Some of them were accessible, and some of those were true.

He had been so grateful for Marisia's return that he had almost come to believe he was glad she had been defeated. She would no longer spend time worrying about Kellerman Unger; she had her own problems with her career. She was less inclined to talk obsessively about Pieter but she kept asking questions – how Pieter had squared Unger, what power he had – and she was beginning to think the power must lie in information. She hadn't asked David Grant to see what he could find out among the dusty FBI reports and intelligence files; he made that decision on his own.

His theory, amateur psychologizing perhaps, was that she would some day need to exorcize the old, grim shadow of her father's death. It was a memory everyone shared, a fact that allowed even the most casual acquaintance to tread cruelly on bruised sensibility. She lived with it, and she lived it, and it seemed to drive both her passion for the bank and the family and her need to keep her distance from Pieter. David Grant could see trouble in that broken-backed desire.

Indexes are conducive to philosophy. There's the need to be precise, but mechanically so; the steady flicking of cards or papers in drawers; the concentration that precludes excitement. He tried the Office of Naval Intelligence. Nothing on their cards in the name index, so far as he could see, but a reference to the island where Georg Van Helding had been killed. He went to Modern Military and shifted through some problematic files. In their research index, he found papers on Nazi money transmission. Interesting, if not perhaps quite relevant. He noted the numbers.

And then the State Department cabinets, stretching back and back in narrow lines under neon lights that you had to turn on one by one to light your way. Each cabinet had drawers with flimsy paper slips, and each slip had to do with a war, a rumour, a visa, a spy, a doubt. State-held FBI files, Intelligence files, anything to do with foreign nationals that had been thought important. David Grant began to search.

There were cards for Georg Van Helding – 'suspected subversive activities of', 'visa application by', 'murder of'. He'd try all those files, although he knew that the visa application would routinely be refused him.

He checked under Unger, Jan. At first he thought there was nothing, and it occurred to him that he might be looking in quite the wrong place. Anything anyone had on Jan Unger most likely came from the war years when he stayed in Holland and most likely was recorded in the long, meticulous attempt to bring Nazis and their friends to judgement.

But then he checked again. There was a card on Jan Unger – 'suspected subversive activities of'. And there was even a batch of papers on Kellerman Unger itself – letters from consulates, a full-blown report, assorted notes. He ordered everything.

He drank metallic coffee in the basement, waiting for his papers to be delivered up or formally refused. He was gratified at the potential size of his haul, but nervous, too. Whatever he found would mean trouble – for Unger or for others. Perhaps it would settle or ruin some myth of Georg Van Helding himself.

He dawdled over the *Washington Post*. When he got back to the Central Research Room, there was noise outside the window – the faint beat of demonstration drums, a column of men and women storming from Capitol to White House. For once, he didn't rise to look out; the reporter's instinct was subdued by a sense of terror.

For the files had arrived. Very well. They would be full

of gossip from FBI informants whose names and credibility were not recorded, and police spies, consular bores, senior men getting on paper exactly what they wanted to hear. It was like opening boxes of snakes.

He checked the lists first. Fifteen files had been refused, for the moment; they needed to be cleared, and he required a Freedom of Information Act request. He filled the forms.

And then, the other papers.

The Americans had kept careful eyes on Georg Van Helding and some of his associates, noticeably Jan Unger back in Europe, because they suspected some kind of money railroad running out of Europe and Nazi territory and the British Empire, and paying off in South and North America to the benefit of Nazi officials, Nazi policy and some lucky, neutral beneficiaries. Money that might have paid for the war effort was siphoned off to places where either it was outside the combat or else could be converted to Nazi uses. There was a brisk memo from Adolf Berle, Coordinator of Intelligence, explaining why a sudden sale of pounds in New York meant the Bank of England had to pay out dollars it badly needed to buy war material. And later there were messages and letters talking about a Nazi campaign to use currency looted from European banks for buying arms, and to deprive the British of hard cash.

The account was detailed and convincing, although Grant was experienced enough to know that reports saying the same thing could derive one from another, in a chain of half-truths. Gold was being moved out of old imperial possessions and into Mexico, for bright new investments in railways and oil, and into Argentina and into Brazil. Cash from bank vaults went by courier or U-boat to South America, often to Recife, and was either shipped north for presentation at American banks or converted into precious stones bought in West Africa. It was a machine for turning European uncertainty and fear into security and dollars.

And there was speculation in the papers. They suggested

Jan Unger had helped set up the money railroads, and his partner Georg Van Helding had been merely a client. Bits of the story were anchored to fact – British banks in Bermuda and the Bahamas taking currency to exchange for dollars, and finding it stamped with the names of banks in Nazi territory, for example – but there were no deposit slips, or cancelled cheques, or eyewitness accounts of U-boats surfacing to take off Van Helding's gold. And it wasn't quite clear where the terminus of this magical railroad lay; there were mentions of two banks in Mexico City, but no suggestion they had been used to store the Van Helding money. David Grant remembered that at the end of the war, the final settlement of the Van Helding estate had revealed missing moneys, unaccounted gaps; but whether the money had gone in secret speculation or to island tricksters or to distant banks, nobody could trace.

It was a dizzying prospect – another war, coming clearer document by document. A war of money and material, smuggling and gold and chance. Yet Grant also realized there had been twenty-five years to lose papers, and there must still be a powerful lobby that wanted silence. If half the names on file – from the American officer so high-ranking he protected Lavall's money all the way through the war and even Roosevelt could not dismiss him, to the English gentlemen who sent their money away to Mexico to provide for the days of Hitler's final victory – were authentic, then that lobby would be formidable opposition.

But he didn't want to reveal. He wanted to know. It was hard for a reporter to remember that.

He photocopied everything that he could, took the papers back to the hotel and filed them in his suitcase before Marisia returned. He didn't want her to know anything until he could tell her everything.

She arrived, tired from the plane, but warm and more

vulnerable and open than he had ever known her. She fell against him, shaped herself to his body and he to hers. The warmth and the sense of completeness soon began to turn to desire.

Afterwards David Grant fell to thinking. He wondered what was in those fifteen other documents that still needed to be checked and declassified. He wondered what they would do to Marisia, to him, to them.

They fell asleep in each other's arms.

'You are sure?' Koolhoven said. He was like *consigliere* to a gangster, lawyer to a lord; he felt no right to impose his views, but every duty to make gentle remonstrances. 'You realize how vulnerable you are?'

Pieter Van Helding shrugged.

'If anything goes wrong, you don't have a management contract or anything – and your shareholding is hopelessly diluted.'

'If anything goes wrong,' Pieter said, 'I wouldn't deserve to be paid off. I would find my own way out. I told you I'd bet the world against success, and I meant it.'

'I am only advising,' Koolhoven said. He lit his pipe, calmly. 'If I was allowed to be a real banking bore, I'd have to say that we know nothing of Rolfe and these people in banking terms.'

'No,' Pieter said. 'No, you're not allowed to be a real banking bore. It's all too exciting, and too immediate.'

'You'll forgive me asking exactly what we do next? After all, you are talking about a massive transformation of the bank. It has to start somewhere.'

'We start with a signal,' Pieter said, 'that we've come from nowhere – and now we're big in the Eurodollar market. Something to make sure people always come to us when they're syndicating a loan.'

'And what do you propose?'

'David Grant used to talk about Providencia. I know

they've been touting a big Eurodollar loan, and I know they haven't got it yet. We're going to do it.'

'And who is coming in with us?'

'Nobody,' Van Helding said.

'But that's far too dangerous for a single bank,' Koolhoven said. 'Don't you think we ought to syndicate the loan?'

'Absolutely not. I want to show that we have the power to swing this. And I want to start the chain – we can go to other people next time to share the loan, because they know they'll need us when they're planning. At the moment, that's something they don't know.'

Koolhoven sucked on his pipe. He wondered, very seriously, how far he would ever again be able to sway and influence Van Helding. The boy now had everything he wanted – funds unlimited for practical purposes and an alliance to outvote anyone else, based on the workings of Jan Unger's conscience. He felt he was talking into the wind, helplessly.

'We are lending on the security of . . . what?'

'If I'm right,' Van Helding said, 'we're lending on the security of Uncle Sam when it comes down to it. The US pays for the IMF, the IMF bales out the Third World and especially the parts the CIA is worried about.'

'You believe your own analysis?'

'I do,' Pieter said. 'And besides, we now have such vast funds available that we can do a deal like this without exposing ourselves too much. We can always sell bits of the loan later – if we want to. And for the time being, remember, we have all that money and it has to get out there fast. People have to know we're in the big time. And we have shareholders to keep happy.'

'Yes, indeed,' Koolhoven said. 'We do.' He looked at Pieter Van Helding and wondered how much longer the boy would allow even the illusion that he could be advised or controlled. He wondered at the wildness; you always syndicate a Third World loan so that nobody is out more than 5 or 10 million on a deal. He wondered at the appetite for attention.

He was losing Van Helding, he thought.

Marisia looked out through green plants to green plants outside, and through that green curtain to trees and boundary hedges, all dappled and kind. There was nothing but green, no life except for the Mexican gardener and the green.

'I hate fucking green,' she said.

It was good to have a retreat in the hills, good to live away from the valley smog and pressure, but only if Bel Air was an escape from another, hectic life in Hollywood. And there was no work at present, more through studio panics, she thought, than any machinations of Pieter, but she couldn't be sure.

And David Grant was away, again.

She would ring Pieter and announce that she was marrying David Grant. She'd saved up the announcement until she was entirely sure it was what she wanted, and until she needed something to shock Pieter back to paying her attention.

She felt uncertain how she should think of Pieter. She thought of finding an analyst, but she mistrusted the ego analysis of American hacks, and felt she did not have time to go deeper. She wanted someone to talk to, someone to resent, fight against, live with.

David Grant would be back. He'd suggested, as a terrible joke, they should be married in the Wee Kirk o' the Heather. It would, he said, remind him of his Scottish blood. And there could be recorded birdsong and all the Los Angeles defiance of the natural.

She wanted something simpler, more direct; a commitment. Both wanted it, in fact, but neither could make it happen. Dilatoriness seemed to be built into humankind.

Marisia Van Helding moped.

She looked at her watch. It would be dinner time in Amsterdam – pudding time for the pudding people. She would call. The telephone would be announced with as much solemnity as a guest; calls from America still impressed the servants.

'Marisia,' she bellowed. Her voice sank and swam in some wild electronic Sargasso.

'Christ,' Pieter said. 'Everything all right?'

'I'm getting married.'

'Yes? I can hardly hear you?'

'Married. To David Grant.'

'I see.'

'I thought I'd tell you. We'll come to Europe soon.'

She heard Pieter begin some answer, perhaps conventional congratulations, perhaps not. She felt cold after telling him; cold in her veins; she was trying to hurt him, saying she was leaving.

'Are you still there, Pieter? O damn these lines.'

The cars came to a halt in Cheapside, grandly. When Kellerman Unger made its move to London, it took a nineteenth-century palazzo with geraniums and occasional Gothic touches, and a great wide clock in the foyer mounted on a globe that had been butterflied like a leg of lamb. It was the right sort of bombast; it told people what Van Helding wanted.

The curiosity, as Koolhoven saw it, was how quickly he simmered down. After a few brief months of self-advertisement, Van Helding's operation was confined to thought, careful talk, and an unpretentious office in the pretentious building. He had let London know he was there – the massive loan to Providencia did that, although it also created trouble for the next time Providencia wanted money. He had begun to build a reputation as a stock-spotter, a market mover.

And now Van Helding was stepping out of his Mercedes on a pale, damp day in London, passing the commissionaires with the paid servility that only the best of them manage, and telling Koolhoven about a dream.

'Neon and tits,' he said, 'street after street of it. Half the windows aren't even clubs – they're ticket offices. Just imagine that lot torn down, and imagine how hard it would be for the worthy local councils to object. Just imagine a massive office development – close to Covent Garden when they rebuild that, close to the City, close to the West End. It's got everything.'

'Except,' Koolhoven said, 'you don't own the site.'

'Mr Joliffe almost does.'

'He does, doesn't he?'

Van Helding and Koolhoven took the stairs – a young, elegant prince with some sort of minder, you might have thought. And behind them, lowering and puffing, came Joliffe in the lift. His parents would not have been able to pronounce the name he now affected, but that hardly worried him. He was gauche and crass, and he talked like a gramophone record slightly distorted – Cockney with Baltic tangs. But he wasn't a supplicant any more, Mr Joliffe; he had almost arranged the biggest property deal in London in ten years – a new area, a vast site, a dream of towers and rents that would skyrocket up beyond even the market's present, 1970 madness.

He could take his time in the lift. They'd arrive out of breath, anyway. All these years he'd bought up shop by shop, site by site, paying off the Maltese with their strip clubs, talking to Bernie Silvers over one dirty bookshop, organizing, patching, scheming. One more little deal, and the property was his. He was king.

'Basically,' Van Helding said, which was a dangerous way for him to start a sentence, 'he's got everything but the last bit of the jigsaw, which is a block on Rector Street. If he gets that, he has the whole thing. If he doesn't get that, he can't build and he's bust. And he's been borrowing with zero return on all this stuff for years – he must be pretty tight for money. I think we can get him out.'

'I didn't know you meant to get him out.'

'Oh yes,' Van Helding said. 'I want this for myself.'

Koolhoven watched his lessons turned into practice. He'd always advised concern for details; Van Helding wanted everything in place. He'd always suggested assuming that people are vulnerable; Van Helding always did. But Koolhoven didn't like the special inspirations Van Helding added.

Joliffe, a little round man with a pale face that should have been rubicund, took a glass of gin and half thought of pinching the bottom of Van Helding's secretary.

'You do have agreements on Rector Street?' Van Helding asked.

'Not entirely final, not yet.'

'You realize London property is good,' Van Helding said, 'but a few streets of strip clubs aren't?'

'Other banks would take a chance. You'll see.'

'You can always go elsewhere . . .'

'But you've seen the scheme. You've seen the site. You know it's good.'

Koolhoven, good at hovering, pounced and let Joliffe from the office.

'Rector Street,' Van Helding said. 'Head leases belong to . . . Hope Estates. Tell me about them.'

'Quoted company, or were. Plantation business, mainly tea in Assam – family company with just enough outside shareholders to make it worth keeping a quote a long time. Then they became inactive. The only surviving owner on record is Mrs Elizabeth Rogerson.'

'Colonial widow?'

'Husband in the Indian army. It was her family's estates, originally. I don't know the story but maybe she inherited and tried to make a go of things and failed. Or maybe she bought out the others and opted for a quiet life. She lives off the west coast of Scotland – one of those islands where the Germans go to shoot.'

'Have you talked to anyone in London?'

'There's a broker, who says she needs the money. And an Edinburgh lawyer – very pompous, very idle. The broker says she's crazy.'

'Odd? Or drink?'

'Drink. And lithium and incipient schizophrenia.'

'And a price?'

'I got the rent-roll figures,' Koolhoven said. 'At arm's length, of course. We don't want people to get excited yet. I think we could offer twenty years' purchase of rents at the next rent review, and they'd be delighted.'

'I guess they couldn't tell the old lady what she owns in any case.'

'I'm not sure she'd care. After all, before they changed the law the girls used to line Rector Street – the best legs in town, even on a wet night.'

'And Joliffe? I assume he's been playing with that site so long nobody believes he'll ever put it together.'

'He's never done anything this big,' Koolhoven said. 'It's a clever idea, of course.'

'I like it very much.'

'I worry if Mrs Rogerson will part with the shares – because they represent property. Property sounds good to a woman like that when money doesn't.'

'You know a lot of colonial widows?'

Koolhoven grinned.

In the car going north through cold shallow London streets, Van Helding had a rush of adrenalin, a sense of winning; one city was no longer enough to contain him but he would change this one – shift its focus and take a profit.

The Van Helding house was in transit between the hotel magnate who built it (1950s colonial, wide driveway, white columns, good, red brick that was wrong for London) and its later, logical owner, a sheik. It had great trees, two Francis Bacons in the drawing room that did nothing for atmosphere, and a decent staff. It was a house that made statements about corporate power, rather than a home.

Katherine Van Helding wore long, sensuous silk. She'd already had a drink, Pieter noticed. His mind was far away, dreaming of bull markets in the early 1970s and property fortunes and the risky world he was invading. He had a sense that people wanted financial adventure, that changing things would be hot; for the moment, people had almost forgotten that adventures come back, called frauds.

'How was your day?' Katherine asked. 'I talked about shrubs with the gardener and talked with the nurse about the children and I joined a committee at the Institut Français. To hold a party for Jacques Lacan.'

'I did business,' Pieter said. 'Do you want me to change for dinner?'

'Don't bother.' Katherine rang for drinks. 'I feel so far from London in Hampstead, I think I might as well be on a farm. Marie Antoinette milking cows.'

'She didn't milk cows,' Pieter said. 'She only dressed as if she might.'

'Georg is learning to shoot a bow and arrow,' Katherine said.

'I have to go to Scotland for a day or so. To get an old lady to sell me a company.'

'I might go to Paris. To spend some money.'

'That's a good idea.'

'You don't mind? I might have a lover in Paris.'

'I don't mind,' Pieter said.

The little plane bumped to a halt on the sheep field. 'Lucky,' the pilot said. 'Usually old MacNab likes to drive a few sheep onto the runway, just to see us sweat.' Van Helding, relaxing as he stepped from the plane, allowed himself to grin.

It was a wonderful day. The rain had washed the air, the sky was a dream of blue, the water was quicksilver spread with peat-dark islands. Iron-grey hills were stippled with conifers. The bracken was beginning to die down in a smouldering brush fire of purples and browns, and when the plane engines shut off, the place seemed clear and undisturbed.

The island taxi came hurtling towards the landing strip, swerving to avoid the implacable island bus which went bucketing and screaming along the one-track road.

'It sounds like mortal combat,' Van Helding said.

'You want to watch what you say on the islands,' the pilot said. 'It's the water and the peat – every sound carries.'

'You know this island?'

'My father was born here. He was in Zaire when I was born, but when the family shop needed him, he came back.'

'Will you come back?'

'I never went away.'

The taxi – a polished, veteran Rover – settled at the gate of the field, and Van Helding boarded. He asked for Scourie, but the driver had already started before he mentioned his destination. He assumed everyone knew.

The land rested on water, peat barely covering old stained depths, the surface blank as a watercolour wash before the detail appears. The taxi climbed a narrow, twisting road between old trees, and then came out into a wide glen. Nothing seemed to move. There were cottages, ruined and with their roofs stripped away. There were trees, the anonymous government forests of sitka spruce and Japanese larch, black and green on the hillsides. At the foot of the glen, the road turned, crossed the peat-dark waters of the sea loch, went past a church and down an unpaved drive.

'Bellart,' said the driver, helpfully.

Stone lions guarded the walk to the house, which was like an overgrown suburban home.

Van Helding picked his way to the door, through genteel disrepair. The dark-green leaves and brambles had been cut back no more than necessary.

'You'll want to mind the vipers,' the driver said, helpfully.

A dog began yammering at the back of the house. The taxi crashed its gears and went on its way, and Van Helding was left enveloped in the soft silence of the place.

In a few minutes, the main door opened.

Van Helding had expected some old, gin-cracked lady, face stained with eighty years. Instead, he saw a tall, slim woman, almost willowy, with long, dancer's legs.

'You must be Mr Van Helding,' the woman said. 'Do come in.'

He was stunned by her, immediately and crushingly stunned. It was in the way she moved, with grace, and in the way she spoke, softly. It was a kind of magic.

She showed him into a drawing room which had been largely unchanged for fifty years. A working fireplace belched a little fragrant smoke, a portrait from the 1920s hung over the mantelshelf, a rack of books stood on one side, mainly Trollope in fine bindings. The place was like an island. In side rooms, Van Helding could see packing cases, suitcases. This room was the one left habitable, with a lit fire for the guest.

'Mummy is leaving Bellart,' the woman said. 'She needs to be somewhere they can look after her properly. I tell you because I don't want you to get the wrong idea. I don't think you ought to do business with Mummy just now. Not until she is better.'

'Forgive me,' said Van Helding. He had reverted to a hand-twisting courtesy. 'I don't know who you are.'

'I'm Sally Rogerson,' the woman said. 'The daughter. Of a late marriage, in case you were wondering – Mummy was forty-two. I'm a dancer.'

'I see.' Van Helding meant it; he could see her grace. But he wondered why people started saying that things were none of his business, and moments later gave him information he had not even asked for.

'You must want whatever Mummy's got pretty badly,' Sally said. 'To come all this way on an old lady's whim.'

'I couldn't expect her to come to London.'

'I suppose the lawyers said Mummy would sell?'

'I'm making an offer as good as anyone is likely to make,' Van Helding said.

'I'm sure,' Sally said. 'I can't tell when people like you are making sense, because it all seems like nonsense to me.'

There was a sound on the floor above of a person lumbering across a room, and what might have been the tip-tap of a cane.

'Your mother,' Van Helding said. 'Where are they taking her?'

'She's not being taken,' Sally said. She answered with too much sharpness and Van Helding knew it. 'She's going of her own free will. And if it was up to me there'd be no sale at all. If it's worth all this trouble to you, it must be worth more than you're offering.'

'I don't think you are on my side.'

Sally offered drink; Van Helding asked for a whisky; Sally said foreigners usually called it Scotch.

'I know,' Van Helding said. 'You're lovely.'

'Thank you,' Sally Rogerson said. 'But you wouldn't want anything to distract from your business, would you?'

'My business is with your mother,' Van Helding said. 'Has she lived here alone for long?'

'There's a maid. A treasure – a sort of Scots halfwit. And a man who does the garden. You can hardly get vegetables in the islands, you know, unless you grow them yourself.'

'Who does she see all year?'

'Ghosts, mainly,' Sally said. 'The minister. Meals on Wheels stopped coming because they said she was drunk and abusive.'

'Is that her reputation?'

'She's difficult,' Sally said. 'But nobody really talks about drink around here. They all drink and they don't want to accuse each other.'

'Can I see her now?'

'She's coming,' Sally said, 'in her own good time.'

There was movement above, and then a sound like rats moving in a stairwell and a little cry. Van Helding looked across at Sally and her eyes – dark, wide, alarmed.

'She's a disturbed woman,' Sally said. 'Remember that.'

Mrs Rogerson entered as though she had always known about entrances – a woman still tall and erect, still full of character although the lovely life recorded in pastel shades above the mantelshelf had been rasped away by age. Her eyes were a little wild, perhaps her dress a little less neat than it might have been, but she seemed rational. Van Helding was sure he could swear she was rational.

Sally said: 'Mr Van Helding is here, Mummy.'

'Bankers never call,' Mrs Rogerson said. 'One has them to dinner occasionally.'

'It's very kind of you to see me.'

'I don't have money any more,' Mrs Rogerson said. 'All gone on drink and doctors. Ask my daughter.'

'I'm going for a walk,' Sally said. 'Be good.'

She pulled on Wellington boots and strode down the pathway to the open, peaty moor.

'Good,' said Mrs Rogerson with contempt. 'What chance have I had to be anything else for the past thirty years?'

She settled in an armchair. She still had some of the physical elegance of her daughter, the high-stepping style. Van Helding tried to imagine her on a tea plantation and he failed.

'Please give me a drink,' Mrs Rogerson said. 'Not sherry – although that's what bankers drink, isn't it? Terrible drink. Gives me a headache and at my age you tend to think the mind's been rubbed out when you have a hangover. I can't risk anything any more.'

Van Helding, through the windows, could see Sally striding off by the loch turning to walk up the glen.

'She's pretty,' Mrs Rogerson said. 'But she's not so clever in business. I let her think I am sillier than I really am.'

Van Helding summoned his formality. 'I've come to put a proposition to you, Mrs Rogerson. I realize it would be ill-mannered to rush matters in any other circumstances, but we don't have much time.'

'You sound like a banker,' she said. 'But you don't look like a banker. You look like a man I used to fuck with.'

She looked proudly at Van Helding waiting for him to show shock.

'You don't look alarmed?'

'Why should I?'

'Because you've come to do business and you find a madwoman full of drink.'

'You sound eminently reasonable.'

'Ah, but I'm not,' she said. 'I really am full of lithium. I shouldn't be drinking. Sometimes, I really am mad. It's got to that point.'

'The business is simple. I'm offering cash for your shares in Hope Estates. I think the price is generous, but you can ask your own lawyers and accountants. At present you can't sell shares, you can't raise the income from the properties very much, and large parts of your resources are tangled up in a dead company. I'm offering a way out of that, and cash, and, if you want it, some help with reinvesting your money profitably.'

'I keep reading your name in the papers,' Mrs Rogerson said. 'You and that man Slater. Coming men in the City. If you smile at a share, it goes through the roof. Am I right?'

'I suppose I am beginning to have some influence.'

'You're supposed to be clever. Are you a Jew?'

'No.'

'Pity. I don't think people make bankers unless they're Scots or Jews. All those stories about meanness are just jealousy at their cleverness. Why do you want Hope Estates?'

'Because I can do something with the Rector Street properties. You can't do it, but I can.'

'I can't do anything,' Mrs Rogerson said. 'Tomorrow they're going to take me away and close up the house. It's supposed to be a very nice home in Argyll. It has bars on the windows.'

'I'm offering you cash,' Van Helding said.

'Notes, Mr Van Helding?'

'A sight draft. Your own banker here could confirm that he will honour it.'

'Old Grieves? He's too busy staring out of his window trying to tell if the people are happy or not. And he'll be at his Gaelic verses for the Mod now, with a bottle.'

'You do talk to your banker, then?'

'I always talk to Grieves. He says if the people look happy, business is good – he can tell exactly how good by the look on their faces. He's the man who's kept me sane all these years, sane as I am.'

Van Helding brought up his briefcase.

'I think you understand the situation,' he said.

'I don't have a lot of choices. At my time of life, and in my condition, doctors make up your mind about everything.'

'If you had cash, you would be free, Mrs Rogerson. You could go where you want to go.'

'That's direct,' Mrs Rogerson said. 'Give me some more whisky. And don't look disapproving. Of course I drink. I'm lonely and I'm daft. And I want you to see what they have done to me.'

Mrs Rogerson rose and Van Helding followed her. High on the side of the glen now he could see Sally treading the moorland, bruising the grasses and heathers, leaving her neat, perfect tracks.

'They made me sell my good silver. Not safe here, they said. Apparently I made a present of the money to dear Sally, or so my lawyers said. Funny I can't remember that.'

The dining room was full of crates and boxes. Walls that were tarnished with years, and carpets full of the smell of long-lost dogs were the last signs of a life lived there. The rest was nailed away.

'I wanted to stay here. They're very tolerant of me, here. And where else would I go? I don't want to have to hide a bottle in the bedpan in some place on the South Coast.'

'You could travel,' Van Helding said. 'Like you used to do. Go to the South of France, go to the Carribean, go to London for the season.'

'There still is a season?' she said. She was reading the labels on crates: 'in care of The Cedars', they said. 'Is it the way it used to be with the balls and the dinners and the dances?'

'Of course.'

Mrs Rogerson had moments of alarming sharpness. 'But they wouldn't want me, would they? Not an old woman who might do anything. I'd drink too much. Nobody would come to take me home.'

'You'd be free to try,' Van Helding said. 'Otherwise, it's nurses in Argyll and a timetable and ping-pong and old people all around you. And shots to keep you quiet and a long, long wait.'

'That frightens me.' She put down her glass. 'I don't whimper. I try to deal with life as best I can.'

'You can deal with it for yourself.'

'Give me the papers,' Mrs Rogerson said. 'Do we need a witness?'

'The minister, perhaps, or the bank manager, if he can come.'

'Call them. Just ask the operator – she'll know.'

Grieves at the bank was leaving for lunch and promised to call on his way. The minister misunderstood the call and thought the strange man must be a doctor summoning him for an emergency at Scourie. Both cars arrived at the same time, both recognized Van Helding's name ('We may be a long way from London, young man,' the minister said, 'but we still keep in touch'), and both primped for the famous London banker. They were only too happy to watch Mrs Rogerson sign and to take a glass of sherry.

Sally Rogerson, high on the hills, saw the cars turn into the driveway. She turned back for home, feeling the wet, springy ground tug at her feet, feeling too slow. She bounded across the last yards of peat and as she came down the path between the stone lions, she was shouting: 'Mother, Mother. I'm not too late, am I?'

Mrs Rogerson, at the door, said sweetly: 'Fuck you, Sally.'

Sally glared at Van Helding, and said: 'I think we'd better talk for a minute.' Van Helding shrugged. 'I suppose you know what you've done? Now she's got money, she won't go into the home. She'll die here – from the drink – not next year but maybe next month. Drink's already got half her mind, even you must be able to see that. She'll die an old, drunk madwoman and you don't give a damn, do you?'

'Psychiatry isn't my business.'

'Really? Then I wonder just how you got Mother to sell so quickly. Did you tell her she wouldn't have to go to the home?'

'We talked business.'

'I'll see my lawyers tomorrow. The deal won't stand up, you know.'

'You're wrong about that,' Van Helding said. 'The price is very reasonable, and it's agreed with the London brokers. Selling now helps your mother's tax position, and it will help yours, eventually. Everybody does well.'

'She's not fit to make decisions.'

'Really? She seemed very rational to me. And she made a very rational choice.'

Van Helding could see Mrs Rogerson coming, stocking-shod, to stand in the doorway, rigid with anger.

'She needs care and protection,' Sally said. 'She needs nursing. If she stays here with some halfwit maid . . .'

'You're not the one to nurse her?'

'I have my own life. I can't be with her every day, day in, day out, for the rest of her life. It's hard enough to take a single day of it.'

'Did you ever ask her what she wanted?'

'No,' said Mrs Rogerson from the doorway, in a terrible, calm voice. 'She never asked. She just assumed – along with that fool doctor.'

'I did ask you, Mother.'

'I don't mind being old. But I will not be labelled old, packed away and set aside as old. I don't mind that I'm not as bright or as fast as I used to be, but I won't be put away for it. I will go where I want to go.'

'You could go to the home. You'd be comfortable.'

'Could I ever get out? Of my own free will, I mean, when and where I wanted?' She faced Sally down, her whisky breath harsh and stale, her eyes bright. 'Or will they keep me quiet with their drugs and let me go into town if my family deigns to pick me up and see me?'

'Just be quiet, Mother,' Sally said. 'You'll upset yourself.'

Van Helding walked away, said his polite goodbyes into the furious silence boiling between mother and daughter, and took the waiting taxi up the glen to the distant seashore airstrip. He asked about lunch at the inn.

He looked back once to Scourie. He could see the front lawn, rough and unweeded, and the open front door, and the tall, elegant figure of Mrs Rogerson, dancing to herself on the grass, trying to coordinate a body that would not always quite obey her any more. She looked like a great stork prancing in a wild field, vulnerable and grim.

Lunch was not good. There was dry salmon, perhaps frozen, and tinned vegetables and a dubious bottle of hock. Knowing the way the island's telephone operators functioned as bush telegraph, he chose not to make the phone calls that mattered. He did call Katherine to say he would be delayed.

At the airstrip there was a little car waiting. Out of it stepped Sally, marching on Van Helding like an avenging army.

'I want that agreement to sell,' she said. 'Now. If you don't produce it, I'll raise such a stink in London . . .'

'Talk to your mother's lawyers,' Van Helding said.

'You wait,' Sally said. 'I can see the headlines – Banker Robs Widow.'

'Sounds good,' Van Helding said. 'Better than an ungrateful daughter putting her mother in a home to keep control of the money.'

'That's so far off course I won't even get angry.'

'Is it really? If it's wrong, why do you care so much that your mother should have no more choices, so that she has to go where you tell her to?'

'I care about her.'

'I expect you do.'

'I have to make some phone calls from the mainland.'

'Yes, I'll give you a lift. I'm leaving immediately. How will you get back?'

'There's no point in my coming back tonight. I need to give mother some time to think things out.'

'Or time to get frightened?'

Sally did not reply.

'I expect you have your case with you?'

'I was packed for tomorrow.'

The plane rose softly over silver waters and bracken-brown hills, turned briefly north to the high mountains of the other islands and then back to the mainland and its dark, deep glens.

Sally Rogerson said: 'I really didn't mean to do this.'

The first thing Marisia noticed about Alexander Fairbairn was that he looked more like a Hollywood agent than any of the agents present – and while they were draped in seemly, uniform black, he had cowboy boots and a look of both California taste and Eastern tailors. He was bluff, awkward-handed, maybe in his sixties, and she knew his name. He had created Security National, after all, and it was the thirteenth largest bank in America.

'You're a Van Helding?' he said, abruptly.

'Marisia Van Helding.'

'You can tell your husband from me . . .'

'He's not my husband. He's my brother.'

Fairbairn was briefly nonplussed, but he had a proper head of steam and he was not going to be deflected by mere facts.

'Your brother. You can tell him I don't appreciate the way he's done business.'

Marisia smiled a little wanly. 'Funny how I hear that everywhere,' she said.

'Really,' Fairbairn said. He steered her away from the

crowds to a more peaceful sitting room. It was a Hollywood A-list party, full of money and tact, where men and women rarely talk to each other and conversations are assigned by status, like a duchess's dance card at a ball. Marisia was feeling too grim to cope, and Fairbairn – the New York banker – was drowning under Californian formality.

'Do women talk to men out here?' Fairbairn said.

'I do,' Marisia said.

'I've just never seen it happen,' Fairbairn said. 'I mean, I see agents talking to agents, and I see executives talking to executives, but what do they do when they get horny?'

'Call Central Casting,' Marisia said. 'This is a dumb broad's town.'

'Then what,' said Fairbairn, with hefty gallantry, 'are you doing here?'

'I'm an actress,' Marisia said. 'Not at the moment a working actress.'

'I'm a banker,' Fairbairn said. 'Security National.'

Marisia looked at his huge, leonine head. He had been designed to be photographed, flatteringly, for an annual report – a figure of authority. She didn't fancy him; she doubted if he fancied her, except in the most general way. It was simply that neither of them fitted the rigid etiquette of Hollywood power.

'I'm surprised you don't have to talk to seventeen people tonight,' Marisia said. 'Bankers are always popular.'

'You don't sound very happy with this town.'

'Is it that obvious? I'm sorry.'

'Trouble at work?'

'Trouble with not having work,' Marisia said. 'Another side of my dear brother and his ways of doing business.'

'I don't understand.'

'My lawyers told me never to explain.'

Fairbairn chuckled. 'You're still fighting.'

'What business did you ever have with Pieter? You sounded as though you wanted me to give him a proper dressing-down the next time I see him.'

'Little bastard did a deal,' Fairbairn said, 'for a client. Sold him a studio for a data-processing business. Trouble was, it was my client in the first place and Van Helding cooked the studio's books. Client wanted the deal, so I couldn't stop him – he was hot to come out here and leave his fat wife and have a good time with his declining money. Client did the deal. Client is furious at me for having let him buy a dud property. I told him he was dealing with the good Dr Rolfe, which is never good news. I told him a studio was a lousy trade for his business, even if he did get stock. I told him, and now he blames me.'

'That sounds like Pieter.'

'And you – what made you so sad?'

Marisia stood up, draped herself against a convenient pillar of dubious design, and struck a tragic pose. 'Life,' she said.

Fairbairn applauded. In the low light of the little room, looking out onto the valley of Los Angeles below, with the water of the swimming pool glinting in the way, they could have been very far from the party and the conventions. But still Marisia was not inclined to confess anything. Her troubles were her own, and she would resolve them; indeed, she knew herself well enough to realize that she had already begun the long, slow scrabble out of depression. She went down, allowed herself to sink, allowed herself to retreat to bed at night and curl up and tense every muscle and cry and scream, and then she knew there would be a change in the cycle, a recovery. She lived with such things.

But she thought of confessing. Fairbairn wasn't kind, not a good man like Koolhoven, but he exuded sense. He was his own man, entirely. If confession had some practical end, she would have told him anything.

'Actually,' Marisia said, 'I used to have a fifth of Kellerman Unger. Until the good doctor intervened.'

'And now?'

Marisia shrugged. 'They put in so much money and took out so much stock, they hardly have to send me an annual report. What's worse, I can't sell the damn stock, and I can't take a dividend because they're not giving. A nice little trap.'

'I take it Pieter Van Helding wanted you to sell.'

'Yes.' Marisia had no intention of explaining that situation.

'We must think of something,' Fairbairn said.

'The last time a banker was nice to me,' Marisia said, 'he turned out to work for Dr Rolfe.'

'Wait till I make an offer before you turn me down.'

Marisia smiled. She said: 'I'm really not picking you up, but if you'd like a drink – I think I've had enough of this party.'

'We could go down the street. There's a pretty basic bar just outside the Beverley Hills limits, if you feel like slumming.'

'Yes,' Marisia said. Fairbairn escorted her through the disapproving women and the scarcely noticing men, and they called for cars and drove in procession down the hill.

'They alarm me,' Fairbairn said, when they had settled in a booth with drinks.

'Me, too,' Marisia said. 'It's the sense that they've got everything basic wrong. They don't make love any more – they don't sleep with their wives, naturally, and they don't love their mistresses, and if they want sex, they make proposals that would make your hair stand on end. There's one credit-card chief who only likes to saddle up his girls and ride them. They say he drools.'

'Everybody has his taste,' Fairbairn said.

'We were probably the only two human beings there,' Marisia said. 'All the rest were like studio chiefs at a screening – they just watch the world and they want it recut. They don't touch; they watch.'

'You're having a bad time here.'

'I'm having a bad time, just for the moment,' Marisia said. 'My husband's away. I'm not working. And you can feel dreadfully isolated in Beverley Hills.'

'You looked – very lovely tonight,' Fairbairn said. 'A real star.'

'Stars are props on these occasions,' Marisia said. 'We're missed if we're not there.'

Fairbairn looked at her very hard. She was lovely, but around the eyes she seemed tense and tired. He didn't want to know what troubled her, but he wanted to ease the troubles.

'I have an idea,' he said. 'Do you want to sell your Kellerman Unger stock? I'd like a stake in that business. And more than that, I'd like to feel I was Pieter Van Helding's boss. If he can rip me off, he can rip off others, and I'd like a share.'

'You sound like a banker in a cartoon.'

'I'm a realist,' Fairbairn said. 'What do you say?'

'You're only doing it to be kind.'

'I don't think so. It makes sense for my operation. It makes sense for me. I like to make trouble.'

'You don't know anything about the bank – or what I have, or anything.'

'I don't plan to write a cheque tonight, either. Our lawyers can talk the details over.'

'Thank you,' Marisia said. 'Thank you very much. I'd like to think about it, but it's very kind. If I was rid of Kellerman Unger . . .'

At home that night she took Dalmane to sleep and in the early hours she woke up suddenly with a vivid memory of a dream: she was on a beach, a white, bright beach, and she was a child. Pieter was there, playing, scheming, making a blood sacrifice, talking quietly. Willem was there, as well. But instead of Willem dying, instead of Pieter triumphing, a broad man in a felt hat came onto the beach and stopped all the games and scooped her up and comforted her and made her know she didn't always have to fight. She called him Father.

The next morning, through the vagueness from the sleeping pills, she was humming. There were things she still had to face down, but she was beginning to know what they were and how they operated. She was beginning to be happy again.

The rooms in the big Glasgow hotel smelled of lint and vacancy. There was dark nylon carpet, tired with age, and a tray of sachets of powdered milk and powdered coffee; everything to drive a travelling salesman to drink. The rooms were simply too big and too vague: a wasteland.

Sally Rogerson slid out of her dress and slip, pulled down her pants and came to bed in stockings.

'I thought you'd like that,' she said.

Pieter Van Helding lay on the bed, hard and passive, letting her take what advantage she wanted. There was a sudden erotic trust between them which electrified them – a playfulness, a readiness.

She swarmed towards him, bent and took his cock in her mouth, gently, with a touch like silk or spiders. He stiffened like iron and she sucked with long, close strokes. He hardly moved, concentrating all his senses, breathless. She began to move again, her body slowly reaching up to him, first allowing his cock to run against her neck, then between her small, firm breasts, then against her belly. Both of them now made no sound, anticipating. She drew herself up and lowered her moist, warm sex onto his, and settled, shifting from side to side luxuriously until he was in her and impaled. And then the waiting was over for both of them, and he began to move with deep, involuntary thrusts, body off the bed, and she moved with him, and the lock of their sudden passion was absolute, bodies melting into one another. They rode each other as partners, and as she began to feel the first violent contractions close to her heart, he was pulsing and pouring himself into her.

Her time seemed to last for ever, a cluster of quakes and spasms, until finally she released him and they slipped gently apart. They growled like fed tigers. A net of fine, wet hair seemed to cover and hold them.

'Anything,' she said, almost anxiously.

The drab afternoon and the Glasgow streets outside made their bed like an island. When everything was finished, Sally Rogerson and Pieter Van Helding looked at each other with something like suspicion.

'This isn't meant to happen,' Sally said.

She dressed quickly, threw spare clothes into a bag and said: 'I'm getting the early train to Oban. I'm not staying the night.'

'I didn't ask you to stay.'

'I'm glad. I left my London telephone number – on the newspaper. You have to decide if you want to keep it.'

'I don't throw numbers away.'

'Maybe,' Sally said. 'If you want, call.'

Van Helding stood up from the bed, still naked and tousled; with great mock solemnity, he shook her hand.

'I'm a busy man,' he said. 'I want to talk to you.'

'Bankers and dancers are an old tradition.'

'I guess.'

And she went quickly down the hall, into the maze of grubby doors and drab carpet crisscrossing in long corridors.

Van Helding lay and rubbed his belly. She was not like anyone else; that was obvious. She was enemy. Friend. Lover. Partner. And she was different.

He felt a wonderful contentment.

* * *

'You can talk to me,' Koolhoven said. He was calm and determined; and he was furious. Van Helding had left him to handle Joliffe – who was scarlet now, a veined redness which threatened imminent cardiac arrest.

'Principals is all I talk to,' Joliffe was saying.

'You can talk to me,' Koolhoven said.

'I know what your Van Helding is doing.'

'And what is that?'

Koolhoven needed time to calculate the scenario; nobody had planned for Joliffe to arrive on the doorstep.

'Hope Estates,' Joliffe said. 'Don't you try to shmeikel me. I know about it all.'

'I was not aware . . .'

'Not bloody aware! Very likely. Six years I work to bring this site together, I offer you a cut, what do you do – you go out and you buy the one missing piece. What do I pay you now? My life? My blood?'

'Could you pay?' Koolhoven asked quietly.

Joliffe seemed like a frog on the point of bursting.

'Because,' said Koolhoven with great patience, 'it seemed to me that we agreed to consider financial arrangements if you could assemble the whole Rector Street site. And now you're telling me the most important part is missing. You've blown your collateral.'

'I can develop without you.'

'Perhaps,' Koolhoven said, 'but not without the land in Hope Estates. Of course, you could always sell to us . . .'

'Six years,' Joliffe said. 'Six years of blood.'

'I gather the clearing banks are pressing you rather hard, and you need the money. And you seem to think we can block your development because we are buying Rector Street. If you're right, then it seems to me you're in trouble.'

'I don't listen to this. I don't listen.'

'Of course we could always pay you a decent market

price for the other property. Then we could simply make the development ourselves.'

'Bloodsucker!' Joliffe howled. 'I got the idea, I got the buildings, I talked with the slumlords and the gangsters and all the boys with the tit shows and I got the goddamn leases, the goddamn drawings, the goddamn plans. Everything I got – except Rector Street, the last block. And now you won't even give me the truth – whether you have the block or not.'

'Your idea was very interesting,' Koolhoven said. 'But it seems to me no more than an idea. You don't have the site. You don't have the money. You're in trouble.'

'You foreign bastards,' Joliffe shrieked. 'You come over here and you snatch, snatch, snatch.'

'Nothing is served by anger,' Koolhoven said. 'We deal in business here. If you want to save your companies, we can help. You just sell the rest of the site to us and the price should clear your financial troubles comfortably.'

'Duress. I won't deal under duress.'

'Logic, Mr Joliffe.'

'Someone will top your bid. You'll see. You won't build.'

'Good day, Mr Joliffe.'

'You may be big news in the City but there are people who are bigger news.'

'Good day, Mr Joliffe. And please don't hesitate to call when you feel better. We're a very forgiving firm.'

Joliffe left, and Koolhoven went to wash his hands. He did it three times before he realized what he was doing.

David Grant returned to find Marisia still anxious and wan, spending too much time in the dull, green prison of the house. He hadn't calculated what to do when all the vitality drained away from her, however briefly, and she became dependent. He wanted to rely on her strength and glamour. Just for a while, that was not going to be possible.

Marisia agonized over selling or not selling her Kellerman Unger stock. It had become a kind of endlessly repeated refrain, no more conclusive the ninetieth time. If she sold to Fairbairn she would never have to worry again. But if she sold to Fairbairn, she would be doing what Pieter wanted, doing it under duress, and cutting herself off from what had been her patrimony too.

What David Grant couldn't get her to face was another possibility: that she needed to divorce herself from the dream of a father never known, and that she had to face the reality of her father's last years. He had schemed, tricked, possibly betrayed in order to make a fortune survive – not people, but money. Marisia took an interest in the Archive papers, but she said they were gossip, old hat, the kind of thing that people on the island said. She had nothing to do with all that.

But she did, and Pieter did, and they all did. They might never ask who killed Georg Van Helding, or why, or what the old man was doing that made him seem to everyone so eminently reasonable a target for murder; but the unresolved question was always close to them and sometimes insistent – like a night bird, circling.

'Talk to me,' David said. 'Just talk to me.'

'Stop being kind,' Marisia said. 'It won't help.'

'You know what I think? If you sold that stock, you'd still be tied to bank and family and history and Pieter. You know that. The only reason you even think of selling is because you want to do Pieter a favour – but not until you have to. Otherwise, it wouldn't even occur to you.'

Marisia said: 'I'm going out.'

'You don't have to go out,' David said. 'I really want to talk.'

'I can't talk,' Marisia said.

She pulled on a coat and took the small Porsche and roared down the twisting canyon. She found the bar where she and Fairbairn had gone. There was a sense of comfort in the shabby red leather booths and the moderate people all around. A waitress, sympathetic, said: 'I'll get you a drink. The movie wasn't that bad.'

'What movie?'

'Aren't you Marisia Van Helding? In *The Music Makers*?'

'I guess so.'

'You have a nice drink, dear.'

There was a nice man, cowboy gear and a warm, wide smile with crooked teeth, smiling at her obliquely, waiting to be invited or not. She didn't feel oppressed by him; in fact, she welcomed him.

'You shouldn't be drinking alone.'

'You mean you're not an alcoholic on the buddy system?'

'You're not a drinker, I can tell.'

'I wish I was, I truly do. I would like to be able to wipe away everything with another shot of bourbon. I guess only men are allowed to do that in public.'

'You like me?'

She looked at him. He was solid, strong, sinewy; he smelled of soap and work. She liked him well enough. And as the bourbon went down, she started to worry that she liked him.

She was drinking too much to drive home. She'd have to ask him for a lift, leave the car. She couldn't do that.

He'd think she was trying to pick him up. She wasn't doing that. But she didn't want to go away, and she didn't want to lose him, and she didn't want to go home, however proper a thing to do that might be.

She wanted to lose control. Now, for good. It was the impulse she'd scorned as masochistic in other people, and it took hard liquor to bring it out in her. She didn't want hurt or pain. She wanted someone else to take responsibility for a while.

He seemed so decent. David Grant was decent. But David Grant was tangled in all the other issues of her life, and this man wasn't. This man existed only at this moment, in this bar, looking brown and smelling of soap. She didn't have to worry about tomorrow.

She wanted him to take her away – for a few hours, for a few days. It wasn't significant; it didn't matter. She wasn't giving her soul along with her body.

God, make it simple. God, make it happen. God, God, God.

'You sure you should be driving?' the cowboy said.

'I don't know,' Marisia said.

'Come home with me,' the cowboy said. 'I'll fix you some coffee and drive you home later.'

'Yes,' Marisia said. 'I'd like that.'

It must be like shooting deer that come in winter for a feed, when the fields are desolate; that was what she thought. He sounded kind, and he was hunting like all the rest.

Only it didn't matter. He had a pick-up outside, and they piled into it. He chewed tobacco and she thought she liked the smell.

This, she thought, was the low. You run away, from the man waiting in the hills, from the decisions you ought to be making, and you drink bourbon until a cowboy takes you home, and then you make an absolute surrender. You let the kind, straightforward cowboy tie a blindfold on you and then you let him – you haven't seen his place; you don't know where you are; you have little choice – tie you apparently to a table. The trouble is, the view through the window when the blindfold comes off is blindingly ordinary, suburban houses in a tacky row and undrawn curtains; and he has such a sense of wonder on his face; and, Marisia thought, you want a cigarette and he is still trying to say he's your master, riding you.

It couldn't go on like that, she knew. She froze the scene, unkindly, and demanded a lift home. She watched the cowboy start worrying as they moved through the more and more expensive canyons. He was out of his depth and petrified.

'Lady, you don't say nothing now, please?'

David Grant was awake when she walked into the house. He'd have heard an engine note not like a Porsche. She thought she had better say something.

'I left the car,' she said. 'I thought I'd had too much to drink.'

David looked up from a sheaf of notes.

'Good,' he said. 'That's a noisy pick-up truck.'

'I got a lift.'

'You smell of chewing tobacco.'

'I can smell of what I goddamn like.'

'Yes,' David said. 'I never tried to stop you. I just wonder why you run away from talking.'

'I'm sorry,' Marisia said. 'I'm so sorry.'

'Being sorry isn't the point,' David said. 'I'm sorry. Dogs are sorry. Anyone can be sorry. It's only with Jewish mothers you score points for being sorry.'

'But I am sorry, terribly . . .'

'I wish you'd talk sense. I'm going to bed. Please shower before you come – you look as though you've been playing basketball for the evening.'

She went into the bathroom and began a meticulous cleaning. It wouldn't do – not the drink, not the evasion, not surrendering control to strangers. The cowboy had a harmless enough fantasy, but the next one – ah, the next one.

She came into the bedroom as warm and clean as innocence.

David Grant put his arms around her and held her very close.

'Don't run away,' he said. 'That scares me. Anything else, but don't run away.'

'It wasn't a great success,' Marisia said.

'It doesn't matter.'

'Please hold me.'

They curled together, like one body. Marisia began to forget.

Koolhoven saw a model – plaster trees flanking a tall, crude tower, symbolizing nothing more than rents. Van Helding, he knew, saw more. Van Helding was imposing a skyline on London. He was making a manifesto of concrete and glass to show he had arrived.

And he was fascinated by the detail. He wanted to know exactly how such a tower could be built from within London's laws, and he wanted to know immediately. The architect, Colonel Henderson, obliged. He was a brilliant, angular man with a gold tooth, and the honorific 'Colonel', a euphemism in 1946, had stuck with him as he acquired more power.

'It's not legally possible, this tower,' the Colonel said, smugly. 'Too much space for the site, too tall. Ratio's illegal. Trouble is, we don't have the tower, we don't have something striking.'

Van Helding peered at the model. It wasn't lovely – a brutal column of coloured glass with concrete details to muddle its shape – but still a proper tower set on a grandiose plinth.

'But it so happens the planners have a problem. They have a map of London traffic, and they need a roundabout just there. It says so on the map. It's said so for twenty years. And we're going to give it to them – public amenity.'

'Why should they want it?'

'Because it's what they want officially. They're committed. Then it's a matter of planners' pride; they call it civic pride. Most of them would tear down a cathedral to keep their master plans – especially if they got their names on the shops.'

'Marvellous,' Van Helding said. 'I leave it to you to understand how the English think.'

'There's one last point. I don't want to be difficult, but I want to be absolutely sure on one point. You have bought old man Joliffe out, haven't you? I mean, he was working the streets for years, and you'll need his land.'

'It's in hand,' Pieter said.

'It had better be a bit more certain than that,' the Colonel said, 'before I go to planning committees. Everybody knows Joliffe was a dreamer.'

'He'll sell,' Van Helding said.

Koolhoven went back to the bank and settled himself in Van Helding's office. At least Pieter couldn't have him make the next call; it needed the Van Helding name. But he wanted to watch. Van Helding, whom once he had loved, now fascinated him.

Van Helding called the senior manager at a correspondent bank – a High-Street chain with an eye to the main chance. The manager kept fingering his bald spot, nervously and enviously aware that full-fledged tigers like Pieter Van Helding roamed the City of London. He was also bored. To be called by Van Helding, a name out of headlines, made his day.

Van Helding said he had made an offer to Joliffe. Joliffe was being difficult.

'Indeed?' the manager said.

'We know he's in trouble. We're just not sure he knows how much.'

'It's difficult to manage Mr Joliffe,' the English banker said. 'He is – one of the old school.'

'As long as he knows,' Van Helding said. 'After all, if you had to foreclose on all the properties he has mortgaged to you . . .'

'I deduce,' said the Englishman, 'you might be a buyer?'

'Cash at valuation. Plus a stake in the development equity, of course.'

'Very tasty.'

'We could give you details of the plans . . .'

'I'm sure your name is enough for the moment,' the banker said. He chanced a seemingly casual 'Pieter' and was not rebuffed. 'We all know your reputation. I mean, if you made an offer directly to Joliffe, we could always . . . reinforce it.'

'I assume your board would rather have ten per cent of an office tower than a hundred per cent of a street or two of strip clubs?'

'We're not happy with the clubs.'

'I do admire Mr Joliffe. But I think his day is past, don't you?'

'I couldn't agree more.'

'We are, after all, a new generation.'

New, the manager thought, and not much time to join it before the bald spot and implacable age raced ahead of ambition. His mind was made up.

And the tower rose, and when the skeleton was finished, a lift cage climbed its side – a platform framed in chicken wire, flimsy against the great, rust-red girders. The tower was now a net of steel, waiting for the glass and stone that would hang from it like wrapping. From the lift, the guests could see all London spread out from the bald and dusty hills of Hampstead to the serpentine bends of the river, glistening under the sun. The building's top, tenuous and raw, was laid out like a command post in war or a banquet – ready for the people who would come to honour the Rector Street tower, and the strategy that built it.

'There isn't even a wall,' Katherine said. 'I don't know why we celebrate now.'

'Topping out,' said Koolhoven, 'is a tradition.'

'I never did understand tradition,' Pieter Van Helding said.

Katherine had the royal role: to take a trowel, lay a tile, accept applause. There were faint sighs of champagne bottles being opened, and the Rector Street development had official existence – proved by the photographs in the evening papers, proved by the little plaque that Katherine had laid.

'I almost wonder if it would pay us to let this building,' Van Helding said. 'If it sits empty, the value goes up each year as rents go up – we can borrow on that value, and we don't have to pay taxes. And we get to write off bits of the costs.'

'You couldn't leave a tower like this empty without getting the wrong sort of attention,' Koolhoven said.

'That's only trouble in the papers,' Van Helding said. 'Not real trouble.'

Pinstripes and hard hats were the order of the day, from the obsequious foremen on the project to City luminaries to occasional journalists from the Sunday City pages. They could look out at the London skyline, now broken more with Seifert towers than Wren churches, and debate the position of Colonel Henderson in the reworking of London. They generally agreed it was not pretty, except in terms of money, but the money was so spectacular, they kept their voices low.

The lift cage suddenly went down.

'Are we expecting anyone else?' Koolhoven asked a secretary who was at the cage entrance with a list. The secretary shook her head.

'Get the guards on the ground to check who called the lift,' he said.

The lift cage had begun to rise from the ground again, grinding slowly upwards, carrying a single man in a yellow helmet. Koolhoven could not identify the figure, but he knew that man should not be there.

'Tell Van Helding, discreetly, we may have trouble,' Koolhoven said to one of the unobtrusive guards on the building's top. 'And get a couple of your men over here.'

The lift cage rose past the surrounding buildings, over

the turrets and pagodas and mock gazebos that nineteenth-century architects added to relieve the respectability of street façades. It clicked into place at the very top of the tower.

'Mr Joliffe,' said Koolhoven. 'What an unexpected pleasure.'

Joliffe grunted, stamped his feet and threw open the lift gates.

'Thought I'd just come and see what you made of it all.'

'Can we offer you a drink?'

Joliffe took in the formal scene and strolled to Van Helding's side. It was almost as though he believed he was host at this party. He did not feel in the slightest bit out of place. He belonged to this high platform, above the tight, narrow streets that were tangled below. It was his dream, after all, and his years. He acknowledged the people he knew, nodded to those he did not. The clearing bank manager was startled and then frostily polite. Van Helding was remote, but courteous. Joliffe asked about the stone cladding, paid compliments on the speed with which the building had risen, asked some technical questions about foundations, and said it all looked very fine.

'I used to walk round here every day,' he said to Pieter. 'I used to dream about this day. And when it came to it, I couldn't make it happen.'

Katherine did not know the whole story, and she was easy with Joliffe. 'You must be proud to see it now,' she said. She thought he was a serious, awkward old man, but she assumed he was important.

'I suppose so,' Joliffe said.

'And what will you work on now?'

'That would be telling, wouldn't it? This time, I'd better keep everything to myself. Safer that way.'

Katherine edged away from him. Pieter asked how Joliffe seemed; Katherine said he seemed sad, but stable.

They had all relaxed about his presence; he did not seem disposed to make trouble.

He had climbed to the top of the scaffolding bars, staring out to the glint of waters in North London by the surprising, marshy territory of the Lea. He seemed fascinated and absorbed. Around the rest of the tower, the party assembled into chattering groups, first puzzled by the old man's presence and then indifferent.

Then they saw what he was doing. Above the scaffolding bars was security wire, but only a thin partition. Joliffe was on top of it. Between him and the street below there was now absolutely nothing but air and wind. The party fell silent as the old man drew himself upright. A jet plane came up the sky like a roll of drums.

Joliffe made what seemed like a child's jump, a little jump, but it took him clear of the building. The party rushed to the side of the tower to watch the fall. He was tumbling for a while until the body steadied itself and then he vanished into the detail and animation of the streets below.

Reporters murmured together. Sudden death was not the point of this party; they had come to talk yields and years' purchase and dividends.

'A terrible accident,' Koolhoven said, firmly.

'He was drunk?' asked a reporter.

'He must have had vertigo,' Koolhoven said.

'But how did he get over the safety rail? He must have jumped deliberately.'

Koolhoven realized at once that they had not quite seen the incident, or, if they had, their memory of it was already tangled. 'Perhaps he was trying to get a better view,' he said.

'Maybe he jumped,' a reporter said, and giggled.

'It was an accident,' Koolhoven said. 'You should have another drink. And, of course, if you want to talk to Pieter Van Helding – perhaps tomorrow?'

'Of course, we don't report suicides,' the reporter said. 'But it is odd he should do that – tycoon in death leap from rival's tower. People are so goddamned superstitious. They'll call it the haunted tower.'

'No,' said Koolhoven. He sounded sharp. Then he recovered his casual manner and said: 'While Mr Van Helding usually doesn't see the press, I'm sure he would make an exception . . .'

'A terrible accident,' said one reporter, shaking his head and seeming serious.

Joliffe, dead, fell on the wrought-iron railings of a basement office and lay there like a furry creature in a shrike's larder. When they passed the railings, Katherine realized that had really happened.

That evening, she lay curled on a sofa watching the fire fall softly. She looked so comfortable, and felt on nails.

'He jumped,' she said.

'He fell.'

'I saw him climb up and jump.'

'He fell.'

Around Pieter, ghosts circled. A corncrake voice had called him late that afternoon, a woman who said she was Mrs Joliffe. 'I told him not to go,' she said. 'I told him. I said they've killed you in the way of business, they'll kill you in life.'

Pieter said to her, too: 'He fell.'

Katherine and Pieter took dinner, estranged and silent. They went into the nursery to see the children and they played for a while. When Pieter felt his house was again in order, he retreated to his study and called the Coliseum.

Yes, Sally Rogerson was on stage that evening. Yes, the stage door manager would be happy to take a message. Yes, they came down around ten thirty-five. Quite sharp, usually. Yes, he'd make sure Miss Rogerson knew that Mr Van Helding was calling for her.

* * *

'Mr Gregory insists,' the secretary said.
'I don't see anybody,' Unger said.
'He won't go away.'
'Then call the guards.'
'I don't think he'll go if I call the guards. Besides, he is one of Mr Van Helding's customers.'
Unger looked baleful. 'I suppose I have to see him,' he said. 'We mustn't offend the young master.'
It was not hard to see why the secretary had thought the guards would find it impossible to budge Noam Gregory. He looked bulky and certain, without melodramatic flourishes.
'Mr Unger,' said Noam Gregory. 'A pleasure to meet you.'
And an irony, Gregory thought. Gregory thought Unger was part traitor, part alchemist, part opportunist. And he had to ask him a favour.
'The matter is urgent,' Noam Gregory said. 'I maintain an account here in Amsterdam as Gregory Enterprises. It has a line of credit attached to it.'
'Indeed?' Unger said. He felt sharp and calm, to his great relief. 'I have no knowledge of this, of course, unless I have the account number and the file.'
'These are they,' said Gregory, pushing a slip across the desk.
There was a pause while the secretary went for coffee, and Unger and Gregory tried uncomfortable small talk. A messenger returned with the file-papers wrapped in legal parchment, tied with red ribbon.
Unger spread the papers before him, and Gregory made his case.
'Payments to a subsidiary in Berne last week were not made,' Gregory said. 'It seems possible that someone here did not realize the extent of the credit I arranged with Mr Van Helding. There was a very unfortunate delay, and some important business was spoiled.'

Unger shook his head. 'I'm sorry,' he said. 'According to the file, the payment would have exceeded the credit limit. Someone must have pulled the file and seen that.'

'Important business,' Gregory repeated, flatly. Unger shifted a little uneasily in his chair. He was face to face with a sort of unblinking power that he particularly disliked and found almost impossible to handle. Gregory was one of Van Helding's curious accounts – no documents, a massive line of credit which had been used again and again, each time with funds coming through within days when payments had been made. It was an account in good order, if you overlooked the oddity that it had no address and the payments in were as often as not in cash.

'I am sorry if a client of the bank was inconvenienced,' Unger said. He had looked into steel eyes like these in little, dark rooms in canalside houses when the Allies started to ask their questions. 'But the figures are quite clear. The credit line would have been exceeded.'

'I should have given you some notice,' Gregory said. 'Time to consult Van Helding, perhaps. But I was unexpectedly in Amsterdam, and . . .'

'You wouldn't object to telling me the nature of this business? Perhaps I could authorize a payment.'

'The circumstances are not important,' Gregory said. 'What matters is that a payment was not made. I have to rely on your services, and if I cannot . . .'

Ten men, two women, would not now come out of Russia because the money had been late. They would sit and face a kind of bitter dissolution over the years. Yet Gregory knew he had to conceal his sense of passion about such things. He was the businessman to Unger, since Unger was choosing to be the perfect banker to him.

'You mean it would be indiscreet of me to ask more?' Unger said. 'In that case, you will have to talk to Mr Van

Helding in London. I regret that I do not know you and I do not know the account. I would obviously like to be able to help, but it is not possible.'

'I understand,' Gregory said.

'I do hope we can resolve the matter.'

'I hope so,' Gregory said.

When he had left, Unger turned the pages of the file. He did not often have the occasion – or the excuse – to look at what Van Helding had done in the years past. On the boy's sole authority, huge sums had been sent round the world, unsecured loans in effect. All the time Pieter Van Helding was risking millions on a man who could not even state his trade, he was also edging Unger out of power, holding him to ransom.

Unger shook his head and reached out into the drawer of his desk for the Valium pills that took the monsters out of his day. He half-drowsed the rest of the working morning before the telephone shrilled. It was Van Helding, snapping that there seemed to be trouble with the Gregory account, peremptorily ordering Unger to do what Gregory wanted, now.

'Pieter, I have seen the file and that would be imprudent.'

'Do it on my responsibility.'

'You will have to give formal authority.'

'You have my authority. I'll telex a confirmation if you want it on paper. Cooperate, can't you?'

'It is not a question of cooperation,' Unger said, very calmly. He was grateful for the pills that soothed his mind. 'It is a question of proper procedure. I cannot make unsecured and unauthorized loans to persons I do not even know – just because they know enough to drop your name.'

'The man is my client,' Van Helding said. Unger, secure in his chemical stillness, thought he detected an edge of hysteria in Van Helding, something very rare. Noam Gregory was obviously important.

'And we should fix a meeting,' Van Helding said. 'This week. We have a lot to discuss.'

'I'm afraid . . .'

'I shall expect you in London on Friday. We can have lunch.'

'But I . . .'

'Be there, Unger,' Van Helding said and put down the phone.

Unger had long ago outgrown resentment at the tone of Van Helding's orders. What fascinated him was the tension in Van Helding's voice before the summons to London. Pieter Van Helding sounded scared.

Why?

Unger scanned the file for clues. There were cancell l cheques, notes of cash payments in and out, an order for a money transfer (the bank's internal document, a pink paper), and a neat pile of official forms. There were a few memoranda, mostly on exact arrangements for big payments in foreign capitals. There was a note on the credit line, the same sort of note that would lie on the file of any account.

There seemed no clues, at first, until Unger began to think about dates. He said out loud to himself what he had only thought casually before – the Gregory account was opened just as Van Helding was dropping a sealed file on Unger's desk, letting the old man know his war history could be public knowledge if he did not step aside. What if Gregory was the source of Van Helding's documents?

Then who was Gregory? Unger knew there were enough groups interested in making life difficult for old associates of what he persisted in thinking was the German Government he had known. Gregory could be with one of those groups. He would be a manufacturer of sacrificial victims, discovering and exposing and ruining people who had done great evil and now were settled in banal, anonymous comfort.

But Gregory had very big money. He disposed of it in surprising ways for a simple Nazi-hunter. Perhaps Gregory was a little more official than he seemed.

Unger poured himself a drink, told his secretary to refuse all calls and arrange flights to London for Friday. He wanted to think sharply, but the tiredness that came from gin and Valium left the same few sentences clicking into place, again and again, like figures on a roundabout. Van Helding wanted him out. Van Helding would make trouble on Friday. Van Helding had a sort of excuse. Yet Van Helding was worried.

Perhaps the files were double-edged, as hurtful to Van Helding's father as to Unger. Or perhaps . . .

It didn't matter. Quite accidentally, Unger had annoyed the enemy. He was trapped – between the old men at the hunting lodge with their deadly desire for quiet and the anger of Gregory and Van Helding. It was all too much for him; his back would break under it. There was this flood of raw information, which could no longer be controlled.

They would come and ask him questions. That was bound to happen. They'd put him under scrutiny. More than a revelation of the moral inadequacies of his war, he feared public knowledge of how empty and powerless the last few years had been. He was more ashamed of the vacuum than of the sins.

He'd been humiliated by Gregory, forced to accept Van Helding as the only true power in Kellerman Unger; even worse, he doubted if his own will survived. He would go to London to be reprimanded, meek as a lamb.

He wished it were over. He wished he could go to some remote, kindly, warm place where nobody would pursue and probe him. He wished he could take his responsibility and lay it on someone else.

Marisia Van Helding.

She had wanted to challenge her brother. She had

talked about it up to the time of the shareholders' meeting that gave the bank to the Palm Springs gentry. She could take it all on now. She was young enough, strong enough.

It was early in the Dorchester bar. Marisia Van Helding sat at a corner table, cramped by the pastel prettiness of the place, passed by waiters bearing little bowls of nuts, watching the door. She disliked public meeting places, but if she had to be in public, she liked the anonymity of this bar.

She drank Perrier against Unger's arrival.

He shuffled in, a dry old man. Marisia greeted him as a loved but failing uncle. He smiled rather wanly and tried to offer her champagne.

'I have to talk quickly,' he said. 'I have to have lunch with your brother.' He seemed to be gulping for air, as though his lungs had withered in him. 'I want to get out of the bank. But I don't want to sell to Pieter or his friends. I want to sell to you.'

Marisia simply stared. Whatever she had expected from this urgent meeting, it was not this.

'I have enough capital for the rest of my days. I don't need the dividends from Kellerman Unger. If I sell, and anything happens to me, it's my business, none of the bank's. And I shan't be involved any more in what your brother does.'

'He tried to push you out?'

'He's tried for a good many years. Mostly, he's succeeded.'

'I'm not a rich woman,' Marisia said. 'I couldn't realize most of my assets if I wanted to. For your part of Kellerman Unger you'd want . . .'

'One dollar. Just enough to make the sale legal. I don't want to be paid at all. I've done well out of the bank and now I want to get out . . . quickly. There isn't a public market to value the shares, so any price I set would be arbitrary. A dollar is unfair – you pay a dollar and you take my burdens from me. I should pay you.'

'I have to decide now?'

'I have to know before lunch.'

Marisia thought furiously. She felt friendless. Pieter was the enemy, David Grant never understood why Kellerman Unger mattered, lawyers patronized her. She felt the cold from the glass in her hand, and set it down on the fancy trelliswork of the table.

'May I go into the park for a minute or two? I'd like to think.'

'I have to be in Cheapside at one,' Unger said. 'I'll wait as long as I can.'

Marisia went out through the busy lobby past the flower shop and the news stand, and crossed Park Lane into the gentle, summer shade of Hyde Park. She sat, very stiff and still, on a bench. A yellow-white butterfly careened around bushes, and breezes caught the pink-purple feathers of the pigeons. She almost felt the rattling of leaves against each other. A squirrel came in long, agile bounds through the grass to see if she had food for him.

'Lovely day, miss,' said a policeman on a horse.

'Yes, yes, it is.'

'Are you all right?'

'Yes, yes, really.'

'I – hope you don't mind me asking, miss, but are you Marisia Van Helding that was in *The Music Makers*?'

Marisia looked up. She did not want to have to put on her official, starlet's smile. 'Yes,' she said. 'That's me.'

'We loved that,' the copper said, 'my missus and me.'

He nodded, and passed on into the park.

Marisia made herself get up. She absently dusted down her dress as though she had been sitting in some distant wood and turned back towards the park gates. There was no choice, really. She had to take what Unger offered.

She needed a drink to say she would buy; and Unger, with his old nervous excitement, shook when she spoke. His energy seemed to come back when Marisia took the burdens.

At Le Poulbot, sharp at one, Van Helding and Unger kept up appearances. They were among chattering pinstripes, occasional public relations persons out wooing, squads of the perfectly dressed and made young men in their upper twenties who had begun to inherit (and to develop) the earth. Settled in their booth, they looked as though their lunch was friendly enough – a guinea fowl made less dry with mushrooms and alcohol, a fish for Van Helding, a bottle of Mersault. Besides, the place was too public and open for serious business.

Except that when the meal was finished, Unger produced an envelope of heavy cream stuff, and put it by Van Helding's plate.

'I'm resigning,' he said. 'You can read my letter.'

Van Helding had prepared a sharp, humiliating little speech which he had meant to deliver quietly over coffee; that way, Unger would squirm, unable to react with anger. Now he was nonplussed.

'And I have sold my shares.'

'I thought we had an agreement that you couldn't sell without the consent of the majority shareholders?'

'I may have said something like that. But that would only apply if there were to be new shareholders. Besides, it was only an informal idea.'

'There are no new shareholders?'

'Your sister,' Unger said, 'is buying me out.'

Van Helding stared, furious that he could not explode in a public place.

'Of course we shall miss your wisdom and counsel at the bank.'

'Bullshit,' Unger said. 'I am going to have a marc – will you join me?'

'And of course you can use your office for as long as you want.'

'My secretary has almost finished moving my things.'

'Nothing has happened? There isn't anything I should know?'

'I am simply tired,' Unger said. 'And I do not like to feel tied to the bank any more – to whatever you and your American friends are proposing to do. There's nothing more I can change. I feel like an old voyeur, trapped in my back room. I can watch, but I can't perform.'

'You kept the bank going during the war,' Van Helding said. 'And you built it up before and after the war.'

'That's true. I worked hard, I risked everything, and I simply gave you a start.'

'You had your friends, too,' Van Helding said. 'My Americans are not so different.'

'I hope they're different, for your sake. You can learn to regret friends. But I don't think you have it in you to reflect like that. Soon you'll be itchy again and London won't be big enough and you'll want Hong Kong or New York or both. Maybe you'll buy your own tax haven.'

'Tax business doesn't make money,' Pieter said. 'It's only for the brass-plate merchants.'

'You have a London merchant bank.'

'Not quite. I bank from London, but that will do.'

'I used to think,' Unger said, 'that some day the London operation might be spun off into a separate company, leaving just the little family bank in Amsterdam. Then I knew it was time for me to go. I was being sentimental. I was starting to think I could get the bank back when I wanted it.'

'I'm not going to stop now,' Van Helding said, 'if that's what you think. You do understand that, don't you? I want all the glory I can get and the power. I want to play every part of the money machine for all it's worth.'

'You play money like chess, as though it were abstract.'

'It is,' Van Helding said. 'It's a game of paper and confidence, it's all in people's heads. And I want to play very hard.'

'I wonder what you would do if you ever failed.'

'It would mean the machine had failed,' Van Helding said. 'I know how the machine operates, and I've changed the machine a little, and I may do more. I know that for as long as the whole business of money, credit, and banks keeps going, I keep going. It isn't a question any more of individuals who make mistakes. Either you understand the way the game is changing, or you get out. We lend to Third World countries that are starving – and we make it pay. They can't go bust because the politicians won't allow it. We lend to Comecon countries like Poland because their economics may fail but their interest payments won't – behind every zloty there's the Russian gold and diamond mines. We lend to little countries like Providencia because ultimately we're lending on Washinton's credit – Washington will make the IMF stop countries dying. Nobody can afford to stop the game any more.'

'I wish I had your youth and your certainty,' Unger said. He reached for the bill and counted out notes. 'I would fight you to the death.'

Van Helding smiled.

'I know,' he said. 'I shan't forget that.'

Van Helding called Marisia from the Coliseum stage door. 'I didn't know you were in London,' he said. 'I got your number from . . .'

'I left my number with Katherine,' Marisia said. 'I thought you'd want to talk.'

'I gather you've doubled your holding in Kellerman Unger.'

'That's true.'

'You're still only a tiny minority in the firm, you know. You can't change anything.'

'We'll see. I shall be at the annual meeting.'

'You still travel with a press agent?'

'For that kind of meeting, yes. Think about it.'

Van Helding thought she was probably bluffing, but it worried him that he might have to call her bluff.

He walked through the dun and green corridors backstage to Sally Rogerson's dressing room, more thoughtful than he had expected. The stage door man had called ahead and reported Miss Rogerson was ready for him. It had been an afternoon dress rehearsal, long and punishing. She sat gauzy and sweating in her room, her small, fine breasts bare, her ballet skirt rolled up as she eased herself out of sodden tights. She wiped white power from her breasts and sat, grateful for air. She smelled like summer, and Pieter was fascinated by the gentle fur around her sex.

'You look like a chorus girl in La Vie Parisienne,' he said.

'I feel like a washerwoman,' Sally said. 'We had a bitch of a day. The Maestrovich was being particularly difficult.' She leaned back, took a little fan from her dressing table and played it over her thighs. 'I need a shower.'

'Wait,' Pieter said. 'I love you.'

'You love my cunt,' Sally Rogerson said, moving a finger to her sex. 'But that'll do for a start.'

He buried his head between her breasts as though he was trying to lose himself, and tongued her belly and the hot, saline depths of her sex. Sally Rogerson leaned back, spread her legs, let a warm, silly grin spread across her face. She watched Van Helding's head bobbing affectionately and she felt herself cast away from shore, felt herself moving higher and higher.

'Now,' she said.

Van Helding struggled out of a City suit as best he could.

'Now, now, now.'

A corner screen, like something from a hospital, toppled forward. After the thud, a bizarre sight followed – a *danseur noble*, overexcited, listening and watching with almost grim attention, dressed in a Danskin and woolly boots. He looked like a schoolboy satyr.

Pieter looked up, and he grinned broadly. Sally saw the disaster from the corner of her eye. Both, disrupted for a moment, stifled their giggles and began to work together even more furiously, more noisily, performing to the hilt. When they finished, they lay entangled sweetly and the *danseur noble* meandered forward.

'Darlings,' he said, 'you were wonderful.'

Sally picked a dance pump from her table and hurled it at him. He skipped a brisk retreat.

On the plane, flying away from the sun over a peaceful North Sea, Jan Unger considered his plans. There was no longer any point in dallying in Amsterdam. He had given up the charade of going each morning to the bank and returning each evening, like a worker. He had nothing to hold him now in Holland, except a lifetime – and the lifetime was a muddle of terror, gains and losses. So he could go to the house he dreamt of, in Cuernavaca.

He had bought the house in the 1940s from some Mexican investments. He had been there several times, but mostly it was let. Rich people liked the Mexican mountains for the air and the sun and they paid well for the house.

He had nowhere else. He felt half on the lam in Holland, where his liberty depended still on the deals he had done in 1945 with the advancing Allies. He was no longer at home. Home had been broken the first day the Germans came, all bright and beautiful and deadly, into Amsterdam.

How much of a life was it worth packing to take to Cuernavaca? Should he take books, familiar objects, the paintings he had acquired, mostly in the early 1950s when people were still hungry for cash and prepared to dispose of the most surprising riches? Should be go clean and unencumbered, leaving his life behind him?

He was still thinking these muddled thoughts when the plane began circling Schiphol, and he hardly noticed the formalities of collecting baggage and finding a taxi. At the rank, there was a familiar bulky figure.

'Mr Gregory,' Unger said, without pleasure, but also without surprise. There was no reason why he should find the client's presence significant.

'Mr Unger,' said Gregory. 'Perhaps we can share a taxi into Amsterdam?'

'I am going to Haarlem,' Unger said. 'Otherwise . . .'

'But I think we should share a taxi,' Gregory said, 'all the same.'

The car that came was lit brightly inside like a stage, and Unger did not resist it. When he settled in the back seat, he realized the doors were locked against him. The same sort of car once took Pieter Van Helding back from a marshland meeting with Gregory, bearing a folder of papers. Now, it took Jan Unger to a neat, suburban house, and left him with Gregory.

'We have something to discuss,' Gregory said. He had been ominously silent during the journey. Unger would have been grateful for Valium, for any escape from the moment, but he had none at all.

'I hope your business was settled properly,' Unger said. 'I know Mr Van Helding was most concerned.'

'He was,' Gregory said. 'When he's troubled, he moves fast.'

'Yes,' Unger said. He was completely puzzled, and emotionally dazed. He had left the plane feeling he had resolved his life and, within minutes, he had toppled into some kind of melodrama.

'I expect you're familiar with these?'

Gregory pushed across to Unger a set of papers. Unger knew them very well. They were the same files that Pieter Van Helding had once dropped onto his desk.

'I have seen them before.'

'But I don't think you know what is in them?'

'That is true. I have only seen the cover sheets.'

'I'm not a vindictive man, Mr Unger. If I was, those files would have been public knowledge long ago.'

'If they had been public, you would not have had Kellerman Unger to use,' Unger said. 'The scandal would have ruined us.'

'I suppose so,' Gregory said. 'It just goes to show that deals have to benefit both parties.'

'Have you a deal to propose?'

'I think you should look at the papers. There's a report there on the illegal transmission of money during the last war.'

'Pure speculation,' Unger said.

'It has a codicil,' Gregory said. 'It's confidential, of course. It gives some names and some numbers. We've been working on it for some time.'

'Could you explain why I have been brought here – what all this is about?'

'Certainly, Mr Unger. You moved a lot of Nazi money. You moved a lot of Georg Van Helding's money. And you moved a lot of Jewish money, as a favour – just like the Swiss did when they found their wonderful new secret bank accounts could be used by German Jews. Now some of that money is accounted for, and some of it isn't. In fact quite a lot of the Jewish money simply disappeared. Perhaps you thought there would be nobody left to claim it when the Nazis had finished – your Nazi friends.'

'They were no friends of mine,' Unger said. 'People like you miss the distinction. I did nothing to help them, but I tried to keep going and keep alive. It wasn't always obvious which side would win.'

'You salted away some of the missing money in Mexico, and some you brought back through Switzerland. The codicil gives the numbers of some of the accounts – numbers and names. You were Thomas Hastings, once, weren't you – that was Mexico City – and you were with Kredit Anstalt in Lugarno as Henry Dutch. Not subtle.'

'You can't prove any of this,' Unger said. 'And what is more, you're quite wrong.'

'The thing is, Mr Unger, we have two interesting sets of numbers. In one, we can show that parts of Georg Van Helding's fortune did reach Mexico, and you invested the money, and you never told the family or the estates where the money was hidden. You kept it. In the other set of numbers, there are clues to where the money from your Jewish clients ended up, and some of the Nazi big shots, too. You took risks, I'll say that for you. Once upon a time, you must have had nerve.'

'Suppose you're right, and suppose you have the papers? What do you want?'

'I think Pieter Van Helding – and maybe Marisia, too – would be interested to know where their father's money went. Pieter Van Helding has some unpleasant friends. They could make your life miserable – or shorten it, perhaps.'

'Unless what, then? What do you want me to do?'

'I want the full numbers of the accounts where money from Nazis and Jews was lodged – so far as you remember them. I want authority to draw that money. Morally it belongs to the Jewish community. It would be best used to protect Jews in the world.'

'Morality isn't law,' Unger said. 'You don't have a proper claim.'

'We're not talking about left luggage in a railway station,' Gregory said. 'I don't need the claim tag. I already have these papers – and the facts you don't want Pieter Van Helding to know.'

Unger said, flatly, 'I want to go home.' The defiance seemed to drain from him, leaving a dry stem of a man. He reflected bitterly that his burdens had lifted for just six hours, only to return more heavily than ever.

Then he said: 'I will need some time to check the numbers. And the names. I didn't keep a file.'

'We only need the numbers of the accounts. You're sure to have kept those.'

'You know which are Georg Van Helding's?'

'Some of them,' Gregory said. 'But I don't think we need make a distinction, do you? The Van Heldings don't need the money any more.'

Unger nodded. 'You want it all.'

Gregory took back the papers and shuffled them into a file. 'I thought you might want to read them,' he said. 'I don't think Van Helding ever gave you a chance.'

Unger said: 'I wanted to go to Cuernavaca. I wanted to go there to die. Then the money would have been washed clean – it would be my estate, nothing more complicated. The law couldn't touch me in any case. And I gave up Kellerman Unger. I thought that would be my punishment. I lost my power there because of the war, so I'd give it all up because of the war. I meant it to be an act of atonement.'

'I wouldn't have moved against you, yet,' Gregory said. 'But I saw you in your office and I realized you could still do something – you could still block my deals through the bank, for example. I wasn't sure if you blocked them deliberately.'

'No, no,' Unger said. 'I didn't know who you were. I still don't. You might be some adventurer who steals money. I don't know.'

'I might be,' Gregory said. 'That can be your final punishment. You'll never quite know if the money went home – or if you were simply outsmarted.'

'Please.' said Unger. 'I am an old man. I suppose I shall

not be going to Cuernavaca, after all – it gets so damp in winter here, it gets into my bones, the marrow starts to ache.'

Gregory looked at him with contempt – secure in his own moral position, even more secure in winning.

There was a great steam roundabout, all gilt and red and high-toned horses, puffing and whistling as they went around. They could shy for coconuts or ride the dodgems. Little Georg liked the dodgems. He had come through disease almost unmarked, and now he liked risk. He had been safe in nurses' care for long enough.

He and his brother had both wanted to go to the fair. There was candy-floss and loud, recorded music, and a horse ride round and round a tiny field.

'Please have them back by seven,' Katherine had said to the nurse. 'You know my husband likes to see the children before they go to bed.'

She had settled in the drawing room, a proper, elegant lady waiting for her evening to begin. It seemed a price she paid for her neat, smart world that she could not start the evening for herself; it all depended on other people arriving. She flicked the pages of *Harpers Queen* and the French *Vogue*. She thought about a drink and she thought better of it.

The telephone rang. The office at Georg's school asked if he would be taking piano next term. She supposed he would. She supposed this temporary London house would be their settled place for a few more years – place of abode, as it said on passports, very roundly and comfortingly. She and Pieter would never truly settle on a city or a continent, she feared, but for the moment this place had a certain security. The sheltering evergreens along the drive, dense and shiny, confirmed the sense of privacy.

She looked down the lawn. The hoops for croquet were still in place. Border flowers swept each side of the garden, a very English, artful muddle of daisies and wild things, glittering in the evening sun. It seemed very homely, as appropriate as anything she could hope for.

She was nervous, though. She found herself looking out on this great green expanse and feeling a sudden failure of her usual calm. She thought she heard the sound of a car outside, on the narrow lane from which the driveway turned. She felt something close to alarm.

It could be the noise of Nurse's Mini, a struggling, effortful noise like the lady herself.

She thought about the fair and the roundabouts. She should have gone with the children. She was not so massively occupied that she could not spare the time. But they had talked to Nurse, and worked on her, and not on their mother. She wasn't invited.

The house seemed very empty. Perhaps she should walk down the hall to where the kitchen noises were beginning. She wanted to hear Georg on his little mock motorcycle, putt-putting and roaring in his treble voice. Anything would be better than the quiet and the birds.

She did have a drink. She wondered if Pieter would be on time. She wondered about his life outside this house. She wondered in a vague, titillating way if she should take a lover. *Le cinq à sept* in Hampstead.

What she heard was: the sound of an engine: a car moving fast, squealing on corners. Then the sound of a second engine, Nurse's Mini, struggling up the hill in a determined way. A long blare on a car horn. Then a scream of tyres, a howling of brakes, a rending, shattering crash that seemed to last for ever and then abrupt silence. There might have been a shout as well; she was never sure about that.

She pelted to the door, evening-dressed and over-scrupulous, losing her shoes as she got to the driveway, running over the biting gravel.

Nurse's Mini was buried in a flat-nosed van. They had

met head on. Nurse had been thrown bodily out of the car and lay crumpled by the road, legs and arms broken out of shape. Katherine ran to the car. The children, her children, were in that car. Her little life.

Georg must have been in front. He had sailed through the windscreen. Glass had taken out one eye. His head was cracked like a broken vase. Eric had been behind. He had fallen forward, whiplashed by the impact and his half-formed neck was broken.

Katherine fell across the car, as though she wanted to embrace the two of them and shield them, and she sobbed. She remembered nothing until she was in the drawing room again. Then she saw her feet were bleeding from the run over gravel.

She started to ask what had happened.

6

It took Katherine time to grow back into herself – to allow feeling again and acknowledge the past. She was empty, then she seemed angry with her own identity, then she managed the social precision of an automaton, and then the shock began to subside. For two years people thought she was indifferent to the children's death; she set aside everything about them, and told Pieter she wanted to have no more children. It was three years before the sense of curse began to lift from her.

In that time, she seemed angry that being a Grunwald, being the wife of Pieter Van Helding had failed to protect her from loss and pain. She defined herself by men, for men, and the definition no longer worked. She needed support, but she could not imagine herself in dungarees at a woman's meeting talking about men as rapists. She was drifting.

She avoided her family, going only twice to see the Baron Gilles, not seeing her parents at all. Gilles rolled cantankerously around his house, announcing the fall of the family finances in his unflattering growl. Katherine was not sure whether she should take him seriously.

'Damn fool idea,' Gilles said. 'Edouard's of course. Wanted to be the high-street bank – us, for God's sake. As if the French working man would trust us with a sou. First they thought we were too grand. Then they thought we must be in trouble to ask for their money. And now we are in trouble. Real trouble.'

Gilles wouldn't tell her the whole story; he only said it was 'absurd' what had happened, and ruinous. Katherine watched his face for some sign that he was joking. The

Grunwalds were the Grunwalds, after all; the idea that they were at the mercy of a few six-franc depositors was unthinkable. They might not have the depth and grace of the Rothschilds, with their London branch and their scientific relatives, but they had a name that was even more grand, that meant more in itself.

So the summons to Paris, when it came, was shocking. When it came to money, none of the women was officially in the inner councils of the family – not even Seraphine, who had decided to hide her sharp mind early on. Yet there seemed to be an emergency, and Katherine was summoned. Pieter simply looked amused.

'*Ancien régime* crumbling?' he said.

'Don't joke, please.'

She was nervous when the plane reached Paris, and she bungled Charles de Gaulle airport as usual – flying past her earthly destination in a plastic tube that led somewhere else. After two false tries she found the car.

The Baron Gilles said: 'You're not going to like this.'

'You could at least tell me what is happening.'

'That absurd story I thought you didn't want to know,' Gilles said. 'This time, you'd better have the details.'

And the story was absurd. The Grunwalds mined silver in the South Pacific on islands that had newly become independent. The *petits mineurs*, the little businessmen who ran the mines, now ran the country, and they had an instinctive distaste for tax. Instead of income tax or property tax, they decided to tax all silver exported. And instead of paying the tax themselves, they put the burden on companies like Grunwald Argent, which bought it and shipped it. Digging, refining, taking it to the port were tax free. Shipping from the islands was taxed as a privilege.

'The silver market's gone mad,' Gilles said. 'We're supplying tonnes. Some Texan buys everything we can produce. But we're still losing money – hand over fist. The tax takes all the profit and more. We pay more tax than we've got capital invested there and the Bourse is not happy with Grunwald Argent.'

'But it's only a little company,' Katherine said, 'compared with the bank.' Ochre suburbs with red and green shopfronts gave way to cool, grey boulevards.

'The bank is in the doldrums. We're not making money. We're finding it tough to absorb the silver losses. And the more silver is in demand, the more trouble we face.'

'Is that why I'm here?'

'You may as well know,' Gilles said. 'Hugh and Edouard and Alain cooked up this idea. It's nothing to do with me. They want to approach Pieter for some help. But they want to do it strictly through the family. Since the last thing I remember about your husband is the family telling him he wasn't welcome at the bank, I doubt if he'll be too thrilled.'

'He always respected the name,' Katherine said.

'The Holy Trinity reckons if they make an official approach people will hear. The Grunwalds all go to London on the same plane, it's trouble. Van Helding visits the bank, it's trouble. They reckon there are enough rumours already without adding to them.'

'The rumours are bad?'

'It's not a panic,' Gilles said. 'Not yet.'

Katherine stared through the windows of the limousine, blankly. She felt as though she was coming back to parents long neglected, not to a place where she belonged.

She watched Gilles rise on the little elevator to the side of the steps at his house. His face was stiff with concentration. He seemed to will away his helplessness and then feel the pain of not succeeding. She wondered what it was like to be a cripple, to know something irreversible – like the fact of a marriage, the loss of children, a series of empty years in a fine house.

The family were all assembled, Seraphine gushing in a maternal fashion, welcoming the lost daughter home.

Katherine bit her tongue. Seraphine had done nothing after the children died, because she was fond of gloss and certainty. You leave alone anyone involved in scandal or trouble – especially the victim.

Katherine asked for a Perrier. Gilles, back to his usual style of talk after his surprising fluency, said: 'American habits.'

'We are just starting the plans,' Seraphine said. 'When the season starts seriously in Paris, we shall have a grand ball – with a theme, something witty.'

She had drawn Katherine aside, but Gilles pursued them. Perhaps he knew how much Katherine needed protection.

'Dracula,' Gilles said. 'They all think bankers are bloodsuckers, anyway. Give 'em something to object to.'

'I really don't like the idea,' Edouard said. 'It's the wrong time to be ostentatious, what with the Socialists. And the terrorists, too. It's not a good time to be a rich Jew.'

Seraphine attempted to be regal. 'We have a position,' she said, 'and we are going to hold it. We are the Grunwalds and we will not give up our style.'

'Bankruptcy might stop you,' Gilles said.

'Not at all,' Seraphine said. 'Then we would need even more to establish our position.'

'Still don't think it could happen?' Gilles taunted.

'I am sure the bank is in excellent condition.'

There followed a kind of quadrille. Both Hugh and Edouard thought it their duty to lead Katherine outside, walk among the new-cut box hedges smelling body-sweet, and bring up the subject of a meeting with Pieter Van Helding. Katherine remembered all the romances she read as a child in which lovely ladies carry jewels or messages or the fate of kingdoms, secretly across frontiers. Her task was to be rather more mundane, more broker than messenger, with no Musketeers.

Both Hugh and Edouard said: 'We can meet, privately, whenever and wherever Pieter chooses.'

Katherine was struck by that. They must be really worried – to allow themselves such a tone of doubt and supplication, to acknowledge Pieter's power so directly. Gilles's house looked so solid, encrusted and grinning with nineteenth-century grotesqueries and surrounded by formal gardens. But then, Gilles was solid – with his own investments and his vineyard. He could always retire, even if the worst actually happened.

There was a *paté des grives*, brought by Gilles from his vineyard. He was sour on the subject of thrushes, except at table, and the southern pâté was subtle and spicy with the meat from the birds that had fed on vine leaves, but been driven off the grapes. Then there was salmon, baked in a pie with truffles and a pike forcemeat. Then there was a proper sorbet of peaches. It was a wonderfully secure meal.

She wished her family would tell her the truth; only Gilles had tried to come close. She wondered what Pieter would do.

The Croisette was full of bodies – oiled and taut, muscles for sale, smooth and golden skin, and lovely girls, lovely boys. Everyone had a major asset on display – a suite at the Carlton, a nice bottom, a hard winter's work on an ageing body, the price of a good meal, a happy sun-dazed willingness to surrender. Porkier husbands, Sally Rogerson noticed, preened in tiny bikinis, as though the entrance money to the beach and a sense of self-importance would re-establish their flagging virility.

Sally would never have chosen Cannes, not in late July, perhaps not ever, except at the film festival for a joke. She rather thought the long Riviera strip had been filled with fake Provençal houses, cutely angled over marinas. She would have much preferred rockroses and Atlantic waves and little coves in the Algarve.

This was Pieter's choice. It seemed Sally had finally been granted the privileges of *maîtresse en titre*. Their long liaison was companionable now, and almost marriage-like; they were friendly in bed, not mindlessly urgent as they had once been. Sally approved. They made love now instead of indulging a mutual flair for gymnastics. It seemed to threaten nobody and Sally almost came to think of it as a pension for a fading dancer.

But it was curious that Pieter had insisted on such a public place, such a crowded, oily, star-fucking beach. They ate an inevitable salade Niçoise at Chez Felix, stayed inevitably at the Carlton.

And then, horribly, Sally understood what game Pieter was playing.

'I have to have drinks after dinner,' he said, 'with the Grunwalds. They own that other stuffy hotel in town.'

'Isn't that a little tacky, Pieter? When I'm here?'

'I need your moral support.'

'But they're your wife's family.'

'They understand about things like us,' Pieter said. 'You'll see.'

Sally forked anchovy and potato into her mouth. Chez Felix, she noted, did not believe in the pure Niçois version of salade Niçoise. 'Do they want money?' she asked.

'How did you guess?'

'I didn't think the Grunwalds would troop down to Cannes to see you and your mistress if they weren't in some kind of trouble. Besides, I read the financial pages.'

'I'm glad you're on my side. You're bright.'

'I thought bankers liked dumb, fluffy blondes.'

And they ordered coffee.

Somehow, that warm, bright evening, oil still on their lips, they wandered almost by mistake to bed. They undressed each other slowly and affectionately, lay in each other's arms until the wonderful, inevitable urgency of feeling set them toiling pleasurably together.

'My God,' Pieter said, 'the Grunwalds.'

'Where are we meeting them?'

'They're coming here. At ten.'

Their watches said ten minutes to ten. They scrambled, sticky with love, into clothes and settled in the drawing room of their suite looking distinctly tousled. 'Have a drink,' Sally said. 'It'll be a sort of alibi.'

Messieurs les Barons we announced and their entrance was frosty, except for the complications, cross and annoying, of manoeuvring Gilles into a room. 'Very vulgar,' Gilles said, not under his breath. 'Cannes in July, indeed.'

Edouard and Hugh were crisp with rectitude as usual. Hugh asked if perhaps the talk could be in private. He glared at Sally.

'I don't have secrets from Miss Rogerson.'

'But this is family business,' Hugh said. 'In front of a stranger . . .'

'Miss Rogerson knows my business.'

'Christ,' said Gilles, who had found the bar. 'Not knocking off your secretary, are you?'

Sally liked Gilles. In a room stiff with pomposity, he was the only one to bellow when he felt like it. 'I'm a dancer,' she said and smiled sweetly.

'A dancer,' Gilles said, letting the word trail on the air and acquire a string of meanings.

'Very well,' said Hugh. 'I should still prefer to talk in private, but if you insist.'

Pieter smiled.

Hugh cleared his throat and began. 'We have some temporary embarrassment, Pieter. In several parts of our business. We have a minor problem at the bank and, with one or two other things, it seems, quite frankly, that we might have a liquidity problem. Our cash flow position is not favourable.'

'You mean,' said Pieter, 'you're in trouble.'

'And things aren't going to get better,' Gilles said. 'Not without some help.'

'Come now, Gilles, I wouldn't say that.' Edouard was clearly offended. 'Our long-term prospects are excellent. It is only in the short term . . .'

'Things are so bad,' Pieter said, 'you want to keep it in the family.'

'If you had ever been in this kind of trouble, we would have helped.'

'But I never was. And I was never likely to be.'

'I really think,' Edouard said, 'your friend might leave us. We have figures to discuss and I am sure you understand the need for confidentiality.'

'I'd rather go,' Sally said. 'Please let me go, Pieter.'

'No,' Pieter said. 'I want you here.'

There was a moment of risky silence.

'Very well,' said Hugh. There was no grace in his defeat. He shot Sally through with offended glances. He told the story of the silver mines, the *petits mineurs* who were holding the Grunwalds to ransom, the peculiar problem that as the silver markets soared, the cost to the Grunwalds of taking the silver from those distant South Pacific islands soared even faster. And Hugh admitted, with some pain, that the Grunwalds' bank had made mistakes, especially the central mistake of becoming a *banque de dépôts* and playing down its traditional merchant banking.

'You mean you didn't want to do anything new,' Pieter said.

'Pieter, please let me tell you about our position. I'm sure we will disagree about what led to that position.'

'Supplicants,' Gilles snorted. 'That's what we are. And penitents. If the priest wants to lecture us, he can. He's our only hope for absolution.'

'Maybe you should do penance,' Pieter said. 'I don't want to hear the rest of this just now. I don't see the point of my committing money to prop up a losing situation. I need figures – the situation, what you need, what you plan to do about it. This has to have at least the shape of a business deal.'

'Very well,' Edouard said, stirring from his silence. He made himself add: 'Is Katherine well?'

'In excellent health,' Pieter said, 'when I left London.'

'You can have the figures tomorrow morning, if you want,' Hugh said.

The Grunwalds trooped out, followed at an inevitable distance by the wheeling, swearing Gilles. When he was the last left, and in the doorway, he said: 'You shouldn't have done it, you know. Not brought the woman. It makes Hugh understand how bad things are, when he can't afford to walk out.'

'Good night, Gilles,' Pieter said.

'Good night to you and your lady. She has a lot more sense and dignity than you do.'

'You said it yourself. I'm a newcomer. A parvenu.'

'You're a shit,' Gilles said. Down the corridor towards the elevators he was still muttering to himself: 'Shit, shit, shit.'

Van Helding called Paris the next morning, and by the time the Grunwald family had reached the bank, a line of shares in Grunwald Frères had been summarily dumped on the Bourse.

Edouard looked at the tapes. It was one of those sunny mornings when every share price that isn't stable, is up. Only the Grunwalds were visibly bucking the trend.

'Damn the man,' Edouard said.

'We always meet at parties,' Marisia said.

Alexander Fairbairn beamed. This time, now that Marisia's own troubles were under control, he came more clearly into focus. He had the huge bulk of a ruined athlete, a ruddy, short-tempered, forceful man. He would have been a quite usual head of some family conglomerate, but as a banker he jarred. He liked publicity; he had been known to drop the bank's prime rate a day before it was strictly wise for the sake of public attention. A century before, he would have driven railroads across America or built cities of steel or given the Rockefellers a fight for control of oil, but now he lived in a time where the only game for a roaring boy was money. He gave Security National identity and notoriety – made it seem more than the sum total of its electronic transfers.

'And this,' Marisia said, 'is David Grant. My husband.'

They were before dinner on the Upper East Side, drinking champagne and chatting amiably, and Fairbairn seemed rather more interested in David Grant than Marisia could easily explain.

'You're a journalist? London paper?'

David Grant produced the three or four sentences that were his conversational calling card.

'What does someone like you do after forty?' Fairbairn asked. 'Can't be too damn amusing running after battlefields all your life.'

'You edit, I suppose.'

'A paper?'

'That's a different story. Editing a paper is politics. Editing a page or two is journalism.'

'But you'd be happy to stay in journalism?'

'I guess,' David Grant said. 'I suppose all of us get restless . . . have the idea that there's a real world out there that we'd like to be part of. The trouble with journalism is that you're always observing. Things happen to other people and other people make things happen. It's other people that find things out, and we dash along and report what they find. It's why financial writers end up in banks and brokerage – it's because they get frustrated with being the voyeur.'

'I suppose newspapers change things,' Fairbairn said.

'I'm not too keen on being examined myself – not by some tribe of liberal cocksuckers who fake their own expenses and talk about fiscal morals. You're not one of those?'

'As it happens,' Grant said, 'I don't think so. I've tried to make sense of some big financial stories and what I've usually found is that nobody can. The insiders say you get the detail all wrong, but they're so far inside, they don't see what the whole picture means. And the outsiders always claim they can't understand, because the English are proud of not knowing arithmetic. They don't want to see that money shapes all their lives.'

'You ever work for British Intelligence?'

'I couldn't say if I did.'

'You ever take risks – real risks, body risks?'

'I suppose. I've been shot at.'

'Can you shoot back?'

Grant shrugged.

Marisia had drifted off to a knot of friends whom her mother had once known – people in their thirties, too, and fading. They had nice, firm bodies, and their minds had suffered the regular assaults of drugs and therapy and faiths that lasted a year. They had been into Pink Floyd, mescaline, Est, analysis, cocaine, assertiveness training. At twenty, it had looked like experimentation. At thirty, it looked like the next doctor's office or weekend session or needle would solve all problems. At close to forty, their air was becoming desperate.

It wasn't happy, talking to them. Marisia broke away soon. She hated their failure to understand and manage themselves. They felt bottled and constrained if anyone suggested that it might be better if they didn't let out anger, if they moderated themselves. They lashed out like children, tired after a hard life. They believed they were perfectible, and they could not live with anything less; the idea that you are both your virtues and your defects, did not appeal to them.

She found she couldn't any longer deal with them. The jargon grated on an unkind ear, and she missed both irony and self-deprecation. They couldn't imagine the world had not been delivered to them – as in the late 1960s it had, for their consideration, approval, or reorganization. It was arrogance, blind arrogance, and also ignorance, but diffused among so many people that its real nature was made invisible.

Fairbairn welcomed her back. She had the distinct sense she had interrupted something important which couldn't continue while she was there, but he seemed friendly enough. And he had once offered to take away her burdens and buy out her Kellerman Unger shares. She liked him very much for that.

After dinner, Fairbairn proposed drinks at his apartment. David Grant said to Marisia, while the banker went to the men's room: 'It's like a job interview. I don't know what the hell he wants, but he's interviewing me.'

Fairbairn lived in the River House, in style. He apologized for his wife's absence; she was, he said, in Florida. He poured stiff drinks.

He said to David Grant: 'Why the hell haven't you asked me what all this is about?'

Grant shrugged.

'You think I always cross-question people at parties? Part of the image?'

'It's a rough image,' Grant said. 'People say you always carry a pearl-handled Colt.'

'You think that's ridiculous?'

'It doesn't sound likely for the chairman of a bank.'

'You want to see?' Fairbairn dug for a photograph in an album. It was a shot of his New York office – ficus, official taste, corporate art – and of his desk. On it were two things: the Colt and a sign saying 'think'.

David Grant grinned.

'I'll tell you why you're here. I want an assistant. I might want someone like you.'

Marisia said: 'I think I want another drink.'

'If you want to come into the real world, then welcome. I need someone I can trust, someone who can dig, someone who knows about money but isn't snarled up in the money machine. Just like you said.'

'This is very flattering, but . . .'

'You'll hear rumours. Would you tell me what rumours you hear about this bank?'

David Grant said: 'They say you're being raided.'

'Do they say who by?'

Marisia said: 'What do you mean, raided?'

'Someone,' Fairbairn said, 'is buying up parcels of shares in Security National. People with nominee accounts who don't have to say who they are.'

'You know who?' David Grant asked.

'I know what sort of people,' Fairbairn said. 'You only have to look at the banks involved. They're all of them Mob.'

'You couldn't say that in print without being sued to death.'

'But it's true,' Fairbairn said. 'The question is who's behind it and what they want. It wouldn't be the first time the Mob has gone after banks. They did in the 1930s, when the banks didn't have cash and the Mob came in with sacks of nice dollar bills – fresh out of the laundry.'

'And you don't want to risk the Mob walking into Security National through the back door?'

'Listen. We have commissions in this country on organized crime and task forces and God knows what. People say it isn't the Mafia, that's an insult to Italian Americans. They say it doesn't exist, the Mob. But there is such a thing as organized crime, and it has to operate its money at a smart level. It has to hide it, use it, make it earn. I don't want to be used for that.'

'You want me to find out what the FBI and your own people can't?'

'You operate differently. You're not the cops; people won't be scared of you. You're not official, either. You can keep your mouth shut if you have to.'

'If I did this . . .'

'If I offered it,' Fairbairn said.

Neither of them seemed to have any doubts.

It was a curious trail – martini by martini, sometimes Nautilus machine by Nautilus, or lunch by lunch. David Grant was busy tripping up a rumour so he could see its face.

He lunched at the Broad Street, played squash at the New York Athletic Club, had brisk useful drinks with commuters on their way back to Greenwich. He found the process exhilarating – not just the hunt but also the billions riding on it.

At the Harvard Club, in the high-panelled barracks of a dining room, he ate with Regina Gloucester. She was a handsome, fiftyish woman who suckled on substantial vodka rocks, a stock analyst of distinction who knew banks and brokerage houses inside out. She had that brisk, self-effacing intelligence shared by women of her age who had had to play down their brightness early in careers surrounded by anxious men.

'Nobody's buying Security National,' she said. 'Not unless they're up to something. I mean, it's not bail-out time, either, but it's certainly not a time to buy.' She put a fork through the skin of her shad roe. 'They've got problems – usual sort of thing. Capital – not enough equity for the scale of their business – but then Chase has got that problem, too. They're pretty tightly held. Mind you, that would make them a perfect target for a takeover – not many parcels of shares to buy, and all the shares together don't add up to more than a fraction of the assets. Could be a good buy.'

'But is anyone doing that?'

'Maybe. Maybe not. Probably not American, if someone is moving – bank commissioners don't like the idea of raiding, and they don't like the idea that Americans would hide their intentions with nominee accounts. They like warehousing even less. Mind you, it could be someone less than scrupulous over here – a lot of talk about the Mob and the banks who've been involved in buying. You might think the Mob was trying to take over a member of the New York Clearing House. That would be a first.'

'What worries me,' David Grant said, 'is why they want Security National. It's such a complicated manoeuvre taking over a bank, you'd think nobody would start it unless – unless the target was vulnerable for some reason.'

'Vulnerable?' Regina rolled her eyes. 'Where do I start? That bank is twenty years out of date. It doesn't know how to control its junior management – they fire a few from time to time *pour encourager les autres*, but that's all. They've got US oil and gas loans you wouldn't believe, and God help them if the price of oil ever goes down. They've been battered in foreign currency. It isn't even crooks and scandal; it's lousy judgement. And they have the problem everyone else has – they want money market rates, and they don't like old-fashioned industry, so they're heavy in short-term money to companies that can't get cash any other way. When that's over – God help them, again. They're dead in the water.'

'Someone said something about repo deals.'

'They have trouble with repo deals? Maybe. It's a crazy business, that.'

'I didn't know exactly what a repo deal . . .'

'And you a foreign correspondent,' Regina said. 'You

should spend more time on money.' She accepted raspberries. 'That's the end of the seminar. And fair's fair. If you find anything out, you let your old mother know.'

'I will,' David said, 'if I can.'

He walked down Fifth Avenue in pale sunshine to the Century. He had arranged to meet a financial journalist, a patrician from Old New York money who had been wonderfully infected with print at an early age. Since his day's work was almost done, the journalist was expansive, settling on the first landing of the stairs with a grand and marbled view of the entrance below.

'Repos,' he said, thoughtfully. 'I suppose you want to know what they are. They're a good, old-fashioned money shuffle that made sense once – when money was cheap. Now, they're a little like watching a bank play Chinese checkers while pouring money down a well. Other people's money, of course; this is still banking.'

'Fine,' said David Grant. 'If you think I might grasp the point . . .'

'Government bonds. Take a bond. Any bond. What is it? It has a face value, a value at which it can be traded, and interest which it earns. Point one. Point two. If someone bought the bond for three months and then sold it back to the original owner, he'd collect the interest. The original owner might want the interest when he got the bond back, but even so the buyer would have the money for three months or so. If he didn't have to pay the original owner too much for the privilege of doing the deal, he might even be borrowing cheaply. And the original owner, of course, is fine: at the end of three months, he's got interest and bond back in his pocket, plus whatever the buyer paid for the deal.'

'Wait a minute,' David Grant said. 'Why doesn't the original owner just hang on to the bond, draw the interest and invest it in more bonds?'

The journalist beamed. 'You're doing well,' he said.

'Because the original owner is not the original owner. This is like Agatha Christie. The person who does the selling is just the bank. The original owner is some big brokerage house pledging collateral for a loan. And the buyer – the one who has the bond for three months – is a firm that deals in government securities, surprise, surprise. Call them the Dealers, the bank the Bank, the brokers the Brokers.

'Now you see the game. The bonds always belong to the Brokers, who eventually pocket the interest they pay, but the Bank actually holds them. The Bank sells and buys back with the Dealers – lends the bonds, if you like, and the use of the interest. They get maybe four or five points on the deal.'

'But that's about a third of what they would get in the money markets. Isn't it?'

'Yes.'

The journalist had the pleasurable twinkle of a man who knows he is about to prove his great superiority.

'Then why . . .'

'You really should know by now. If there is one thing that rules bankers, it's habit. It was once a good thing to do repo deals, so they go on doing them. A credit record is really only a banker making sure he has the habit of lending to you.'

'And why is it that every time I hear the word repo, I hear the word trouble? It can't just be that banks are losing out on a few points of interest.'

'Lord, no,' the journalist said. 'The real problem is the people they're dealing with. Here they are, lending someone else's property for a profit, and the people who get it – they're relatively small. Banks lend billions to little firms with a capital base of maybe five million at best. Nothing will ever stop a banker's habit – not sense, not prudence, not nothing.'

'So if they went wrong . . .'

'Think of it,' the journalist said. 'Banks lose millions. Face lost everywhere. And worst of all, if the dealers didn't pay the interest on the bonds, there'd be open war between big brokers and big banks. It's the kind of scenario Wall Street learns to fear. Except, of course, in this case, nobody will ever understand repos if there is a collapse.'

'And names?'

'I shouldn't tell you this . . .' the journalist had begun to twinkle quite alarmingly '. . . but yes, one. Ironside Securities. Run by my first cousin four times removed. Backed by Security National. Big loans to a slack young man.'

Grant thanked him effusively and caught a cab to the 13th Street Health and Racquets club. He crossed the astroturf, was duly dazzled by the girls and chrome, and met his opponent for squash – a young broker, slightly wrecked from his noontime line of cocaine bought in Trinity churchyard (like other brokers, he took his lunch there).

'Big money,' the broker said. 'Someone big is after your new boss.'

'American?'

The broker was having a moment of acrobatic difficulty with a jockstrap that tangled itself around feet and legs.

'Damn it,' he said. 'No. European. Foreign, anyway. Or laundered money.'

And at six thirty, tired and brisk, Grant had hared uptown again to the Oak Room in the Plaza.

'Funny you asking all this,' his contact said. 'There was a man called Koolhoven from Kellerman Unger asking me all about Security National. More about the bank than the bid, though. I suppose your wife would know him, wouldn't she?'

It took character to avoid whistling, or frowning, or leaping up.

'Really,' David Grant said. He thanked God for an English accent; to Americans, even English surprise sounds laconic and drawled.

'Of course,' he said. 'It couldn't be Kellerman Unger who want Security National?'

And he knew the answer, already.

The chandeliers at the Metropolitan fly upwards, as they once did in Viennese theatres, but instead of a practical splutter of candles rising out of sightlines, there is the vision of ugly electric lights with a life of their own. It is hard to forget the chandeliers weren't needed in the first place.

There was no time to talk. David Grant had dressed for the eight o'clock gala, and Marisia was ready for him. They had arrived in time to be polite to their companions, barely. The chandeliers rose, the curtains parted, and a social obligation began.

Nureyev was dancing, a gala performance. Marisia remembered the old London days when girls waited three thick at Covent Garden stage doors, fainting and writhing. She remembered, also, Nureyev's extraordinary presence on the stage – a romantic body full of romantic powers. It had been like watching dreams, concentrated into one man. It was a little less like that, now. The elevations, the turns were there, but sometimes the movement did not have the elasticity she remembered. And yet the man soared; he took the stage by a moment of force and held it, he danced in glory.

There was a partner of his in a Merce Cunningham piece – Sally Rogerson. She intrigued Marisia. She had the utter lack of fuss and ostentation that Fonteyn once had – no signals that great technique was to be expected, only moments of wonder when it appeared. She was tall, lovely, agile in the lights. Marisia wondered why she mattered.

Afterwards, there were obligatory drinks. Nureyev came off stage with the thick, white pancake make-up streaked and sweated, like a pantomime clown *in extremis*, and Marisia watched, amid congratulations, the process by which he changed. The paint was stripped, the face restored to high Tartar cheekbones and warm, charming eyes, and a clear capacity for imperious will. And Nureyev wanted to go dancing, now. Dancing somewhere sociable, coming down from the high of the exertion on the stage.

Sally Rogerson was a few doors down the wasteland corridor. Marisia had been taken enough with her performance to want to acknowledge her. With David in tow she knocked on Sally's door.

The door opened after a minute. A dresser held it. Inside, Sally Rogerson was talking to Pieter Van Helding. They seemed like intimate companions, sure of each other, and very close. Their movements, their standing suggested not simply friends and lovers but also – something Marisia could not, would not tolerate. Someone else had blurred the lines – between sister and lover, lover and friend. This time, it was a woman who seemed to be lover first and sister second.

Marisia couldn't speak. Pieter saw her, and he knew what was happening in her heart and mind. She was jealous, unable to articulate any feeling and furious that she had made herself so open and exposed. She was standing at a door where she expected nothing except to give polite congratulations to an artist, and her life had been presented to her in one moment.

'Marisia,' Pieter said. 'I had no idea . . .'

'No,' Marisia said. 'I didn't either.'

'You know Sally Rogerson: Prima ballerina *assoluta*?'

'*Assolutamente* not,' Sally said.

'You were,' Marisia said, her sentence breaking its back, 'wonderful.'

'Thank you. I feel like a tired bitch.'
'You'll come to supper?' Marisia asked.
Pieter and Sally looked at each other. Marisia was capable in her own right of moments of great imperiousness and this was one. She stood rigid, insistent, fierce. She was angry at the thought that Pieter and Sally might disappear together. She wouldn't tolerate it.
'I'd love supper,' Sally said. 'But I think I have to sleep. It's like after a workout, you know.'
'Nureyev was thinking of going on.'
'Nureyev,' Sally said, 'won't get up until five tomorrow and I have to do a publicity interview.'
The dresser closed the door. David Grant took Marisia's hand, and she pulled away from him. Damn it, someone else had taken her place as Pieter's heart and centre. That was it. She didn't care if it was foolish to want exactly the role she had rejected again and again; it made her no happier that someone else had assumed it.
On the way back to the inevitable party, Grant told Marisia about his day of sleuthing. He said Pieter was after Security National.
Marisia was steely. 'He's good,' she said. 'He ought to have a New York bank.'
'You know who he is. You know who backs him.'
'I don't much care,' Marisia said. 'I'm not responsible for civic morals. I'll change if ever I'm elected president.'
'But think of those Palm Springs people . . .'
'They're clever. They're fine. It is no business of mine even to think that I should improve the way they do business. I don't feel responsible for that. The rules change, but they change themselves, and I'm sure Pieter has to operate within the rules more or less. Why shouldn't he have a New York bank? Perhaps he could make the New York Clearing House efficient. Nobody else can.'
'But on moral grounds . . .'

'You never have talked morality to me,' Marisia said, 'and you never should. It doesn't concern me. I worry a little about how well my money is invested, and that is that. I don't need your suburban troubles.'

'You call it suburban if . . .'

'For God's sake,' Marisia said. 'Drop the whole subject. Just because Alexander Fairbairn writes your cheques, you think you owe him everything.'

'You don't want Pieter to triumph, do you? Pieter who tried to ruin your career?'

'You want me to act for revenge if I won't think morality?'

'He tried to wreck you. Now you could ruin his plans.'

'Why should I want to?'

'I don't know exactly,' David Grant said. 'I just know that you do.'

Marisia stared ahead. The lights of the avenues dazzled her, and when they dived through Central Park towards the party, the darkness was almost a blessing. In the moments between the walls of the road across the park she said: 'What can I do?'

'Make a fuss. Vote your shares. Go public with any doubts you have. Make it a matter of banker's movie sister tells all. You can get the Press to listen; I know that.'

'What good would that do?'

'Any delay means people can start asking questions – about where Pieter's money comes from, about the Palm Springs connection, all of that. The more questions, the less the authorities will feel they can rubber-stamp the deal. The less rubber-stamping, the more chance the whole deal fails.'

'You're asking more patience than I ever had,' Marisia said.

But she remembered the sight of Sally Rogerson and Pieter, and she remembered Pieter in the studio park lot telling her she would never work again, and she was sure she was going to fight.

It was a night when the city seemed darker, richer, warmer – like some terrible image in an Old Master held under varnish. Jan Unger walked out into the streets and crossed a bridge and began to stride out. He loved Amsterdam. He regretted that his escape to Cuernavaca had been at least delayed. He regretted that he was still in the city where his own bank stood, now under a kind of alien control. But he loved the city. He had done almost anything to survive there. They could take away almost anything from him, but that would remain.

The streets seemed peculiarly empty. He was aware of the faces and shapes of the few people walking with him; they were so few that they could not blur into a crowd.

He could even hear the black Mercedes.

It was Koch, he thought, and the people from the hunting lodge, who seemed to pursue him now in dreams and substance. All around him, the familiar, friendly city seemed to be a trap. He couldn't leave; Gregory had seen to that. He couldn't win; Van Helding had seen to that. But he needed to go; without escape, he was destroyed; his friends, the old men at the hunting lodge, had seen to that. He couldn't explain to them why he knew Noam Gregory. He couldn't . . .

'I think,' the big man said, 'you'd better get in.'

When it happened, the realization of a paranoiac dream, he was quite unsurprised. Of course they would take him in a dark car, through empty streets to meet his fate. Of course they would confront him with his derelictions and his failures.

But he didn't know who they were. He sat in the back of the black Mercedes, and he did not even guess. They could be Gregory's men, Van Helding's men, the men from the hunting lodge. They could be anyone at all. He had been taken into a kind of limbo, as interrogators try to take their victims into a place without time or identity. He was vulnerable to anyone. He did not know the right thing to say. They had taken him and put him outside any rules he understood.

Then all that happened was a mission, an errand. He was to deliver a parcel of files to Gilles de Grunwald. He could deliver them, if he wished, at the Grunwald's ball. There was no need for ostentation; a quiet, discreet delivery was all that was necessary. But it must be personal.

That was all they wanted.

He tried to ask if they knew Koch, if they were from the hunting lodge, who they were. But he realized that in talking with Gregory, in seeming alarmed at the moves against Van Helding, he had forfeited the right to be admitted any longer to the reasons why things happen. He could only act as he was told, uncertain who would act against him if he did not.

He held the envelope cautiously as he left. He knew what it must be. If he was curious to open it, he would die. If he left it to the Baron Gilles, the Baron Gilles would die. Only on a night like the Grunwalds' ball would a personal gift from Jan Unger go unnoticed, until it was too late.

Then he could no longer love the streets and canals of Amsterdam. He was too aware that now he was not a man; he was a shadow, made and manipulated by someone else.

He walked down a street he knew, and did not fit it any more. He had been made less than a stick-man; he was transparent, without substance, as good as dead. And yet the envelope fascinated him. Perhaps it was not a bomb, after all, only files that were important.

He found he could believe anything.

* * *

The townhouse of the Baron Gilles de Grunwald was bathed in a wash of sinister light. Red carpet became a dark stain, overlooked by gargoyles, and roses turned black like old blood. In a high wall, vampires assembled through the metal detectors and entered a high-ceilinged world of images – hologram bats circling and shrilling around dimmed chandeliers, retainers dressed like humpbacked monks or mindless men or girls with single eyes, dry ice in the air and round the food. At the head of the grand stairway, a hologram woman dressed in wide skirts from the eighteenth century beckoned soundlessly to the crowds below, repeating her invitation every 2.92 minutes.

Gilles de Grunwald thought the place would be hard to defend. He didn't understand why none of his sources said the party would be attacked. There was always at least one rumour about so ostentatious an event, particularly when it involved old Jewish money. He wondered why all the people, from the post-punk monsters to the dowagers, felt so secure.

Seraphine dressed as lady of the manor, the role she played best in life. 'I don't see Pieter or Katherine,' she said, anxiously. 'I do think people will talk if they don't come.'

'They will come together, I suppose?' Edouard asked. 'I really think Pieter might come with that dancer again.'

'They know what is appropriate,' Seraphine said grimly. She had almost dropped her aristocratic pose by saying 'respectable'.

She knew who would make this party work as an affirmation of the Grunwalds' power – which bankers, ministers, industrial barons, young persons who are noticed, would together guarantee success. She checked them off a mental list. But nobody was more needed than the Van Heldings. Nobody.

A predator lady, sharp like a shark, moved through the crowd in a stunning frock and said to Seraphine: 'I don't see Katherine. I did so want to tell her about the new collections.'

'I think.' Seraphine said bitchily, 'she mostly wears Jean Muir.'

Creatures and tuxedos spilled into the garden, in a scent of perfume and roses and arc lights. It looked like old money building its follies and fantasies. Nobody grasped that the money was the greatest fantasy of all.

Gilles thought to call the Georges Cinq, but there was no answer from the Van Heldings' suite. He asked Edouard if they expected an answer about the bank that night, and Edouard said they did. No, nobody had talked about terms. Yes, it was odd that Van Helding had not yet made a proposal.

Seraphine threw open the library doors. Her wide, white gown was partly silhouetted, party glowing under one of the designer's ill-placed lamps.

'Come along,' she said to the men. 'Business can wait. We are all on duty tonight.'

Pieter was being sweet – kind and attentive, pleasant in manner, and pleasantly allowing his hands to stray. Katherine was appreciative. She moved sensuously under her satin gown, giggled a little, watched for his friendly reaction. On the way to the party, she snuggled on the back seat of the limousine and said, 'Now, now, now.'

Pieter smiled.

'I mean it,' she said.

When they finally arrived, the Baron Gilles stalked Pieter as much as his wheelchair would allow. He couldn't trap him easily, but he could follow. The Van Heldings worked each room with almost professional ease, making sure everyone knew they were there, and confirming all that the Grunwalds wanted.

'And perhaps we could offer you cognac?' Edouard said. 'In the library.'

Pieter said: 'It's such a good party, I hate to leave.'

'It's been so difficult to get hold of you.'

'I had business. In America.'

'We do seem to have rather a deadline. If we could talk . . .'

'You're sure the Countess Seraphine would want the others to know you were huddling with your banker – on a night like this?'

'With our friend,' Edouard said. 'Our family. Of whom we see far too little.'

The door shut out the party noises.

'Armagnac,' Pieter said. 'No cigar. I wouldn't insult your brandy.'

Pieter said: 'Kellerman Unger has commitments all over the world. We are very active. We don't have great pools of money waiting to be used. So you'll understand if I turn down your proposals.'

Edouard blanched – an unlovely endive yellow and white.

'But I do have another thought. We can provide the resources you need for operating expenses for the next eighteen months. Provided, that is, those expenses stay at the level you forecast in your papers.'

'I don't know how to thank you,' Edouard said.

'However,' Pieter said, and he waited for the conditional clause to strike proper terror. 'You'll understand that a deal of this size can't just be a matter of family. I can't cash your affection at any bank I know. And keeping the good name of European banking isn't a job for one small Dutch bank.'

Hugh squirmed sycophantically, as though to say that, of course, Kellerman Unger was so much more than a mere small Dutch bank.

'Don't keep us waiting,' Gilles said. 'Tell us the worst.'

'You can have the loan for three years. If you don't pay interest and capital in full at the end of that time, the title, name and business of the bank Grunwald Frères will revert to the original family holding company. And the collateral we want is fifty-one per cent of the family holding company.'

It took a minute for the brothers to think through the implications of Van Helding's offer. Gilles saw it first.

'Clever,' he said. 'We have cash for eighteen months. If we can't make that cash back in eighteen months after that, we lose our name. Is that it?'

'Our name,' said Hugh. This was slightly more than he could stomach, even at a moment of despair.

'I'm not interested in your industrial holding companies,' Pieter said. 'This deal is meant to save the name of the bank, and I want that name as collateral.'

'Very fair,' Gilles said. 'Almost too fair. If we can't save the name, he gets it. Of course, what it'll be worth if we can't save it is another question.'

'I'm sure Grunwald Frères will be an admirable subsidiary in France of Kellerman Unger,' Pieter said.

'Unthinkable,' Hugh said. 'To reduce the bank . . .'

'The bank's dying,' Gilles said. 'Don't try to dictate terms. We can't, not now.'

Pieter set down his glass and, with it, a bundle of papers.

'I am in no hurry for an answer,' he said. 'But then I imagine you're in a hurry to strike a deal.'

The library doors admitted the rush of the party, and then closed to shut it out again, as though a tide had passed. Van Helding was again among the pretty, and the disguised, and the rich.

'Shut up, Hugh,' Gilles said. It was all he would say.

The house was like a theatre Wurlitzer – all noise and tunes, effects and lights, glories rising with furies from the floor. Inside it, everyone knew the money machine that kept such parties rolling, but nobody wanted to think too closely about it. It was a fact, though, as tangible as the champagne or the caviar (Beluga, not Sevruga, Pieter noticed).

Katherine went to the bathroom by the garden, appointed for women. She soothed a make-up ruffled by strenuous dancing, and thought how young she looked. In a lavatory next door, there was a sudden sharp gurgling noise; an abandoned little animal sound. It might have been pleasure, but Katherine's instincts told her it was pain.

She pushed the lavatory door, carefully.

Her cousin Alain was sprawled, alone, with a hypodermic in his hand.

'Hello, Katherine,' he said. 'I'm going on holiday.'

There were new, red marks on Alain's arms, and signs of earlier bruising. The hypodermic tumbled out of his hand, and he grimaced as though his blood was rushing too fast and hard for his veins, and then he collapsed, smiling.

The leather man from the hallway, source of the glittering eyes, barged into the room and scooped Alain up. He flushed away a paper stained with powder, and the hypodermic. 'Go away, lady,' he said. 'There's nothing you can do. He's a fool speedballing here.'

Katherine went quickly. Things seemed to go wrong when they were going most right. She found Pieter again, smiled almost shyly, went out with him to the terrace behind the house, looking over metallic roses and open, glittering sky.

'Can we go home?' she said.

Gilles was at the door. Katherine remembered he was always near the door at parties, and she wondered why; she was very innocent about threats and security. He seemed vulnerable, scuttling like a land crab. He seemed to suffer something besides pain.

'Pieter,' Gilles said. 'I need a minute.'

'We were going . . .'

'This isn't business. Did you ask Unger to come? He's arrived on the steps and the guards don't know what to do.'

'I'm sure it's all right,' Pieter said.

'Oh yes,' Gilles said. 'I'm almost sure, too. You mean you didn't? You didn't ask him?'

'I didn't say anything. We don't have much to say to each other any more.'

'He says he has something to deliver to me.'

'Maybe he does.' Pieter shrugged. With Katherine, holding hands, he went down the steps past the little guard post where Unger was delayed. He did not acknowledge the man. Unger saw him pass and wondered yet again at how he had lost all power to choose, so late in his career. Nobody ever told him what to do, but he was here on orders, carrying out a commission, doing as he was told. Pieter was right to pass him by; it was hardly Jan Unger who stood here, waiting for the net of walkie-talkies and guards to pass on his admission.

Gilles let him in. He said he would meet him in the library, then changed his mind and set the garden. He had Unger shuffled through corridors along a distant route.

Out in the garden, Unger could see the wheelchair, for once without its attendant. Gilles seemed more shapeless and baggy than usual. It must be tiredness and the night.

Unger put his hand into the envelope to pull out whatever the hunting lodge wanted him to deliver.

'Here,' he almost said.

The blast was immediate and furious, but since it happened at a distance from the house – and by a wheelchair where a stuffed, straw dummy sat – it was hardly noticed.

It could have made Jan Unger a martyr.

Fairbairn would not use a lobbyist, yet. He disapproved of the new shingles hanging all over Washington, the new respectability of the paid persuaders. He thought of them as pimps, or worse, and not as servants of democracy. He preferred to rely on his own network.

Grant thought his methods too close to the golf-club locker room, too unsophisticated. Fairbairn liked to tell the truth, more or less, and not always spell out the advantage to a Congressman of helping him. He tried to argue ideas, in a simple, basic fashion. It would not have worked on some Congressmen, but it seemed to get Fairbairn one audience: Ryder, Representative from New York, a man like a sparrow, citywise and slightly seedy, with a protective coat of brown anonymity and sudden, birdy gestures when under stress. Ward bosses put him in power, a reward for long silence, and he was good at calculating when to say nothing. It was his major talent. But behind the vacant lot of a face, a mind did work – in slogans.

'I'm here,' Fairbairn said, over lunch, 'to express my concern. As a citizen talking to his Congressman, you understand.'

'And as a banker with problems,' Ryder said.

'We all have problems, God knows,' Fairbairn said. 'And God knows I would never ask for government help, in any way. We have to stand on our own two feet. Except, of course, we don't expect to hunt murderers or defend frontiers for ourselves, and I reckon when it's a question of defending national interests and preventing crime, a man can go to his Congressman. Don't you think?'

Ryder nodded. It was a good time to say nothing.

'Now if we allow foreign banks to take over our big banks,' Fairbairn said, 'you know what that means. It means control of who gets money in America – in your district, Congressman – has passed to Tokyo or London or Amsterdam or Hong Kong. They're the ones who decide where jobs go, which firms stay alive, what cities can borrow to keep going. Now American banks can't even operate in more than one state, in case they stop serving the state they belong to. Imagine what happens when an American bank isn't even sure it wants to be in America. It can take American money from depositors and put it anywhere in the world.'

'Like Chase Manhattan now,' Ryder said, with great reasonableness.

Fairbairn snorted. 'Hardly,' he said. 'Chase or Citibank or any of the others may do foreign business but when it comes down to it, they're still responsible to the Federal Reserve or the State Banking Superintendent. Who knows who these foreign banks will obey in an emergency?'

'We can always stop them doing business in America.'

'I wonder,' Fairbairn said. 'They'd say that was illegal interference with trade. You could be in court for a decade on that. Besides, who knows about these companies that come in? They have cash, sure, but they don't have to tell Washington where they get it or how much they've got. They don't even tell their own central banks. They might have any number of businesses that aren't banks, and they might give them all their money – which is something we can't do and we can't stop them doing. We don't know if money in those banks is safe or not. Why, London merchant banks are allowed to keep two sets of accounts: the ones they publish and the ones with the real profit and loss, that they keep very quiet. Who knows about institutions that can do that?'

Fairbairn had no shame. He had always criticized the ban on interstate banking – which confines banks to only one state of the union – and now he was praising the regulation as though it were the only thing preventing a pinstriped horde from descending on America and stripping away all her money. David Grant watched the old chameleon adjust his protective colours to the terrain. If he wanted new rules, he would have to praise the old ones.

'You don't, I suppose, have some immediate reason for all this?' Ryder said. 'Like someone trying to take over Security National?'

'Something's up,' Fairbairn conceded, grinning.

'It's an important issue,' Ryder said. 'I could schedule hearings but I don't want it to look as though I'm doing Alex Fairbairn's dirty work. Because,' Ryder said firmly, 'I'm not.'

'We'll have our own PR people and our shareholder outreach people working on this,' Fairbairn said. 'I'm not asking for a Congressional defence, just a chance to have these issues aired. So the next time that, say, a Hong Kong and Shanghai Bank wants to take over Marine Midland, we'll at least have thought about the national interest.'

'Or the next time someone comes raiding Security National?'

'It's the national interest, Bob,' Fairbairn said. He raised a glass, and Ryder raised his Perrier in a little claw. 'To the national interest.'

At eleven each morning, the officers of Kellerman Unger held their review meeting. Usually, it was a sparse affair. On Thursday, by tradition, everyone tried to attend. That Thursday, despite the bomb blast at the Grunwalds' the night before, there was the usual crowd in the grand, third-floor boardroom. There was an odd, marked disparity between the melodramatic standing of the bank – succouring the Grunwalds, trying to grab control of a major American bank, expanding to make reality out of long-nursed technicolour dreams – and the dull matter of the meeting. There were a pair of lacklustre loans to be debated, and that was almost that.

'Just so you all know how things stand in America,'

Koolhoven said, 'I gather our friends at Security National have started to ask questions.'

'I gather more,' Van Helding said. 'I think we can take it that they now know we're behind the buying. They can't prove it, of course, and I don't think they'll accuse us of organizing a warehouse for our stock. They can't go public quite yet.'

'Perhaps we should talk about Ironside,' Koolhoven said.

Pieter Van Helding frowned at him. 'Very well, gentlemen. Thank you for coming in this morning. I'm sorry there was nothing more exciting to discuss. I think Koolhoven and I can handle the other business.'

The other gentlemen left in a murmuring herd.

'I don't want Ironside talked about too publicly,' Van Helding said. 'Even inside the bank. I don't want to appear too Machiavellian.'

Koolhoven said: 'Sorry.'

'Not that it really matters,' Van Helding said. 'We may have laid the trap, but Security National walked right into it. It's their fault for being so heavy in the repo business without proper credit checks on their customers. It's their fault for trusting Ironside. Nobody told any lies about the company, after all.'

'If it's a trap,' Koolhoven said, 'is it time to spring it?'

'I think so. I want Security National to have some embarrassment before we go public with a bid. The weaker the management the more chance the stockholders will welcome us with open arms.'

'It's not that easy to force the issue,' Koolhoven said. 'I mean, Ironside has some capital, although not enough. If our friends failed to come up with the money they promised, Ironside might just mention the fact. That wouldn't look good – too calculated.'

'You should look at the books,' Van Helding said. 'I'm sure by now young Ironside is as stretched as he could be.

Hurting bad. It's just a question of whether deals are going his way, and since the market in T-bills isn't, I don't see much of a problem.'

'It's a risk,' Koolhoven said.

'It always was,' Van Helding said. 'It was just possible Ironside would make a brilliant success of it. The market was on his side for a long time. But I don't think he has done anything of the sort. I think he's ballsed it up, like we hoped.'

'His exposure must be appalling – twenty, thirty times his capital.'

'That'll look good when it's reported. Security National lends someone else's bonds to a dud company. That should make the network news.'

'I just worry if we can pull the rug.'

'We will,' Van Helding said. 'Leave it to me.'

There were tall varnished door and they were locked shut. The cleaners at eight had found the office barred. Nobody arrived for work at nine. At ten, the building's guards called the managing agents and at ten minutes past ten, a Federal Marshal arrived with a writ.

Ironside Investments were dead. It had become insolvent and the principals were not rushing to pick up the pieces. In fact, the principals seemed to be out of the country.

It took a little time for the news to reach Wall Street, but only a little. A frantic junior manager at Security National kept calling the Ironside number, to press for repayment of $110 million in interest that Ironside had taken from government bonds that now had to go back, with their earnings, to their original owner.

By eleven there was a sudden lull and then a panic in the government bond market. The hysteria of dealers in the pit, bellowing and mauling to do their deals, was quieted, and then redoubled. Nobody was sure quite what had happened, but they knew there was very bad news.

By eleven thirty, the *Post* and *News* business pages were pressing Security National for comment. By two that afternoon, the bank had declined comment to the *Wall Street Journal*, the *New York Times*, UP, API, the Dow Jones news service and a couple of TV stations.

Security National's management committee met at two fifteen. Stock in the bank tumbled $1.95 to $39.50, a low for the year. They had to get out a statement, however short and laconic, to specify how great the damage was. Rumour had put it up to $200 million and analysts like Regina were busily figuring what a dent the loss could make in Security National's profits. Other people were trying to work out the consequences if Security National decided to be strictly legalistic – to insist that it was Ironside's problem to pay the interest, and Security was only a middle man.

They puzzled over that possibility at Grant, FitzSimmons Lind, a massive Wall Street house whose chairman, Walter Gollinger, was an old friend of Alexander Fairbairn's. Gollinger went to Fairbairn's home at nine in the evening for drinks. He said he was concerned about the Ironside collapse. He said that, after all, the bonds in question belonged to Grant, FitzSimmons Lind.

'It isn't to be construed as a threat,' Gollinger said. 'You know that, Alex. But we are worried about the scale of the Ironside loss. If you couldn't make it good, we might have to think again about all that Security National paper in our money market funds. In fact, if we don't get the one hundred and ten million dollars, I think we wouldn't be able to keep any of that paper.'

'You mean you'd bounce us – from your whole funds?'

'I never threaten, Alex. I do hope we can come to an understanding.'

The management committee met twelve hours later, at

Security National's tower, and agreed that in the circumstances – Gollinger was an important circumstance – they would make good the loss. If Ironside couldn't pay over the interest it had been given, then Security National would. There was a lengthy memorandum about who had done what and why, written partly to calm staff fears and partly for leaking to an eager press. In it, Fairbairn said the bank took no responsibility for Ironside's collapse. However, since they had no wish to see the government interfering in the market, and they wanted to protect other brokers, they would magnanimously underwrite the loss – more, the memo implied, from a sense of civic duty than anything else.

At eleven thirty that morning the men from the Federal Reserve arrived. David Grant had never seen the deep anger of Alexander Fairbairn, but it came roaring up now like a twister on the plains.

'I don't know how to keep my temper with them,' Fairbairn said, 'I never have done. Maybe you'd better take my gun.'

Grant wondered how much Fairbairn was playing to the gallery, pretending a menace he did not plan to practise. He could sense the man's fury.

The two young officials had the blank faces of bureaucratic authority, impervious to displays of emotion in their clients or subjects.

'Naturally,' they said, 'we are very concerned.'

'A loss of one hundred and ten million,' Fairbairn said, icily, 'does not threaten the solvency of Security National.'

'Naturally not.'

'I should damn well think so.'

'Although we do detect some weakness in the balance sheet, which . . .'

'Please,' said Fairbairn, 'get to your point.'

'The matter of Ironside Securities,' the man from the Fed. intoned. 'We assume you will be absorbing the loss.'

'I dislike civil servants who make assumptions.'

'Perhaps we should be a little more direct. You lent large sums of money, including other people's bonds, to a tiny company with insufficient capital and no track record. I can't say that sounds prudent to me.'

'Have you ever run a bank? Eh?'

'Mr Fairbairn, I'm trying to be reasonable. Because of the lending, the firm thrived for a while. Because it has now collapsed, a number of institutions are seriously embarrassed. They can't absorb the trouble and you can. They might go under and take half a market with them. You won't. We're paying a tribute to your strength just by being here.'

'Just as well,' Fairbairn said.

'However,' said the man from the Fed., 'if you don't absorb the losses, we fear very disruptive effects. That is why we are talking to you as a matter of urgency.'

Fairbairn called for the memorandum and brandished it at the men from the Fed. They read, and although their faces remained impassive, you could almost detect disappointment. They had come for confrontation, not agreement.

'Well,' said the senior man, 'this does seem satisfactory.'

Fairbairn grinned.

'You bet your ass,' he said, injudiciously.

'Quite a flurry in New York,' Koolhoven said. 'Talk about the future of capital markets. And some very rude words for Security National.'

'It's like the best sort of clockwork toy,' Van Helding said. 'You wind it up, set it down, and let it destroy cities. I really thought it wouldn't be this simple.'

'You knew the men at the other end,' Koolhoven said. 'And you were absolutely right about them. They rushed into the trap.'

'I thought they'd go for anything that looked good in the money market, however bad the foundations. They're and old-fashioned bank and they don't have thc muscles for change. So they change desperately.'

'We ought to think about the formal offer now.'

'Not yet,' Van Helding said. 'I don't want to look as though I'm buying a dead bank, for a start. And I don't want to look as though I'm exploiting this sort of share-price weakness. We've got time, after all, and I'm fairly sure the share price won't recover for a bit. Isn't there some capital issue in the next month?'

'Like the Chase notes,' Koolhoven said. 'Fifteen per cent on the note, but you also sign a contract to buy shares in the bank within ten years – at a fixed price.'

'They're not going to sell those, not at the sort of share price Fairbairn's ego could stand. They'll find people paying other people to take the contract off their hands.'

'It sounds like the kind of issue that might remind sellers how much they want to sell,' Koolhoven said thoughtfully.

Van Helding helped that process. He and Katherine went whirling off in pursuit of assorted social and rich people, most of them, but not all, happened to be shareholders in Security National. They went from the Hamptons up to Maine, from Maine to Palm Beach, and back to the Mainline suburbs of Philadelphia. They had a weekend in the moneyed suburb of Pittsburgh, they went hunting in West Virginia and they absorbed the obligatory outdoor culture and the racing at Saratoga. Katherine spent the day draped in cold, wet sheets at the spa, in pursuit of the cure. She giggled about it a lot.

It was an almost royal progress. They went from the colonnades and great estates of Newport to the grotesqueries of Palm Beach. They coped with mannequin ladies of uncertain age who lived to dress and sharp old biddies who lived for money. There were men of business with political ambitions, and one politician from an old Social Register family who longed to be a cellist. It was rigorous work – social life, but also listening and prompting. They heard worries about Ironside, the effect on Security National, most of all the fact that the shareholders might have to make up their minds – or even make changes – about how the bank was run. For most of these people, the bank shares were an old holding. They liked the dividends, they wanted the stock price to rise, they thought of the bank as a kind of family heirloom, but they did not want to take an interest in it. Even when it was a sizeable part of their fortunes, they considered it the dull part of the portfolio.

By the end of the month, both Katherine and Pieter were longing to dine without evening dress, to eat food that was unpretentious, and to talk something short of the assorted apocalypses that the American rich lived to fear. Katherine had begun to develop car sickness, a defence against another tea party, another lady of a certain age.

And when Katherine went home – by Concorde, to assure attention, and with the gossip columnists told that Pieter had gone with her – Van Helding made a retreat. He needed somewhere anonymous, where nobody would even want to know who he was. He also needed somewhere to have meetings of utter discretion. He chose a string of motels in New Jersey, a few minutes from Manhattan and out of bounds to anyone using their real name. He paid his bills in cash, and took phone calls only as 'Mr Fairbairn'. He lived in tacky, unlikely neon palaces with water beds and adult movies and short-order diners. He refined the basic bid, took advice on valuations, reviewed his own information on the weaknesses of Fairbairn's position. He also asked intermediaries to find out, tactfully and generally, what view the New York State Banking Commission and the Federal Reserve might take of any bid.

He talked cold figures nightly, in the wet, flashy suburbs, numbed by the honky-tonk neon that winked in the motel windows.

It took three days. When he was satisfied he went back to London, anonymously. He was beginning to think of himself as a guerrilla, a financial fighter; he was beginning to take seriously the idea that he saved institutions, made things work. By the time he touched down in London, exhausted and overfull of gin on the daylight flight, he had an almost Messianic glow.

Koolhoven's big grey head was full of sleep. He turned in his chair and sighed. He wanted to sleep away his fears, but somehow they came bubbling back through the dreams and stayed with him.

Pieter Van Helding. He loved the man, he had taught the man, and now the man had taken an insignificant bank, and made it a power in London, and now he was aiming for New York. Koolhoven should have been proud, and in fact he was miserable. It had all become too violent, too cunning for him. He heard of Jan Unger's death, blown apart by some letter-bomb device in an outhouse in Paris and he could hardly believe his ears. He watched Pieter set traps for Security National and, although he admired the strategy and the elegance, he no longer felt confident that the next stage would not be some horror. There seemed very little Pieter Van Helding would not do to keep and expand his empire.

Koolhoven told himself he was being sentimental. Pieter was simply effective; he knew what games to play, and how to play them. Pieter was brilliant. Pieter was . . .

Of course, it hardly mattered now what happened in the distant past. Once Van Helding had made the move to London, all the curiosities of Amsterdam began to seem remote, even the death of Jan Unger. Once Van Helding was in New York no doubt the oddities of London would seem equally remote – exactly who was Dr Rolfe, and why was his control of the bank so carefully masked through Liechtenstein and Panama, and who, if anyone, ran Dr Rolfe? Each success – the great tower block in London, the company takeovers, the deals to buy firms, sell off their property assets, and start to run the business – made the origins of Van Helding's power seem less important. He was the right man to have power. Of course he was. It was silly to imagine anything else.

And then Marisia Van Helding had called. She wanted to know what notice had to be given of a shareholders' meeting. She wanted to demand one.

Koolhoven had gone back to the articles of association, usually a document from pure theory, and he discovered that with more than 5 per cent of the voting shares under her control she could ask for a meeting at any time.

What the hell was she doing? Wasn't she close to Pieter? If she had turned to the other side, followed David Grant to Fairbairn's camp, then there could be serious and nasty trouble.

He couldn't sleep. He could shut his eyes and watch a zoatrope of animated monsters parading in an endless circle. He remembered the Widow Van Helding, and the children on the beach – always that image, the children so innocent and so deadly on the beach – and Pieter in the gold vaults, and a whole, shared history that meant also a shared responsibility. Pieter Van Helding had been Koolhoven's creation, until he broke loose. He was Koolhoven's fault.

He startled himself awake.

7

'It's war,' David Grant said. 'I saw it on the tapes.'

Alexander Fairbairn pushed a heavy buff envelope across his desk, as cautiously as he might handle a letter bomb. 'This just arrived,' he said. 'See what you think.'

'He's generous,' David said. 'Cash for thirty-one per cent, he reckons he has twenty, and stock for the rest. That's not bad at all.'

'It's good to know we got the right enemy.'

'What do we do officially?'

'Listen,' said Fairbairn, 'to a lot of fat-assed lawyers. You can't begin to imagine how many of them are going to come here in the next twelve hours. Lawyers and brokers and bankers and the shareholder outreach people – bastards. They take a fee to ring up all the people they say we should have known better all along. They speak for us.'

'And, of course, our case is ready.'

'Of course not. I need a day with the lawyers just to find out what I'm allowed to say. I think the law says you can't call your enemy a Mafia thug without proof.'

Fairbairn was tense like wire, and dangerous. The big man radiated anger, in part to hide his sense of real fear.

Lawyers did arrive, in bluebottle battalions, expensive as sin. They proposed alternatives. Complaints to the Securities and Exchange Commission about dealings in Security National stock before the bid was announced; a sniff of insider trading excited the watchdogs. An informal approach, also, to the New York State Banking Commission, since unlike other big Eastern banks, Security National was not a National Association answering to

Washington but a bank under State regulations. They talked with their friends at the Federal Reserve office in New York, rather stiffly. They proposed searches in London and Amsterdam, of extreme sophistication and expense. Then they told Fairbairn he would lose, eventually, unless he could swing the shareholders in a public campaign. He had to work the phone like the shareholder outreach people were doing. He had to make public statements that made sense. He might even consider announcements that otherwise would have been delayed – good news announcements, of course; and he might delay those which put the bank's management in a less good light.

They were not optimistic about Fairbairn's suggestion that he tell the truth about Pieter Van Helding. A libel suit was not impossible, they said; while Van Helding was a public figure, Fairbairn's own position made almost anything he said open to the construction of malice. That could cost a great deal of money, and shut up discussion just when it needed to be most open and heated.

Fairbairn was like a child with teachers. He listened, he learned, and he resented. When the lawyers left, he spat very deliberately in the corner of his carefully carpeted office, with its civic art and its Bloomingdale's taste. He needed to blaspheme against the proprieties that hemmed him in.

At nine he expected a friend for drinks. Alex Fairbairn was old-fashioned enough to reckon he had friends and enemies, not just class analogues. He thought Gorringer of Grant, FitzSimmons Lind was such a friend. Gorringer had the massive brokerage house, a sense of politics and a conventionally handsome fiftyish face, kept taut by tennis, yachting and its failure to show emotion. He could show intelligence but not his motives; and that was a huge advantage.

Gorringer liked Fairbairn, but did not admire him. Fairbairn seemed part of a lost generation – born to be a Commodore Vanderbilt or an Andrew Carnegie or an original Rockefeller. Born in a time of mogul power, Fairbairn had lived to the time of the multinationals, whose personality outshone their bosses'. Fairbairn was out of date. Yet Gorringer would humour him. He went remembering a ten o'clock dinner date and determined to arrive on time.

'I suppose,' he said, after a few polite preliminaries, 'you want to know if we want to buy a bank.'

Fairbairn said: 'I'm glad I don't have to sell myself.'

'It's an idea,' Gorringer said. 'Maybe we do need a bank. We work through one in Ohio just now, but I suppose we could work through one we owned.'

'And very soon, when interstate banking becomes legal, you'd already have a bank to expand nationwide. Not just New York State, like now.'

'Maybe, ' Gorringer said.

'I want to level with you,' Fairbairn said. 'We're an outfit with huge assets and a capitalization in the market that doesn't match. Anyone who buys us gets something cheap. But if someone unfriendly, who doesn't know the New York rules, gets control of Security National, then it's the end of our comfortable system here. And that someone could get us for virtually nothing.'

'I'm glad you sorted out the Ironside business,' Gorringer said. He tried not to look at his watch too ostentatiously. 'I didn't want to fall out over something so trivial.'

'It wasn't trivial,' Fairbairn said. 'I changed the way we look at middle managers' decisions because of that. We train them, we prepare them, and then we trust them, and maybe that's our mistake.'

'I don't think I know what my retail brokers do in my name half the time,' Gorringer said.

'We still have the deposit base, the branch network, the overseas business. We still have the balance sheet.'

'I couldn't do a sweetheart deal. It would be much too big. I need some legal advice, as well. As the law stands, the same company can't lend and borrow in the same state unless it settles for operating in just one state. That would limit us very nastily.'

'I'm not suggesting a full-scale takeover,' Fairbairn said. 'I simply would like someone to tender for a percentage of the shares, so control stays on my side.'

'How strong is your side?'

'At least twenty-eight per cent. I own eight myself, and the rest I vote.'

'So you need someone to vote with you on twenty-three per cent.'

'Exactly.'

'It's going to be hard to stop people selling to Van Helding,' Gorringer said. 'He's offering them more for a share in Security National than the market ever would. It may be cheap, but on the Exchange it's cheaper still.'

'People have their doubts about Van Helding.'

'Maybe. They have their doubts about big brokers taking over big banks, as well. Unless, of course, we could show that the whole deal was a salvage operation – that the bank would go under without us.'

'No,' Fairbairn said to the implicit suggestion. 'No, no, no.'

'And another thing. Van Helding can't hurt us because we're too big. We're the world and he's a fly on it. But he might hurt you. He's a good dirty fighter and I wouldn't like to be in his line of fire. I think he's found out that fighting clean takes too long. Anyway, if you win clean or dirty, you still get to rewrite history.'

'We have a defensible position,' Fairbairn said. 'We want to defend it.'

'Then let me have papers tomorrow. All I'll promise is a friendly reception and a serious one. The figures don't worry me half as much as the politics.'

The two men rose and crossed the broad acres of the drawing room. They asked politely after each other's wives – Fairbairn's wife was now almost always away, but convention required that nobody notice the fact. And Gorringer said:

'There's one outside problem. One of the candidates for November asked me to think about being Treasury Secretary. It's early days, and he's a dark horse, but I'm backing him. That means I'm getting a little careful about anything I might have to consider in Washington.'

'I never heard you use racing talk before.'

'I always liked winners,' Gorringer smiled, not kindly. 'And only winners. You understand that, don't you? Old friend?'

'You can't win,' the lawyers told Marisia over and over again. 'The only issue you can raise is the stock issue in the bid. You can oppose that, if you want to. But Van Helding only needs fifty-one per cent of the votes to win, and he's got them. You could ask for a vote of confidence in the board, but he'd win that too. You just don't have the power in Kellerman Unger any more.'

'I'm sure you're right,' Marisia said, dangerously serious and straight-faced. 'You're right about what you know. But I don't think you know very much about this kind of battle.'

'Really, Miss Van Helding . . .'

'This battle is about publicity. About what appears in the Press, what grabs people's attention. The more questions people ask, the weaker Pieter's position. The facts don't matter so much as the feeling that people ought to be looking for the facts. Don't you see that?'

'This is going to be extremely expensive. I'm not sure people will understand.'

'I understand,' Marisia said. 'If there is one thing I know from Hollywood, it's publicity. I know that brother and sister clashing in a billion-dollar deal is headline stuff. I know that if people begin to think there's an issue in this bid which goes beyond a foreign bank taking over a domestic one, they'll start wondering about Dr Rolfe and the Palm Springs gentry and all the other things that Pieter needs to hide.'

'You realize the legal implications of saying any of this out loud? You're fighting a deal which would reduce your power in Kellerman Unger even further, and anything you say would be judged in court by your motives. You have every reason for malice – the courts would assume that motivated you.'

'I want that shareholders' meeting. Who gets to fix the date and where would it be?'

'They fix the date. And it would have to be in Amsterdam. That is still the corporate headquarters.'

'Damn,' Marisia said. 'It couldn't be shifted to New York?'

'I doubt it.'

'New York would be better for the Press.'

'That won't concern the Kellerman Unger board. They're not going to go out of their way to help you.'

'Except,' Marisia said, 'except that I guess the Holland correspondents of US papers aren't exactly overworked. And it's not so far from London.'

'If you're sure you want to go ahead . . .'

'Of course I'm sure. I just have to do some preliminary work to make sure the meeting gets all the attention it deserves.'

Marisia took the car out to JFK that afternoon for a flight to Rome and the final week of dubbing on a long, sensuous saga of a film. Her imperious director, a Marxist aristocrat called de Gregorio who expressed his sympathy for the working classes mostly in bed and sometimes with a cane, had sealed the set while shooting to excite the Press. Marisia had waited for the paparazzi to break through the studio doors, but de Gregorio had been clever; no unauthorized person got in, but the rumours built and built. The movie was said to be blasphemous, pornographic, vicious; a petition was started against it; demonstrators came on the Rome underground to wave placards at the studio gates. De Gregorio, *il Maestro*, kept his distance from all this, grandly affecting not to notice how well his campaign was working. He was the great artist, the genius, the operatic figure in cape and beard, and he was naturally unconcerned with the vulgar details of selling a movie. Art was being forged in the studio. That was all that counted.

Marisia's chance was obvious and she seized it. Any talk about the film was front-page copy, and the Rome press corps was happy to take an interest. If there could also be a photograph, they would be even happier.

Of course, Marisia could never have defied de Gregorio and admitted a photographer to the set, but a dubbing hangar was different. On one side of a great room, she flickered in image, a great, golden presence, still without sound. She stood before the screen, in her more workaday clothes – on screen she was first *belle époque* clothed, and then *belle époque* naked – and the picture was stunning. It took five tries and then the studio guards were called, but the photographer got away.

Stage one, Marisia thought.

The reporter called that afternoon. He'd stop by the Hassler that evening to talk to her, if he might. He was most grateful for her help. It was a story that would run everywhere. And no, of course, he would never say how it had been arranged. The official story, if anyone asked, was that the photographer was working on his own initiative and the reporter had almost blackmailed Marisia into talking, in order to minimize the damage from the leak.

Of course, Marisia told the reporter – confidentially – about Kellerman Unger and how she was fighting to have the bank remain in her family's fortune and life, and how she worried that her brother was rushing into America and ruining them all, and how his friends in Palm Springs did not seem to have the most orthodox of business backgrounds.

She didn't know exactly how much the man would use but she knew she had made a start.

It was a golden evening in the soft Virginian hills, and Fairbairn and Grant rode together on great stallions. They were spirited animals, the emblems of Fairbairn's estate, but their power was tamed that evening. As they edged through the fields back to the great manorial house there was business to talk.

'I need something else,' Fairbairn said.

'The SEC isn't helping, much,' Grant said. 'But there is one scandal brewing – something about Magnum Studios and a movie called *The Music Makers*. Starring my wife, as it happens.'

'Get on with it.'

'The SEC has tip-offs. They also get cussed, as you know, and they've thought something was wrong with Magnum ever since it was sold.'

'That was one reason,' Fairbairn said, 'I took against Pieter Van Helding. Do they reckon they can spot the fraud?'

'Fraud,' Grant said, 'may be overstating it. They do say that *The Music Makers* was apparently sold off to Helios

SA for twenty-eight million in Helios stock which promptly became worthless. They say the deal was sweetened – that Helios was actually paid another ten million in cash to buy the film, and issued stock to cover that as well. Yet Magnum still released the film, and took a distributor's fee – which was purely theoretical, since the film did slightly less than zero business.'

'I never liked the movie business,' Fairbairn said.

'Then,' Grant said, 'the SEC started asking where the thirty-eight million write-off was – why that stock hadn't been written down to zero when Helios went bust. They found the stock had been fixed to the deeds on a set of property deals. If you were selling to Magnum's property arm, then you got your cash price, your Magnum stock, whatever – and you got a parcel of Helios shares. You could keep them or you could light fires with them. Your choice.'

'And?'

'Every development on Magnum's books was written up by the amount of the stock. So the thirty-eight million was added to the value of a bunch of shopping malls. Magnum seems to have thought the worst anyone could say was that they had overvalued their property.'

'It's a story,' Fairbairn said, grudgingly. 'But that must be . . . fourteen years ago.'

'Just when Van Helding got his first big American money,' Grant said. 'Just when Dr Rolfe's chums at Seed had bought Magnum. Just when . . .'

'I do understand,' Fairbairn said. 'I'm not as much of a damn fool as I look.'

The horses were impatient with the talk and the pace, whinnying restlessly, and Fairbairn nodded to Grant. They should give the horses their head on the narrow lanes, and they slackened the reins; the horses went forward in a flex of great muscles, like the thoroughbred Arabians they were.

And after the brief exhilaration, the violent wind against the face, the pace softened again.

'Is the SEC going to Magnum?' Fairbairn asked.

'They think so. They'll spell out the deal. They'll have to mention Van Helding, of course. It won't look good for him. Even if you like creative accounting, he's still got to explain how he was working both sides of a dud deal – helping Helios and helping Magnum all at once.'

Fairbairn allowed the sway of the horse to take him for a moment and he said: 'It's not enough.'

'It's more than I expected in America. Van Helding just hasn't been that active here.'

'The trouble is . . .' Fairbairn shifted in the saddle, '. . . it makes me look like a fool, too. I can go to the shareholders and say – do you want to be taken over by a crook who defrauded your bank's client? And they can say right back – yes, he sounds better protection than you ever were.'

'There is another thing,' Grant said. 'If you think you need Gorringer again, at Grant, FitzSimmons Lind – they were the brokers when Seed sold Magnum.'

'I know. We all owe each other so much it's hard to pick sides at times like this. You can't count on anyone staying loyal – and that's not cynicism, it's the fact that after years on the Street you have many different loyalties.'

'The best you can say is that Van Helding looks a crook.'

They were on a rough course through the woods to the house. There was a metalled surface, enough for cars, but they rose alongside it among the scuffed leaves. Sunset glittered through the passing branches and there was late birdsong, a sense of a fine day going to its orderly rest.

The shot was unexpected.

It came from very close. Fairbairn held tightly to the reins. His horse reared up in blind alarm and came down like a trick horse in the movies, hard on its front legs, buckling and then struggling back up. Fairbairn was caught, tight-muscled, in the reins and bridle, his leg pulled out of joint, hanging.

'Get me out of here,' Fairbairn said. He sounded cold, not frightened, despite his dangerous position, head down from the stirrups. 'That wasn't an accident. These are private woods. Nobody shoots here without my knowing.'

Grant fumbled with the straps. He wished he was more competent with horses, but he was hard pressed to hold his own mount, restless now, and work on the harness of the other. And he could hear the brusque, sudden roar of a powerful engine, a car, close by, and Fairbairn's horse tried to rear again at the sound. When the old man was freed, he sat down heavily by the roadside. He seemed crumpled, unwilling to trust his legs with his weight, as unsure of his joints and tendons as a drunk or a child.

He wanted to know who shot. He knew his horse; high spirited, strong, easy to panic. Someone had fired, knowing what would happen.

The car engine note came out of the trees, and a silver-grey Porsche nosed up to them. It drew up by Fairbairn, huddled on the verge, and the driver got out.

'An accident,' the driver said, unnecessarily.

His companion also left the car – with a camera.

'No pictures,' Grant said.

The cameraman stepped forward, and Grant tried to rush him, hearing the sound of a motor drive clicking, pushing the film forward, image by image. He threw himself at the photographer, tried to bring the man down with a rugby tackle, and found a boot in his face.

'Don't hurt a fellow journalist,' the driver said.

'Give me the film,' Grant said.

Fairbairn on the verge, was trying to rise, uncertain and ungainly. He wanted to hit out at someone. He wished he had his gun.

The driver held Grant by the collar. 'You're lucky,' he said. 'We won't do you for assault. This time.'

Grant stood in the track, watching the little car bump away and he jumped back onto his horse as Fairbairn stood by his. He wanted to ride after the car and snatch back the film but it was a hopeless hunt, a violent moment with no use. After a few minutes, he wheeled around and rode back.

The pictures ran in every gossip column. Fairbairn looked puffy and blotched; he might have been full of drink. Even the kindest of Wall Street people saw the item and shook their heads. You couldn't see this shambles of a man, fallen from a horse, and not compare him with the Van Heldings.

Grant's friend Regina said quite simply: 'Three points off the share price any day. This isn't a town to look over thirty in the first place.'

'We seem to have a lot of bad luck.'

Regina shrugged. 'You can't afford bad luck. Mind you, the Security National price still isn't anywhere near the bid. Someone still thinks it isn't going to happen.'

'Explain that if you can. I thought Van Helding had all the cards.'

'Politics,' Regina said. 'You're the second case, after all – that makes you look like a trend, and a trend worries people. When Hong Kong and Shanghai came in to take Marine Midland that was different. It was first. It was an agreed bid. They checked out the bidder and they didn't even come up with mystery. They were clean. Now maybe you can spot a few differences between that and the Van Helding business? I'm not giving prizes.'

'We might win.'

'You might,' Regina said. 'It depends on what else Van Helding has in store for you – Van Helding and luck, of course. And it might well depend on Fairbairn's leaving the board.'

'If Fairbairn went, there wouldn't be anything left – he is the bank.'

'And there's the bank,' Regina said, cuffing the inside pages of the *New York Post*. 'An old drunk who can't keep his seat on a horse.'

'Van Helding fights very dirty.'

'He fights well,' Regina said, complacently. 'Same thing.'

Koolhoven had something close to stage fright. He had inherited authority in the bank at Jan Unger's fall, and titles when Jan Unger died. He was elder statesman now, the face of the bank in public moments, and he was not happy with the role. He liked to make things work; he hated to sit at a shareholders' meeting.

It was clever of Marisia Van Helding; he didn't know whether to respect or loathe the woman or both. She was going to lose the vote, but she was going to win the publicity battle. There were newsmen outside in the bank halls being handled politely by security staff; Koolhoven realized he should have done something formal about public relations but it was hardly what one expected at a private meeting in a small Dutch bank. Still, the dozen men with notepads and cameras were a distinct embarrassment.

They used the smallest room available, of course, and scattered the gilt chairs as usual. No cameras in the room; that rule seemed sensible. No special provision for the Press, and seats reserved for shareholders even if it was obvious they would never come. One nominee account had six seats, and Koolhoven held the proxies in his pocket.

It had to be decorous, because noise and fury would set off headlines. Koolhoven was scared.

He was already at the table with the other board members – Pieter Van Helding, as managing director, to his left – when Marisia entered. The doors swung open on a lightning storm of flashbulbs and a woman who had grown into the power and the glory of a star. Marisia Van Helding walked into the room and stole it. She denied anyone the possibility of looking away. She was dressed in a formal suit, but an explosion of a hat, all dark feathers and crested like some fierce, predatory bird. She smiled at Koolhoven, and at Pieter, and she took her seat.

'The business of the day,' Koolhoven said, 'is to respond to Mrs Grant's request for a meeting. Mrs Grant has given proper notice of a motion, which I shall read in a moment. Your board opposes this motion, and since Mrs Grant is proposing only a negative, I suggest we first debate the official motion from the board. Now it will not be necessary to read this out, I am sure. It is clear to everyone, isn't it?'

The Press grew murmurous. They had not been given copies.

Marisia stood up and said: 'Mr Koolhoven, if I may?' She stepped forward and turned to face her audience. 'I asked for this meeting in order to prevent a deal. Our board is proposing to take this relatively small, relatively successful bank into a business it neither knows nor cares about – banking for the people in America. A merchant bank suddenly runs accounts for New York farmers and cashes welfare cheques. A European bank tries to compete for business even American banks can't make pay. This makes no sense. Worse still, when we go into America, we become yet more dependent on our – our friends, our hidden friends, the shareholders who are represented here by empty chairs and proxy votes and nominee accounts in other countries. They have no names – but they have control.' Marisia let eyes and hands sweep across the vista of the room as the Press corps scribbled furiously. 'We, the shareholders of Kellerman Unger, are being outvoted by numbered bank accounts and post office boxes in Panama and these empty chairs. We are giving up even what little power we have left, and we are giving it up to . . . whom?'

Koolhoven tried to say: 'Marisia, the order of business . . .' but Pieter tapped his elbow and shook his head. It was better to let her make the speech she would only, otherwise, make outside the doors.

'I wish we knew,' she said, 'who now controls this bank. I wish we knew why they want a major retail bank in America. I wish I understood why my own brother insists on doing what these faceless people want. I hope they're happy, but the shareholders at large are not. We don't know what interests are served by buying Security National. We only know the deal will not serve our interests. Someone, somewhere, is getting just what they want – at our expense.'

'Thank you, Miss Van Helding,' Koolhoven said.

'I haven't finished,' Marisia said.

'But I really feel . . .'

'I have a statement to make.'

'We agreed,' Koolhoven said, 'that speeches would be limited to three minutes.'

Marisia turned to the Press corps and said: 'I will not be silenced. I want to tell the other shareholders what I know of the people who are really running Kellerman Unger. I want to say . . .'

'Marisia,' Koolhoven said, 'you are over time.'

'What are you afraid of?' Marisia said. 'Are you afraid I'll say something you can't deny – something too bad for you to dismiss?'

'I'm afraid we said that speeches would be limited to three minutes. That is all. I must insist . . .'

'They are trying to stop me talking,' Marisia said.

Pieter groaned inwardly. Nothing could better serve Marisia than this intervention by Koolhoven; she could promise revelations, fail to deliver, and emerge as a martyr. Koolhoven was handing her the game.

'Are there any other speeches from the floor?' Koolhoven asked.

There were none.

'Then I shall do what I planned to do in the first place,' Koolhoven said, 'and ask Mr Van Helding to support our own official motion to this meeting – which is, you will recall . . .'

'They've got copies,' Marisia shouted.

'But if I can read out . . .'

'You didn't read my motion. And that was what this whole meeting is about.'

'Order,' Koolhoven said. 'Order, please.' He felt he was watching a stage from the audience, and not taking part. Marisia was acting for the notebook with the authority and skill she brought to acting for the screen.

'Mr Van Helding,' Koolhoven said.

Pieter rose. 'I realize,' he said, 'ladies and gentlemen, that all new departures can seem alarming to the more conservative among us, especially those with a well-developed instinct for the dramatic.' Marisia glared at him; of course, he would try to put her down as a mere actress, and of course, she would resent it bitterly. 'But this is quite a simple deal. We have a chance to make a vast leap – in terms of assets, power, authority, and our worldwide operations. We can do so relatively cheaply. It is true that your individual shareholdings will be diluted but you will have a share of an infinitely larger, more diversified, more flexible bank. We can go to the very big leagues this way, ladies and gentlemen. We can't turn our backs on that.' He took a sip of water. 'As for those shareholders who prefer to maintain their privacy – I'm sure we all understand that. If I were to call a register here today for the benefit of the Press, would all of you be happy? Where a man's money goes is his business, and only his. I can assure you there is no occult power behind Kellerman Unger. We are a young business, a growing business, and we are just coming into our own.'

He wasn't even speaking for the shareholders, Marisia knew, but for the Press. Defuse Marisia, make her seem hysterical and scared, alarmist beyond reason.

But she knew they would have to ask questions now, when they could. Even when the votes were tallied and her side defeated, she knew she had won the attention Pieter Van Helding could not stand.

Fairbairn, like a boy with some new toy, would not listen to Grant.

'This cigarette pack,' he said, 'lights when there's a tape recorder in the room. And this pen lights up if anyone is bugging the room. And the case itself stops a .357 magnum bullet.' Fairbairn opened the briefcase wide, displaying an electronic workshop with a scrambler phone, a dazzling flashlight, and what he said was a 'voice stress analyser. You can tell when the bastard is lying at the other end of the phone.'

Grant said it was all impressive.

'Weighs twenty-two pounds,' Fairbairn said.

'But I don't think it answers our problems. You think Pieter Van Helding has stress when he tells lies?'

Fairbairn shrugged. His new toy seemed to offer him protection, a shield against the sense of being manipulated which he resented almost more than losing the battle.

'There's a bomb sniffer,' Fairbairn said. 'And if anyone

steals the thing, there's an alarm – goes off six seconds after they get it out of your hands.'

Grant said: 'I hear Van Helding is in the Mainline tonight.'

'I beg your pardon?'

'He's at Villanova, in the Philadelphia Mainline.'

'I know where the Mainline is. I'm surprised an Englishman does. You must follow the doings of the rich very carefully.'

'I know about the Mainline,' Grant said. 'The richest suburbs in the world.'

'Who knows?' Fairbairn said. He snapped his shield and briefcase shut.

'It seems a few people got together for drinks last night.'

Fairbairn was suddenly attentive.

'Who?'

'Van Helding. His wife. Some shareholders. Some friends. Just a social gathering.'

'Damn it, that man does nothing that isn't deliberate.'

'Shareholders are entitled to a social life.'

'They're acting as if they can just change sides at will.'

'They can,' Grant reminded him.

Fairbairn turned on the computer terminal in his outer office, a toy he enjoyed but still did not find reassuring.

'We had better do some sums,' he said.

He explained the program – two columns, one red and one blue, raced on the screen from zero to one hundred. The first to pass fifty-one made the whole screen pulse and its rival disappear.

'Red is Van Helding's lot,' Fairbairn explained. 'Blue is our side. And fifty-one per cent, I don't have to say, is victory.'

He made the blue column rise to twenty-eight.

'That's the good news,' he said. 'Eight per cent in my

holdings, twenty in family and allied trusts that I can vote. Nobody's withdrawn any proxies yet and I don't think they will, so that's my base.'

Grant said: 'And if Van Helding is telling the truth, he and his allies have twenty-two per cent in their hands.'

The red column rose to twenty-two. It seemed terribly close to Fairbairn's figures.

'And now,' Fairbairn said, 'for commitments. No point in discussing who might go over to Van Helding until we know where we stand.'

Fairbairn saw the struggle in trench terms – Flanders trenches from the first World War, where only the desperate would go out over the top to change sides.

'Clients and holdings of Grant, FitzSimmons Lind,' David Grant said.

'Not a commitment.'

'But they were talking about a counterbid.'

'They weren't talking figures. Besides they'd be in a mess if they suddenly had to buy out their own clients – it wouldn't look good.'

'In limbo, then?'

'Eight per cent in limbo, yes. It might be even less than eight per cent – they tend to have new money and new money hasn't bought Security National for a long time. We haven't exactly been a hot stock.'

'So if Gorringer did decide at the last minute to vote with Van Helding, if the worst came to the worst, we'd need fifty-nine per cent to be sure of victory.'

'We don't have to face that yet,' Fairbairn said.

Old names, grand names came tumbling out like a litany of class in America. The first five were sure to vote for Fairbairn, so he said; loyalties were involved. Besides, they had given their word and between them they held 11 per cent.

Blue moved to thirty-nine per cent. Grant was impressed until he realized commitments had no legal force, people could always change their minds, and there were dozens out there who might already have thrown their votes behind Van Helding.

Grant asked the computer for shareholders on record with 3 per cent or more of the company. There were only seven, but none of them had yet been accounted for.

'Start calling,' Fairbairn said.

He brought the pen from his briefcase, the one that detected phone bugs. It did not light.

'You're doing the talking, I assume?' Grant said.

There was a doctor in the Mainline who would be taking dinner. Was it politic to risk interrupting his meal? But why not; the boss of a massive bank is entitled to take some liberties.

'Doctor Thompson, please.'

A servant scurried to find the doctor and prise him away from soup.

'God, Fairbairn,' the doctor said. It was not a promising start.

'I'm sorry to interupt your dinner like this.'

'So am I, Fairbairn.'

'My colleagues have asked me to check with our most important shareholders. We want to see if anyone will commit to supporting the board – which, as you know, is opposing the Kellerman Unger bid.'

'Your fellows rang me,' the doctor said. 'Whatever you call them – professional shareholder botherers. This is all very embarrassing. Nothing against you, Fairbairn, but we have Van Helding here for dinner, and I don't feel . . .'

'Naturally,' Fairbairn said. 'If you do make a decision, please call me at any time. We'd be most grateful to know.'

'Glad you understand,' said the doctor.

Fairbairn slammed down the phone and punched the

computer keyboard. Van Helding's red went to twenty-six; Fairbairn's blue was stuck at thirty-nine.

'Give me the other East Coast people. We might as well catch them at dinner.'

A Palm Beach matron was away from her newly recovered mansion, in the Bahamas with Mr Haley, a voice said. Fairbairn and Grant struggled with the Caribbean 809 exchange until they got through.

'I'm with you,' the lady said. 'Absolutely.'

She sounded ginny, but she had given her word.

Red twenty-six; Blue so close to success at forty-two.

The next three calls were noncommittal until it became clear the indecision was politeness, and the decisions had actually been made – against the board.

Red thirty-five now; Blue still at forty-two. The gap on the little computer screen had stopped seeming significant.

Merciless technology reached a golf-playing lawyer in Palm Springs, victim of his own self-important taste for mobile phones. He said the Van Helding operation looked attractive; his neighbours spoke well of the man. He said he was not committing himself.

Red thirty-eight, Blue forty-two. All the advantage was fading away.

In San Francisco, the call woke a grande dame from her afternoon nap.

'I simply will not be disturbed on matters of business,' she said. 'I thought you knew that, Fairbairn. I suppose you really are losing your touch.'

Red forty-one, Blue forty-two; only just a lead, only just. The faint blink of the computer screens made the columns seem alive and level, racing of their own volition.

'We could call Gorringer,' Grant said.

'We can't press him. He's too important. He has the brokerage and he has the power to save us.'

'We could sound him out.'

Fairbairn dialled Gorringer's number.

'I'm sorry,' a woman said. 'He isn't here. He's in Philadelphia. If it's urgent, I could give you that number?'

Fairbairn wrote it down. Digit by digit he began to know the number. 'This is a silly question,' he said to Grant, 'but this isn't by any chance the number for Doctor Thompson?'

Grant took the slip of paper and looked. He nodded.

'Then that's where Gorringer is. He's eating with Pieter Van Helding.'

Red forty-nine, Blue forty-two.

'Is there anyone else with as much as two per cent?' Fairbairn asked. 'Calling the smaller fry would take hours, and we don't have hours.'

Grant checked the shareholder register. There was one unlikely name, a Long Island dentist who had bought in the past year – and bought massively, up to 1.8 per cent.

'We stockholders don't usually get this kind of attention,' he said. 'I'm flattered.'

'I should be happy to give you any information you need – and I should like very much to know how you're thinking of acting.'

'I shouldn't tell you this,' the dentist said, 'not after you've been so courteous. But I bought Security National as a takeover situation. I guess that says it all.'

Fairbairn was stone-faced. Without speaking he stirred the computer columns, Blue stayed at 42 per cent, unsafe and vulnerable. But with the extra 1.8 per cent, red climbed over 50 per cent. It salved Fairbairn's ego that the screen did not begin to pulse. Van Helding, on these figures, was just shy of 51 per cent.

'There isn't anything to say,' Fairbairn said. He almost felt relieved. 'If Van Helding wants Security National, he's got it.'

* * *

At eight in the morning Eleanor Brown was staring from her office window high in the World Trade Centre. She was a stiff backed woman who affected oversized tinted eyeglasses, a raffish touch on a schoolmarm's face – like a little old lady from Kansas, in New York on a package razzle. She was as stiff in her mind as she was in her back, and she was Alexander Fairbairn's last hope.

She was Banking Commissioner for New York State, the regulatrix of the money shops, the scourge of usurers, and the blocker of sudden changes. She liked the early morning office for its quiet and the sense of the city stirring around her. Exiled to the grandiose blankness of Albany, the state capital, she felt insecure.

Before ten, nothing much could happen. At ten the cheques from all the city's banks were taken to the clearing house, sorted, and sent back to the banks on which they were drawn. Yesterday's business became payments, not just paper. Until then Eleanor Brown expected quiet.

The telephone rang.

'This is Alexander Fairbairn of Security National.'

'Good morning.' Miss Brown did not sound friendly.

'I would be very grateful if you could see me this morning. Before the New York Stock Exchange opens.'

'Is it urgent?'

'Obviously I think so,' Fairbairn said.

Miss Brown watched her secretary arrive and begin bustling in the outer office, making coffee, shuffling papers. She could never understand why people were so addicted to pointless movement.

'Come as soon as you can,' Miss Brown said. 'I presume this concerns the Kellerman Unger bid?'

'It does. I wanted to raise some issues.'

Like saving the skin of a grand old man of New York banking, Eleanor Brown thought, cynically.

She had read the *Wall Street Journal* by the time Fairbairn arrived, bursting through the various cordons of security and secretaries.

'I'll tell you what worries me,' Fairbairn said. 'We may lose our independence to a foreign institution that doesn't have to take any account of the laws of the United States. You know as well as I do that London merchant banks are allowed to keep double books – and God knows what they do in Amsterdam. Nobody will ever really be sure how strong Kellerman Unger is – and how much they can be trusted.'

Eleanor Brown sighed. 'You have disturbing news,' she said, and Fairbairn had to ride over the faint irony in her voice. 'But I don't quite see what I'm supposed to do. I've never been one to stop foreign takeovers for the sake of it. This is supposed to be some sort of free market, after all.'

'Of course,' Fairbairn said. 'But when a company has an approach like this, it naturally tries to find out as much as possible about its suitor.'

'You mean it digs up all the dirt it can find?'

Fairbairn grinned. 'Exactly,' he said. 'Now my staff has developed a dossier . . .' he threw down a bundle of legal-sized pages '. . . and what we discovered about Kellerman Unger was not exactly flattering.'

'I take it you would have been disappointed if the record was clean.'

'We're so close to being taken over, we might have been relieved,' Fairbairn said, in a rare burst of honesty.

'But you're not exactly neutral investigators?'

'We didn't exaggerate anything,' Fairbairn said. 'This is a record that goes from aiding the Nazis in World War Two to links with the Mafia now to deals the SEC is investigating.'

'Sounds interesting,' Eleanor Brown said, choosing her

words with caution. She flipped through the pages. 'Can you prove any of this?'

'Beyond reasonable doubt.'

'I mean in a court of law. If Van Helding knew you had given me this material.'

'I'm sure of it.'

'I need to know the strength of the evidence before I dare use any of this. I know you want all this to be true, but I can't be so certain.'

'There is another point,' Fairbairn said. 'London wouldn't allow a New York bank to take over a major clearer. You can be sure of that. And Security National isn't exactly some tiny downtown operation that you won't miss; it is a vital part of the clearing system. You could always say the principle of reciprocity had been broken. I happen to think this dossier is a good reason for acting on principle.'

Brown smiled. 'Very clever,' she said. 'Of course, that way none of these allegations would ever be brought to the test.'

Fairbairn was expansive. 'Test them as much and as long as you want,' he said. 'We'll help you.'

Brown's tone was not entirely friendly. 'Really,' she said. 'Are you absolutely sure you have that much time?'

Villanova dinners had cheered Van Helding, allowed him a sense of being already an insider. Gorringer broke easily. He had come full of loyalty to Fairbairn – five weeks before, a senior Grant, FitzSimmons Lind analyst had wanted to pull out a sell recommendation on Security National and Gorringer, loyal still, had blocked it; now, he was ready to be told it was all right to change sides, and he did so, swiftly. Now, he was admitting incidents like the suppressed report.

'Although,' he said, 'I was right. If people had sold then, they wouldn't have got your bid.'

Van Helding was out of his expedient New Jersey motels, in a Fifth Avenue apartment lent him by Palm Springs friends. He was open at last, available to occasional persons from the Press and frank about the bid. Every time a journalist called him 'brilliant' in print, or 'dynamic', he reckoned another thousand Security National shares tipped his way. He gave Koolhoven champagne the night he returned to New York from Villanova, to celebrate the sweet certainty that the bank was his.

Now, he had to run the obstacle course. He looked down on his view of midtown – the neon cap of the Chrysler building, the red white and blue of the Empire State, that austere dull prism up at Citibank. He could see the city sparkle at night, and the lines of urgent people fall into simple, ordered place. Reality was a grid, a plan, apparent from up high. Van Helding saw no individual move below; he had climbed above all that. He sat on a terrace whose walls of glass came vertiginously to the ground. He thought, hard.

People missed Van Helding's intelligence. They saw his deals, and considered him a dealer, without wondering if the deals were part of a strategy; and then, when the deals suddenly added up to a grand achievement, they were faintly surprised. Van Helding thought in ways very different from them. He second-guessed a man like Fairbairn, not because he was so like him, but because he had almost nothing in common with him. Van Helding knew the abstract wonders of his money game, and took joy in them, but he also knew their limits.

Fairbairn had to be playing the regulatory card by now. He had been foolish enough to find out how strong his support was, and the call to Dr Thompson must have been an unpleasant moment. Almost certainly he would have discovered where Gorringer was dining.

Van Helding considered Fairbairn's hand. He had the foreigner card – being foreign is something many Americans have had to transcend in their own lifetimes, something they deeply suspect in others. He could always try to persuade the New York State Banking Commissioner of some public policy offended by Kellerman Unger. Or he could assemble a dossier on the bank, full of hints at the murder of Van Helding's father, the truth that Jan Unger smuggled gold for the Nazis and the history of the bank in Van Helding's time. But the real dirt, Van Helding thought, was historical; the rest would be ambiguous. Jan Unger was dead. Kellerman Unger had clearly changed since the war years. It would be hard to show a court that the bank was still in any important way the institution that helped load U-boats with other people's fortunes.

Van Helding knew the information game. It was the foundation of his own fortune. He had usually known too much at the right time about the right rivals. He also knew its rules were more subtle than simple blackmail. Fairbairn's logical course was to allow some regulator to see the dossier, privately, as a reason for taking more seriously what issues of public policy the bid might raise. Since the first place where the bid could be stopped was the State Banking Commissioner, that was where Fairbairn would show his papers first.

Van Helding allowed his gaze to drift over the city stretched out before him. He had always liked maps. He remembered the map, like a concertina of vellum, that went with a book his father had on Sir Walter Raleigh's search for Eldorado. There had been wide, snaking rivers linked like veins. There were coastlines only half mapped where intricate bays would suddenly stop and a flat, blank line appear for a while. There were suggestions of frontiers between empires that would have been hazardous to cross, and names of great cities that somehow had not been on the ground when intrepid explorers arrived. And there had been, in red, Raleigh's route, in search of a city of gold. It had seemed so certain.

He tugged his mind back from childhood memories. There was one simple solution to the state problem. Banks could be organized under state law, or they could be national associations under federal law, answering to Washington. Federal ideas of what was acceptable might be far more sophisticated. Security National would have to become a national association – take the NA after its name, like Chase and Citibank and the rest.

It would take time. It would also take the consent of the Security National board. He would have to ask the board to override the cantankerous, rowdy old man while he was still in power. But he needed only five votes, since the board was very small.

That evening, it was Pieter Van Helding's turn to work the phones.

Fairbairn thought of them as gargoyles – a gallery of them, ranked along a table in a soulless modern room. He could tell them apart with some difficulty, and mostly by their symbolic function: a burnished, blonde woman who had once been a consumer advocate on TV; a black Congressman; a man who was a director of Security National because he had been a director before; an old-money New York lawyer who once made four underground films of startling obscurity; a dry-eyed lawyer; the managing director of the bank itself; a stockholder representative who owed his position more to gin and golf than to ambition, a mining engineer, vastly rich, but walleyed like a landed pike, whom Fairbairn had once invited to the board for South African connections that afterwards proved a huge embarrassment; and an official from an insurance company who had the bland, unsurprised features of a man who expects history to be written without him. That was the board of Security National.

Fairbairn suggested they talk about reorganization of the north-eastern sector of the branch network. The gargoyles came to animated life and bickered, mostly because they wanted to discuss the coming merger. Some talked of a lack of capital, some of a change of style, some made apologetic references to 'recent events' and looked away when Fairbairn glared at them directly.

It was a preliminary skirmish, all of it, shapeless and pointless, until the professional director broke the chaos with a simple motion: to approve the merger with Kellerman Unger. And to apply to become a national association – to leave the supervision of the state of New York and take orders from Washington.

'The motion is irregular,' Fairbairn said.

'Sorry, Al,' said the professional director. 'We've all discussed it before. We just didn't want to rush things.'

These nine absurd figures were taking his life away from him. At least they had not said to his face that he was old and irrelevant and that they wanted change. They would not dare push him out.

'Do you,' he said, 'want me to resign?'

There was an awkward moment. Feet scuffed under the table, a pencil tapped, there were nervous coughs.

'I don't think,' the professional director said, 'that is for us to say. The new owners . . .'

'We have not been bought,' Fairbairn said. 'Not yet. We have the same owners we had last week and last month. I ask again: do you want me to go?'

'Perhaps – but then of course for the sake of continuity . . .'

Fairbairn glared at the professional director. 'I am

sure,' he said, 'some of you have continuity on your minds.'

'We ought to talk about it,' the consumerist lady said.

Fairbairn left the room. He sat like a visitor in a deep armchair. There were magazines, and he wondered what the bank provided for its guests – the *New Yorker*, of course, which had a brief note on the merger, nicely turned, ironic, not substantial.

Fairbairn wanted to know what those fools were saying. They were judging him. They thought they could cooperate with Pieter Van Helding and not get hurt or burned. They didn't know that Alexander Fairbairn, with his 28 per cent of the bank, might be needed to protect them.

'Al,' said the professional director, 'please come back.'

Perhaps it would be like a court martial, where brother officers lay a sword on the table as you enter – point toward you if they find you guilty, scabbard if they find you innocent.

There was no talking, and no sign. Fairbairn refused to wait in the corner of the room; he walked to his seat and looked down at the yellow legal pad before him, covered in doodles of spiders' webs.

'Al,' the professional director said, 'we thought it might be a good idea if you'd stay until the merger is complete. Kellerman Unger might not go through with it, after all, and they might want you to stay. We shouldn't be too hasty.'

Fairbairn looked grim.

'But you'll have to recommend the merger.'

'Al,' said the lady consumerist, her perfect, plastic features formed into what she thought looked like compassion (could 5 million New York viewers be wrong?), 'I thought we'd never shift you without something like this – it was hard for us, too. Believe me. We do have to change, you know. Change is growth. For the sake of the bank and the stockholders and the depositors . . .'

Fairbairn rose. The meeting must now be over; a moment longer, and all his emotions would boil within him, and ruin the balance to which he was precariously clinging. One by one, the directors filed out.

'Of course,' said the professional director, 'we have to ask for your complete discretion.'

Fairbairn was left alone. David Grant walked into the boardroom, in part for instructions, in part to offer comfort. Fairbairn was looking ahead of him, quite blank.

He couldn't, now, find in the casual violence of his words in ordinary circumstances anything that matched what he felt. He couldn't stay – not at the whim of those gargoyles and jackanapes, the ones he had put into power. But he couldn't go – not just surrender the bank, and particularly not to Pieter Van Helding, not until the last option had closed.

'Get out,' he said to Grant. He spoke so flatly that Grant did not think of disobeying.

Fairbairn felt himself tied, from heart to pocketbook, to the bank. Like a sea captain who goes down with his ship, he had no life beyond the failure of the great machine he had made and ran.

Anger came up inside him like bile and he cursed Van Helding. He bellowed his pain and his loss. They were taking his life away, slowly, and the bastard would not even give him a clean confrontation, a chance to do battle. The options were closing on him, even as he thought. He could discredit Kellerman Unger; but that was a dream, with too little time to find and prove some monstrous crime. He would have to sign the announcement that Security National wanted to be a National Association, was recommending the Kellerman Unger bid. He would go on record as chairman of a bank in such trouble that it needed to sell itself, even to an outfit the chairman could not approve.

Fairbairn saw the trap at last. If the merger went through he could resign with dignity, claim he had done it all for the sake of the bank and retire to Palm Beach. He was not excited by the idea.

But if the merger failed, his troubles had just begun. Security National was admitting its problems by accepting the bid – saying it needed help. Nobody would forget that. If the merger failed the market would know how weak Security National really was. Share price and future would be in eclipse. Now it had gone so far, a failed merger would be ruinous.

That was the trap Van Helding had set: Fairbairn needed his own defeat, just to survive.

Security National Bank made formal application to the Office of the Comptroller of the Currency, pursuant to 12 USC ¶35 and as permitted by Section 137 of the New York State banking law, to convert from a state to a national charter and thereby become a national banking association.

Eleanor Brown walked into her ladies' room, threw a water glass to the floor; stamped for a while and, when she had perfectly composed herself, put on her oversized glasses, and came into her office.

'Explain it, Al Fairbairn,' she said. 'Five days ago, you give me some thick dossier on the evils of Kellerman Unger and you beg me to help you. Now you're trying to take the whole damn thing out of my jurisdiction and you're selling yourself to these crooks.'

'I don't have an explanation,' Fairbairn seemed profoundly unhappy.

'I like the bit,' said Brown, 'this bit where you say that the bank has often considered becoming national, that the idea didn't just come up with the bid. Do you like that bit?'

'It's true,' Fairbairn said. 'As it's written, it's true.'

'I feel a fool,' Eleanor Brown said. 'I wanted to be helpful and I wanted to stop something terrible happening to Security National. And now I'm on my own. The man who built the bank doesn't give a shit if it's sold to the Mafia.'

'Eleanor . . .'

'You'll have bank inspectors swarming through Security National and I hope you're ready for them. They'll write down and they'll publish just how strong you are. And then they'll start trying to get some information out of Kellerman Unger. Public information, you understand, the kind public officials can base decisions on.'

'We're not worried.'

'Public hearings,' Brown said, 'everything out in the open – not in a private dossier for my eyes only.'

'Nobody will go,' Fairbairn said. 'When they held the hearings on Marine Midland Bank, when Hong Kong and Shanghai wanted to take them over, just seven people went. They left the file open for fourteen days to get public comment – and nobody said a thing. The public doesn't give a damn who owns the banks as long as their money is safe.'

'You think it's safe with Kellerman Unger?'

Fairbairn shrugged.

'I worry about this deal,' Brown said. 'We don't know about Kellerman Unger. We don't know how they lend money and how scrupulous they are. We don't know how heavily committed they might be to a single borrower or how much they might siphon out of Security National in a crisis. Who knows? It's all that innocent upstate money at the mercy of an international hustler.'

'Van Helding is an entrepreneur,' Fairbairn said.

'He's also the main support of the Grunwald family, if your own dossier is right. Imagine the Grunwalds as your biggest debtors and tell me if that's healthy.'

'Kellerman Unger has cash enough to make the bid. That makes them liquid.'

'And afterwards? And where does the money come from?'

'I have to stick with the board, Eleanor. If I don't, I create problems for the bank itself – and the bank is my history and my life. It's not just a living and an office. It's who I am.'

'Van Helding is going to take it away from you,' Eleanor Brown said, very evenly and deliberately. 'You know that. I know that. Why hide the facts from yourself?'

The strategy worked simply for Marisia: reporters came to ask about the new movie, worried that she wouldn't answer the questions about the bank their editors had prepared. She would make a show of reluctance but she would talk. There wasn't anything in the family history she kept back: she talked about her father's death, said she'd rather not talk about where his fortune went (which made reporters think of something they might otherwise have missed), and allowed herself to be cajoled into talking about 'My Brother the Billion-Dollar Playboy' and worse. Every time Pieter Van Helding managed to present himself as responsible, serious, brilliant even, Marisia engineered another story on the Van Helding family curse, the background to Van Helding's sudden rise. All this had to be done with great care, with guarded references which suggested the spidery hand of a lawyer had crept across the copy, but still with mention of the rumours that breathed in City places and El Vino's and the Third Avenue bars. Dossiers, files, hints of intrigue were all around. A heavy London Sunday newspaper cobbled together one of its group journalism exercises and bought TV time to plug it before the story was written;

what appeared was anodyne, but heavy-breathing, and heavily promoted. The sense of scandal around the Van Heldings was cumulative.

One thing Marisia could not do, but the Press, as it happened, did it for her: a serious look at Van Helding's actual impact on the City of London. Again, a heavy Sunday decided to look at what effect the man had in the long term, after the flashy deals had been forgotten. He had said he was only selling off the unneeded assets of the companies he bought, making them more efficient; in fact, it seemed he had not even been concerned with real running of a business. He had come in, made his profit by selling off property usually for more than his share stake had cost, and then left the companies floundering. The kind of industries on which small, pleasant towns depend – nothing grand or vast, only the lifeblood of little communities – had been taken apart, as a child might disembowel a watch, and not reassembled at all. The game was over quickly for Pieter Van Helding and he did not care to retrace his tracks.

Marisia accumulated material, and it frustrated her. 'It's only words,' she said to David Grant on the phone from London. 'There isn't any legal action left to take. I can't believe Pieter would run rings around a man with twenty-eight per cent of a bank. It doesn't make sense.'

David Grant said: 'It does, you know. Nobody thought anyone would dare attack an institution like Security National, so it wasn't guarded. It's that simple.'

'Has Fairbairn given up?'

'I don't think so,' David said. 'He doesn't have much room for manoeuvre. His board think he's lost, so they've backed Pieter's bid. That means they've admitted they need Pieter. If the bid didn't go through, they'd be in terrible trouble. People would think that Security National was in such a mess it couldn't find itself a buyer.'

'I'll send the cuttings,' Marisia said.

Something curious happened in the act of Telefaxing copy across the Atlantic. Newspaper stories on one side became evidence on the other. Repetition of a rumour, an innuendo, a memory of a Caribbean murder or a Hollywood deal now became something more than different versions of the same story. They became an impressive heap of material that could be carried into a courtroom or a Congressional hearing.

'And Fairbairn duly took the pile to Congressman Ryder, who chirruped approval. He looked sparrowlike at Fairbairn and said: 'I thought you supported this bid.'

'Yes,' Fairbairn said.

'But you give me all this material. I wonder why.'

'There is a public interest,' Fairbairn said stuffily. 'I think all this material should at least be evaluated.'

'Ha,' Ryder said. 'You mean you've done everything, lost everything, and now you want a new sort of Congressional bale-out.'

'I have the best interests of the bank at heart. Naturally.'

Ryder turned the pages of the file. 'Noble,' he said, 'but gnomic.' His political pulse was already racing: big money, foreign power, little people's savings at stake, glamorous film star champions the cause of justice, billionaire financier fights own sister. He could see a hearing the networks would cover, a national issue which could give a junior Congressman stardom he could not hope to buy or plot.

'I don't suppose,' he said, 'Marisia Van Helding would testify?'

'I know she would be happy to.'

Ryder sucked his teeth. 'I guess,' he said, 'if Van Helding won't listen to minority shareholders in his own bank, what chance is there for depositors with Security National?'

'And the fact that unknown foreign owners . . .'

'It's a good story,' Ryder said. 'It's a scandal, too.'

'Tell that to Dan Rather,' Fairbairn said.
'I will,' Ryder said, 'God willing.'

'I am sorry for him,' Van Helding said to Koolhoven. 'Just sorry. If he thinks he can get anyone to intervene at this late stage . . .'

'Full scale Congressional hearings,' Koolhoven said. 'You do understand that, don't you? It's like a trial, except without a judge. It means in effect that anyone can say anything, and it gets reported.'

'I suppose we'd better be represented properly – Washington lawyers as well as New York?'

'At least,' Koolhoven said.

'Will it mean much delay?'

'It all depends,' Koolhoven said, 'on what the committee decides to do.'

'You realize if they turn us down they're ruining Security National?'

'Possibly.'

'Definitely,' Van Helding said. 'I don't like the little, fiddling plots. I like to have a strategy. Either people go my way or else they face the consequences, and while we couldn't bankrupt Security National, we could sure as hell spoil it.'

'We're trying to take over a workable bank,' Koolhoven said. 'We don't have an interest in spoiling.'

Van Helding glowered at him. 'You really don't understand, do you? What the hell do you think I've been working for, all these years – just the privilege of taking over some workable bank? I want to be a power in America, too. And I can do it. I have the backing and the brains. And if anyone gets in my way, then I don't care if I shake the whole system down with me.'

Koolhoven began to fill his pipe. Van Helding must be tired, of course, and the strain of Congressional hearings on top of a prolonged campaign – but Koolhoven looked again, listened to the ice in Van Helding's voice and knew that was not the explanation. What he'd thought was ambition was actually fanaticism. What he'd thought was ruthlessness was actually megalomania. All that was fine for as long as Van Helding could hold power and expand his empire, without interference or ill luck. But if his luck changed, then the worst side would be visible, as it was now. Nobody had trained Van Helding for either frustration or disappointment. If Van Helding lost momentum he wouldn't even understand what had happened.

Pieter seemed calmer for a moment and he rang for coffee.

'I once said . . . ' he turned to Koolhoven, '. . . that if I fell, I would bring the whole system down with me. You thought it was a young man shouting off his mouth. Don't deny it; I know you did.' A tray was brought. 'You should know better. If people ceased to believe in financial stars like me, they would cease to believe in the prospects for their money. If big banks go down, all big banks go down – people don't know enough to tell the difference, just enough to panic. If I go down, the system goes down – because I am the system, the profitable, public side of the system.'

'It's possible,' Koolhoven said, 'that you're not that important.'

Van Helding had a flash of fire-hot anger which he cooled by sheer will.

'We'll see,' he said.

Koolhoven went back to his own quarters, puzzling. He thought a skein of curious thoughts – what happened when the Palm Springs gentry, who held all the cards and strings, decided what they wanted from Kellerman Unger and Security National? What happened if one of those other involvements – Jan Unger's friends, Mr Gregory's friends, the Grunwalds, the massive, egotistical loans to Providencia – went sour or sinister or simply conflicted with the orders from Palm Springs? Van Helding had been allowed such autonomy he no longer understood how much he was controlled.

At five past ten, the subcommittee of the Committee on Government Operations of the 96th Congress, first Session came to order. There were six Congressmen at a horseshoe table, with their witnesses in the centre before them; there were staff aides, a flurry of reporters, a mass of ENG operators toting cameras in the hallways of the Rayburn House Office, waiting for something to happen on Capitol Hill. Old hands did not trouble too much with Ryder's opening remarks nor with the evidence of a Press-hungry Washington lawyer who had decided to give evidence on the law without fee or client, in the public interest. 'It's an unnatural act for a lawyer,' one cameraman said. 'And you can't put unnatural acts on the seven o'clock news.'

Eleanor Brown testified. It was deplorable, she said, that Security National could simply switch laws when it suited them – from state to national. Lawyers for the bank, part of a hefty posse lying in wait for witnesses with loose tongues, intervened; there were documents to show how often the bank had considered going national, and they would be produced.

Fairbairn was called. By then, the lawyers had worked the territory like dogs – barking, snapping, pissing to mark their grounds. The battery of the committee and its friends and enemies was ready.

The old man looked as he always did – bluff. But he talked in a very subdued fashion about Kellerman Unger, picking over his words carefully. He said Kellerman Unger was a substantial bank. He said that the merger held great possibilities.

'Tell me, Mr Fairbairn . . .' Ryder was like a sparrow on a ledge, but aggressive '. . . do you really have any choice about this bid? Surely if it were to fail, your share price would tumble? And your only defence, if shareholders liked the sound of the bidder, would be government regulators?'

'If one wanted a defence . . .'

'And you might find a strong defence a little difficult? I mean, you have your problems like other banks with overseas loans, and you don't have the choicest of business, do you?'

'We have been prudent.'

'And the figures suggest you are short of capital – that if someone could reorganize your capital structure that might be healthy?'

'Perhaps. Most bank balance sheets look like that. If your raw material is money you tend to have vast assets on a relatively small equity base. Just like a car firm has lots of steel in its balance sheet.'

'And those assets – weren't you badly hit when the rules on overnight deposits were changed?'

'No worse than the other big New York banks.'

'Let me explain for the benefit of the committee. Money in people's accounts overnight, not yet paid out, used to count as part of your assets, didn't it? Overseas money, that is. You cleared the payments at ten in the morning, but until then, the money was counted as yours. And when that rule was changed and deals were cleared at five in the afternoon, your assets dropped by one-ninth?'

'Like other banks', like other banks'.'

'But you did not look quite as strong as other banks – with all your retail branches?'

'The change was purely technical.'

Fairbairn hated to be pressed or cornered. He couldn't roar with anger here; it would make him vulnerable. But

Ryder was deliberately grating on his nerves. He wanted indiscretions.

'Kellerman Unger is offering substantial cash, I see.'

'Yes.'

'It must be a very liquid bank.'

'Awash,' Fairbairn said, crisply. 'A company that's growing and advancing attracts support.'

'What do you know about Mr Van Helding's shareholders and his sources of capital?'

'Only what I read in the balance sheet – and that looks healthy enough.'

'Don't you think you ought to know? After all, you're handing over your bank to Kellerman Unger. Doesn't that make their real owners your new bosses? Don't you want to know their names?'

'Our concern,' Fairbairn said, 'is with the business. Not who owns it. You wouldn't think the less of Kellerman Unger if it was owned by nuns.'

'But it isn't, is it?'

'I do not know.'

'Do you have any concerns at all about the sources of Kellerman Unger's money?'

The silence was long. Ryder looked expectant and then worried. He had hoped to build to some moment of indiscreet revelation but the old man was not yet off balance. He had reverted to his oldest trick – simply sitting, sipping at a glass of water, pausing. Then he said:

'No.' Fairbairn's old bear expression, quizzical and a little forlorn, gave him away, but the single word was clear and anticlimatic.

'Very well,' Ryder said. He leaned back. 'We are, of course, grateful for your testimony.'

Marisia Van Helding and David Grant caught up with Alexander Fairbairn as he stalked along the corridor, ignoring the crowd with cameras perched on their shoulders and microphones out like a forest of thorns.

'Lunch,' Marisia said.

They went for veal and white wine and roasted peppers.

'I've been finessed, haven't I?' Fairbairn said.

He pushed the meat on his plate to one side.

'Are you going to give testimony?' he asked Marisia.

'Of course.'

'I don't even know if I want you to do that, even after all we've done. The way Van Helding is seen on Wall Street, you'll seem like a sideshow – neurotic film star seeks publicity.' He was pale under the reddened veins on his cheeks and the blustering manner had become quiet. 'I never wanted power like the Rockefellers. I was never a patron of the arts, or governor of a state. I wanted to be Fairbairn of Security National. And now – either Van Helding gets the bank and I lose, or Van Helding drops the bank and it falls apart. I lose.'

'Are you telling me not to speak?'

'No,' Fairbairn said. 'I wouldn't presume. You're the one person who seems to have come through all this with some dignity and some standing. I wouldn't want you to give up now. I just don't know if I can be there to listen.'

In the afternoon they listened to official paranoia – how could Americans know a bank was sound, if it wasn't run according to American law? The idea that Kellerman Unger might obey Dutch law was produced as a great condemnation.

There was more. There might not be information on the bank's affairs, and when the New York Clearing Banks already had their problems, commingling with whatever dark secrets Kellerman Unger hid might be disastrous.

'Highly speculative,' Ryder said.

A lawyer warned about loans to Third World countries that couldn't pay interest, let alone capital, and deposits from oil producing countries that might be withdrawn at a moment's notice (the lawyer mentioned several sensational novels), and the lack of regulation in the Eurodollar market, and the lack of profit in retail banking.

'And how,' Ryder asked, 'does this apply to Security National?'

The arguments never quite became specific.

At three thirty, four members of the United States Labor United and Socialist Workers' (Marxist-Leninist) Party advanced in cardboard suits, unhappy in a temple of capitalist power, uneasily aware they were asking the enemy for a favour and maybe serving at least some of his interests.

The Mafia, they warned, was infiltrating trade unions and corporations and banks. Now they wanted Security National so that they could exploit the savings of honest working men. Kellerman Unger and Pieter Van Helding were nothing more than a front of respectability for organized crime.

David Grant watched the men stand to give evidence, eyes fierce, bodies stiff. The very fact that these men were making the accusations made it almost impossible for Ryder to give them credence. For the first time, the committee was hearing the literal truth. And in hearing the truth, it was being given an excellent reason to set truth aside.

Grant had an ice dagger in his heart. His life, after all, had been concerned with getting and sharing information, as though that act in itself would clean and improve. Yet sometimes the worst thing is the wrong person, telling the truth at the wrong moment.

Ryder put a guillotine of silence on the fraternal delegates and they trooped stiffly away, as though they had never expected more.

In the corridor, Marisia stared over David's shoulder at

a familiar walk. Odd how you could recognize the rhythms of a lover or brother, long before the face was clear.

She could always duck into a side room, deny that she saw him; but she decided she would not. She had come to face him out, after all, and she would take her chance.

'Hello', Van Helding said, chattily, and made David Grant's stomach turn over with self-righteous anger. 'I didn't know you were here. Are you cheerleading for the opposition?'

Marisia seemed quite cool. To David Grant, her lack of fury was mysterious. This was the man she denounced and despised; she was trying to ruin his plans. And yet she accepted his presence peacefully and without a murmur.

'And David,' Pieter said. 'It's good to see you. I'm relieved Fairbairn came over to my side before we ended up with a family feud.'

'Yes,' David Grant said, vacuously, completely unable to deal with Pieter's numbing self-assurance.

'It would have been so difficult,' Pieter said. 'For Marisia, I mean.'

Marisia had a grim little smile. 'Where's Katherine?' she asked.

'New York,' Pieter said. 'There's not much reason for her to be here.'

Grant felt like the victim of the schoolyard bully – except that adult rules forbade him either to hit out or to cry.

'I would very much like you to come for drinks,' Pieter said. 'I've taken a house in Georgetown for a month or so, until this whole business is over.'

The house was on the curious block where Henry Kissinger lives and which at night serves double duty as a gay cruising spot. Local dowagers say the gay men keep the streets safe; Kissinger's secret service escorts, however, do not help the neighbourhood.

There was a long, cool garden, mostly a basalt-black reflecting pool which sent back the blue sky and the high, scudding clouds. Trees drifted to the walks at the edge of the pool, and tall, ethereal flowers, pale and spiky, grew in the shade. It was urban landscape trimmed and perfected into décor. And there was a bottle of a Bollinger RD and there were comfortable chairs; and it was wrong, David Grant thought. Marisia, faced with the man she sometimes considered her enemy, seemed perfectly relaxed and unperturbed.

'David thinks we shouldn't talk,' Pieter said. 'I can tell.'

'He thinks we're opposing generals,' Marisia said.

David Grant felt profoundly uneasy. 'Of course not.' he said. 'After all, you're brother and sister.'

'You can tell it bothers him,' Pieter said.

'You know I'm appearing before the committee?' Marisia said.

'What in hell are you going to tell them?'

'Family secrets,' Marisia said, 'I expect. People talk about you a lot. You don't ever seem to do anything wrong.'

'I lost some money on horses. At Saratoga.'

'That's a start,' Marisia said.

David had wandered to the other end of the pool and he looked back at brother and sister, so close and intimate together. He spoke quietly to the surface of the water.

'It's like a whispering gallery,' he said. 'I can hear whatever you say.'

Brother and sister stared down the pool at him, profiles matched as neatly as coins from the same disc.

'I want to know,' David Grant said, 'why you don't fight.'

'Don't be silly,' Marisia said crisply. 'We can do that in the committee room.'

'But you call yourselves enemies . . .'

'Like nineteenth-century generals,' Pieter said. 'We fight wars, but we come from the same stock. We know the same people.'

'Marisia will tell all,' David said.

There was no response.

'It's a question of duty,' David Grant said. 'She has a duty to the American people – to tell what she knows.'

Brother and sister had risen from their chairs and were advancing down the narrow paving, a boisterous little committee of two.

'As for you, Van Helding,' Grant said, 'I expect you'll follow your usual standards.'

The committee reached David. He felt attacked by a single person with two faces, two bodies.

'Fairbairn and I . . .' he began.

The committee tumbled David off his guard and into the shallow waters of the dark pool, still in his black banker's suit and club tie.

'Pompous git,' Marisia said.

'Let me ring for another bottle,' Pieter said.

The water was shockingly chill, and in the sun David Grant was a wan, subdued figure.

'Borrow a suit,' Pieter said. 'Or my driver could take you home.'

'I'll get a taxi.'

'Don't be silly,' Pieter said. He went away to organize transport.

'I have some things I want to say to Pieter,' Marisia said. 'I'll follow you.'

David Grant shuffled wetly from the garden and into the car.

'I am going to talk tomorrow,' Marisia said. 'Seriously.'

'You're sure they are prepared to listen to you seriously?'

'Oh yes,' Marisia said. 'Ryder needs some action in that

committee. It's much too dull and proper for the headlines.'

'I understand.'

Pieter kissed her, very gently, a brotherly and not at all erotic kiss. It was so ambiguous, she felt chilled.

A bare half hour after David Grant went back to the hotel, Marisia said her farewells and called to say she was taking Pieter's car into town. David Grant was relieved. He wanted the fleshy, warm, familiar reassurance of Marisia curled around and with him. He wanted Marisia to come back to him from her conspiracy with her brother.

But after almost an hour, Marisia had not come. The journey back had taken David Grant fifteen minutes, presumably in the same car.

He thought: perhaps she has run away. He considered himself dull alongside her splendour. She needed a life of her own. Perhaps she had gone to claim it and her links with him had snapped.

One hour since the phone call. Something was wrong.

Car and driver skidded to a halt close to the FBI building, in an ugly ring of porn shops and blank, wine-blasted faces.

'Transmission, miss,' the driver said.

He stood by the hood of the car and shook his head. A second car drew up, and the drivers seemed to know each other.

'He could take you on, miss,' her man explained.

Marisia climbed out. Hot as the night was, the sidewalks were unfriendly. There were broken buildings, like dead teeth, in the line of the road, and occasional curious signs (GO-GO DANCERS FEMALE UNTIL EIGHT). She felt more comfortable in the back of the other limousine.

The new driver never asked her where she was going

but she assumed that the first man had told him. The journey began to seem very long, not the few blocks she vaguely remembered between the FBI building and the hotel. There was a bridge across a wide river; that was certainly wrong. And the sound of jets coming in to land at National Airport. Then there was parkway, trees and careful landscape, billowing like ribbons along an endless road.

She rapped on the partition to talk to the driver. He said nothing, simply drove ahead. The line of commuter traffic out of Washington kept them moving at a steady pace. Marisia thought about jumping from the car, but the doors were locked. She felt for a reading light in the back of the limousine; with a light, she might be visible even through the tinted glass and she might be able to signal. There was no light. All she could see was the road ahead, the pattern of lights, a little rain that came to smear the glass, and the clean, tall woodland on either side.

Distract the driver. But he looked only straight ahead. Take down the partition somehow, with an electric button, with a fist. The partition was solid. Get out of the car; no, that was impossible and, as the car picked up speed on the open parkway, dangerous. Watch the road to see where she was being taken. But she had not noticed the road as they came out of Washington itself. And she did not know the city or the surrounding country well. This parkway could lead to hell or Boston – or both.

She was in a kind of capsule, spinning away from the real world. She knew, all at once, she had been kidnapped.

It was easy to see why. Someone wanted to stop her from talking. Someone thought she had something important to say. This was Pieter's car, and she had been put in it after leaving Pieter's house; she had told Pieter she planned to cooperate with Ryder's committee. This was Pieter's plan.

Then it would be subtle. It would be right. Whatever he

planned, it would be what she feared, what perhaps she wanted. She stopped herself. Her train of thought was half logical, half erotic, when she most needed to think sharply.

She thought for a moment they might kill her. It was a calm thought, born not of panic but of meticulously thinking through her situation. So she must be ready to defend herself.

She looked at the driver. He was nondescript enough, an anonymous man in middle years, the kind who will always drive people to an execution if it pays the mortgage.

They would have to take her from the limousine. That was obvious enough. She doubted if there were still Raymond Chandler wagons that pumped poison gas at passengers while the drivers went miraculously unscathed.

The car turned without warning into the driveway of a large house. There were notice boards by the gate, but they were ill-lit and obscured by the trees. Marisia rattled the door of the car, thumped on the windows, cried out and tried to force both locks and catches.

The nurses smiled patiently, as though they understood too well.

'I want to speak to Pieter Van Helding.'

David Grant waited patiently, realizing that it was almost dinner time and Van Helding would probably be out in Washington on business.

'David,' Van Helding said.

'Marisia hasn't arrived,' Grant said. 'What the hell happened?'

'What do you mean? She left here more than an hour ago. My driver had some kind of transmission trouble, but she took another car.'

'I told you. She hasn't arrived.'

'I'll talk to the drivers. I don't understand.'

'If you harmed her . . .'

'Don't be ridiculous, Grant. She is my sister, after all.'

'Then where is she?'

'Perhaps she had business somewhere else . . .'

Grant heard the phrase and slammed down the phone in exasperation.

He didn't know where to start. He could check Fairbairn, of course, and perhaps Congressman Ryder's office. And after that – she could be anywhere. After this long hour and a half, she need not even be in the Washington area any more.

'Call me,' he said aloud. 'For God's sake call me.'

The room was neat, white, and full of flowers, and there were three other women – excited, joking about sex and faces. One said she'd always wanted bigger breasts. One said she'd worried so long that her face just wasn't her, that it didn't fit her personality. One said she reckoned her man was going off to a younger woman and she'd finally decided to have it done. The three of them giggled and chattered and they thought Marisia very strange. She looked grim and she didn't say a word.

She wanted to speak, though; it was just that when she tried to force words up through her thoat she felt muscles clench around the sound and kill it. Nothing came out except gutteral sounds, and she could not even predict what sounds.

She wondered what the other women thought, what sense they could make of her soundlessness. Maybe they thought she needed an operation on the vocal chords; that would make sense. But the clinic seemed to be for plastic surgery. Maybe they thought she was in for a face-lift as the first stage of some therapy to bring back her voice.

'Funny,' said one of the three, who felt she could speak

as if Marisia was not there. 'She looks just like that Marisia Van Helding. You know, the film star – the one on the seven o'clock news?'

Marisia nodded, and the women ignored her.

'Can't be, though,' said the woman who wanted bigger breasts. 'I looked at her charts. She's plain Mrs Grant.'

Marisia was alarmed by her sense of calm. They had injected her as she came in, some tranquillizing shot. Then they had taken advantage of her brief quiet to persuade her to take two red pills. Now she was aware that everything was utterly, alarmingly wrong, and her mind, through the curtain of drugs, knew she was somewhere to be hurt.

The nurses were sweetly reasonable, although they had never had a patient like Mrs Grant before. The ladies came in all excited and nervous, full of vitamins C, B, and E, and ready for the surgeon to make them lovely again, to beat off age with a cut. This woman did not seem excited. She seemed frightened and delirious, by turns.

The women chattered mercilessly. 'The one thing is,' said one, 'I had my nose done and what they don't tell you is, you hear it. You really do. They start with the knives and the saws and everything and, of course, you don't feel a thing but then they break the nose. Whoomp. And you really hear it crack. I remember so well.'

'And the way you look after the operation – my God!' said the woman who wanted to be younger. 'The first few days they keep you in that big football helmet bandage and then, when they take it off, it looks like you've been in a gang fight.'

'I asked him if I'd still have feeling in my nipples,' said the woman who wanted larger breasts. 'He said it would be just like before. They'd get nice and hard if Harold stroked them. I said I'd thank him if he could do the same for my H[illegible]old.'

Everyone laughed. Marisia found the drugs wanted her to laugh, to giggle happily. It was such a happy place and people were going to achieve such dreams. Except that she did not have such a dream; she was happy with body, face and age. They were her living and her identity and she didn't want anyone to change them.

The nurse bustled in, her face a neatly-tucked homage to the hospital's business. She distributed pills, warned that there must be no drinking, said the doctor would be along in a moment.

Something lodged in Marisia's mind, the kind of irrational idea that will not go away. If she could evade the doctor, it would all be fine. If she could just stay out of his way when he came on his rounds, they could not do anything to her.

She tried to get out of her thick, white bed. It was harder than she had expected. The drugs had taken away the resilience of knees, the balance of limbs. But she managed to get herself to the edge of the bed.

'You all right, dear, Mrs Grant? You don't look well.'

She wanted them to be quiet, all of them, to stop their talk about knives and operations, and allow her peace to make her mind and body lift, so she could walk down the corridor and escape the doctor.

'And you know, you're awake all the time. I mean you don't really feel anything and you forget it all afterwards, but at the same time you can see the knife and everything. Four hours they took with me.'

Get up. Get walking. Get into the corridor. Make yourself walk steadily so that nobody thinks anything is wrong. It's your evening constitutional. It's your right.

'I know. I heard all the stories, of course. They say there was this woman and they were lifting her face – only a young woman, mind – and they cut the facial nerve. She had no expression on that side of her face, ever again. They couldn't do anything about it.'

'I don't believe it.'

'I do. You think where the nerve comes out under the ear and it spreads across the cheeks – like this.' The woman held spread fingers against her face. 'That would be terrible.'

Marisia thought: that's what they're going to do. They don't have to make excuses. I checked into a clinic because of vanity, the operation, tragically, went wrong; that is all. She had never been a vain woman, but what they could do here with a slip of a knife was to take away soul, expression, and performance from her face. She had a sudden horror of what would happen. She imagined the four, five, six hours under a local anaesthetic while the surgeon worked, telling her to lift her eyes, raise her eyebrows, whatever was needed. Six hours sitting, half comatose, feeling as she did now – terrified at heart, smiling still.

If only the drugs would wear off. But, of course, they would not. She wondered how they had stopped her talking. She felt momentarily angry, and then she felt elated. Damn the drugs. She could no longer count on the loyalty of her mind or body.

She left the ward and wandered into the corridor, using one hand to steady herself against the wall. She went slowly, and she tried to seem certain of where she was going. She had no idea what to do when she reached a door, an exit to the outside world. Perhaps she could run, call for a taxi, call David, call Pieter – Pieter who could do something, who had the power, but who was the one who had sent her here.

And how to call?

She couldn't call a hotel. She would have to say the number she wanted, and she couldn't speak.

She couldn't tell anyone.

At the corner of the corridor, a tall, white-coated figure, elegant of face, said: 'Mrs Grant, isn't it?'

Marisia looked up at him. He seemed hugely, unreasonably tall, and even the friendly drugs could not take away her sense of terror. On the surface, she couldn't show anger or fear; she was only a light-headed, wandering girl, foolish and floating.

She beamed up at the doctor. She tried to say: 'Do you want to dance?'

David Grant paced the room. He didn't how to start. The only possibility was Van Helding and why should Van Helding be telling what he knew?

But if Van Helding knew, there was at least one other person who sometimes showed signs of caring equally for Marisia and Pieter, and who was in Pieter's confidence. He could call Koolhoven.

'Marisia's gone,' he said. 'She left Pieter Van Helding's house in Pieter Van Helding's car and she disappeared into thin air.'

'How long ago was that?'

'Almost two hours.'

'Won't Pieter say anything? Doesn't he know?'

'Pieter isn't very helpful. All I know is it would suit him if Marisia didn't give evidence tomorrow and Marisia gets into his car and she disappears. I don't want to sound paranoid . . .'

Koolhoven said: 'Don't say anything like that. Just don't say it.'

'I want her back. Now. I want to know that she's safe.'

'I don't know how to find her,' Koolhoven said. 'Believe me. If I could find her, I would. If Pieter's friends in Palm Springs have decided to do him a favour – God knows where she could be.'

'It doesn't have to be Rolfe and his friends,' David Grant said. 'It could be Van Helding himself.'

'I don't want to think so,' Koolhoven said.

Jan Unger broken. Jan Unger dead. Willem dead. Marisia gone. The trapping and humiliation of Alexander Fairbairn. The ruining of that poor bluff Joliffe in London. The rigging of the gold market. The list was now a catalogue of horrors, and in it there was nothing to make Koolhoven believe what he hoped: that Pieter Van Helding would never turn in violence against Marisia.

'I don't want to think so,' Koolhoven said again. 'I'll see if I can find out anything.'

She had one number still. It was on a slip of paper she was holding when they undressed her and drugged her and got her ready for bed. She didn't know whose number it was, but at least it lacked the string of zeros that a hotel would likely have. She might get a human voice to answer.

She didn't know what to do then. But she had one idea.

There were pay phones in the corridor. The ladies sometimes wanted to make private calls, away from the chatter of their roommates, and the booths were soundproofed.

She sat down. She dialled a number. Nothing happened. She had no change.

She opened the booth door a little, and gestured to a passing nurse. She didn't have to say anything; the nurse produced a handful of dimes.

'Put it on the account, dear,' she said. 'They never think you need things like dimes, do they?'

She dialled again.

After eight rings, when she was about to abandon the project, Koolhoven answered.

She touched the touch-tone buttons at random. Three short bursts; pause; three long bursts; pause; three short bursts. She hoped whoever had answered was friendly, and she hoped to God they knew Morse code.

'I hear SOS,' Koolhoven said. 'Is this Marisia?'

She tried to speak. Nothing came out.

'Tap once for yes, twice for no.'

She tapped once.

'OK,' Koolhoven said. 'Can you say where you are?'

Marisia tapped twice: No.

'Look at the telephone,' Koolhoven said. 'Is there a number?'

One tap: Yes.

'Is the area code 202?'

One tap: Yes.

'Thank God, you must still be close. Can you speak at all?'

Two taps: No.

Marisia could see the doctor returning in his long, white coat, imperiously shooing his subject women into their proper rooms. She had to move fast.

'Are you all right?'

Two taps: No.

Don't waste time, she said to herself, for God's sake don't waste time. Tell me what to do next.

'There's one thing we could try,' Koolhoven said. 'Tap out the number on the telephone. Tap it out like this – quick burst of dots five for the number five, nine for nine. Like that.' He demonstrated.

She watched the corridor and tried to hunch herself over the receiver so that nobody could see precisely what she was doing.

'Five-five-five,' so far so good. It seemed to be taking an age. She felt she had to make long pauses between the bursts of dots, simply to make sure that they were properly understood.

'Seven.'

The doctor was coming closer.

'One.'

'Four.'

Damn, the last figure was zero. She'd have to tap to ten. She'd never get to finish. The doctor was almost at the door of the phone booth and he wouldn't be tolerant of his patient's odd behaviour.

'One-two-three-four . . .'

'Mrs Grant,' the doctor said. opening the door, 'come along now.'

'five-six-seven . . .'

The doctor leaned forward, cut the phone line by pressing down, and smiled.

'Come along, my dear. You're in no state to make telephone calls. Why, you can hardly speak.' He summoned a nurse.

Koolhoven was left staring at the receiver. 202.555.714 . . . and then a number that could be seven, eight, or nine.

Very well, they had a clue to where Marisia Van Helding was. But how could they use it?

He called David Grant.

'One thousand milligrams vitamin C, 500 of pantothenic acid, 20 each of vitamins B_2 and B_6. That helps the antibodies. Then there's 2500 units of D, 300 of E and 500 of calcium lactate. That's to make sure your blood clots when we've finished with you.' The doctor grinned, but his speech was a routine. 'You'll be rattling with all those pills inside you.'

He guided her along the corridor.

'I just want one last look at you, to be sure. Just before we tuck you in. We've got you down for eight tomorrow morning, you know.'

The doctor's room was lit so brilliantly that Marisia's lazy eyes could hardly deal with the brightness. The doctor put her in a raised chair and stood back. He brought out pencil, ruler, pad, and markers, and he said: 'Of course, your case is unusual, my dear. Not at all what we're used to.'

Marisia wanted to see the drawings he was making, to see what he planned, but he would not show them. She wriggled a little in the chair.

'Keep still, dear,' the doctor said, patronizingly.

He took up a marker, and he began to make crosses on the skin of her face. Marisia drew back involuntarily from the felt tip marker. 'Upper lip blepharoplasty,' he said. 'A platysma lift for the neck – better a stitch in time, dear. And . . .' he passed a fingertip gently, tingling Marisia's temple, '. . . chemical peel. Dermabrasion is so very effective.'

Eight tomorrow morning, they were going to kill her face – do it with surgical razors and needles and chemicals that burn off the skin. The doctor seemed so sweetly reasonable as he talked. She couldn't say that she knew, that she didn't want it. She was left spluttering.

The purple pen marked where the surgeon would cut. And then the doctor half-lifted her, groggy as she was, from the chair.

'I expect you're nervous,' he said.

'Dance,' Marisia tried to say.

She wished she could just feel clearcut fear.

'The telephone company won't do it,' Grant said. 'I know that. We have to find someone who's got a reverse directory of some kind – numbers and then addresses. I can't think who would need one.'

'I suppose,' Koolhoven said, 'we do need a reverse directory. I mean, anyone who had a telephone directory in a computer program – couldn't they just ask it the question the other way round? Ask for the number in the data base, and get it to print out information? The telephone company must do that.'

'Anyone who did direct mail ads,' Grant said, 'if they did them from telephone numbers.'

'Or anyone with the DC phone book in a data base.'

It took twenty minutes, but they found such a data base – someone with access to the telephone company's data base, indeed.

202 555 7147.

Unlisted.

202 555 7148.

A clinic close to Baltimore.

202 555 7149.

A bookstore.

'If you'd called back I guess we would know which number,' Grant said.

'Possibly,' Koolhoven said. 'By the way, there is one other logical number. If Marisia wanted to punch out zero, she'd have to punch out ten. So we'd need to check 555 7140. And maybe 555 7150 as well.'

It was 555 7140 that convinced them. Another clinic, but this time a number listed as a patients' line.

'Out on the parkway,' Koolhoven said.

'It still could be the bookstore. Or the other clinic.'

'She must have been taken somewhere she could be hidden,' Koolhoven said. 'If that's a bookstore, we're stumped; we can't break in. But if it's somewhere like a clinic, where anyone might come and go . . .'

'We've got a set of chances.'

'And which do we try first?'

'The patients' number,' Grant said. 'I've never heard of the clinic. Most major hospitals have a switchboard with separate lines for separate rooms. This could be somewhere small – maybe an abortion clinic, something like that. Somewhere you could easily hide someone overnight.'

The logic convinced them. Koolhoven summoned a car.

'You must understand,' he said, 'I can't believe Pieter had anything to do with this.

'But you're still coming to help me.'

Koolhoven sighed. 'I don't know anything any more,' he said. 'It pays to assume the worst.'

The women in the room were sharp when Marisia returned. They thought she'd done well to get another private consultation with the doctor; they all rather fancied him.

The nurse came in. She had a pair of clippers and a comb and a businesslike expression. She was wary of Marisia, as someone might be of a dog of unpredictable temperament.

'Time to get you ready, dear,' she said. 'You're first for the chop in the morning.'

She parted Marisia's long, fine hair an inch back from the hairline all around the head, and she set the clippers whirring. Marisia's lovely hair tumbled randomly to the floor.

She felt like a prisoner. She could half see her face in a mirror, and it was scared and naked. And still the chemicals denied her the feeling of fear, and her frozen voice could articulate nothing, and she watched the nurse take away the thick clippings.

There was a last red pill, shaped like a lozenge. She might as well take it. Nobody was going to help, since the only person she had reached by phone was Koolhoven, and while he was decent enough, he was also Pieter's man.

She began to drift off. It was like sleeping, but also it was like being mad, and in the night figures crept and set siege to her mind. She was almost sure she saw Pieter, but she was also almost sure she saw Koolhoven and David. She was sure she went walking for a while.

'I'm Mr Grant,' Koolhoven said. 'And you've got my wife here. I demand to see her.'

The woman at the desk said: 'It's a long time after visiting hours, sir. Your wife will be asleep by now. She may even be sedated.'

'I don't think you understand,' Koolhoven said. 'I'm not paying for her to have this operation. I want her out of here tonight.'

'But sir, I'm sure . . .'

'Put yourself in my position,' Koolhoven said. 'I have to pay out all this money and you must have seen her when she arrived – did she look all right to you?'

'She was struggling a bit.'

'And the nurses, do they think she's all right?'

'They think she's a bit odd,' the woman said. 'Actually, she has a bit of trouble talking.'

'I'm happy to settle the bills,' Koolhoven said. 'I just don't want her to do something she'll regret and I'll have to pay for.'

He allowed a hundred dollar bill to show between his fingers.

'Besides,' Koolhoven said, 'I'd like to see her.'

'There are four other women in that room.'

'Just for a minute.'

'They'd be very alarmed.'

'I have ID.'

Grant had slipped out of the receptionist's field of vision, and down a corridor where no guards stirred. He waited for Koolhoven to persuade the woman to give the room number.

'She's in 4F. But I didn't say that . . .'

And then Grant kicked over a fire bucket, loudly.

'What the . . .' The receptionist was alarmed. She went to see what was happening, and as she did so, Koolhoven brushed past her. He ran down the corridor, waited for a bend, and then slowed down as though he belonged to the premises.

She went back to her desk to call security, and found the hundred-dollar note. It was quite a romantic idea for a man to want to see his wife, and, besides, he had seemed so reasonable. She hesitated.

They tried a side door. It opened on a dimly lit room. On a starched bed lay a woman in her middle years, body draped in satin, face hideously bruised and blotched. It looked as though her nose had been broken, her eyes had been torn, and despite the subtle placing of the scars and lines, the hurt around each set of stitches was apparent. The woman looked like a victim, beaten and set aside.

'They'll do that to Marisia?' Koolhoven said.

'They'll do something worse,' Grant said. 'That's just what people look like when they take the bandages off. She'll be better in a few days.'

The image hung in Grant's mind, for all that.

The next door opened into a nurse's office.

'Yes?' said the nurse, aggressively.

'We were looking for Mrs Grant. In 4F.'

'This is 4. F is on your right. Who are you?'

'I'm her husband,' David Grant said.

'She's signed the consent forms,' said the nurse. 'We're operating at eight.'

'You don't understand,' Grant said.

'I understand very well,' the nurse said. 'We get lots of husbands who decide they can't afford the surgery or they don't want their wife to go through with it. Then they start to make trouble. Well, I told you. It's too late.'

'Can I see her?'

Koolhoven came forward again, a hundred-dollar note turned to show the figure clearly.

'I suppose so,' said the nurse. 'But you mustn't disturb her. She's under sedation.'

'There's nobody else in the room?'

'Three others. But she's in the bed next to the door. On

the left. If you're not back here in three minutes, I'm calling the guards.'

'Thank you.'

'Just be here in three minutes.'

Grant and Koolhoven opened the door of 4F. Marisia lay behind curtains, asleep and apparently peaceful, but with her half-smiling face ringed by shaved flesh. She looked angelic and she looked ravished.

'Wake up.'

They could not wake her. She simply turned, smiled, and never moved her heavy eyelids. They had to pull her out of bed, and Grant took her in a fireman's lift. If anyone saw them in the corridor they would look a bizarre trio, impossible simply to pass by.

They got to the nurse's station. Koolhoven asked the nurse to see if Marisia was all right, saying she had seemed a little restless. The nurse titupped to the ward, clucking. If people came at this time of night to disturb the patients, was it any wonder they were restless?

When she had gone, Grant hefted Marisia through the nurses' station and out into the corridor.

The alarm bells started just as they reached the bend in the corridor before the elevators. They drilled insistently into the night, stunning the two men but not waking Marisia. The desk clerk must have given them a hundred dollars' worth of peace and then, when they had not reappeared, decided her job was at risk if she did nothing.

'Will security have guns?' Grant sounded urgent.

'I don't know. I mean, I don't know if they run this place as a simple clinic or . . .'

There was a scrambling of feet behind them.

Grant and Koolhoven, with the still comatose Marisia, ducked into a side room. There were white gowns, and a surgical trolley, and a porter sitting, smoking, with a copy of *Hustler*. He looked alarmed as the three entered, and got up protesting. Koolhoven slugged him; there seemed no choice.

Gowned, and with Marisia on the trolley, they came back into the corridor, moving urgently, as a pair of guards went by.

'Sir,' said one of the guards. 'What is that, sir?'

'Emergency. Cardiac trouble we can't handle here.'

'Do you need an ambulance ?'

'We've ordered one.'

The desk clerk recognized the faces, went to the alarm again and shouted as the two men bumped the trolley down the clinic steps. They unloaded Marisia without ceremony into the back of the Porsche and drove furiously away.

'That's kidnapping,' Koolhoven said.

'Thank you,' Grant said. 'I couldn't have found her without you.'

'I guess.'

They bundled Marisia's head in towels and set her on the sofa in the hotel room. They called a doctor, who tutted at the cocktail of drugs she had taken, began a lecture on indiscriminate drug abuse, and was told to be quiet; unused to such treatment, being an American doctor, he tried to leave, but money helped persuade him to stay.

'She's feeling no pain,' the doctor said. 'And she won't until late tomorrow. You can move her if you want to – no physical reason not to.'

In the hotel room, Marisia lay snoring and smiling, and half bald, while David Grant took himself to a sofa to sleep.

In his apartment, Koolhoven took a drink. After tonight, there was little prospect of Marisia appearing before the committee. She would take days to recover. She would have to explain to reporters her shaved head.

She might even be grounded by vanity. And she had had a simple warning: stay out of Kellerman Unger's affairs.

'I would like to thank this committee,' Pieter Van Helding read from typewritten sheets before him, 'for the detailed and fair examination of the issues involved in Kellerman Unger's bid for Security National. I appreciate your concerns. I understand your anxiety that American banks should be operated in the American interest. And I want to give this assurance.' Van Helding set aside his papers which served him only as a prop, so that he could signal by ignoring them some statement with special force of sincerity. 'I shall invite Mr Alexander Fairbairn to remain as President of Security National.'

Fairbairn glowed. It was instant salvation from the prospect of limbo.

'I shall remove no person from the board, although I shall appoint representatives of my own.'

A weasel promise, Grant thought. Van Helding could – probably would – double the size of the Security National board to reflect his new power and appoint more than half the votes. Some of the shareholders' representatives would be left without shareholders and would have to resign.

'And we shall maintain sizeable parts of the present management, although naturally I think Kellerman Unger will have something substantial to contribute to the running of the bank. This is after all an American bank, and it will continue to be run by Americans for Americans, in America.'

The committee room shivered with a brief round of applause.

'Thank you,' said Pieter Van Helding.

He had told no lies. He had simply not addressed the wild charges thrown against his bank, and the livid faces of the cardboard-suited Socialists at the back of the room showed how effective that strategy had been. And he had staged a proper climax to the hearings. Even Ryder, piqued that he had not brought Marisia Van Helding to give evidence, was delighted. He could rewrite his news-letter to constituents now: RYDER SECURES FUTURE OF GREAT AMERICAN BANK. He had a pause, no more than a pang of gas, when it occurred to him that most of his constituents owed more to banks than they loaned them – more mortgages and car loans than CDs and money market funds. It would look good, though; good enough.

David Grant sneezed violently.

'I can't go to Pieter's party this evening,' he said to Marisia when he returned to the hotel. 'I've got flu from falling in that bloody pool.'

'You didn't fall,' Marisia said. 'You were pushed.'

David Grant glared from below a billow of handker-chief.

Marisia looked a little curious with her new, high hairline and the first prickles of stubble growing back, but she had come through her ordeal with surprising strength. The near-coma ended bathetically in hangover. She looked in the bathroom mirror and for the first time in her life, she did not take her face for granted.

'Are you really going to Pieter's party?'

Marisia nodded. 'I saw Nancy Reagan's hairdresser,' she said. 'We've fixed a sort of wig and mantilla. It'll look a little odd but less odd than this.'

'I don't know how you can be so calm about what happened.'

'I don't know how much of the menace was in my mind,' Marisia said. 'Everything seemed to add up to a threat, and yet nobody ever said anything. Or did me much harm, apart from the hair.'

'Just because Koolhoven helped save you . . .'

'That confuses me, too. But I can't let Pieter down now.'

David Grant sneezed again.

The long black pool had been obliquely lit, so that its surface glittered a little but was not broken. Imported staff had organized the house into sociability and dematerialized with prim efficiency. It was a victory party, but discreetly so, and the only curiosity was the TV crew.

'*Sixty Minutes*,' Pieter explained. 'They're doing a profile of me.'

Marisia said: 'Shouldn't you have Katherine at your side?'

'She's not in the movies,' Pieter said. 'Besides, we look just like a great big old-fashioned family this way.'

He had the grace to laugh.

Marisia watched the crowd arriving. There were Congresspersons, sometimes with their own spouses; lobbyists, including some that Pieter did not employ; a handful of bureaucrats; some people from the *Washington Post* (Ben Bradlee thought of Van Helding as brilliant, aggressive, thrusting, much like himself); a man who came to parties because nobody could disprove his claim to work for the Ear column; some bankers, local and from New York; and a brace of grandes dames, surprising in this alien territory.

Fairbairn came at ten. He drank hard.

There were academics, mostly from the various free enterprise think-tanks that had followed Reagan to Washington; some people from the British embassy, and some from the unofficial British clan in New York, including a hairdresser and a minor rock luminary; and an exquisite Nigerian model. Bob Colacello was there with the style junkies; Andy Warhol was not.

And there were figures from the Hollywood that Marisia had tried to outgrow, including the banker Henry Klein.

He was surprised to see her, but he smiled. He had a forgiving nature. After all, Pieter had once asked him to ruin her career because she refused to cooperate with the Palm Spring gentry. He felt this was an imposition and that Marisia had been unnecessarily difficult. However, he was willing to let bygones be bygones.

Marisia circled with the guests, now acknowledging a compliment from a New York frockmaker who had taken to dressing only and always in black, now ducking a knot of identical, still-featured California matrons. The utter lack of warmth in the place amazed her. The only subject which animated all these disparate people was power – who had it, who was losing it, who was gaining it.

Pieter Van Helding obviously had it.

Marisia suddenly wanted air, and she drifted out to the poolside with Henry Klein in tow. It was cooler by the water and less fraught.

'Its, er, so nice to see you again,' said Henry Klein. He seemed a little nervous.

Pieter was also in the garden. He was talking to Sally Rogerson, tall, lovely Sally whose face seemed drawn and tight. They were very quiet, very intense, not at all social.

'We leave for San Francisco on Tuesday,' Sally said. 'The whole company is going.'

'You can't stay in Washington for a while?'

'Only tonight.'

'I'll see you in London, then?'

'I'm not sure any more, Pieter. It's been fun, but now it doesn't make much sense.'

'I don't understand.'

'You'll think I'm being silly. It's just that I need a little more certainty. In my trade, we get nervous when we get older. The muscles get slack. The body doesn't sing as it used to. It's worse for the men, but we all worry.'

'You have your allowance.'

'It isn't money,' Sally said. 'I worry about feelings and I worry about career.'

'You can teach.'

'I want to teach. And I want to settle in London.'

'That can be arranged.'

'I mean, settle. Someone, the same someone, in my bed every night. All night.'

Marisia thought of walking down by the pool to talk with the couple, but something in their seriousness stopped her. She guided Henry Klein away. She was afraid that something was happening that would make Pieter angry, and she did not want to see his cold eyes.

'And I'm pregnant.'

'You don't have to explain.'

'It's getting late for me, Pieter. For a baby. For everything. I'd better go.'

'People don't just leave,' Pieter said. 'They don't leave me.'

Sally smiled and pushed past him.

Van Helding went back to the party as sombre as mourning. He had lost, and the feeling was unfamilar. He was losing his sense of control. He never wanted to feel this way again.

Marisia watched him, carefully. Perhaps he was vulnerable, at last; but she doubted that. He recovered quickly and slipped back into the party, talking subtly and persuasively to a Colombian in a corner. A lobbyist had pinned a Congressman like a butterfly and was crucifying him with gin; Marisia sailed to the rescue.

And then she took Pieter to a corner.

'I don't know why you didn't come back to the committee,' he said.

She looked at him with no visible emotion, a calmness that she could hardly feel. 'You know,' she said. 'Besides, I can't attack you on moral grounds. You have no shame.'

'You flatter me.'

'I have one thing to tell you, now we've done this party.'

'Go ahead.'

'I'm going to kill you.'

Pieter looked at her, serious and cool, and he said with immense complacency: 'Good luck'.

8

It was respectable, glamorous financial power – money with black Halston dresses and sharp minds and proper connections. It was exactly what the Palm Springs gentlemen had wanted Pieter Van Helding to deliver and he had done them proud. He looked coldly self-contained as he waited for the New York shuttle at National, among solemn businessmen telling overloud jokes, pecking at calculators, shuffling files, anything to mask their fear of flying. One boy said he recognized him from the pictures in the paper and he had always admired Mr Van Helding. Van Helding stayed cold. He had won himself an empire, but with tricky obligations – and the Palm Spring gentry could not be trusted to behave discreetly. He had to take control briskly and remorselessly. He had to take control, in fact, when he landed in New York.

The papers were full of his party and his triumph, and for once they failed to mention his father's murder. Pieter Van Helding was known at last.

The last few passengers scrambled onto the plane, glaring at the filled seats with unconcealed resentment. A neat, blank man asked Van Helding to move his briefcase.

'Gregory,' the man said. 'Mr Gregory.'

'How good to see you.'

'I have some papers for you.'

The plane began taxiing gently to the runway.

'You once saw a file on your father. Parts of it, anyway. Now you can have the whole thing. We've talked about it, and there's nothing more we can do with it. You might as well know all we know.'

'Isn't it a little indiscreet to talk here?'

'Nowhere better,' Gregory said. 'Nobody can listen to you at takeoff. They're too scared and it's too noisy.

The plane began to gather speed.

'You have one copy and so do we,' Gregory said. 'You can publish if it helps you, but you can't suppress it. We still have the files if we need them.'

'I don't understand why . . .'

'We like to help friends,' Gregory said, 'even if they have friends already.'

The plane roared up into the sky.

'And now,' said Gregory, as their fellow passengers relaxed and the 'fasten seat belts" sign went off, 'now we shall talk of something else. Your party last night was a great success, I hear. And your lovely sister? How is she?'

'It's like the first day of school,' Fairbairn said. He was harrumphing like a wounded beast, uncertain if he had to give up territory, worried about his powers. 'Where the hell is he?'

Fairbairn's secretary reported that the Eastern shuttle was running late. 'Again,' she said.

'Why can't he get a corporate jet?' Fairbairn sniffed.

Van Helding took Gregory to the taxi rank at LaGuardia and left him by a health spa just past the midtown tunnel. Gregory never said where he was going or why, and he never seemed to have an address.

In front of the Security National building was a public space, lined with the city lost, some smoking generous spliffs, some clutching bottles wrapped in brown paper, some looking douce and decent, only out of place. Van Helding passed them into the building.

'I am Pieter Van Helding,' he said to the guard. 'And what's your name?'

'Fred,' said the guard. 'Who do you want to see?'

'I'm the new boss,' Van Helding said, gently.

The guard was startled. 'Yes, sir,' he said. 'Can I help you, sir?'

Van Helding caught the elevator to Fairbairn's office. It amused him to take the old man slightly by surprise. He was recognized in the elevator, and he caused a silence which crushed the most spirited secretarial tattling. He stalked to Fairbairn's territory and was greeted by the old man as though he were a restaurant guest enticed by a *maître d'*; the old man offered the arrangements of the day like a menu, offered coffee, offered his office.

'That won't be necessary,' Van Helding said. 'I just need a small office when I'm in New York. Somewhere to work from. I know if you start moving people's offices in a place like this you upset the perks and promotions of a hundred years.'

Fairbairn chattered. He was clearly nervous, and grateful that he would not have to cede territory as he abandoned control.

'I have some ideas,' Van Helding said. He took from his briefcase a list of twenty points, typed as a memorandum. He read through them, allowing no interruptions. They were immediate, necessary actions like firing the men responsible for the Ironside débâcle, softening the currency dealers so they would not be offended by a new and brighter boss from London, startling a committee on the retail banking side with a memo that did not flatter their results or prospects, and arranging drinks with a few leading brokers to press the case for the new Security National as corporate underwriters. He would start, Van Helding thought, with Bob Fomon at E. F. Hutton. He admired the man, and he liked his leafy office.

'He's working,' Fairbairn admitted to his secretary.

'You don't know the half of it,' his secretary said.

There was also a call from Henry Klein. Van Helding

had expected it, but he hardly knew how to handle it. He had gone into this long alliance knowing the nature of the people who shipped him funds when he needed them. He remembered the corpse-sour smells from the Thunderbird in a Safeway parking lot, when a property deal went wrong.

He said nothing to Henry Klein.

'Congratulations,' Klein said. 'We gave you a pretty clear run because we don't like to use our contacts when we don't need them. And you pulled off a very clean deal.'

'Thank you.'

'There's one thing. We need to deposit some money. Usual sort of thing. We thought we might open a few accounts under ten thousand dollars. Just so you wouldn't have to tell the IRS. Then we thought we might arrange a few letters of patronage for some offshore companies. We need to find a less cumbersome way to move money.'

'You're calling from New York?'

'Of course,' Klein said. 'I wouldn't be so indiscreet as to talk like this on a long-distance call. I know what the FBI always listen to.'

'And you want comfort letters for offshore companies, so they can borrow? Secured against a scatter of deposits in upstate New York?'

'Exactly. It's better to keep this sort of thing close to home, don't you think?'

'You want me to handle it?'

'I'm sure you have other things to do.'

'I have six months' work making sense of this place. Then I can start worrying about London and Amsterdam.'

'So find some trusted people. We could find them for you, if you like.'

'I like to control my own people.'

'So do we, Pieter,' Klein said. 'Congratulations on the merger.'

Money doesn't have morals, Pieter reflected, hearing

still the click as the line went dead. So it's drug money out of Miami and the Keys, or it's something in New Jersey – dumping toxic waste, construction payola, union kick-backs. Or it's mozzarella or some monopoly of tomato paste, or maybe it really comes from crime that involves guns and violence and menace. It's clean when it reaches us, Van Helding thought; or at least it is no dirtier than any other money. He would not know how to card wool, build looms, draw patterns if he was putting money into a textile firm somewhere, or helping the firm borrow money; and he did not need to understand the business of his friends. He only wanted them to keep the business far from him. He had come this far on their whim and they could put him back to zero with their indiscretions.

But they needed him, and he was secure in that comfort. They had other relationships with banks – fraud, for example – and they had other Wall Street allies. But they needed his special visibility and his fame.

It was six thirty in the evening before he had time to look at the papers Gregory had left with him.

He asked for drinks, and he thought. Even though he might have special power over the names in the file, it was arbitrary knowledge, hard to use. He had power enough over people he had long suspected; he had a position whose bulwarks were fortune and empire. He wasn't sure what else he needed.

He wasn't used to declarations of independence; either they made him angry or he could not quite believe them. Sally Rogerson had gone. And now Klein chose to call him and pull the strings, a reminder that his power was conditional. His world seemed a little less than perfect even as he made his triumphal entry into Security National. And less than perfect wasn't what he wanted.

He dreamed of risky expeditions for great wealth, up forest rivers, between strange midnight creatures; of Eldorado, of hacking a way to gold. He wanted to be something more than the efficient architect of Dr Rolfe's aspirations.

He could go to Providencia, go into the bush for a while and come back with some fabulous riches, stones that gave special powers, the impediments of a fairy tale.

He stared at the file again.

Sometimes he thought the killing of his father haunted him and Marisia, and shaped their lives. But at other times he could admit that he himself chose to keep the memory alive, because it was useful.

He told himself to stop thinking in grandiose terms. He should think only of how the file could be used.

Koolhoven called at eleven, and it was not like him to make unexpected calls.

Marisia was away in a crystal high of her own where David, on mere alcohol, could not quite follow. She was bright and sharp and short-tempered and she was thinking, more than anything, of breaking finally with Pieter Van Helding and establishing her own independence. She was thinking of doing it with a gun.

And David Grant, gentle and philosophic, was watching and tending her. He thought he understood less and less of what drove her, and even so he was more and more fascinated. She had been assaulted, terrified, and she needed comfort; but within a few hours, it seemed, she was strong enough to embarrass the man who had organized her hurt. She seemed to want no obvious revenge, no simple confrontations. The tensions between brother and sister were almost palpable, cords of contact that seemed to muddle love and hate. It puzzled David Grant and he knew there could be no simple explanation.

Koolhoven was announced.

'I'm sorry it's so late,' he said. 'I had to see you both.'

They offered drinks.

'I'm very worried,' Koolhoven said. 'I expect that's obvious.'

Marisia said: 'You're never worried.'

Koolhoven shrugged. 'I try to be of service,' he said. 'Senior eunuch, that's my role. Everybody listens and nobody expects me to do anything.'

'You've run the bank for years.'

'I'm glad someone sees that,' Koolhoven said. 'I thought I was pretty much invisible.'

He hadn't come to complain he was too little appreciated, Marisia thought. Whatever he wanted to say involved pain and difficulty; he could not bring himself to say it directly.

'You love Pieter, don't you, still?' he said, after a pause.

'He's my brother.'

'Even after what he had done to you . . .'

'We don't know who actually organized that.'

'It must have been Pieter.'

'It could have been his friends. After all, they only had to keep me out of the way for a day or two, so I couldn't talk to the committee. Maybe they didn't mean harm.'

'They held you,' Koolhoven said. 'They threatened you. They left you for a whole night without a voice, and you must have been terrified.'

'Yes,' Marisia said. 'I was.'

'And you're so calm about the whole thing.'

'I don't waste my energy,' Marisia said, 'any more than Pieter does. There's no point in anger if you can't do anything with it.'

'Pieter terrifies me,' Koolhoven said. 'There's been so much that I hardly wanted to believe. And I always thought I was ultimately in control – that the game was the one I knew and studied. And now, things seem very different.'

His voice was flat as his words.

'You could quit,' David Grant said.

'No,' Koolhoven said. 'That's the one thing I can't do. First of all, someone has to watch over Pieter Van Helding, for all our sakes. I've done it so long I doubt if I could hand over the job to anyone else. And then, what would I be without Kellerman Unger?'

'We all seem to owe our lives to that bank,' Marisia said.

'I had to say all this,' Koolhoven said. 'Please forgive me. I didn't know anyone else who would even begin to understand.'

'Talk as much as you want to. Stay the night, if you want.'

'You know,' Koolhoven said, warming a little, 'I remember you and Pieter as children – you, from the time you were born. I feel like a family retainer. I shall have to write my memoirs one day – The Van Heldings as I Knew Them.'

Marisia said: 'God forbid,' which came out rather more sharply than she had intended.

'Do you remember Pieter talking about Eldorado – about wanting to go and look for a city of gold in the forest? He's started to talk that way again. It sounds to me as though he is serious.'

'I can't imagine Van Helding out of a city and a city suit,' David Grant said.

'He'd wrestle alligators in a pinstripe suit,' Marisia said. 'That's who and what he is.'

'But he's tired of who he is,' Koolhoven said. 'It's as though he has ambitions that could never possibly be fulfilled – in any imaginable world.'

Marisia shrugged. 'Maybe it would be good for him to go up a river and get bitten by mosquitoes. Who knows?'

'If he went,' Koolhoven said, 'I couldn't go with him. But somebody should. I mean, he is not – not quite sane, I think, any more. Somebody ought to be with him.'

David Grant shuffled his feet. 'You mean me.'

'You're young enough,' Koolhoven said. 'I don't like to admit it, but I'm not.'

'Has he bought the plane tickets?' Grant asked. 'I mean, should I start packing?'

'No,' Koolhoven said, 'no, no. It's not that close. It's just – I wanted to ask if you would go.'

Marisia began to laugh like falling ice.

'Don't laugh at me,' Koolhoven was desperately serious, his anger and his hopelessness merged together. 'Please. I have to protect him. I thought you loved him, too.'

'It's possible he tried to kill me.'

'But he's . . . Pieter.'

Marisia shrugged. 'Some day that magic is going to wear off,' she said.

'Senior eunuch,' Koolhoven said again, because he liked the line. 'That's my role. Everybody listens but nobody expects me to do anything.' In the great hall of mirrors, shimmering with volleyed reflections of candles and crystal, the Sun King had long passed. His successors this night were the finance ministers and bankers and bureaucrats who make up the International Monetary Fund.

Koolhoven fitted. The Dutch liked to listen to him and the British politely deferred. Van Helding had no taste for this kind of diplomacy and Koolhoven did it well; but, more importantly, he did it seriously.

At Koolhoven's table were two topics. Only one was money. The United States had again been told to contribute more to IMF, and IMF had announced its willingness to distribute such money to Third World countries whose debt had passed reason. This arrangement was regarded as highly satisfactory by the commercial banks, who gratefully saw assorted taxpayers, mainly American, assume the burdens they had taken on without due thought. It was liked less among the American bureaucrats, who failed to see why one nation should prop up the world's economies, especially when many of them seemed singularly ungrateful to their benefactor. It also seemed rough to the Third World countries themselves, who knew only too well the prim programmes of conventional austerity which IMF demanded as the condition of loans. A man from Bangladesh, who remembered the genocide of the early 1970s, said very quietly that it was ironic that the price of getting money to pay American Express was cutting food subsidies to his people.

There was another topic, more electric, less detailed. An enterprising American banker had organized a night's entertainment after the banquet, at the house of the lady who had succeeded Madame Claude.

'These meetings are good for the ego,' Arthur Miller said. He was a dapper, middle-aged black man, Inner Temple trained, who had ruled Providencia like a socialist emperor since the revolution. A judicious use of pipe bombs had discouraged his opponents from reminding him too loudly that the CIA had put him in office originally to keep the left at bay. Now, he liked to talk about the Providencia Experiment, hung banners across his airport which for a full year had welcomed the Cuban table tennis team, and made much of his standing in the Third World. 'I think', he said, 'we are scorned by most first world people, the second world has doubts about us, and our own people make occasional revolts. But here, everyone wants to know us. Everyone wants to lend to us. Only the bankers love us.'

'It's the new world economic order,' Koolhoven said cheerfully. 'The banks have let themselves be expropriated. For a profit, of course.'

'But I still believe the wealth of the world has to be redistributed.'

'Don't say that while you owe us money,' Koolhoven said. 'Imagine the panic if people suddenly lost confidence in all our Third World loans. Imagine the money we'd have to write off.'

'Tax advantages,' Miller said. When he was a London lawyer he had known about such things.

'Bankruptcy, more like,' Koolhoven said. 'If the confidence goes, we don't have anything else. If all the unreal loans were called in, who'd eat? If all the risky lending were stopped, there wouldn't be a factory or a rice paddy south of El Paso or east of Berlin.' He was tearing a piece of bread between broad fingers. 'I can imagine that the whole machine will dissolve one morning. We'll find that all the businesses aren't making money, and all the governments are heavily in debt, and all the Third World can't pay us back, even the interest, and the whole system tumbles down. It's only paper and faith, after all.'

'Nonsense.' There was a solid New Yorker with a Brahmin voice, a banker of substance. 'Don't depress yourselves. If banks had to worry about the real world, we couldn't do business. We could never take a risk. And if we didn't take risks, then the Third World wouldn't have what little it does, East and West would be even more at odds than they are, and I doubt if there would have been peace in Europe for the past thirty-five years. Large sums of money have a wonderfully healing effect, if you spread them wide enough.'

'But that leaves you with the power,' Miller said. 'You pull the strings. It's your whim and your judgement whether I can buy rice on the open market this fall. It's like going back to being a colony – except instead of paying tribute, we pay interest, and nobody builds our hospitals any more.'

'So does Washington,' the New York Brahmin said. 'Every government pays interest when it borrows money. There's no reason why you should be different.'

'It is different, though,' Miller said. 'You buy a T-bill and you don't buy the right to make economic policy. But when the IMF lends us pennies, it can dictate what it wants – because we need those pennies so desperately.'

'I would love to write economic policy,' the Brahmin said.

'But not for my government,' Miller said.

'We just want a return on our money.'

'Tush,' Miller said. 'You lend to us because we pay more. Your interest rates are controlled in your own country. You make a loan in Simonstown and the rules are different, and besides, the money's safe. Your own government stands behind the IMF who stand behind us. You're guaranteed.'

'Of course,' said the Brahmin thoughtfully, 'the whole game could end if one country went bust. I do see that.' He wondered how bad Providencia's troubles really were. Miller and Koolhoven seemed awfully chummy, but no other bankers were dashing to woo Miller. That in itself was unusual; a Third World country with credit and heavy loans, was normally in social demand at an IMF meeting. Now it was no secret that Kellerman Unger was heavily committed to Providencia, and none that Providencia had its own problems – like an economy dead in the water. The Brahmin fished for clues.

From the far quadrant of the circular table, all men, a plangent voice was raised. 'What happened,' it said, 'to Madame Claude's girls?'

'I'm sure they found work,' Koolhoven said. 'They had talent and experience, after all.'

'And double joints, some of them,' said the plangent

voice, digressing to a long, lewd anecdote. The high talk of finance subsided in favour of lickerish anticipation.

After the last *digestif* the long limousines surged up to palace steps, took in the diners and swept them away from the sparkling dream of Versailles. The evening could officially begin.

Koolhoven was beginning to unwind. It had been a slightly disconcerting conference. He knew Providencia had problems, but the meeting gave him his first chance to see how many other people knew. And the Grunwalds had been conspicuous by their absence. Of course, the old families of money were out of fashion in Paris, but still the Grunwalds usually had business to do. Koolhoven sensed the bank had two clients who were unlikely to thrive.

From the moment the limousine pulled away – bearing Koolhoven, Miller and some others – a new game had begun. In the thicker trees along the roadway, the driver seemed to make out the shape of a girl, high skirt, tight blouse, booted, hitchhiking back into Paris. He drew to a halt.

'What the hell is he doing?' Miller asked. 'Doesn't he know about security?'

'Don't worry,' Koolhoven said. 'This is the start of the entertainment.'

The girl was tall, loose-limbed, blonde hair flying, and a pretty, almost childish face. 'Charmed, I'm sure,' she said with a faint Blackpool accent, as she settled in the car. She let her hands drift over her nipples, brown, and indented. 'Such nice gentlemen,' she said.

Miller giggled. The limousine went on sedately through the empty streets, its world made private with dark glass. Inside, one of the men put out an exploring hand, and ran the girl's short skirt a little up her thighs, and then further, until he saw a fine, blonde bush. She wriggled a little, pleasurably, on the seat. Galsworthy adjusted his dress, self-consciously, and the girl saw the gesture and put out a hand to his cock. She took it deep into her mouth, stroking with her tongue, and Miller buried his own tongue, very suddenly, in her blonde bush. She passed like an icon from lips to lips, mouth to mouth, hand to hand.

Koolhoven was amused. The girl made the rules and the men hardly knew it. She was playing victim but actually controlling everything.

She opened her blouse and let it fall away. The men reached out for nipples, for clitoris, for the fine, runner's backside, and a faint whiff of brandy and cigar and warm, wet lust filled up the car.

The car came to a soft halt by a large suburban house and the girl disentangled herself carefully, leading the way naked up the steps and past shrubbery into a bourgeois stolid home.

The place had great decorum, and women. The Brahmin was tugged upstairs with the girl for a healthy, unsubtle fuck, tugged by instinct. The others sat on sofas in an Empire drawing room, chatting, being amused by the girls, drinking champagne, amusing themselves with the gestures of hand and lip that would have been unforgivable at a more proper party.

And when the first, furious bout of sex was over, and Koolhoven had returned to the drawing room, he talked long and decorously with the Madame. She was an old friend, an associate of the legendary Madame Claude whose girls were the enticement and the wonder of generations of diplomats, persons worthy of unofficial reward or bribe, politicians and the men who could not possibly be thought to belong to hoi polloi.

'It's good to see you,' the Madame said,

Koolhoven loved such moments. His appetites were satisfied and he could enjoy the satisfaction in the glow of friendship. There was none of the postcoital coldness and distance of other brothels. Madame Claude had always been a social person and her successors worked the same way.

Miller had taken a strapping blonde woman upstairs, and when he returned, he moved a little awkwardly. He also seemed serious and glum in the car returning to Paris.

'It won't last,' Miller said.

'Are you always this depressed when you've had a woman?'

'I mean Providencia. It's going to go wrong. You go on giving money and we try to pretend to pay back loans, but it can't last.'

'Sex doesn't seem to agree with you.'

'I'll tell you what doesn't agree with me. It's the idea that I might never go to Madame's house again.'

'You have money.'

'I am a socialist.'

'Even socialists are allowed to be prudent about the future.'

Miller thought for a moment. Nobody ever suggested he was like some other Caribbean leaders – whose IMF loans are shipped in Vuitton suitcases to numbered accounts on Bahnhofstrasse in Zurich, sending money back to its natural home. But he was also not a fool. Men who play with the CIA are wise to have bank accounts away from home.

'You don't understand,' Miller said. 'I could have a retreat and servants and a rich man's life, I suppose, but I would be sad if that was all I had. I did want more, you know.'

Koolhoven stared out of the car window, embarrassed by the compassion he felt.

Marisia Van Helding dressed to dazzle, armour against the battle. She was going to break away, battle for herself, free herself from the all-involving ties with Pieter, with family, with the bank. She felt as though the family, since her mother died, had been a snare.

She was almost sure what she wanted, in the elevator rising to Van Helding's office. Almost, because she was still a little nervous that her body would betray her will, that she might momentarily weaken when she faced Pieter and fail. In her handbag, she carried a gun.

Inside the executive maze, there was calm. Bland walls, fair art, large ficus trees. No junior persons, harried and tousled, dashed through corridors. Nobody was bonhomous by the elevator, dreaming of early lunch. She had time to collect herself. She was sure she would end it all now.

'Marisia, darling.'

Marisia allowed herself to be led into his office. It was surprisingly small, not on a corner, lacking all the signs of corporate power that she had become used to seeing and weighing while in Hollywood. And she looked at Pieter. He was spare, strong, able to concentrate will upon objects like a burning glass. She wondered how she looked to his still, formidable eyes.

Van Helding brought out the usual Bollinger RD.

'This isn't really a social call,' Marisia said, but she took wine anyway. 'I'd like to get to the point.'

'Please do.'

'I want to sell my shares in Kellerman Unger. I've decided that I don't want anything more to do with the bank.'

'Again?' Pieter said. He smiled. 'Why don't you just cash the dividend cheques and forget about it? The cheques should be good this year.'

'I've decided. It's too complicated to explain.'

'You want to break away, is that it? To be free of family and of me?'

'I'm an independent woman.'

'That's not in doubt. It's a lousy reason for giving up your assets.'

The champagne bubbles spent themselves gently in her nose. She wanted to giggle.

'I don't know where to sell them,' Marisia said. 'I assumed the bank might want to buy them in. They must be almost the only independent shareholding left in Kellerman Unger.'

'There are a handful of shares in trust for Georg – for any children I might have, I mean.'

'I want to get away from all the past. I don't want to be part of father's murder and Unger's war and your dubious friends. I thought that before, but after what happened during the hearings – someone wanted to destroy me, hurt me, because I dared to argue with you. Well, if that's the new rules of the game, I'm not willing to be a martyr. I want out.'

'I didn't have anything to do with the kidnapping,' Pieter said. 'Believe me.'

'But it spared you some embarrassment. Didn't it?'

'I'm very sorry it happened.'

'I'm sorrier. Because it's an academic question whether you planned it or not. You showed once before you'd be happy to ruin my career if I didn't do as you said. You're quite capable of organizing something like that.'

'Do you need the money? I mean, you come here and announce some great dramatic statement, and all you want to do is sell some shares. You could do that without telling me.'

'Hardly,' Marisia said. 'It's still a significant bloc, and besides, there's hardly any open market for KU shares.

'They'd be hot,' Pieter said, 'if anyone knew they were available.'

'Nobody does, yet. I'm trying to end all this calmly and neatly.'

'You can't end family ties. You can't get away from being father's daughter. All you can do is make a fuss about the shares – which in reality are a nice income and no moral problem. They don't hold you back.'

Marisia felt herself slipping, losing the certainties she had brought with her, sensing that the more they talked the less easy it would be to take decisive action. Perhaps she was making an absurd fuss, perhaps nobody understood the huge symbolic weight she made the shares in Kellerman Unger bear. She really felt that in selling them, she could be morally distanced from Pieter. And yet selling them looked so very much like a device to seize his attention again. She watched her motives with a cold, clear inner eye.

'I don't like the way you do business.'

'We do business like other people.'

'I just want out of the whole thing.'

Damn feeling. It ought to be possible to set it aside when you need to be cold. Her glass of champagne slipped a little, and her hands went down to blot away a few beads of liquid, and Pieter caught her hands.

'Your hair grew back beautifully,' he said.

'I . . .'

'You have beautiful hair. When you've been swimming, it's beautiful even then. Soft, wet, long, strong hair.'

The moment seemed to hang endlessly. Marisia waited for the adrenalin to rush and her body to welcome him, as it had done before, but this time she felt separate. That moment, she knew she had truly won her independence.

But Pieter did not know it. Or if he knew it, his hands and his eyes did not give the fact away. He was fooling with her hair, and then with her breasts. It was the right motion, the one that suspended sense and breath for a moment, but it did not work. He must sense that, she thought. Yet he keeps coming at me, as though to punish me. This is the price I have to pay for doing it before . . . never being able to say 'No' with conviction.

Sometimes when you hate most, you lust most. Marisia was terrified as she felt more and more of Pieter's weight pressed against her. She would break in a moment, surrender, gladly. That would be the worst thing. She would thrust and moan and cry out and – if only she could hold on to the will she brought with her, which now seemed as certain and substantial as discarded wrappings from a present.

He had uncovered her breasts and his fingers were playing along the inside of her thighs. She thought of jamming her thighs together. When she did it, his hand simply forced a way, up to her sex. An unfriendly hand, that had expected to triumph and would not admit defeat, a fist close to her vitals.

Marisia leant back to gain the momentum for a swing at Pieter. It was then that Katherine arrived.

Katherine had meant to speak her husband's name to tell him she was there, but she'd hoped to surprise him, perhaps put a hand over his eyes as he finished a phone call. Well, she thought, she'd surprised him. The scene before her seemed unequivocal. There was Pieter, dishevelled, importunate, and there was a woman, arching back, a fist at her sex. Then Katherine recognized Marisia. It was odd how it took minutes to recognize someone so close to blood. Katherine lost expression in her face. Pieter and his sister, in a skein of undone clothes and wild hair, on a sofa in the morning.

Pieter tensed and Marisia took advantage of his shock, pulling away, cradling clothes around herself as though she were swaddling a baby. She felt violated.

Pieter said: 'You know Marisia, of course.'

His apparent assurance startled both women.

'I know Marisia,' Katherine said.

'Katherine,' Marisia said, 'it's not what . . .'

'Please don't tell me. I don't want to know.'

Pieter simply watched. His diplomatic skill was intact. Marisia was apologizing to Katherine for Pieter's assault, and Katherine was forgiving Marisia. Pieter was clear. In time, Katherine might come to take some vague, unspecified but killing responsibility for what had happened. Pieter could walk away from his own crime.

Yet Marisia wanted most of all to comfort Katherine. Katherine had so little feeling left; of all the grotesque moments she had lived with Pieter Van Helding, to find him making love to his own sister seemed only a mild exaggeration of the norm.

'We'd better not explain,' Pieter said. 'People misinterpret things.'

'I want a divorce,' Katherine said.

'You're hysterical.' But Pieter thought Katherine was remarkably rational. She had evidently reached her breaking point, very late.

'I'll go,' Marisia said.

'I've thought about it for months,' Katherine said, 'and it doesn't have anything to do with what I just saw.'

'I thought you came for lunch.'

'I was going to see my lawyers, and I wanted to see you first.'

'Are you,' Pieter said, settling back into his chair behind a fortress desk, 'going to cite my sister as co-respondent?'

Marisia froze on her way to the door. Her face read horror.

'I don't know.'

'People will think that's a rather sad fantasy, from a rather sad woman. You do realize that?'

'It wasn't a fantasy.'

'You've been under such strain. You never recovered from the death of the children. I can hear what they'll say.'

'It was real. And it doesn't matter. I want to divorce you because you live off other people. You suck their blood.'

'And you also realize . . .' Pieter was insultingly calm '. . . that there would be no question of my continuing to help your family if there was a divorce? It would end my obligations.'

'You're lending them money. You're not supporting them.'

'If you looked at the figures, you'd think it was support. They won't survive without me. If I'm outside the family, of course, that won't matter as much. I can just reflect on the failure of a weak link in European banking.'

'I've done enough for my family,' Katherine said. She ran a catalogue of insults and hurts through her mind, the things she had ignored or tolerated for the family's sake. 'I can't do everything.'

'You wouldn't mind seeing Grunwald Frères tumbling down? You'd be on your own, you realize. They couldn't look after you.'

'I don't know. I shouldn't have to choose.'

Marisia came back from the door, stalking to the desk.

'Pieter,' she said. 'Don't do this.'

Pieter simply ignored her. 'So please do go and see your lawyer. But understand what they'll say about you in court when you tell your story. And understand your family will be ruined. I doubt if either event will make you happy.'

Katherine stood rebellious but subdued, head down, straining to produce words of defiance under her breath as a talisman against Pieter's threats.

'Stop it now,' Marisia said.

'I like to have things settled,' Pieter said. 'I like decisions.'

'I am not going to live for my family,' Katherine said. 'I want to be free now.' The words came thin and deliberate. 'I don't have children to hold me. I don't have a husband except on special days. I don't have a social life I like and I'm in a strange country. And you all of you live on the edge with your risks and your drugs and your . . .' she produced the word with Gallic distaste '. . . screwing. I like order in my life, Pieter. I do not want to live on the edge. I am a Grunwald.'

'I wonder what that means,' Pieter said. 'Not much, I think. If you want freedom, the Grunwalds lose their empire. It's that simple.'

'You, you . . .' Katherine raised her head for a brief moment of rage '. . . you . . . newcomer. We have a past. A name. A place.'

'Glory doesn't earn fourteen per cent,' Pieter snapped.

'I'm going to Paris tonight.'

'You could still make the two o'clock Concorde.'

Marisia watched them and she started to fumble in her handbag as though she was hunting for a paper tissue to comfort Katherine. He had wronged them both; they were allies. He had built a machine of blackmail and pressure and fear – Marisia could hardly complain, without confessing the earlier affair, and Katherine could not protest without ruining her family.

Marisia pulled out the gun.

'I really am going,' Katherine was saying to Pieter. She turned back to Marisia, went to hug her and then saw the little gun.

'You ought to get out more,' Pieter was saying, staring out of the window. 'When you get back. I'll arrange it.'

Katherine and Marisia were conspirators now, knowing

the advantage they held while Pieter still looked down from his window to the orderly streets.

'Pieter,' Marisia said, softly. 'Turn around.'

She fired three times. The sound was not loud, but it was improper, it rocked the quiet corridors. A secretary stamped on a panic button.

Pieter dived beneath his desk. Marisia fired her last three shots and turned to the door.

The security guards were there. The gun was back in her handbag, the women were douce and elegant and calm, and the man Van Helding was emerging from behind his desk.

'We thought we heard shots, sir,' the guards said.

'Nothing at all,' Van Helding said.

'It was me,' Marisia said, 'I . . .'

'It was nothing at all,' Pieter said. 'A silly accident. A joke.'

Marisia felt sick to her stomach that she had failed to kill him. Maybe she couldn't kill him; maybe, like some legend, nobody could kill him without special rituals.

'You'd better go,' Pieter said. 'Both of you. I shan't say anything.'

Marisia smoothed her dress and followed Katherine out, and the secretaries, recovered from their alarm, smiled with professional sweetness.

'Sometimes,' Katherine said, 'there is nothing I can do.'

Marisia held her.

Koolhoven liked paper and slide rule, not computer screen and disks. He liked the satisfaction of uncovering webs and patterns in figures, a subtle process which computer exercises could not match.

He needed those satisfactions, since the figures gave him none.

From the IMF meeting he had carried home a sense of

gloom. Not only was Providencia on the point of collapse, almost every bank in the world except Kellerman Unger could afford to see it go. It wasn't Brazil, with twenty-five devaluations in a year but with friends, or Mexico, monstrously borrowed but with oil. And if Providencia went, Kellerman Unger was in trouble. Money to cover bad debts would be scarce and buying Security National took massive cash. The Palm Springs gentry would want a return on their capital; Kellerman Unger was meant to make money, not just be a fireworks display. And the fact was that for years, Van Helding had run the bank for a grandstand – so that there was always some new advance to justify any temporary hiccup in profits, some new demand for capital with immediate and tangible results – like getting control of Security National. But the scale of the last deal was such that sensible investors – the Palm Springs gentry certainly had sense – would want time to make it work. So instead of dealing that could mask brief uncertainties in the balance sheet, the figures would be scrutinized with care. And a careful accountant would label the loans to Grunwald Frères and to Providencia as bad debt; they were remarkable because the bank had taken the burden itself rather than syndicating it.

If Koolhoven made the figures read that way, the story was alarming. KU was going to be hurt, badly, and it was so heavily involved in high-risk, high-profit lending that a failure of confidence could be disastrous. It could steal away the good name of the bank, which now made people pile in recklessly to shares that interested Van Helding. At present, only glamour hid the technical weaknesses.

Koolhoven added the provisions he thought were prudent for Providencia and for the Grunwalds. He shook his head. Together, and in Kellerman Unger's state, they left two choices: bleed Security National, not wholly within the law, or else ruin.

He wondered if Van Helding would listen. The man was brilliant at short-term calculation, and at building a name on a succession of successes. Koolhoven had always tried to balance that genius. But Van Helding had weaknesses. He only knew the paper world of finance where raising capital for a new venture, investing in actual plant, was very remote. He played the equities market like a chessboard, and he had not been there when the equity market was genuinely a way in which companies started, built, and rewarded their friends.

He called Van Helding's office and arranged to see him immediately.

'I think,' Van Helding said, 'it's time for me to take a break from all this. I've started putting Security National in order, and a few weeks or months wouldn't make any difference now.'

'Maybe,' Koolhoven said. He did not want his sense of urgency deflected.

'And we've got so damned respectable. We used to take risks and now we just have corporations. It's all a machine.'

'I think you'll find we do have risks,' Koolhoven said. He intended irony, but he sounded reassuring.

'When I was a child,' Van Helding said, 'I used to dream of Eldorado – going through the jungle and up great rivers to a kingdom of gold. It wasn't a greedy dream. It wasn't even about the fabulous treasure at the end of the road. It was all about the risk and the adventure of getting there and the fact that everyone else had failed.'

'Eldorado,' said Koolhoven, 'is not going to answer the bank's cash-flow problems.'

'I don't want to think about the bank's problems. I want to think about my problems, and I'm getting stale.'

'Go to Eldorado,' Koolhoven said. 'Myself, I go to Tuscany this year as usual. Choose what you want. But in the meantime, I have something to tell you. Urgently.'

'Eldorado is urgent,' Van Helding said. 'If I can get away, I shall feel much more sane and complete.'

'You probably have three months,' Koolhoven said. 'If you don't find Eldorado in that time, and you don't do anything here, you might come back to find you don't have a bank.'

'You sound like a schoolmaster.'

'I'm worried.'

'Let me have one fantasy – one special fantasy.'

'I've been doing sums,' Van Helding settled reluctantly into a show of attention. 'One, we have serious problems of cash flow and credibility if Providencia defaults. Two, Providencia is going to default.'

Van Helding seemed remote, slightly shocked. 'Eldorado was near Providencia, wasn't it? Didn't Walter Raleigh set out by way of Guyana and the Orinoco?'

'Listen,' Koolhoven said. He wanted to slap Van Helding, to anchor his wandering mind. 'There's a third point. It would be bad if Providencia went down. It would be even worse if the Grunwalds went down at the same time. We can't bale out anyone else, not after a cash bid for Security National.'

'We could undo the Grunwald deal.'

'It's committed.'

'But it's private and informal.'

'Better not.'

'When I agreed to that loan,' Van Helding said, 'I thought the name would be worth something, whatever happened. But if the French nationalize the banks, it'll be very different – not like owning a bank under Giscard d'Estaing at all.'

'You mean,' Koolhoven said, 'that you understand we don't have collateral on that loan any more – nothing worth a damn?'

'Exactly,' Van Helding said.

'I suppose you also realize that even if we were to be sticky about protocol, cut them off if they were a day late with anything, we'd simply lose what we've already paid out?'

'We could do some stalling,' Van Helding said. 'Say we put Providencia on a nonaccrued basis, forgot about interest payments and still treated the loan as though there was no blinding rain or sudden dark, or else eager to escape it.'

'Except that when you go nonaccrued, word will get around. The banks will all want out and countries will all want the same terms.'

'We'll be fine,' Van Helding said. 'If we have a little time.'

'If the Grunwalds collapse . . .'

'It's not like you to be so pessimistic.'

'It's a treacherous time. You've pulled off a great coup, you've taken control of a great American bank, but the bank needs work and you can't use its assets for your own purposes until it's back on an even keel.'

'It might be better if I was away for a time,' Van Helding said. 'You could delay things.'

'I can't guarantee that. I think we're in trouble and I think you have to help get us out.'

'I'm going,' Van Helding said. 'I need to go.'

'Your name might be enough. You could make some excitement around the bank, make people think things are all well. Otherwise, I also have a duty to depositors and clients and shareholders. I will have to tell the truth about the problems, sooner or later.'

'That's blackmail.' Van Helding said.

'Of course it isn't,' Koolhoven said. 'It's a warning. Soon all these problems will be visible through the balance sheet.'

'You'll just have to keep the balance sheet looking good

until I get back,' Van Helding said. 'If I decide to go off now, people will assume the banks are safe – otherwise, how could I go? I reckon people know how much they mean to me, how much the banks are my identity. They'll think I wouldn't go away if the empire was crumbling.'

Koolhoven felt desolate. It was as though some curtain had come between Van Helding and reality, a barrier which stopped him acknowledging the true state of things. By going away, he might seem to be confident, but actually he would be admitting defeat – telling himself there was nothing he could do if he stayed.

'I'm going to Eldorado,' Van Helding said. 'It's my last childhood dream. You couldn't deny me that, now, could you?'

'Shabby,' said Baron Gilles de Grunwald. 'That's the word. Everything is a little more damp than you remember. A couple of good paintings gone. Little things.'

Katherine nodded. 'And it all feels so lifeless, my parents' house.'

'Not much joy around. Doesn't worry me. I have my vineyard and my investments. The others are feeling it quite hard.'

'Mother keeps behaving like a grande dame. Then I find her crying into the sorbet.'

'Seraphine and Nicole have it worst. They're more Grunwald than the Grunwalds. They thought of themselves as old money. Well, it's dead money now, not just old. Fortunes have a life span, too.'

'What do we do?'

'We lean on Pieter Van Helding, that's what. Nothing else to do.'

'I suppose so.'

'Nothing wrong, is there?'

'Wrong? I don't know. Pieter and I had a very business-like marriage. The children – '

'Don't say anything.'

'I want to, Uncle. I never say anything about what really matters. I never said how much I mourned the children, or how much I would have liked other children.'

'You don't even say that to Pieter?'

'We've come apart. It happens.'

'Find a lover, then.'

'I don't know the rules in New York. In Paris there'd be someone who called in the afternoons – *cinq à sept.* In New York they want risk. I don't like that.'

'And Pieter?'

Katherine shrugged.

'Damn it, you could look after your own interests more.'

'If I did that, Pieter might divorce me.' She spoke with visible effort, her neck muscles tense. 'If that happened, he wouldn't support the family any more.'

'He said that was business.'

'It was pride. He wanted to humble the great Grunwalds and make them – us – dependent on him. He liked that. Now, he's not sure he can afford such luxuries and he's getting cold.'

'Time for lunch,' Gilles said. 'That's one appetite you can always indulge. Nobody divorces for overfeeding.'

'You're the only one in the family who doesn't sound as if he was drowning.'

Gilles said: 'Perhaps I have less at stake. I know who I am, and it's not just a Grunwald.'

'I have my life at stake,' Katherine said, very simply.

'Just a little fine tuning, that's all,' Gilles said.

'I want you to talk about it,' David Grant said.

'I told you what I meant to tell him,' Marisia said. 'I

meant to say he lived off conflict and dealing, other people's energy and fears. I was going to tell him he'd die without his network and his plots and his machinations. All that.'

'Did you say that?'

'I didn't say that. I told him I wanted to get rid of the shares, though.'

'And . . . ?'

'He didn't say much. He said it was like denying my past and my family and I couldn't do that. He said it was hard to market Kellerman Unger shares.'

'But what happened? You've been tense like a cat out hunting ever since you came back from the bank. You cry out in your sleep. If I lean over to hold you, you throw me off.'

'You wouldn't understand.'

'Something must have happened. I know that.'

'David, this is not a courtroom. I'm not on trial.'

'You only have to tell me once, just tell me so I can help.' David Grant held her hands, first comforting and then more firmly, eyes blithe with an innocent compassion. 'Tell me now.'

Marisia pulled away from him. 'If you really want to know,' she said, 'Pieter tried to rape me.'

David stared at her.

'It wouldn't have been the first time. But the other times, I said yes.'

'The other times . . .'

'It's my life, David. It's part of me. I didn't think it mattered to us, and I wanted to get rid of the shares to get rid of the family and Pieter and the past all at once. Isn't that something? I went to make the final break and he cheated me out of it.'

David Grant, usually so voluble, sat clawing at air, an animal who suddenly senses its cage.

'Say something,' Marisia said.

'I don't know,' David said. 'Hold me.'

She put her arms around him and he was trembling.

'I have to go out,' he said.

'I understand.'

'I have to go,' David said. He put on a coat like a disguise and walked out of the building anonymously. He took a cab to the brownstone where Pieter and Katherine Van Helding now lived. He paid off the cab and began to walk in the brisk evening. He thought how New York streets seem darker than other streets, lit brilliantly but sporadically, with buildings to take away the starless, blind sky.

He stood outside the Van Heldings' house, under the dappling of the last leaves. He watched the lights, wondering if anyone was there, and if so, who, and if they knew what had happened and could explain it all to him. He walked away a little, then returned, wanting to know and not wanting to know, heart tugged back and forth by tides of feeling and doubt.

Van Helding saw him, but only as an anonymous trench-coated figure, who could have been a man from the Palm Springs gentry keeping protective or custodial watch, or a friend of Mr Gregory or perhaps a bomb-throwing enemy of Mr Gregory, or even a reporter staking out the house.

He pulled the curtains shut and, in Katherine's absence, called quite peremptorily for dinner.

By the time the plane landed, Katherine had had more than enough time to think, to let the troubles race through her mind. She could not make sense of them, or put them into order. She felt at their mercy. And when the driver found her, and they began the slow progress through outer boroughs back to Manhattan, she was very still and quiet.

She was in a trap which even the sympathetic Baron

Gilles was inclined to take for granted. None of her family could bear to think what might happen if she broke from her marriage. Since she was a Grunwald, and proud of the fact, she would deal with the world as she was told. She returned to her husband, ready to go on. Yet all the history and fame in the family seemed nowhere near as strong as the burden they imposed.

Van Helding had his own ideas.

'You really should get out more,' he said. 'People say you're a recluse. You should have a social life, make a column item for *Women's Wear Daily*, go dancing with some nice young men and meet some frockmakers.'

He grinned.

'You know I'd hate that,' Katherine said.

'You'll like it,' Pieter said. 'You'll be famous and glamorous – the talk of New York. I've arranged it.'

He was serious, she realized, and he meant her to go out and glitter like the other lost wives, with a phalanx of good, gay men and a card marked for the *louche* ways of the New York overclass. That was what he wanted, and she understood without any need to spell it out that it was a condition of taking her back. She squared her shoulders. He wanted her to be a social whore and she would do it. There was nothing left to lose. She would act out whatever fantasy was in his mind, tremble on the right dance floors, chatter at the right dinner tables.

'Good girl,' Van Helding said. 'Good girl.'

Telephones rang, although Van Helding wanted all calls held. First Henry Klein came on blustering.

'We're hearing good things,' Klein said. 'Also, we're hearing bad things.'

'What things do you hear?'

'You have some troubles, they say. Providencia. A private deal with the Grunwald family.'

'Do they say how serious the trouble is?'

'Any trouble,' said Klein, 'upsets my principals. Especially now there's so much committed to you. We like returns, and we don't like mistakes. And while we might make excuses for a mistake or two, a disaster is something else again. The doctor, in particular, has a short temper. You remember Mr Ferrara.'

'I remember.'

'If anything goes wrong, we'd like to know first – tell me, and I'll see what I can do. But if it goes badly wrong, expect us to pull the rug. We control the banks; you don't. You have power just as long as we say sc.'

'You're very direct.'

'I'm a direct man. My principals have very direct methods.'

'You want to be more explicit?'

'I'm not that crude. You know me.'

'You never say anything that might be taken down and used in evidence against you.'

'Just listen to me. You have a month and then we want a full report. A full, favourable report.'

Before Van Helding could even grunt acknowledgement, Klein had put down the phone.

Van Helding put the palms of his hands onto the papers before him, and traced with his fingers like a blind man reading braille. There were plans and maps, the strategy for a journey up the great, snaking rivers of Providencia, to places where a dreamer might put Eldorado. There was also, hidden in a document case, the file on the Van Helding murder and on Jan Unger, the papers that Gregory had produced so suddenly and casually on the flight from Washington.

It was time to talk to Koolhoven, Van Helding thought.

Before he could call, his phone rang again. He wanted

to ignore it, to shout angrily at the secretary who was failing to shield him. Instead he took the call.

Marisia: 'I just want to say I need to know how you want me to deliver the share certificates, and how I get paid.'

'Where are you?'

'I'm at JFK. I'm going out to Los Angeles – three days on a movie, a cameo bit they wanted Jane Fonda for. They say I'm just as thin.'

'Is David going?'

'David's staying. We need some time to think.'

'Where can I get you?'

'My lawyers can call you if you can't tell me now.'

'Have them do that. We'll buy the shares in at our valuation, and you get to check the figures. I mean, your lawyers do.'

'Thanks. That's all, Pieter.'

'You don't mean that.'

'I'm very tired,' Marisia said. 'I'm glad we can get the shares settled.'

Again, Van Helding heard a click, a silence, the return of the dial tone. It seemed to be his day for hearing home truths and being dealt with by one-time friends, now cooled.

He had an initiative to take himself, though. He bundled up his papers, took the leather document case and walked to Koolhoven's office. The accountant was immersed in paper, his leonine grey head bowed over calculations. He saw Van Helding come in and motioned him to sit down while he finished a sum. But Van Helding was impatient.

'I've fixed my departure date,' he said.

'You can't have done,' said Koolhoven. 'Damn, you've made me lose the thread of this.'

'I'm going in two weeks.'

'Pieter, that isn't possible.'

Van Helding put tickets before Koolhoven with a great dumb show of explanation and proof.

'It's imperative you remain here,' Koolhoven said. 'If you don't stay, we have no way of preventing a disaster.'

'I can't solve our problems while I'm dull and tired. I need relaxation, refreshment. I need some adventure.'

'You're not going to St Tropez. You're going into the wilds for an indefinite period. Sometimes it seems to me the more you find out about the state of things here, the more determined you are to go.'

'I can't always run both Security National and Kellerman Unger,' Pieter said, arrogance helping him skid over Koolhoven's anger. 'I have to get away to show there are other people here, that the banks are not just me. What would happen if I was run over in a car crash tomorrow?'

'You have to stay,' Koolhoven said. 'In my judgement you are the only person who can bail us out. If you can't stay, if you won't stay, then I'll have to start telling the world just how bad things are. I shall – how do you say it – blow the whole story.'

Van Helding said, thoughtfully: 'But it wouldn't do you any good. You've been around all the time I've run these banks. You've known everything. If things are as bad as you say, it reflects no credit on you. You'd be telling the world about your own mistakes.'

'If the banks go down, my credibility is in pieces anyway. The question is whether to save the bank's good name for a month or so, or save the world from the consequences of a failure.'

'You sound like a comic-strip character – saving the world.'

'Not at all,' Koolhoven said. 'The whole business of world banking is like a net. If you keep it tense, people can trust it. If it once tears, it tears for ever. And if

Kellerman Unger and Security National hit trouble, it's going to be the start of a chain reaction like 1929. Only this time it won't be some small bank in Flint, Michigan that starts the whole thing. It'll be a major bank in the heart of Wall Street. We're talking the biggest bank crash in history.'

'Keep talking,' Pieter said. 'You might talk it into happening.'

'I want to stop it,' Koolhoven said. 'But I need your help. You're the one with the glamour and the name. The markets will listen to you.'

'Politicians listen to you,' Van Helding said.

'I went to Washington yesterday. I stayed around after a meeting and I went to see some people on Jim Baker's staff at the White House. It wasn't official, just drinks. I asked if the administration knew the problems we were all having with loans to the Third World. He said of course they did. I asked if the administration would bale us out. He said of course they wouldn't. They've decided that just at the moment the US isn't in the business of saving commercial banks who make mistakes. That's why you have to stay.'

'Koolhoven,' Van Helding said. 'I used to love you like a father. I hated to raise my voice to you.'

'You're using the past tense?'

'Now, I'm going. What is more, you are going to keep your mouth shut about Kellerman Unger's private business. We don't have to announce our problems, especially as I'm sure they will heal themselves.'

'Nothing will keep me quiet.'

Van Helding produced the leather document case. He said. 'Have a look at what is in here.'

Koolhoven took the case as though such menace was a matter of course, and he turned the papers, one by one, very neatly. He lost his rage. He seemed to be in fear.

'I know about you and my mother,' Van Helding said. 'I know who paid for my father's murder. I know you hired . . .'

'Somebody is giving birthday presents early,' Koolhoven said.

'I'm sure a lot of people would be interested in this file,' Van Helding said.

'Oh yes,' Koolhoven said, sounding tired. 'Yes, they are always interested in the murder of Georg Van Helding. It fascinates them.'

'And if you decide to talk, then this file is public. Immediately. I don't know about the statute of limitations – I'm not even sure which country would want to prosecute – but the scandal should be enough to bring you down. I'm quite prepared to do it.

'It's for the sake of the family,' Pieter Van Helding said. 'I'm sure you understand.'

He never asked himself if it had all been a grand design; in retrospect, he could justify anything. And now that the Eldorado expedition was close, he wanted two final details.

He wanted a witness – someone to see what happened on those great rivers, someone who hated him enough to tell the truth.

And he needed to put someone in charge of Security National while he was away – someone acceptable to the Palm Springs gentry, for a while, and someone who would not have the strength to upset his power.

He called Marisia. She could hardly bring herself to speak to him, but he promised to forgive her, to take no action. Then he made his offer.

'We should have shared things before,' he said. 'This time, I want you to represent me in the bank. You're the biggest shareholder on public record still, apart from the

Palm Spring gentry. It won't be for long, and it's mostly ceremonial.'

He waited for the proposition to take effect. She wanted it, he knew that. She wanted power. And he was giving her a brief authority that was more spectacular than anything she could hope to build for herself. And besides, he was forgiving her what an unkind DA might call attempted murder.

He also asked for David Grant.

'Why David?' Marisia asked. 'You wouldn't harm him?'

'I want someone to write the story of the expedition. He's good.'

'I don't think he'd go with you. He knows too much.'

'David?' Pieter said. 'He couldn't even imagine what there is to know.'

'I don't trust you.'

'You get the bank, for a while. You get forgiveness, little sister. And your husband gets a good story.'

'Why?'

Pieter Van Helding did not answer. He could hardly tell her the truth: that it amused him to twist people out of their comfortable positions. And he had won the power to amuse himself; he had played the money game to the point where he controlled the rules.

'Let me know,' Pieter said, but he knew she couldn't say no.

9

The drive was long – out past old colonial houses, built of wood, as gaudy and turreted as some gingerbread fantasy and all grown over with vines. They saw men walking to work, wire-sharp cutlasses at their side, as common as briefcases in a city. David Grant knew it from earlier visits, knew the air conditioning that roared and failed all night, knew the drained hotel pool and the breakfast of curious fruit and boiled coffee, but Van Helding glinted at the sight of it all. He looked like a fascinated child at the boxes on thin bird legs from which children came tumbling, ready to net fish in the canals. He stared at the dun-white cows that went wandering in gardens, under the protection of the red and white Hindu prayer flags. The sense of overwhelming life did not oppress him and the heat seemed to stimulate him. He was mad for the place, David Grant began to realize; and the idea of this urbane, manipulative man where no city skill was relevant began to make awkward sense. Pieter Van Helding had entered a dream.

There were courtesy visits – diplomatic visits, like presenting credentials. It was ponderous, but important. He had made his appointment with the prime minister, and dragged along David Grant, and now the car was at the great shaded courtyard of the house, overhung with poincianas, and on a balcony they settled to wait for Arthur Miller. A tiny green treefrog leaped in graceful arcs, side to side, peeing as it went.

Miller arrived in a bustle of secretaries, quickly shooed away. He had decided that the occasion was social.

'I wish you luck,' he said. 'Our photographers went over the bush the last time you loaned us money – for a hydroelectric plant. We seem to have missed all the cities of gold.'

'A good socialist wouldn't see them,' Van Helding said.

'A good socialist would expropriate them,' Miller said. 'I suppose that's really what you're seeking, is it? Cities and legends of gold? Forgive me, but when a senior banker and a solid white journalist go walkabout in the bush we often suspect they must have other motives.'

Miller looked mischievous.

'Arthur,' Van Helding said, 'what can you mean? I would love to be Daniel Ludwig and build a world in the rain forest. But I'm afraid even I am not that rich.'

'You'll be happy with the sloths and the anacondas and the waterfalls?'

'Yes,' Van Helding said. 'It's the journey that matters.'

'You'll forgive me the suggestion, of course, but in California they have dude ranches for the inexperienced. I suppose this is a kind of dude expedition – a kind of game?'

'I am very serious.' Van Helding said. 'I've dreamed of coming here since I was a child and I learned about Walter Raleigh's expeditions. It doesn't matter to me that the Indians really went to Colombia with their gold, and perhaps Walter Raleigh went exploring further to the north. I want to be the explorer, you see. Where the risks are real.'

'I have to lecture you about that,' Miller said. 'There was a time we thought of staging expeditions to Eldorado for the tourists.' He sighed. 'A fixed itinerary, guesthouse meals, that sort of thing. But we couldn't have guaranteed the safety of all those people. And I didn't want to run a nation of waiters.'

'You could have sacrificed Eldorado every time,' David Grant said. 'Like Disneyland.'

Miller ignored him. 'We can't be responsible for you in the bush, you know. There may be guerrillas there. We can't tell. Your American friends are curiously reluctant to let us know what their spy satellites see.'

'I am told,' Van Helding said, 'the risk is minimal.'

Miller ordered ice and gin, and made an ironic toast. 'For the sake of our colonial heritage,' he said, 'Dutch and English. I think gin is what we all have in common.'

Then he turned serious.

'Rivers here aren't like your rivers,' he said. 'They change channels every day. All the rapids and the rocks and the shallows – people know them only by instinct. You couldn't chart them, unless you charted them like a newspaper – every day.'

Van Helding could hear a scuffling in the courtyard and he noticed that Miller was impatient, trying to peer unobtrusively over the balcony to see what preparations were being made below.

'We know it is dangerous,' he said, quietly.

Miller recovered his concentration. 'There really are anacondas. And piranha, and great waterfalls, and the land is impassable – except to the cats.'

'I know,' Van Helding said. 'Someone told me a story about a prison you have in the interior – on an island in a river, with no bars?'

'Nobody would try to escape,' Miller said. 'They all know the dangers.' He rose and paced along the balcony, looking down as though expecting a signal. 'They say, gentlemen, we have more varieties of life than any other country on earth.' He grinned complacently.

Down below in the courtyard, a whistle blew.

'My morning diversion,' Miller said. 'Please pull up a chair. I call it – the youth of Providencia salutes.'

He was posed like a prime minister, he saluted, and then the schoolgirls below scrambled for places and began their morning drill. Skirts flew over long, fine legs and there were occasional glimpses of bright white knickers and sometimes tight black hair, and Miller was rapt. He remembered gymslips.

The girls lay back and began to bicycle in the air, and Miller licked his lips. He would hate to leave all this, the power to see out his fantasies. Yet he knew it was bound to come; his sharp LSE mind thought Providencia must fall, now bauxite and sugar and rice were all too cheap to sell and coca too dangerous. And when Providencia fell, a chain reaction would start. Even the money in Switzerland would suffer. The only hope was the selfsame 'they' he had always denounced – the international capitalist conspiracy which now, God willing, could not afford to let his dreams fall apart.

He was sweating a little.

Airborne, the stewardess brought orange juice, and sprayed the plane against flies and mosquitoes. David Grant coughed and stared out of the windows at the land below.

There was forest without end. Sometimes it rose, broken-backed, like a loaf, and sometimes there was a scatter of purple and red flowers in the high branches, and sometimes a river curled back and forth, and sometimes an airstrip showed like a rust-red wound where the green had been stripped away from the rich bauxite in the earth. For a good twenty miles, a silvery lake, man-made, filled the view; under it, Indians had been washed away or left to bloat. At its fringes, twigs appeared, then branches, then trunks, then whole trees until some could stand clear from the water. The forest crept everywhere.

The Otter bumped to earth on grass and was mobbed by small, naked children. In the guesthouse, Van Helding's men stole mosquito nets; windowpanes and air conditioners were both officially there, although long vanished in reality, and officially the nets were not needed. Once supper was finished, they had nothing to do but listen – to each other, to the night.

Van Helding looked out from the veranda as though he was trying to find his bearings among the eerie howls of the monkeys and the piercing song of frogs.

'Tomorrow,' he said, lifting a beer.

David Grant sat down beside him.

'You want to talk?' he asked.

Van Helding smiled. 'If you like.'

'The boatmen aren't here yet.'

'They're supposed to arrive at dawn. They're coming from a village upstream.'

'Is the government man going with us?'

'No,' Van Helding said. 'I think he can't wait to get back to the coast.'

Grant lit a cigarette. 'We just follow the river?'

'There's no other course. As far as I can see, the river is everything here – it's road, and it's water and it's food – everything.'

Grant nodded. 'We follow the river,' he said. He was trying to nerve himself to ask the questions that troubled him, and he tried crabwise tactics.

'We ought to have some ancient treasure map,' he said. 'A map someone found in a library somewhere, and only we understood it.'

Van Helding looked at him sharply. 'You're catching the spirit of it,' he said.

'It's a game, isn't it?'

'In a way.' Van Helding seemed for a moment prepared to be expansive, but the moment passed. 'You can think of it as a game, if you like.'

He never gave away any feeling; he never revealed himself. Grant was infuriated.

In the morning, the air was cool and washed, the colours rain-clear. There was a line of dugouts at the landing stage, hard, dark wood, painted with gaudy blues and reds, each with a man to run the motor and another with a pole to stand in the bows and fine-tune the steering.

By eight the boats were loaded and wallowing, and the sun had begun to beat down. The government representative busied himself with the radio, consulted with the boatmen, made sure as he could be that these curious white men would have no grounds for complaint. He didn't give a damn if they lived or died, but he cared very much that he couldn't be blamed.

'I am sorry I cannot accompany you,' he lied. 'I shall expect to hear from you, though, each morning at nine. On the agreed frequency.'

He was aboard the little Otter even before the luggage hold in the nose had been slammed shut.

On the first boat travelled Van Helding and Grant; behind them were a photographer; a kind of quartermaster; a guide who spoke English; and a naturalist, a portly man who made a career out of staying clear of England, where an unlikely erotic appetite had made him responsible for a half-dozen wildly assorted children.

They rode on a river that seemed to have muscles like an animal's flank, and the boatmen concentrated furiously on the ripples and turns of surface water that showed where the currents now ran. Sometimes there was spume on the water, surprising flecks, and sometimes the boats came achingly close to the rocks.

Grant watched the others, with a vacant but careful look. There was nothing to see, except the photographer, who shot every move, every lift, every mile. Nothing was going to be forgotten and everything could be proved.

Along the banks of the wide river, there was always a blank green wall. Sometimes the mangrove roots crept out into the water like a spider's legs, and sometimes there were great, high, feathery fountains of bamboo. There were dead trees hung with elaborate nests of bowerbirds, and macaws went squawking and clattering past, a clash of red and blue and green and yellow. There was a luminous, huge turquoise butterfly, like a paper dream, that went over their heads, and the howler monkeys paced the little fleet through the trees, silent as the boats went by, and starting to cry like nervous dogs if the boats got too far ahead.

Van Helding trailed his hand in the water, for the sake of the cool.

The boatman shrieked.

'*Fisi*,' he said, holding up his own hand. Three fingers had gone from it, bitten away, and the flesh had grown back like a shell. He mimed the action of sharp teeth. '*Fisi*. Fish.'

And Van Helding learned not to be a tourist.

There was nothing kind in this air, Grant thought, nothing friendly. You die, the river won't mourn; you live, the forest will still eat. And he watched Pieter, looking still for clues. Van Helding, up against that great indifference, seemed implacable.

They could hear the first falls long before the river turned to show them – a sound like the rain that goes with thunder. When the boats came round the bend they could see a shallow curtain of water that was wider than the course of the river. Water boomed among boulders and crashed around plants that looked like dried hyacinth. The boats came alongside each other.

'You see falls?' the boatman asked.

Van Helding nodded at the invitation, and the lead boat edged ahead into the low waters of the falls. Van Helding stood, and Grant stood to match him, and the boatman motioned that one of them could stand on the rocks and look out to the falls.

Grant went. He picked his way over the edge of the boat onto mossy boulders, and slowly he straightened up. The sound of the water bothered and confused him. He heard Van Helding say: 'Look back.'

He turned too suddenly and he felt his legs go away from him, sliding down the rock into the rush of water. He tried to hold on, snatching at brittle stems of water plants, trying to anchor his flat hands on the lichen of the rocks.

'Hang on,' Van Helding shouted.

Grant slid further, and he found his feet catching the gravelly riverbed. If he went down just inches further, he could stand; but he would drown in the rush and the scum of the dark brown water. If he clung to the plants he could feel himself being tugged downstream.

Each tensing of muscles made things go wrong – put him into the water to drown or to float away. He snatched at Van Helding's arm and pulled, working his feet with a paddling motion against the rocks, and slowly emerged from the water.

'You're all right?'

Grant spluttered and said he was fine. The little boats made for a natural harbour at the edge of the falls where there were rails to haul the boats over and round the rise in the river. Grant rested in the shade of the trees, and felt his damp clinging clothes begin to dry and fall free of his body. He knew nothing would dry completely in this rain-sodden air.

'They say,' the guide began, brightly, 'that he who drinks creek water will come back to Providencia.'

'If he lives,' Grant said. He was watching Van Helding eat his lunch, and puzzling. Van Helding had pulled him out of the water with sudden strength, and yet there had been just a moment when Grant really wondered if Van Helding would help him at all. He had been caught between drowning and falling into the force of the river and he really did not know.

'What will you settle for?' he asked.

'I don't understand,' Van Helding said.

'When there isn't a city, and there isn't any wonder. What is going to make you turn back?'

Van Helding shrugged. 'Time, I suppose.'

They cast off on the new waters, and within a half-hour the sky went basalt black and seemed to fall in needles. Van Helding and Grant baled with spirit. They looked up to see a canoe passing in the storm, with four bare-breasted women in a row, children between them, paddling with red-blue paddles as though there was no blinding rain or sudden dark, or else eager to escape it.

Nights they could spend close to villages, with their prism-shaped huts and their intricate, abstract designs on the triangular doors. They climbed slick red mud to the village captain's hut, talked politely to the old man in his riverboat captain's hat, and waited for the proper invitation. When it came, it was properly acknowledged and properly accepted, and the tents went up among the great green calabash that hung from bushes.

David Grant liked to talk with the captains, in broken French. The first told him that Adam and Jesus would come rowing back on Judgement Day in a little boat, and they'd hit the sinners with the paddle, and ferry the good to salvation. Grant listened scrupulously.

He wondered how Van Helding would react if anyone brought him a problem from the outside world – banks or London or New York. Pieter watched, looked for advantage, checked, just as he would in some city boardroom, but here he was exhilarated as Grant had never seen him. In the monkey screams and the flash of gaudy birds he had found something.

Risk, Grant thought to himself. It's like drink or

heroin – something to take in big doses to forget the world.

He felt the expedition had already turned claustrophobic. Everything was photographed, noted, recorded. Van Helding's progress could be charted frame by frame. And the subject matter, Grant knew, was Pieter Van Helding's psychodrama. They all had to hope it was not being staged at someone's expense.

Grant tried to strike up talk with the portly naturalist, but the man went walking by the river where his was the only human sound, and stood unalarmed by sudden slithering noises in the underbrush and the spoor of big forest cats – sometimes dung, sometimes footprints on a sandbank where iguanas had come to lay their eggs. Grant insisted on talking and the naturalist turned petulant. He wanted silence. The last thing he wanted was more human problems, like a man who wanted to escape the cool perversity of Van Helding.

Night came down suddenly, and by nine the village lights had died. A fire burned on the margins of the village, to scare the big cats, but it was low. The kerosene lamp in David's tent began to splutter and he decided to do without it.

He lay on sleeping bags, under a rough mosquito net, staring at nothingness and listening to the lively, chattering night. There was movement everywhere – tiny frogs, jewel-bright, making sudden flights, and something slow-moving, heavy, hanging from branches, perhaps furry, perhaps scaled; and the monkeys, clashing and screeching in their perpetual, sociable terror. The expedition's tents were arranged in a circle with a fire between them, and last shadows played on the tent walls.

Van Helding was still reading in his tent. He had a flashlight and he was looking at maps and papers, like a schoolboy under the covers at night, checking particularly the course of the next five or six days' travel. It was always the line of the same great river, which would take them on a sinuous course through the rain forest and out to the savannah on the Brazilian border. Van Helding thought of the Indians fleeing the conquistadores, laden with gold, and how that column of men and women, children and priests, and stone and precious metal, went high across mountains and skirted great lakes and settled eventually in some forest. Eldorado had to be a forest place, guarded by the forest creatures of legends like the great yehus, whose backward feet crashed through the underbrush while their monkey minds swing through the high branches.

And then it was time for him, too, to douse his light.

He came awake to hear a hubbub in the village, a child crying something universal like 'mama, mama'.

The monkeys were quiet, and the quiet seemed most ominous. Van Helding pulled back the flap of his tent. Dawn had not yet come, but there was a mêlée of tall, confusing shadows under the risen moon. One shadow went stealthily, hugging the ground.

Van Helding shouted: 'David Grant.'

Grant stirred, then muttered, then came awake in panic. He heard the quiet of the monkeys first, and it occurred to him that some great predator must be around. There was a scream, high and anthropoid, and then the silence grew up again; it seemed that somewhere a monkey had been in the path of a great cat and some witness monkey had sung out the funeral cry.

Grant dressed immediately, and reflexively tied up strong boots. He reached for the revolver.

Van Helding was already out of his tent, his flashlight tracking along the ground, a Purdy shotgun ready in his right hand. There was a low shadow moving on the village. He could see it, almost, and he imagined the last of the moonlight caught its sleek, black body and the markings coded in the black fur. A child was shouting, 'Tiger, tiger.' Van Helding crept forward, watching, wondering if a cat would turn and panic, wondering what it could be hunting – or whether even the great black tigers of the forest came scavenging for cans of bully beef and leftover flesh.

Then the shadow was close to a hut and Van Helding's hair rose, and he was cold as diamonds. A thin-faced brown and black dog tethered to a pole began to bark shrilly. There was movement in the other huts. The barking had become a high howl of fear, and the ground-hugging panther slunk along and then – Van Helding saw the movement – it came down in one bound on the dog's back, claws out, teeth bared, cutting and tearing.

Van Helding raised his shotgun and cocked it. He could hear someone moving across from the big cat, but he had to take the risk. He fired twice, and the shots splayed the panther's head open, and it slumped. In its mouth, the dog was bloody, and opened, purples and sinew-whites all clear in the lights that the village had suddenly brought.

There were lit brands, kerosene lamps, torches, all dancing in the village and moving to the sound of the shots. David Grant said, very quietly: 'I'm here.' Van Helding swung his flashlight past the panther's body, and saw Grant standing close on the other side, revolver drawn.

And Grant, blinded for a moment by the light, found himself staring down the barrels of Van Helding's shotgun.

Dawn hit the sky like theatre footlights suddenly brought up.

At nine Van Helding made the morning call to the coast, reporting that all was well. The village captain broke out drink from a tiny refrigerator, which held beer and batteries. Van Helding was intrigued by the batteries;

the captain explained they lost their power in heat and a good freeze often brought them back.

Van Helding refused to be a hero. Something cold in him made the villagers too nervous to applaud. The boatmen simply collected more blenkies – five gallon cans of gasoline – and they set out again upstream.

Although the passengers in the boat had nothing to do, no responsibility and little choice, they still kept silence as though they were occupied. David Grant had images running in his mind: the water, and Van Helding towering over him as he slipped, and Van Helding in a dark place with a shotgun pointed at Grant's belly. He wondered what the unspoken agenda of this expedition really was. And he had a half-image from an old movie in his mind, a lost classic that Marisia and Marty Genovese had made him see. There was an island, a vaguely Baltic count, a gaggle of shipwrecked people; and the count planned a hunt. Grant remembered the great hounds and the mist. And what the count loved to hunt was man – the most dangerous game, a decadent pursuit that had to do with extremes of experience. Like watching a man drown, or blowing out his guts with a shotgun, David thought. He wished he saw fewer movies.

Every morning at nine they made their call to the coast. The radio in the early hours was full of creole chatter – chief calling chief. Nobody had secrets any more. The morning call began to seem quite ordinary, like striking camp and casting off and moving slowly on the great, wide beast of a river; and with familiarity came consolations. Night seemed more sweet and more cool. Noises seemed less oppressive.

It was hard to remember that this was a quest, a search for a golden city. Gold came to them once, and by accident.

Great falls came up just before noon on the fifth day.

The river water turned to smoke and rainbows hung in the air. The boatmen struggled as far as they could and when engine and paddles would take them no further, they took to the banks, clearing a way with machetes. They struggled up a narrow path with the boats on their heads, fighting through sticky vines that seemed to have an almost muscular strength.

Above the falls was a broad lake, with men diving. They slid into the river and stayed there until Grant could almost feel the crushing pressure in his chest. Two saw white men and fluttered old damp bits of paper, permits they once won.

'Pork knockers,' the guide shouted. 'They find gold.'

'They work as a team?' Van Helding asked.

'No,' the guide shouted. 'One gets stuck in vine, the others walk on. It's the only way.'

Van Helding watched them and a man broke surface, carrying a lump of brown riverbed that was tangled in weeds. As the man held it aloft, Van Helding thought he saw the veins of metal and the sparkle of mica. He thought he saw gold.

He had come so far from his entanglements – Katherine, Marisia, the Grunwalds, the banks, the idea of David Grant as a rival – that he could live only in the moment. It was enough for him, and after it, he could be a power again when he returned.

He hadn't expected the worst to happen.

David Grant went to watch the river in the early morning light. The macaws were staging one of their dawn raids, sounding like gunfire in the air, and glittering in their flight. Something was floating out in the stream, within reach of the bank; something carved and wooden. Grant was intrigued.

'You're awake early,' Van Helding said, startling David Grant.

'It's a fine morning,' Grant said. 'There's something out in the stream that I don't recognize. Can you make it out?'

'Looks like wood,' Van Helding said.

'Are there villages this far up?'

'There's even a border post twenty miles upstream – where the French territory comes close to Providencia.'

'I'd like to see what that thing is.'

Van Helding shrugged. 'Don't you think you've taken enough risks?'

The wooden object bobbed away across the stream, and then returned to their bank with the turn of the current.

'I wonder how Marisia is.'

'Yes,' said Van Helding. 'So do I.'

'You know she almost sold out of Kellerman Unger before you said you were leaving? She wanted to be free of the whole thing.'

'But she's not free, is she?' Van Helding said. 'In fact, she's got exactly what she wanted – control of the banks.'

'She really did want to be free.'

'I can't think why,' Van Helding said. 'We've always got on so well.'

There was a moment of silence. The wooden paddle – if that was what it was – had lodged by the bank in a knot of roots. Grant thought he would have a chance to get it, and he squatted down, carefully avoiding the water.

'You know,' Grant said, concentrating on his reach, 'I thought of you as a rival once.'

'Really?' Van Helding said. He was watching Grant's uncertain balance over the water. Then Grant stepped forward, because it seemed one step would bring him closer to the paddle, and then he took another step because the paddle had shifted slightly as the run of the river tugged it away from the bank.

'I never thought of you as a rival,' Pieter Van Helding said.

David Grant took one more step. He was cautious in the water but he knew piranhas only liked the mouth of creeks and responded to blood, so he assumed that he was safe enough.

His scream tore across the morning like an electric current, and his big, muscular body rose and shivered and fell back. Van Helding pelted out to him, churning the water.

'What the hell happened?'

Grant could say nothing. His eyes were rolled up and fixed open, as though he had been deeply shocked, and his body was too stiff. Van Helding tugged him back to the bank and shouted for help.

The portly naturalist came waddling up from his tent, saw Grant's body on the ground and began to run. He checked Grant's legs and found what looked like a tiny puncture wound close to the ankle.

'Stingray,' he said.

'What the hell do you mean?' Van Helding said, his agitation obvious.

'There are freshwater stingray and they keep to the banks and the shallow waters. You can't see them in the mud. They're the worst.'

'What do we do?'

'We get him somewhere he can be airlifted out. He needs a hospital.'

Van Helding looked down at David Grant who was fragile and stiff all at once, his eyes still terrified and wide. For a moment, Van Helding showed emotion: annoyance, even anger. This was not meant to happen. The photographer was dashing around recording the scene and Van Helding told him to stop.

'What happens if he doesn't get to hospital?'

'He's got tetanus shots, so the puncture wound shouldn't be too much problem. I can dress that. It's the venom in the sting that gets people different ways. Sometimes it produces paralysis, sometimes it doesn't. That's why he needs doctors.'

'We have antibiotics . . .'

'They're not what we need.'

David Grant lay on the ground, unmoving, and Van Helding knelt to brush away a wandering squadron of ants.

'Get the radio,' Van Helding said.

They called the coast and an alarmed government official said he would call back in fifteen minutes. A full half-hour later, he came back on the air in a splutter of static.

'We can't land an Otter at the border post,' he said, 'and we don't have helicopters. You'll have to send boatmen downstream.'

'But we're seven days from the last airfield.'

'It can't be helped. You'll make better time with the current.'

'Are you telling me there is nothing at all that you can do for this man?'

'Give him an additional tetanus shot. Give him any muscle relaxant you have. Try him on antibiotics just in case the wound gets infected. And keep him covered from the sun. That's all you can do.'

'If we get to the border post, could the French do any better?'

The Providencia official said: 'I hope you will not consider doing such a thing. It would be a most unfortunate diplomatic . . .'

'I am not,' said Van Helding, icily, 'a diplomat, nor am I concerned with the niceties of your relations with the French. I am only concerned for the safety of this man.'

On the coast, the civil servant engineered a long burst of static. Van Helding was power, but Van Helding was isolated. The civil servant calculated what he could, and could not, get away with.

'Try the border post,' the voice from Simonstown said, at last. 'That's not official, of course. And if the French can't do anything, you're another day upstream.'

Van Helding shut off the radio.

They put David Grant in the bottom of the dugout on piles of bedding, with Van Helding and the naturalist for attendants.

'The pain looked terrible,' Van Helding said. 'He screamed, and he seemed to go up in the air.'

The naturalist shrugged. 'When the women go down to wash or to bathe they always beat the water.'

He worked on the puncture wound, trying to press out venom, and dressing the bloody mess carefully. He said: 'What worries me is that if he screamed like that, and went rigid, the poison must have affected the central nervous system.'

'Christ,' Van Helding said.

The little fleet began to edge out into the river, trying for speed, but held back by the power of the waters. Van Helding seemed utterly preoccupied, in ways the naturalist found surprising. Sharp eyes in his pudgy face saw that Van Helding was trying to make up his mind about some complex and difficult issue. At the time, the naturalist assumed the problem was whether or not to advance upstream in search of Eldorado, or whether the reality of Grant's pain and possible death was enough to wipe out the allure of the myth. Later, everybody knew: he had lost his witness.

At the end of the day they had still not reached the border post. Van Helding asked if the boatmen would go on by night, but they were reluctant. They could not judge the course of the river in the dark, even with a moon, and besides, the forest was black at night in the charge of angular, sharp-toothed creatures, and things of scale and fur that are not to be found in natural history books. At night, the boatmen wanted fire to protect them.

Overnight, Grant seemed to relax, but his eyes were still fixed. Van Helding closed them, gently. The naturalist shot antibiotics around the wound to hold infection, and announced that he could do nothing else. The next morning, they moved before dawn, in the great, cool stillness of the forest, and finally they came within sight of the border post.

There were three wooden houses strung along the bank – a flag of the French republic over a guardhouse, a store, and a wooden bungalow before which a tall, full woman was washing her long hair in the river. She stood and watched them pass without concern. She was blonde, and she had adopted the river women's single piece of cloth. She draped it for decency around her belly, and not, as the boatmen's people do, around the ultimate erogenous zone of the thighs. She looked vacant and accepting.

Nobody answered in the guardhouse, and Van Helding ran to the store. The fact of a man running seemed to surprise the woman in the river, and she tugged at her hair, and climbed out to the bank.

The store had rough wooden shelves, and among the objects familiar from the downstream stores – cans of sardines, packets of birdseed for singing birds – there were curious exotica. There were three cans of cassoulet, and five bottles, stored upright, of a sweet pink champagne that must long ago have lost its life in the heat and damp.

'*Vous desirez?*' said the storekeeper, who was short and dark.

Van Helding explained what had happened to David Grant. The storekeeper said he was desolated, but what could he do? Perhaps, Van Helding suggested, the guard could call to the coast and see if the French authorities could move a helicopter into the interior – anything to make the journey back to a hospital faster and simpler. The storekeeper was desolate again, but he could not speak for the guard. Perhaps his wife could speak for the guard.

Van Helding was infuriated now.

'There's a man's life at stake,' he said.

The storekeeper said he regretted but he had no means of official communication to the coast.

Van Helding ran again to the guardhouse. From inside, there were gutteral noises, grunts and growls. He pushed the guardhouse door and stared. The woman from the river had slipped out of her *panga* and presented herself to the gendarme, who was strenuously humping her from behind. The couple were completely unconcerned by Van Helding's presence, until they clung to each other as though with claws and bucked around, and then fell quiet and a little embarrassed.

The gendarme said: '*Vous desirez, m'sieur?*'

Van Helding laughed. Out here, with nobody for miles and no other neighbours but the life of the river, three people had contrived a little suburban, sexual war of their own. He wondered how it had started, whether the storekeeper offered his wife as consolation to the gendarme, or the gendarme was the wild seducer, or if the woman simply thought it reasonable that she should share herself. But he saw why the storekeeper was not that morning on speaking terms with officialdom.

Offialdom buttoned his fly, and the woman walked, happy and proud, off into the back rooms of the tiny guardhouse.

'We have a man in great pain in the boats,' Van Helding said. 'An important British writer . . .' he knew better than to say journalist to a flic '. . . and we need to call the coast.'

The gendarme was cooperative. He called the coast in the French territories and they agreed to send out a helicopter from one of the inland bauxite mines. They insisted that it was at the expense of the injured party, and Van Helding gave his name.

There was nothing to do now but wait. The long day stretched out with no diversion. The boatmen sat by the river, watching and thinking, smoking an old pipe and drinking an occasional Alsatian beer from the store. Van Helding had been invited to a formal coffee with the gendarme but the moment the official ceremony was completed, Van Helding found himself waiting again. The naturalist had found a pile of ancient cans and bones and bottles, half-buried, at the back of the settlement, and in it he found little rock boas, lovely and slim, twisting and turning in pursuit of small rodents.

The great heat of midday came on them, and then the rain of the afternoon and the sudden dousing of light that went with it, and then the noise of a helicopter engine was clear in the air. The boatmen looked up in alarm and took prudent refuge in the store, over a few more Alsatian beers.

The French team were from a mining company and they were brisk and efficient. They lifted David Grant from his roach-worked bedding in the store and took him to the copter straight away. They asked if Van Helding was coming with them, and he said no. He said he would tell the next of kin.

'He'll live,' said the doctor who had come with the helicopter. 'We'll get back to base tonight, and then we'll get him to the coast tomorrow.'

'It might be better if he returned to Simonstown,' Van Helding said.

The doctor said, 'Don't you believe it. They've got a hospital the British built in 1920. We've got the hospital the French built for the space centre. He'll be better off with us.'

Van Helding nodded.

The only problem that remained was how to tell New York what had happened without causing terrible alarms. He settled down to compose a radio message that Marisia – or better yet, Koolhoven – would be able to comprehend and handle.

And the sound of the helicopter droned up into the sky, and was quickly lost round the river bend, and the guide and the naturalist took on the job of negotiating a camp site and a dinner.

Marisia settled back into the back of the limousine and read the papers. She tried to set her mind for the day in the bank offices, and she realized how little she knew about the daily detail of the business. She was presenting herself for a ceremonial role, a star performance, and she hoped the detail would not spoil things.

There was a moderately bitchy paragraph by James Brady in the *Post* about Katherine dancing at the Red Parrot while her husband toiled up rivers in the jungle. Marisia frowned. Nobody said 'jungle'; she knew that.

As she passed the guards at the Security National tower, there was a flurry of messages sent upstairs so that she could be expected and escorted. Fairbairn himself came to the elevator doors.

'My dear,' he said. 'We don't see enough of you.'

'My dear,' Marisia said, 'you will.'

She knew that Fairbairn had time for patrician social graces, and she knew she could spare no time. God knew how long Pieter would stay in the bush on his fool's errand, but it was always possible he would suddenly tire of the idea and come rushing back to New York. She had only weeks, at best, to use the advantage he had so casually given her and take real power.

For she was sure now that she wanted the power from which Pieter had contrived to exclude her for years. Now, she was coming into her own.

Fairbairn tagged her like a friendly dog, and only at her office door did she shake him off. She said she would not lunch at Four Seasons. She said she would not be leaving the office. She asked her secretaries to hold calls, and she summoned Koolhoven.

'I'm really very busy,' he said.

Marisia smiled. 'Of course,' she said. 'But you do understand that for the next few weeks, I am in Pieter's place. I have his votes, and his proxies, and his shares, until he comes back. So you must imagine that I am he.'

Koolhoven said: 'We usually have a morning meeting at nine, to review things. You want that?'

'Of course.'

'You're familiar with the most pressing deals? Or do I have to explain them?'

'Today you have to explain them. Tomorrow, I'll understand.'

Koolhoven cleared his throat. He looked impatient with this new situation. 'It hardly seems worthwhile,' he began, but Marisia had stood up, come from behind her desk and settled by him on the sofa.

'We've known each other many years,' Marisia said. 'I've known you all my life. Now, you wouldn't want to disappoint me, would you? I need to know from you what is happening, and together we'll make decisions. Just like you do with Pieter.'

She was fishing, and she knew it.

'Pieter makes decisions,' Koolhoven said. 'I advise.'

'Exactly,' Marisia said, rising from the sofa. 'Exactly. And that is how it is going to be now.'

'But you know nothing about the bank and its business.'

'I know a great deal and I learn fast. Besides, I have you to help me. I'm sure we will make a great team.'

Koolhoven smiled, thinly and disagreeably.

'How much do you want to know?' he said. 'I suppose I can tell you since you're standing in for Pieter, who knows it all.'

Marisia said: 'I hear we have our problems.' She was casual, but she had the actress's trick of making each syllable crisp. 'It had occurred to me to ask for a half-yearly audit, just so I can be sure where we stand. There's the matter of the loans to the Grunwalds, for example, and to Providencia.' She managed her own thin smile. 'The more I know, the more sensible I can be.'

Koolhoven said: 'You weren't thinking of bringing in outsiders?'

'Of course I trust you,' Marisia said. 'You've been like a father to me. You wouldn't lie. But it would be better if I know objectively what the problems are, don't you think? I mean, if anything happens to Pieter, they're really my problems.'

'I really don't think you should bring in outsiders.'

'Arthur Andersen, I was thinking,' Marisia said. 'They're very discreet.'

'They are,' said Koolhoven. 'But I still think it might be better if . . .'

'I have made an appointment with them for eleven this morning,' Marisia said.

Koolhoven leaned back against the sofa, and whistled very softly for a moment. 'Very well,' he said, 'what do you want to know?'

'There,' Marisia said, comfortingly, 'I was sure you would see it that way. I just wanted to be sure that I had full and accurate information.'

It wasn't very subtle blackmail, Koolhoven thought, but

it was effective. She was clearly quite as sharp as he had feared. The prospect of a new bank president calling for a midterm audit of the business would start rumours the length of Wall Street. Kellerman Unger and Security National were still, after all, outsiders in New York, albeit rich and influential. Money could buy them position, it couldn't buy them full membership of the established banking class.

Marisia smiled her starry smile and said: 'We should begin.'

In the field hospital on the bauxite mine, David Grant had come back to a kind of consciousness, in which he remembered the moment of stabbing pain and envisioned coiled snakes and biting fish that could pass through air with terrible red eyes, and fierce cats prowling in the night, and Van Helding, the predator of them all, with shotgun, with waterfalls, with some special, secret, terrible device that had sent all the constant pain of the forest to jar his spine and set all his nerves a millimetre off pace and . . .

They shot him full of painkillers and said there was nothing else they could do. Probably the coastal hospitals could handle the case. They didn't quite know whom to consult, since all other members of the expedition were now presumably making their way upstream with limited radio contact. From what they knew, the journey must have started in Simonstown, and it seemed logical to send him back there. A helicopter crossing from French territory would not be thought friendly, so they decided Grant would have to go first to the coast, and then along the coast by a commercial flight.

'We can send a rocket to the stratosphere,' the doctor said, 'and we can't get this man to a proper hospital.'

'No politics once the rocket's launched,' an orderly said. 'The space centre people will know what to do.'

And the helicopter duly went up to Korou.

Grant felt the rumbling and bumping of the flight, and the hard impact when it landed, and then his mind flashed onto a scene that was wholly surreal. In place of forest, river, macaws, and cats, and then the field hospital, white and simple, he had woken up in a rocket-launching area. There was even an Ariadne rocket on the launch pad, ready to go. It was like time-travelling and hallucinating, all at once, on some virulent mescalin. And the more he could focus on the rockets, the more he could feel pain; and the more he was shot full of painkiller, the more his mind raced back to forest menace. He was dodging in and out of nightmares, feverish, and lost.

Marisia came to the end of her week with a sense of glory. She felt she could truly control this curious empire. So much of it had been built to allow Pieter unquestioned authority at the centre that its workings seemed lucid and clear from where she sat. People reported and deferred to Pieter, and needed his imprimatur for major decisions, and feared his arbitrary interventions in minor ones. It was his institution, a personal fief, and she had inherited it.

She was exhilarated, and she needed some social excitement that could match her feelings. David Grant was up some damn river, and Pieter was not there to see her triumph, and she was in imminent danger of losing impetus. It was like the weeks after a publicity tour and a successful opening, when the movie does well and there's nothing more to do, and the mind starts pondering the next job while the body wants to go dancing.

Dancing, Marisia thought. Call Katherine. No reason why they should not be sisters, after all.

Katherine sounded uncertain. She didn't want to see Marisia. Marisia was a kind of rival that she didn't understand and had rather not handle. But still she could hardly say no. And evening out in sisterhood, a column item just like Pieter wanted, and maybe also a shoulder to cry on. Marisia knew Pieter, after all, and she had fought him so long that now she must have thrown off any warmer feeling.

They knew it was a mistake from the first drink. Marisia was up, sharp and high, and Katherine was fuelling herself for the night. The bar was latter-day Art Deco, and a tough place to be down; the blacks and silvers required a proper degree of posing. Marisia loved it; Katherine hated it.

'Could we speak French?' Katherine asked.

Marisia said, 'Certainly.'

'You worry about David Grant? In the forests?'

'Sometimes. There are other things to occupy me.'

'I worry about Pieter. Not so much what might happen to him – physically – but what might change him. Do you understand?'

'Perhaps,' said Marisia. She was looking around. Two rather junior persons from some magazine in London that she'd met at a party were just in view – angular in black and white, with coifs of hair. She wondered if they were interested in each other, or if they could be interested in Katherine and her. Perhaps it was a night for a little slumming.

'I mean,' Katherine said, 'he never did such an extreme thing before.'

Marisia said: 'He likes extremes.'

'Not risks like this – not going away. It's as though he was running away. And he leaves the bank to you, which is extraordinary.'

'Not at all,' Marisia said. 'I know what that's about. I've always resented the fact that we don't share the power from our father's will and he wants to remind me what I'm missing.' Did one beckon to young men in bars if one knew them a little? She had always moved in proper parties in public places and she was not at all sure. She decided that yes, she would.

'You know them?' Katherine asked sharply.

'Of course, I don't pick up strange men in bars.'

Katherine sighed. 'But I expect you could.'

'I could,' Marisia said. 'That's true.'

The two youngsters were late twenties English, sharp-shouldered and not at all reassuring, one in a pinstripe suit and a T-shirt, the other in a modified zoot suit. They beamed, and spoke most politely, and their faintly punk air dissolved instantly.

'Mrs Grant,' said one, called Peter.

'How good to see you,' said the other, called Kevin.

'Do sit down,' Marisia said. 'We're playing at wicked old women and we must get you a drink.'

'Rather,' said Peter.

Marisia made introductions and Katherine looked resentfully at her, knowing that the prospects of intimate talk had gone. But Marisia was happy, and eager to be courted, and nothing less than seduction would suit her.

'We were going to Mudd,' Peter said. 'Or somewhere. I don't suppose that would interest you?'

Marisia beamed.

Kevin launched into a convoluted theory of class and clubs in New York, with special reference to the early role of the Rhode Island School of Design. Marisia listened for a while, laughed and then ordered more drinks. She enjoyed the control she felt: two pretty men, an evening ahead and the knowledge that she was hot – with power as well as beauty, money as well as grace.

And Katherine responded. It was curious, but Katherine responded almost as she would have done to Pieter, picking up cues, helping with conversational moments, supporting and even flirting. Katherine liked power.

They found the car outside the bar, and told the driver to head downtown to White Street. Peter rather shyly produced a little snuff box – Victorian, a family pride, enamelled – with cocaine and the necessary implements. Katherine produced a mirror, Marisia sparkled.

At Mudd, they watched the crowd for a while, and then danced, and then drank again. Kevin and Peter had discovered new steps which they taught – laboriously to Katherine, who wanted to be right, and easily to Marisia, who wanted only to perform. On the floor, people cleared space for them, as a phenomenon – one that didn't fit, and wasn't at all usual – and Marisia found herself grateful in the centre of a net of eyes. She bathed in their attention, gloried in their stares. This was stardom, she thought, not the contrived kind, the press-agent kind, but a moment like this – when people know your authority and your beauty without having to know who and what you are.

The music went slow for a moment. Marisia leaned across to Katherine, who was wearing a fine, romantic evening frock that was mainly white. She stirred the neckline just a little, and Katherine smiled. She sat the boys down on the sidelines, and she raised Katherine up from her chair like a suitor at a formal ball, and led her to the dance floor.

Everyone sensed event. Lights that had been random and wild now focused on the floor, and the dub music changed to a kind of gentle, insistent, waltz-like ska. Marisia was bright and glamorous, and Katherine followed, fascinated, now settling the neckline for herself and even more seductively. The two women stepped out and began a perfect waltz. At turns, Katherine let her whole body drift back gracefully, and Marisia held her, and they moved together in a romantic, spotlit fantasy. People held their breath.

At the end of the number, Marisia bowed to Katherine, who was suddenly confused. She didn't know where she was, what she was doing, why she was with Marisia, and yet Marisia was all she had to cling to. Marisia, the one Pieter wanted, the one who wanted Pieter, who wanted her, and she – it spun for her, the whole conundrum, and she let herself be guided back toward the bar. There was applause on the way back, gentle but felt, and there was a moment before the music began again in earnest and other people moved to take up the space on the dance floor in which the women had left some kind of wafting, tousled ghost of feeling and grace.

Katherine said: 'What happens next?'

Marisia said: 'I feel like some old-fashioned disco.'

Peter and Kevin, having at first thought it might be time for them to make farewells, now racked their brains for appropriate places to go on. The driver was in the doorway, even as they left, and he pulled at Marisia's sleeve.

'Telephone message,' he said. 'Private.'

'I don't understand.'

'Koolhoven, Mr Koolhoven called – on the car phone. He'd like you to call him back directly.'

The driver knew his business. With practised discretion, he organized the coats so that Marisia had time to take her call without interruption.

'There's news from Providencia,' Koolhoven said.

'Bad news?'

'David Grant. He's been injured.'

'By Pieter?'

'I don't know why you think that,' Koolhoven said, but it was a hollow token protest.

'Just tell me what happened,' Marisia said.

'It seems he trod on some kind of stinging fish in the river. They have stingrays, apparently. He's been taken to a field hospital and then to the clinic at the French space centre, and they're flying him on to Simonstown. Apparently there's some diplomatic problem.'

'He is all right, isn't he?'

'As far as we know,' Koolhoven said. 'If you want to go down . . .'

Marisia said: 'You mean, if I want to leave you alone in charge of the bank. Isn't that it? You mean, if I want to clear out of the way.'

'I thought you might want to be with your husband.'

'And you booked the flights.'

'Listen to me, Marisia. There are flights – one a day from Miami, one a day from New York. The Miami flight is more direct.'

'Thank you.'

'I didn't know this would happen, Marisia. I didn't plan it.'

'I said thank you.'

'If you leave tomorrow morning, and bring David back, you could be in New York on Sunday evening. It's possible.'

'Is that what you booked?'

'I don't know what happened to David or what the effects are. You have to believe me. The message from Pieter was very short and very garbled.'

'We know he's all right then?'

The boys and Katherine were at the limousine door.

'Yes,' Koolhoven said.

'Get the tickets to me this morning,' and Marisia, caught in her high and her concern and her ambition all at once, added, 'please', and then worried in case it sounded too much like a supplication.

She put the phone back in place and the others swarmed

in like puppies. Katherine was soft-eyed and absurdly compliant. Marisia took a malign pleasure in announcing that she had to go home, that something had come up, that – wasn't that the final playing-out of the role Katherine demanded? – business called.

'The drugs and the boys and the night', she said to Katherine, 'are yours.'

Katherine took a blank-eyed moment to respond at all, and then sighed. 'Van Heldings,' she said, and she turned her attention to young Kevin, whose fingers were making unmannerly and pleasant advances under her pure white frock.

On her return, Marisia mobilized the household. It might be two in the morning, the bleariness of the maids too obvious, but there was work to be done. She packed, she organized. She left instructions. And by nine the next morning she was on the Providencia flight to Simonstown.

She would not give up the bank. She refused the American champagne, iced out any man who attempted conversation. She had her own matter to resolve. She was going to return immediately from Simonstown, be in the bank on Monday morning, but also she was damned if she would give Pieter and Koolhoven the satisfaction of seeing her apparently indifferent to David Grant. She did love him, constantly, even if the feeling was no longer an ache.

And she remembered Pieter. There was Pieter on the beach, Pieter willing Willem to his death, Pieter smiling so confidingly at the funeral. Those were childhood images she had long repressed, that had been the exotic centre of her one attempt at psychoanalysis. She knew Pieter killed people, not with guns or knives but with the mind. And she knew David Grant had suffered in the forest.

What else could she think?

She thought maybe she was being paranoid, giving Pieter powers no man possessed. Then she remembered his will. He would bend the world if he had to. And she was flying now, into his territory.

The runway at Simonstown had a tenuous look, with bush surrounding it. When the plane doors opened, the technical cool gave way to warm damp air. Marisia's peace was over.

'Business?' immigration asked.

'I have come to see my husband. He's in hospital here.'

'Visa.'

'I have no visa. Your New York consulate does not issue visas.'

Immigration clicked his tongue against his teeth. 'Are you expected here?'

'I have come to see my husband.'

'Ah yes. And which hospital is he in?'

'I don't know, yet.'

Immigration said: 'Then how do you know he is here?'

Marisia stared at immigration, a whole department and a frontier personified in a cropped-head boy in his twenties, rehearsing set lines, unwilling to chance making a mistake, happy enough to keep the rich white lady waiting a while.

'Do you have a ticket out?'

'Of course.'

'Please let me see it.'

The boy pored over the ticket for a while.

'How do you plan to support yourself?'

Marisia produced a sheaf of notes and cheques and cards.

'American money,' the boy said, triumphantly. 'You do not have Providencia money. You cannot support yourself.'

Marisia wanted, she thought, to respect the People's Republic of Providencia, but she was annoyed. More, the boy seemed determined and she had little time. She smiled, explained the difficulties of buying Providencia currency, and then began to talk in a high, clear actor's voice that filled up the terminal.

'I am Marisia Grant,' she said. 'Marisia Van Helding,' Pause. 'I have come to see my husband who is in hospital and to make contact with my brother, Pieter Van Helding.' She looked around. 'I am invited by your prime minister, Mr Miller.'

'Do you have a letter?' immigration asked.

But Marisia's ploy had worked. A tall man in white broke out of the crowd and came to the immigration desk. He spoke briskly to the boy, who complained it was all irregular, and Marisia's passport was stamped for a twenty-four hour visit. She also had an escort into Simonstown.

The trees parted just enough for a concrete road, rutted and unpredictable, menaced by bush on both sides. There were shack houses on stilts with pie-dogs rambling between them, and sometimes the glint of cooking fires under the houses. The car swerved often to avoid bright-eyed men and bright-eyed dogs.

'You'll want to go directly to the hospital?'

Marisia nodded.

The hospital was a quadrangle of colonial wood, set on scrubbed tile that rang with the sound of heels. Off a modern corridor there were a few discreet rooms which were almost private, well hidden from the main wards; such privilege was not supposed to be.

'Mr Grant is sleeping,' the nurse said.

Marisia went very quietly to his bedside. He was pale, and his body still had the unnatural contours of shock, but his eyes flickered open and he saw her. He wanted water; she gave it to him. Such simple needs had gone from their lives, and Marisia was alarmed at how moved she was.

'They didn't tell me about stingrays,' Grant said. Marisia helped him sit up against the harsh, horsehair pillows.

'How do you feel?'

Grant tried to shrug.

'The doctors say I ought to be paralysed,' he said. 'I can't move my legs yet.'

'We can go back to New York.'

'I want to get back to Pieter,' Grant said. 'I feel I let him down. I was supposed to be his companion. I was supposed to chronicle the expedition.'

'You did all that,' Marisia said. 'Now you have to rest.'

'You don't understand. He saved my life and I always suspected him.'

Marisia walked to the window which was heavily shaded by old bougainvillaea vines. She turned and said: 'With Pieter, that's always the safest thing.'

She argued with the doctors in the corridor. They wouldn't understand that she had to return to America; they thought her duty lay with her husband. It was pointless to explain that she ran a bank; women do not do such things. They warned her that Grant had already been moved too much and they couldn't predict what another move would do.

'Besides,' said one East Indian doctor, 'the airlines wouldn't take him.'

'I don't think you realize,' Marisia said, 'I shall charter a plane if I need to.'

And the doctors went blank before such assurance.

They had come to fit the river, so that big bucklike capybaras played on the margins without fear of the clumsy boats. Van Helding watched the forest pass with fascination. It was like staring at the night sky, waiting for more and more stars to appear as you look.

That night, they found a patch of open land that might once have been a growing ground and was not yet overgrown. The trees around had been hacked back so that there was comfortable room to make fire and pitch tents and still have a *cordon sanitaire* between the men and the bush.

'Beautiful night,' the naturalist said, conversationally, tackling his supper out of a can.

'Like the other nights,' Van Helding said. He was relaxed no longer, not the peaceful, drifting man of the river. He seemed to be waiting.

'It seems a pity not to use the photographer more for natural history pictures, don't you think?' The naturalist wiped his mouth on his sleeve. 'Such variety. Why, the two-toed sloth . . .'

'I'm sorry,' Van Helding said, and he got up. 'I didn't mean to interrupt you . . .'

But the naturalist was blissfully unaware of other people's reactions and talked on.

'. . . extraordinary creature which needs no defence since it simply never moves more than it has to, and stays clinging to the end of branches. It doesn't eat much or often, and for as long as it sleeps where cats can't get it, it's safe. Now if only we understood more about how that creature lives in the wild . . .'

There was a new note in the night sky, and the boatmen caught it first – something mechanical and powerful. They squatted by the river, agitated, and looked up into what had become a crystal sky, briefly streaked by the fiery tail of a shooting star. The monkeys were not as noisy as usual, Van Helding could tell, and their quiet made the engine note more audible.

'There couldn't be another boat on the river?' Van Helding asked the guide.

'Not at night, sir,' the guide said. 'Nobody travels at night. And that sounds like a big engine – and big boats can't get up the falls to here.'

'Maybe it's a plane,' the naturalist said. 'Could just be someone overflying the forest – no reason why not.'

The river went very quiet, just as the monkeys had fallen silent when a great cat passed, and the men on the riverbank were straining to hear. The green forest walls blanketed and deflected sound as effectively as any man-made device, and they swallowed all the echoes of the engine. But there was something, coming closer.

'It sounds,' the naturalist said, 'almost like a helicopter.'

Van Helding roused the photographer and made him start shooting pictures downstream. The naturalist looked puzzled. He had never understood the obsession with recording the minutiae of this trip, and he understood it even less now. His instinct was to reach for a gun, not a camera. The unexpected was always dangerous in the forest.

And suddenly, round a river bend some 300 yards away, came red and green lights in formation and the violent sound of engines.

'Christ Jesus!' said the naturalist. 'What the hell is this?'

Van Helding stood staring at the helicopter, a bulky Westmoreland gunship. He had a camera to his eye, and the sound he heard most strongly was the creak of the motor drive.

'Do you know who that is?' asked the naturalist. 'Damn it, do you know?'

Van Helding shook his head. 'I didn't think those things had much range, though,' he said. 'They must have a base quite close. And it's got to be military – nobody else would dare risk a copter in a forest. Too likely to go down.'

'But whose military?' the naturalist said. 'Whose military?'

'The guerrillas don't have copters,' Van Helding said.

'According to the people in Simonstown, anyway. It could be military from across the border.'

'And what are they doing in the middle of nowhere?' The naturalist was squealing now.

The guide and the boatmen had started to douse the fires, using canvas and water and anything else they could find. They didn't want to be seen by the military machine that hung now at the bend of the river, and they feared that they were already in gunsights.

The helicopter was still, and suddenly it spat out a beam of white, blinding light that stirred the cautious life of the riverbank into scampering flight. Like a great bird, with a searchlight for its talons, the copter began to move steadily towards them, checking each side of the river in turn.

Van Helding organized the men with guns. The photographer tried to put down his camera for a moment to pick up a rifle, but Van Helding motioned to him to go on taking pictures.

'Don't shoot yet,' Van Helding said. 'It might be something peaceful, something official.'

'It's not the helicopter that took Grant away,' the naturalist said, 'that's for sure. It's too big and too powerful.'

Van Helding shouted against the rising noise of the engines: 'We just don't know. So hold your fire, for God's sake.'

The boatmen had made for the water and the cover of the boats, and they seemed to be preparing to slip soundlessly down the stream, abandoning the others. They knew about helicopters from television on the coast.

'It seems so slow,' Van Helding said.

'It's hunting,' the naturalist said. 'It must be hunting for you. You're the only target in the forest that would be worth this much effort.'

'They couldn't know where we are.'

'The boatmen could have told them. They know how far you can go with so many gallons of gas and so many pounds of cargo. And they know where the camp sites are, too, and the breaks in the forest wall. I bet the boatmen could tell them where we'd be within half a mile.'

The great iron creature, scaly with defences, moved slowly towards them, its flat, merciless light teasing out the life in mangrove and bamboo, making spiky shadows behind dead trees, and sometimes catching snakelike movements in the water, or lighting the black-green forest boundary. Everything now was still except for the deafening racket of the engines and as that noise filled up the quiet a great magnified voice spoke out across the water.

'Drop your weapons,' it said.

The men looked to Van Helding, and he lifted his Purdy to his shoulder.

'Throw down your guns,' the metallic, booming voice repeated. 'If you throw down your guns, nobody gets killed.'

Van Helding fired twice, but he fired wild.

The answer was a rain of machine-gun fire that made lace of the river. The men standing in the tiny forest clearing might as well have been naked. They were lit as neatly as actors on a stage, and each one's movements were visible.

'This is your last chance,' the metal voice said.

The men on the riverbank waited for Van Helding's lead. They were unsettled, unsure what defence they had against the great iron hawk that had blinded them and pinned them to their little refuge. They couldn't run back through the cordon of dying fires into the bush, because vines and cats and death awaited them. They couldn't dive forward into the river, because quite apart from the danger of the waters, there would be no safe place to make landfall. The boatmen already had the boats edging gently downstream, motorless and silent. Their faint, dark shadows could hardly be seen.

And the helicopter came to stand close to the camp site, the searchlight focused and vicious as it came closer. Everybody dived for the ground. The helicopter swung away from them for a moment, turned, and came in low, aiming for the bank. It passed over, banked up sharply, as though checking to see if it had room to land. Nobody moved. It turned back and spat out warning shots as it passed. The bullets took the head off the guide, quite neatly.

The portly naturalist saw one last thing: Van Helding, standing, photographing for himself now the photographer was lying on the ground. He chronicled the guide's dead body, the blank riverbank where the boats had once been, the helicopter coming down in an epiphany of white light. And only when the machine had made its landing did Van Helding pitch away his camera. Now, it was too late. Whatever awaited him was coming down from the helicopter with guns.

The naturalist had found the best cover he could, judging that the light and commotion would scare away any animals that could run. He watched as the helicopter doors were pushed back, and he took his rifle to open fire. He shot four times, and then, to his horror, he saw Van Helding turn on him with the shotgun. Van Helding aimed directly for the point where he had seen the riflefire.

And the men came down from the helicopter, uniforms black against the white light, faces unseen.

'You are taking a terrible risk,' the doctor said. 'I can sign a certificate that your husband is fit to fly, but I can't guarantee that he really is. These things can end in paralysis, you realize. Paralysis or even death. We don't move patients with shock – we keep them warm and quiet.'

'I have to return to New York,' Marisia said. 'There really is nothing more to discuss.'

Providencia Air sold Marisia six first-class seats and strapped David Grant across three of them in his stretcher. There was a brief fight when the pilot, superstitious, refused to take a sick man on board; Marisia simply had Grant put physically on the plane with the help of the government men, who were only too keen to see their responsibility fly out. Then it was a fight between white pilot and black government, and Marisia could withdraw.

The government man in his dapper white suit watched the plane take off, and the police buttonholed him.

'Prime Minister's orders,' they said.

That morning, the Van Helding expedition had not made its nine o'clock call to the coast, and the minister had heard talk among the chiefs of some upstream incident involving great iron birds and lights in the sky and gunfire. The chiefs had built a fine rumour on this flimsy evidence.

'Say nothing,' was the prime minister's order.

The government man and his colleagues prepared grimly to obey.

Koolhoven never wasted time, and in the early morning he sat square and upright at his office desk. He was staring into space. For so many years he had controlled the bank, made things happen, turned other people's dreams and plans into machinery that worked, and directed things – subtly, he thought. Now he realized there was another side to what Pieter Van Helding had done with the banks. It was a side about which Koolhoven had been all too complaisant.

Why the hell was the man in Providencia? He knew the banks were in danger. It was pure luck that Marisia hadn't asked directly yet about the Grunwalds or Providencia, and perhaps he could keep back the bad news until Pieter returned. If only he would return, make sense out of the tottering figures Koolhoven had before him, explain it all so that Koolhoven could understand.

He had to wait for Pieter.

Only: some simpler voice kept challenging him. If you say nothing there will be no action and people will go on depositing their dreams and futures in two banks that are rotten, and trusting the name and glamour on company prospectuses and calculating their lives on the credit lines the bank could promise. Other banks, other businesses, other people depended on the banks' survival. They needed early warnings of trouble, to disentangle their lives.

Easy to think, Koolhoven knew, and not so easy to act upon. Banks are name, image, goodwill, reputation; if their image is tarnished, they start to decline. Worry feeds on worry. And if people speak out of turn, then it becomes all the more difficult to sort things out, find the kind of brilliant, improvised solution that was Pieter Van Helding's greatest skill.

Speak out, Koolhoven thought, and the clients might save something, but the banks would be in terrible, wrecking trouble.

Keep quiet, he thought, and there is a possibility – remote but real – that the banks will crash.

He didn't usually feel self-pity. He hated the idea of analysing himself. But he knew he missed Pieter desperately. He would do nothing until he had spoken with Pieter; he owed him that, as he owed him almost everything. He admired his quicksilver, his brightness, and more than that, Pieter was the one he had nurtured and loved. Even, at times, controlled like a father, with something like a father's love.

Such thoughts were unproductive, and Koolhoven tried to set them aside. He went back to the sheets of print-out before him, and when he had finished he erased the program and shredded the papers.

Nobody else must know, but a rumour could be fatal.

After three days, the Ministry of the Interior held a wrangle in its great wooden palace by the canal. There were those who said the whole thing was some simple accident and didn't matter; they had better things to do than look after dumb white men. There were those who reckoned the imperialist beasts had found something in the forest and were deliberately keeping radio silence. And there were those who feared guerrilla activity from across the border, a new bite from an old enemy that could now cloak territorial ambition in the struggle to oppose socialism.

And there was Arthur Miller who arrived in a flurry of aides and said: 'If he's lost, we're embarrassed. If we try to pretend he's not, we're fucked. This isn't some white madman, this is the nation's banker, for God's sake. And will someone please tell me if we have one single theory about who made him disappear?'

'Anyone with friends across the border could get a helicopter in,' the man in the white suit said. 'And anyone with a few riverman contacts would be able to work out how far the Van Helding party had gone.'

'So you think someone was hunting Van Helding?'

The man in the white suit said nothing.

'The boatmen won't talk to us,' a cop in stripes and medals said.

'They'll talk to the chiefs,' Miller said.

'The chiefs won't say anything.'

'Then break a few heads. Fire a few guns. Lose a few friends. Just find out what happened.'

The cop said: 'Tell us what you want to find.'

Miller bellowed back, face purple: 'Find the truth. That's all. Leave me to worry about the consequences, later.'

Koolhoven was infuriating Marisia. He was sad, withdrawn, and crabby. She dealt with him brusquely.

'Is there anything I should know?'

'Nothing.'

'Our two endemic problems – the Grunwalds and Providencia. I hadn't forgotten them.'

'I didn't suppose you had.'

Marisia glared at him.

'Very well,' Koolhoven snapped. 'Providencia is now on a nonaccrued basis, if you know what that means.'

'Trouble,' Marisia said.

'Exactly. It means they can't pay interest and we're stalling repayment of capital. It can't last.'

'Can we afford to write them off?'

Koolhoven shrugged. 'Politically or financially?'

'Both.'

'Financially, we could be embarrassed. We have minimum liquidity requirements and we have to have cash deposits. Some of that is in Providencia paper, and it would make a nasty hole in the balance sheet if we had to write it down. And we're like everybody else in this mad business – every time the price of oil goes down, we shudder. If the oil-producing countries have to take any of their billions away from us, just to feed the nomads, we have a crisis. It's sure as hell Providencia and the like won't pay back on demand.'

'And will anyone else bail out Providencia?'

'Possibly the IMF still. Possibly the generous US Government if they really understand what trouble it will cause if Providencia goes bust. All that is possible.'

'It'll hurt us if any of this is known?'

'It'll hurt. It's not the worst, though. Everyone is overstretched in the Third World; it's a fact of life. We didn't know what to do with those damn petrodollars when they came flooding in, so we drained the vaults as fast as we could to the only people who were desperate to borrow. We'll get sympathy for that.'

'Give it to me straight,' Marisia said. For a brief, glorious moment she saw what she was doing: Mildred Pierce. 'Tell me exactly what will hurt and embarrass us.'

'The Grunwalds,' Koolhoven said. 'If they had been allowed to go down years ago, they'd be back in business by now and thriving. As it is, they're a kind of trans-European bomb that could go off anywhere, any time.'

'How bad are things?'

'We've rolled over loans again and again. Our main collateral is their name. That's what Pieter wanted, and that's what he's likely to get very soon – if there are no miracles. If the damn French Government would hurry up and nationalize them we could at least claim it was all bad luck.'

'If both went down together – would we survive?'

Koolhoven shrugged. 'It's not possible to calculate until it happens. If it was a good day – we might keep the building.'

'You want a drink?'

'It's very early. Yes, I do.'

'You want Pieter to come back?'

'If only he would. It's possible I'm misreading the figures, or seeing things the wrong way. He may have some elaborate ploy he didn't spell out to me.'

Marisia put a full tumbler of Scotch in Koolhoven's big hand.

'That can't have happened often, can it? I mean, you were Pieter's right hand.'

'It did happen,' Koolhoven said. 'You know I love that man. I've watched him all these years as he built the bank and moved into London and then into New York. There's always been bluff and cheek in him – there had to be, otherwise Kellerman Unger would still be hunkered down by a canal in Amsterdam worrying about loans to Indonesia or some such nonsense.' Koolhoven sucked at his drink. 'But now – now I'm having to reread his career, and I'm having to make myself think that he may have made some terrible mistakes. It's all – different angles, if you see what I mean. And I still think that perhaps he was planning something.' Koolhoven looked at her as a great dog looks at a loved person, hoping for reassurance. 'Besides . . .' he paused '. . . I don't know how to say this to you without being offensive. For as long as Pieter Van Helding was here, we could trade on his name. People believed in him, were impressed by him. They'd follow him. People knew he'd find some clever somersault that would make the oddest figures suddenly look right. And if he's away – I'm afraid if anything happens when he's away.'

Marisia handed Koolhoven a phone.

'Call Providencia,' she said. 'It isn't that difficult. Ask him to come back.'

'That would not be appropriate,' Koolhoven said.

'You're talking as though if he stays away, it's the end of his whole empire.'

'He knew the situation. He chose to go away.'

'He knew how bad things were?'

'Oh yes,' Koolhoven said, and he smiled his wide, frank smile. 'Yes, he knew before he went off to Providencia. Everything that I've told you today.'

Marisia summoned a secretary and told him to make

contact with Pieter Van Helding – or at least with Providencia Government officials who were in contact with him.

'Bring him back,' Marisia said. 'If you're right, we'll need him. If you're wrong – if this turns out to be some ploy to put me out – I'm tough enough to fight.'

'I know,' Koolhoven said. 'If he won't come back, Marisia, you're our only hope.'

He was obviously from the interior; the city streets made him nervous and unsure, and he looked around with a sense of puzzlement. Man-made noise wasn't in his world, and here it was everywhere. Inland you didn't wait for a bus, you took the river; and the girls never showed their thighs, as here they did, seemingly without meaning the invitation; he didn't have to contend with all the city choices. He didn't have to worry, for example, if the policeman behind him was friendly or hostile.

He wanted to see the museum. There were supposed to be ancient things there, from his people, finer than they made today; he had heard that from the missionaries as they obstinately built what they said was a truly traditional hut while the *graman* chief was putting up his nice European bungalow. He walked up the museum steps and looked inside.

It was like a storehouse, he thought, a disordered storehouse. You couldn't see where things were, and there was no sense of organization. There was a family of armadillos, dead; some hammocks, from the Indians; a scale model of some kind of mine; a diagram on the wall which showed the structure of politics in Providencia. He couldn't read, but he saw the familiar picture of Arthur Miller, looking like a spider in a web with all the lines that came from his head. Someone had scratched out Miller's eyes.

It was odd the policeman had followed him. They were strange in the city, he knew, and he also knew he didn't have the skills to hide here. Give him bush or river, and he could be hidden even from the wild things he hunted, but not on streets and in rooms like these – brown, lifeless rooms that smelled of hot dust, enclosures he could barely stand.

He began to move faster. Better not run; cops were like animals, they scented fear.

The policeman behind him had also speeded up. He wasn't one of the ornamental street cops either, there to send the traffic that way and this; he was in black, with a light, peaked cap. The boatman had never seen a cop like that before.

He wished he hadn't come to the city. It always meant trouble. Once he came back with his guts turning after too much stuff they called wine, made out of rice, and once he got the clap, and this time he was being followed by a policeman. He should have taken the money and run. They'd got paid well for taking the white men upstream, and he could have bought a new boat or kept the money for gas, or even bought a generator – like the chief's, for light to keep away the night spirits.

'I'm an honest man,' he thought. 'No point in running.'

They'd been asking what happened to the white men. They asked the chiefs, and they wouldn't say anything, because after all there was nothing they knew first-hand. They might think the boatmen had done away with them. These city people believed anything of the inlanders – thought they were savage, called them bush people, treated them like the niggers of a black country. And he'd come into town with money, damn fool, and that would make them even more sure.

Better not let the cop get him. Better get down those stairs just as fast as he could, and get lost somewhere – in a bar, in a public building. There was a big door ahead, and rooms coming off it where he could dodge and hide.

There were books everywhere. It was like a storehouse of books, on shelves, a grander version of the riverside schoolroom. People seemed to be looking for particular books. He thought he would follow their example.

Only the cop had found him.

'You like to read,' the cop asked.

The boatman nodded.

'You're holding that upside down,' the cop said.

And since the cop had a night stick and a gun, the boatman agreed to go down to the main police station, and after a talk of two hours in which he was only slightly bruised he agreed that he had been on the white man's expedition.

'We knew that,' the cop said, although in that case, the boatman reasoned, he had no right to beat the confession out with a stick. 'We saw you with your roll of money.'

'I'll tell you,' the boatman said, because he was understandably anxious about the enthusiasm the cop showed for wielding his night stick. And he explained about the helicopter, and how they had slipped away because of the gunfire and left the others.

'You know that's murder, don't you?' the policeman said.

'We never touched them.'

'It's murder. You left them there and you took the boats and they couldn't escape. You one guerrilla, man?'

'I don't know about guerrillas,' the boatman said, unhappily.

'You got one chance,' the cop said. 'You take us back to where you saw the helicopter land. If your story looks true, you're fine. If it doesn't, we'll hang you.'

The boatman was silent.

They kept him in a cell overnight with a couple of

drunks, and one of them threw up over him, and he still felt dirty the next morning – very far from the river. They made him get into a plane and they flew inland, and he felt nauseous and terrified. He started to think that maybe he wouldn't find the place again – and then he thought that he was a boatman, after all, and nobody knew the river better than he did – and then he thought that he knew the river from being in a boat. It was knowledge in his muscles, not his mind. He didn't know if he could work out a location except in terms of gallons of gasoline and travelling time.

'The day before the night,' he said to the cop suddenly, 'we were at the French station.

The cop nodded. It was the first really useful information.

They radioed ahead to see if it was feasible to land a small plane at the French station and they were told it was possible, but rough. They took on board two canoes – unlikely things to find at a station run by white people – and travelled at treetop height, the plane seeming to graze the forest ceiling until it flopped down to earth.

And they started up the river.

'Two days,' the boatman said. They wouldn't let him work the pole or the engine; they'd brought other boatmen for that. He felt strange as a passenger on his own river, strange and unsettled. Maybe that was what they wanted. He could see that the policeman, full of city starch, was none too happy, either.

But the boatman knew he might not recognize the spot. He might go past it, and then they'd hang him. It would be so easy to get it wrong in a place where the bush rushes back to repair the slightest break in its green-black defences. He watched the bank with a madman's eye, determined to miss nothing. It was the right bank, he knew, and they had stopped at four – on the second day upstream from the French station.

The cop had his own thoughts. It was odd the way the trail was marked like a paper chase. Here a man fell in the falls, and here a panther was shot at night. Van Helding did not mean to go unnoticed.

There was silence in the boats as they travelled. The boatman looked at the cop's gun and he started to sweat. The cop had his own embarrassments. What exactly was he supposed to do if Van Helding was alive and well, and wanted to keep quiet? And what if those helicopter stories were the nonsense they sounded, and he was out here alone with the river people? People told stories, at night, about the river people.

The river made one of its revolutions, a serpentine turn that almost doubled back on itself, and opened a tunnel of green that stretched for a quarter mile. The cop saw condors – more than one. The boatman suddenly smiled.

'What the hell you smile for?'

The boatman didn't think he should bother to explain. If there were condors, there must be carrion on the ground. Carrion would mark the campsite. The boatman was sure, at last, that he wouldn't hang.

'You best go into the shore,' he said.

The ground was covered with a bitter prickle of red ants, and what the condors had not snatched, the ants were bearing away in systematic convoys. The tents still flapped open, and there was plastic sheeting everywhere, some torn with bullet holes, and broken branches, and signs of old fire.

Also, there was a man. The policeman went to him very gingerly, afraid of what he might find, and the boatman would not even approach. After these days, with the ants marching, the remains would not be pleasant. There was flesh clinging to bones which had gone grey and used-looking where they were exposed, and the broken stock of a shotgun. The cop knew the shotgun was a grand one; a Purdy.

'Christ,' he said.

The boatman was looking out to the river.

'You see what you did,' the cop shouted.

The trees seemed to have been hacked, perhaps by rotor blades; but the policeman thought he had heard that helicopter blades were fragile and liable to fail if they hit against solid objects. There were no signs of boats – that again fitted the boatman's story – but some of the cloth and skin suggested that not all the boatmen had got away. For the policeman realized that he was standing on the site of more than one murder. He saw the flattened area, close to the hacked trees, where there had been a landing, and an oil spill, harsh-smelling, which could not have been the commercial gasoline the boatmen used.

'There was a helicopter here,' the cop said.

'I told you.'

'But it couldn't have been the helicopter that hacked the bush away – that would break the blades. Did you hack the bush?'

'No, sir.'

'Did the white men?'

'I didn't see.'

'Then who did? Someone must have prepared this site – made it big enough for a helicopter to come down.'

'I don't know, sir.'

'Shit,' the cop said. He didn't like the place, its sweet deadly smell and its bodies. They'd have to take the bodies downstream in this heat, day after day, carrying the rot in the pit of the boats. It would be better to leave them for the forest to take its course, but the coast would never stand for that. These men had to be identified. They mattered.

The policeman prodded the greenery, brushing away

the column of ants that mechanically took to the air bridge he was giving them. There were shotgun shells under leaves.

'I'm going to look around,' he said. 'Come with.'

The boatman said nothing.

'Come with,' the cop said, and drew his gun.

He couldn't force his way far into the bush. It had closed again over its wound, and vine and creeper had seethed back into places where they had briefly been cut. The boatman used his machete to make a way where it seemed there had been a path cut before. The macaws clattered up from high branches, and monkeys fell quiet at the intrusion. Very high in the branches of the purple heart tree, just audible on the forest floor, animals crashed from branch to branch, running from the new forces they could sense moving in their lower kingdom. Beyond the marks of the helicopter landing and the rough clearing, there was little light, and no sign of movement, and not much trace of any man.

The cop could see nothing at all, and he motioned to turn back. Then the guide saw ants moving slowly, swarming upwards.

Shadowy in the grasp of vines was what once had been a man – a white man, with a camera around his neck, and red ants seething from the foot to the naked skull. As the cop looked up, a column of ants marched out through the fleshy parts of the mouth, like a tongue.

The cop curled himself up as though he had been struck in the stomach. 'Cut him down,' he said to the boatman.

The boatman did not move.

The cop fired twice at the boatman's feet, and the machete flew into the air to take out the vines and free the body; he had to use his gun three times more before the worst of the bones and flesh had been put into a canoe, under tarpaulin. The smell was charnel-sickly and insidious, seeming to perfume all the hot, sweaty air with death, and the men retched, They would not take the dugout with the bodies until the cop agreed to travel in it himself, and take the boatman from the city with him.

And the funeral barges set out down the river.

The cop said, under his breath, '*Pater noster qui es in caelis . . .*'

'It must be possible,' Koolhove said. 'They had radios when they set out and plans to contact the coast at regular intervals. Someone must be able to make contact.'

The Providenica consul, stationed at the UN Mission in New York, very much regretted it, but the telex said nothing of the sort. It said contact had been lost and a search party had been sent.

'Are you confident,' Koolhoven said, 'that every means has been used?'

'We have a search party out even now,' the consul said.

'We want to send our own representatives,' Koolhoven said. 'Naturally.'

'That will not be necessary,' the consul said and regretted the phrase immediately. 'We do not know if the loss of radio contact is significant. It is often difficult to transmit from deep forest. Sometimes batteries fail.'

Koolhoven said: 'I would not like to think that the Government of Providencia was covering up.'

'We shall report,' said the consul, 'immediately we know what has happened.'

Koolhoven wanted to intervene, to find and save Pieter Van Helding. He blamed himself for allowing such an expedition. And he realized that he had only a brief time to prepare for the morning meeting with Marisia.

'Is there anything to report about the Grunwalds?' she asked.

Koolhoven said: 'There's one chance, which is to find

out what is really happening with the French Government's nationalization plans. One of my assistants was at Vincennes in 1968 – when the riots happened, you remember. Dope, sociologists, and theoretical Marxism. It seems he has a friend in the right *Cabinet du Ministre*. I never thought I'd be grateful for the Vincennes old-boy network, but I am. He's in Paris now.'

'That's good,' Marisia said. 'I looked over the papers on the flight – it struck me as odd that the loans weren't syndicated at all. Didn't other people get a share? Are we really alone?'

'We're alone.'

'That doesn't seem very prudent.'

'Pieter isn't always very prudent,' Koolhoven said. 'He usually delivers larger profits that way.'

'He seems to have got it wrong this time,' Marisia said.

'Tax and currency. That's what will bring the Grunwalds down. They borrowed in weak dollars and they've got to pay back strong ones – after a franc devaluation, in the middle of a recession. There's a thirty per cent difference there. Then there's tax. They've not always been as cautious as they might have been in tax provisions, and the present French Government won't give such a capitalist institution the benefit of the doubt. And since they're such a grand name of money, the French will no doubt nationalize them with great glee. Dancing in the streets, I expect.'

'You're saying it's politics more than money?'

'It would look good – France now owns the Grunwalds. They can't even guess how bad a bargain they'd be getting.'

'Is anyone going to help us? Citibank and Chase and the rest – they don't want a banking crisis, and they can't like the idea of their brother banks being taken over by the state.'

Koolhoven said: 'We're the outsiders, you know. More to the point, everything we did with the Grunwalds was very private and very special. If we let out now how bad things are in Paris, our Wall Street friends would do the sums in a half-hour – and they'd know how much trouble we're in. If that was public knowledge we'd never get out of this hole.'

'Friends are the last option possible.'

'That's it, exactly.'

'And Pieter's partners – the ones he called the Palm Springs people?'

'I can try. That is, if they don't start screaming at us first.'

'I wish,' Marisia said, 'they could get through to Pieter.'

'They've sent a search party.'

'A search party? Isn't that drastic?'

'I don't know how else you make contact with someone in a rain forest, if their radio isn't working or they don't want to call.'

Marisia looked at Koolhoven and she realized he was terrified.

Under that stolid front, Koolhoven had a sense that things were dissolving, calamitously.

Marisia held out her hands and said: 'He let you down, didn't he? He wasn't there when you needed him?'

'I wouldn't say that,' Koolhoven said. 'No.'

But his eyes were watery instead of cold, and he had to look away.

The boxes with their terrible freight of skin and bones and flesh and cloth had been put into cold store in Simonstown, and the policeman had been sent to the Prime Minister's office.

Miller said: 'What was left in the camp?'

The cop explained. 'Tents, bedding, plastic sheets.

Cooking gear. That sort of thing. And there was a case, metal, sir, with camera and film.'

'Exposed film?'

'Unwrapped, sir.'

'It's in the cold store?'

'I imagine so, sir.' The cop looked puzzled. 'Could I ask a question, sir?' Miller nodded. 'Does the Government really know who did this? Or where Mr Van Helding is?'

'No,' Miller said. 'We don't. Not officially and not unofficially. He's either in those boxes, or he's in the forest, or he's being held by someone who can run a helicopter into our territory without us knowing. I'll be honest with you. I hope to God the man is in those boxes.'

When the policeman left, Miller slammed his fist against the little table of rattan at his side until it buckled. Damn all white imperialist bastards who could make such trouble even in their tragic ends. Miller knew he could call New York for dental records, but then everyone would know there were bodies, and bodies too far gone for usual means of identification, like features or papers. He could keep quiet, but sooner or later the story would emerge, and Providencia would look bad all through the West. And debtors need all the respectability they can get.

He went out to police headquarters and demanded to see the film. The police didn't want to open the cold room, which was poorly sealed and carried a charnel smell. On Prime Minister's orders, they did it.

Miller found the camera quickly, with the lenses and the pile of film. He could destroy it now. He could pretend there never had been such vital evidence. The cop said the photograhper still had his camera, and that meant the last minutes had been recorded. Without the evidence, Providencia could announce one of those tragic accidents in the wily bush – unfortunate, but nobody's fault.

But he couldn't do that, not really. The film had been

mentioned already in reports to New York. The best he could do was send it north as fast as possible, get it away from here, let it tell its story where the details at least would not hurt him personally.

He gave Prime Minister's orders.

Think of the evening, Katherine Van Helding told herself. Shuffle the invitations as they come – some gaudy, some precise, one mayoral, two for the greater glory of frock-makers on the turn (when their boyfriends' faces replace their own on advertisements), and one for a fund-raiser at the New York Public Library; and beyond them, a nicely embossed, nicely printed line that stretched out from the Helmsleys to the New York society of the 1900s. You considered your evening, and your frock and your escort – a safe man, a walker, for a safe evening.

She wondered if out-of-towners went to an agency for gown and face and escort. Perhaps she should set one up.

Koolhoven told her they'd lost radio contact with the expedition. Straight away, she wondered if Van Helding was dead – and what she felt, if he was dead. He hadn't made her happy, nor even fulfilled the social contract that a wife expects, but she still responded to him, power and presence, and he was not at all dispensable. The pain of him was sometimes all that reminded her she was truly alive, in between the frocks and the invitations.

He was dead. Think: if he was dead, then she could fly back to London or Paris in a great show of mourning and take her chances. She would be *femme seule* instead of *femme couverte*. She needn't play any more of these public social games. She could have her life back – whatever her life was, without Pieter.

'You'd better carry on,' Koolhoven had said. 'For the moment. We don't want rumours.'

So she settled for a day that was about looks and

attitude and lunch – a little time looking at paintings on 57th Street, lunch at the Russian Tea Rooms with a friend, an hour at the beauty salon. She knew the time, the woman who would work her skin and the nature of the treatment and the glow it would produce – all planned, all known. A terrible soft trap.

'I think we just got a warning,' Koolhoven said.

Someone was selling out of Security National CDs, and selling stock in the market just enough to depress the share price on a day when everything else was conspicuously sunny. At the same time there was a series of withdrawals from upstate branches. There was nothing to wreck the balance sheet, but there was three dollars off the share price, and when you looked at the statistical probabilities of all these things happening together, Koolhoven knew it was a message.

'The bastards are getting out,' he said.

Fairbairn was heavy with lunch at six in the evening, and he made an avuncular round of farewells.

'Anything I can do?'

'Yes,' Koolhoven said, surprisingly. 'Make a trip to Washington for me.'

'And see who?'

'Anyone you can reach in the White House. We're very close to a disaster here, but at least we can minimize its effects. Get them to say who would be the lender of last resort if a country went down – it isn't obvious at all, especially with Eurodollar deals.'

'We want the Federal Reserve to step in?'

Koolhoven said: 'Or a consortium of central banks. Whatever. The fact is Providencia has gone nonaccrued, so we do without the interest, and if we can stall a total default for a few weeks, we might just find a safety net.'

'But we haven't even started talking yet.'

'Then start,' Koolhoven said, his fury at the old man's patrician idleness spilling out. 'I mean, please start. Please.'

The telephone rang shortly after Fairbairn left; it was the office of the UN mission from Providencia.

'This is a little irregular,' said a starched black voice, 'but we have some material which Mr Miller wanted someone senior to see.'

'Yes?'

'We have evidence that Pieter Van Helding's party was intercepted on the river. We found a quantity of human remains but of course without dental records . . .'

Koolhoven put down his head on the desk for a brief moment and banged it, hard.

'Are you there?'

He recovered for a moment. 'Of course, of course. Do you know if Mr Van Helding is dead?'

'The probability . . .'

Was that going to be all? Probability? Death and ending were bad enough, but the prospect of doubt and anonymity and random bones was intolerable.

'There is also some photographic film which we felt should be returned.'

'Yes,' Koolhoven said. 'I'll be here.'

He thanked God it was too late to call the women.

They garlanded the lions on either side of the Public Library steps and brushed the dope-pushers back into the dark heart of Bryant Park, and Fifth Avenue looked washed and splendid. The evening of the seventh annual Fargo Awards had been stage-managed, brushed and teased until, like a blue-rinsed head, it was perfect, in its own terms.

Photographers clattered their lights at Vreeland who was imperious, and Halston who was in black, and assorted journalists, a part of the Warhol empire, and a handful of politicians who were following their wives.

Katherine Van Helding mounted the steps like a figure from an album. She was grand, beautiful, picture-perfect, born to this social world and born to use it. She was not Mrs Van Helding, but Katherine de Grunwald Van Helding. She could survive Pieter, gloriously, if she wanted.

People asked how Pieter was, and Katherine was polite, and a famous dress designer who liked to look and listen asked if Katherine and her walker would care to come back for cocktails, afterwards, and the manicured, stylish crowds went in to dinner.

They had put Katherine next to Gorringer of the brokers, the same Gorringer who had helped engineer Van Helding's triumph in America. He drank a little too much, feeling out of place, and numbed by a wife who gushed about art. She had a good eye, but a suburban matron's way of talking about it, as though pictures were children with a talent. Gorringer wanted to talk politics, and Katherine felt inclined to oblige.

'It's got to stop, you know,' Gorringer said, looking at her as though he felt sorry. 'The IMF is just the International Marxist Foundation. They're bankers to the world's failed revolutions. And we have to draw the line.'

Katherine had a good political sense. She knew when someone was blustering and when someone was preparing, rehearsing policy. And Gorringer was serious, enough to pain his wife who wanted a flippant evening. Katherine encouraged him. Now Pieter was gone they all of them – Marisia, David, Koolhoven and Katherine – had to live on their nerve and their instincts and save themselves.

'We'll make an example,' Gorringer said. 'We'll let a country go. Take somewhere like Providencia, where they mortgaged oil they never found and the banks lend them money to pay interest on their interest. We'll let them go. And we'll tell the IMF: one penny to that country and we'll pull out.' Gorringer warmed to his subject and Katherine made a pretty, painted audience. 'We'll show the banks they can't come running to us when they make mistakes. They should have put all that money in American industry, not drowned it offshore. Besides, they wouldn't help us when we needed them. Wall Street made the whole country think Reaganomics wouldn't work and we're not going to help out Wall Street now. We're going to clean the whole mess up.'

Katherine smiled.

'And believe me,' said Gorringer, with that wonderful smugness that is reserved for Americans, 'the people of Providencia will thank us one day. They truly will.'

Katherine smiled again, and she turned the conversation and kept it light and she let the glitter of the night sweep around her; and she didn't forget a word. She rose to applaud the winning designer, she scuttled home, sent the chauffeur and the walker away with equal briskness and called Koolhoven.

She left a message on his machine. 'They're going to let Providencia go. They won't help us, now.'

The packet of films was opened once by the guards on the door, who were fearful of something so curious, so late in the evening. Eventually they agreed to send it up to Mr Koolhoven, and they insisted the Providencia messenger go with it. They made a fuss with Koolhoven's secretary, demanded he call them before opening the package.

Koolhoven agreed. When they had gone, his secretary brought coffee and he waved it away, and she produced the address of a photographer close by.

'He's discreet?'

'He does grand people's naughty pictures,' she said. 'He has to be discreet.'

'No Press links?'

'How many nudes from the Four Hundred have you ever seen in the *Post*?'

Koolhoven grinned.

When the secretary had bustled out with the films, he went back to papers and calculations and the computer screen. Night after night, he had been tracking elusive things, omissions rather than errors, slips rather than disasters – things that did not quite make sense. If Providencia and the Grunwalds both collapsed, he would need to know exactly where the bank stood, and it seemed that the whole picture would be hard to build. It had been carefully fudged, not so much that auditors would ring alarm bells, but enough to make exactness impossible.

It could mean someone had been sloppy. It could mean there was a kind of accounting netherworld beyond the respectable public figures. If it was the latter, someone had managed to run deals and arrangements without Koolhoven knowing, and that could be nobody junior to Pieter Van Helding.

At eleven the phone rang. The photographer had finished his work – 'Industrial job,' he said. 'I'm on an assembly line here. I'm starting to print up if you want to come down.'

Koolhoven took the limousine to an apartment on 16th Street, and told the driver to wait.

'What's all this about?' the photographer asked. He was a tall, gangling Pepsodent boy, an unlikely candidate for discretion or dirty pictures. 'This isn't exactly my usual line of country.'

'But we're paying your usual rates,' Koolhoven said, 'for what I gather is your usual silence.'

The red light burned still in the darkroom, suffusing the air.

'There are fifty-two films, at least,' the boy said. 'I don't know the order so I can't begin to make a story of them. There's some scout-camp stuff. And there's a reel or two of *Apocalypse Now*.'

Koolhoven stared at the endless spools of film, the equipment, the first contact sheets hanging up to dry.

'All this film,' he said. 'It must have been exposed to heat and damp.'

'Yes,' the photographer said. He was pouring tart-smelling chemicals. 'Yes, you can say that again. Some of the shots look like old granny's sepia. And whoever did the shoot was good – but insane. He covered everything, every angle. He got twenty times what he needed on absolutely everything.'

'Maybe he was paid to.'

The photographer drew the papers through their chemical bath.

'You really won't tell me what all this is about?'

'We're paying you to know nothing,' Koolhoven said.

'I'm just trying to help.'

Koolhoven looked quickly at the scattered contact sheets as they came down from the line. He saw Van Helding in the dugouts, Van Helding visiting the Prime Minister, Van Helding on an island, Van Helding on the plane (interminably – of the plane alone there were almost a hundred shots). He saw the plane landed, the boats casting off, the assorted expressions of Van Helding against the forest and in clearings and by tents. Once, there were a dozen shots, badly faded by light, which seemed to be taken at night and to show animal guts spilled on the ground. Immediately after, there was Pieter Van Helding and his Purdy, like a game hunter at his moment of triumph.

And the last film began to come alive in turn, the shapes forming in negative, the negative set aside, the prints beginning.

'Christ,' said the photographer. 'It is *Apocalypse Now.*'

Koolhoven had difficulty with the little viewing glass, but he struggled to hold it in place over the contacts.

There was a great light. Then through the great light there was the shadow of rotor blades and a metal flank. Then there were men coming down from the helicopter with guns. Then there was Van Helding, standing with a gun – all this was on one film and the order was clear. Then there was a little fat man, silhouetted, and a flash of gunfire. Then there was a confused series of out of focus shots which seemed to show gunfire, or perhaps flares. Then there were shots through leaves.

Then there was a last shot of the thirty-four left on the film – a shot of a man who could have been Van Helding, silhouetted against the light, gun down.

Koolhoven almost cried. If his gun was down, he had given up – stopped the bloody business of defending himself and admitted it was time to surrender.

It might be someone else.

But it was someone in very Western clothes, skin flashing white. The photographer took the picture. The little fat man must have been the naturalist and he was accounted for by gunfire on the other side of the clearing.

Koolhoven had seen Van Helding at the moment he gave up.

Koolhoven read the inspector's report again and again. He would have liked to find some flaw in it, a link of evidence that was missing, and since he could not, he wanted to cope with its flat, prosaic account of horror by constant repetition. He thought after many readings it would lose its power to tangle with his dreams.

He summoned the family – Katherine, Marisia – as he had to do.

'I think,' he said, 'we can assume Pieter is dead.' He could say it to Marisia directly, while they were alone.

'Is there any doubt?'

'In law, yes. It may take seven years to get a legal presumption of death. But we have photographs.'

'Photographs?'

'Someone took pictures right up to the end. You can see there's a heavy military helicopter – it could be a Chinook – coming up the river, then searchlights, then gunfire, or at least flashes and men falling. Then nothing.'

'I don't see how the film survived.'

'Waterproof bags, they say – and it takes even ants time to get through space cloth. The heat did some damage, and the last film of all was ruined. It was in the camera.'

'It's odd anyone had time to unload a camera and put the film away.'

'The photographer was an old combat hand, apparently. And who knows what people do in a crisis?'

'And what happens now?'

'Wait for Katherine, and I'll explain it all. For the minute, it doesn't look good. Pieter is only legally missing until the bodies are identified.'

'We'll need to appoint a chairman, not just have one acting.'

'I'm not fighting you, Marisia. I need someone to do the public appearances – like the press conference – we'll need to announce what we know. People will listen to you.'

'You're giving me Pieter's bank?'

'I'm staying. Someone has to do the management work of salvaging this whole mess.'

Katherine arrived. She quickly acknowledged how

much she knew, and how much she wanted to know, and she said she only wanted to talk about the future.

'Thanks for the message last night,' Koolhoven said. 'You're sure Gorringer meant Providencia?'

'He said Providencia,' Katherine said. 'He talks a lot of truth when he's drinking.'

Koolhoven said: 'I wish they'd find another country to slaughter. They can teach the whole of the Third World lessons as far as I'm concerned – if they'll only leave Providencia alone.'

And when Fairbairn had arrived, Koolhoven began his explanation of how bad things were. It was like a revision of history. Instead of the wild excitement of the Eurodollar business, and its middle-life, middle-aged respectability, there was suddenly a network of loans with no central banks to guarantee them in the last resort, and no national laws to protect the lenders. Instead of freedom from regulation, there was freedom from safety. The paper deals which Van Helding had executed with such brilliance were all likely to tumble when confidence lapsed, even for a moment, and the vital signs of faith suggested that people wanted no more of paper. Kellerman Unger's buccaneering was now more like the extravagant wildness of a boy in a wine cellar – and the cavalier attitude to local banking law, on which loans could be which part of the portfolio, now left the bank exposed, not the regulators. Lending to Third World countries, such a clever way to slip profitably outside the gentle restraints of any country's banking law, now foundered on the fact that many of those countries were never worthy of credit. All this was happening to hundreds of banks in various countries all at once, so the two special problems of Kellerman Unger – the Grunwalds and Providencia – could not and would not be covered.

'What I'm saying,' Koolhoven said, very solemnly, 'is

not to be repeated outside this room. For the moment, we have to put on the best face we can. If we admit anything, we may lose everything – it's a house of cards.'

'My bank,' Fairbairn said.

'There's some curious lending, too,' Koolhoven added, compounding Fairbairn's misery. 'Most of it after we took over, but not all of it.'

Fairbairn looked sharply at him. 'Not all of it?'

'Your middle management probably has friends in low places, too.'

When the meeting broke up, Koolhoven nerved himself to call Henry Klein. The Palm Springs gentry had better have an official statement that Van Helding was considered missing; they would not want to learn it from the network news.

Klein said: 'I rarely leave the Coast nowadays.'

'Indeed.'

'When I do, it is for important matters. Like liquidating positions in certain stocks for my principals.'

'Nothing has changed,' Koolhoven said, 'because Van Helding has gone.'

Klein sighed. 'We don't feel we've been kept fully informed,' he said. 'We were hoping you would come to us sooner.'

'I always thought it was Van Helding's prerogative to talk with you.'

'We would certainly value his advice. But he's lost on a river in South America, you say.'

'We don't know, not for certain. We hope . . .'

'Yes,' Klein said. 'We all hope. However, you have ten days. We require proof – proof, mark you – that all is well.'

'I shall do my best,' Koolhoven said.

He went back to the computer terminal. This time, he asked for uninterrupted real time for a fussy series of calculations. He wanted to know if one of the two banks could be salvaged – if moving Kellerman Unger assets into Security National would protect them, if the American bank authorities could be satisfied and the Dutch and British kept at bay. At least Security National was only marginally involved in Providencia and the failed attempt to salvage the Grunwalds. Absent, Koolhoven thought, a handful of personal loans for speculation on the New York market, which were run as tightly as any margin account with a broker, and some mortgages on Fifth Avenue co-ops.

The figures would still not add, and the process of shifting assets would be difficult to achieve, more difficult still to explain to outside accountants.

He tried the figures over again. He looked for some pattern, some logic that he had missed. Perhaps Van Helding had known exactly what he was doing, and had simply hidden the key to his plans. But perhaps he had known there was no hope at all, had run away from the implicit, street-rough threats of Henry Klein, the pressure of shareholders, the impending collapses, into a dream world where the irrational pursuit of Eldorado wiped out his coming failure. It was curious that he had suddenly developed that overwhelming desire for physical risk. Middle age might explain it, but a simple quest for excitement would not. Van Helding was not like that. His kicks came from what he could calculate and what he was good at – skiing, for example, where he could make himself expert, and then surrender to the sensuality of speed and wind.

The body was an image that Koolhoven could not shake – caught in vines, almost eaten, ants like the motion of a tongue in the mouth of a skeleton.

Perhaps Pieter Van Helding had finished liked that. Perhaps he was a kind of suicide.

* * *

Marisia took the press conference, with the solemn, familiar board members around her. She never had stage fright, except that morning. They asked her about Pieter Van Helding, whom she hated, whom she loved, and she answered as coolly as she could.

Within an hour, trading in Security National shares had been suspended on the New York Stock Exchange. The specialists couldn't make a market with so much panic-selling, and a trickle of opportunistic buying. There was no two-way process, and the flood of orders set the traders bellowing until the share was taken off the market.

Two hours later, trading resumed. Security National announced that its managment would continue as before, that Koolhoven would step up, and that Marisia Van Helding would act as chairman on behalf of minority shareholders. Shares in Security National dropped $4.25 on the day, not helped by an unexpected analysts' report from a big broker's that cast doubt on the bank's next earnings.

At five, Koolhoven reviewed the day. They would be clearing international transactions now, down on Church Street in the New York clearing house, with everyone paying up and collecting. They had survived.

He had one thing that worried him. Three of his brighter assistants had been let loose on the files, with a brief to act like adversaries. They were to dig out anything that might look bad when the files fell into unfriendly hands.

They found twenty-seven transactions unaccounted for. The files were simply missing. There was not even the sort of skimpy detail that marked the more suspect loans in Van Helding's time – money flooding out as letters of credit to the Caymans, or being collected in America for some brass-plate Bahamas company. Some of those, at least, might be straight; no reason why investors shouldn't incorporate in the British Virgin Islands, pay a 15 per cent business tax and a few thousand to a local lawyer, and export their American earnings without paying withholding tax. Since the British Virgin Islands are covered by British tax laws and treaties, the Americans had to let the money go. That kind of deal was legitimate, however much it offended the IRS.

But the twenty-seven were simply not documented. There were skips like erasures in the computer record and gaps in the paper files.

Koolhoven puzzled over the missing material. The last thing they needed now was a problem that could not be quantified.

He watched the figures, line by line, coursing across the video screen, and when the material was assembled, he asked for hard copy. They might yet survive. He would need to strip Kellerman Unger for a while, but that could be hidden. If they were lucky.

'He's relatively dead,' David Grant said. 'Is that what you mean? Not quite alive and not quite absolutely dead. Just enough of both to be embarrassing.'

'If you want to look at it like that,' Marisia had curled in front of a wood fire that cast gentle shadows around the room. She watched the castles form and crumble in red ash, and landscapes dissolve in flame. She knew she had to talk with David Grant, and she hardly knew how to do it. They had never discussed Pieter and Marisia; Grant could hardly imagine it, Marisia could hardly articulate it. In a curious way, Grant did not seem violently upset, and that made Marisia concerned. Perhaps he had always known about brother and sister, or perhaps he could never face the fact.

'It always comes back to Pieter,' Grant said.

'I have the banks now. That makes a difference. There's nobody to challenge me.'

'Would anyone dare, given the state they're in?'

Marisia shifted herself. 'Did he make any sense in the forest – Pieter?'

'He never gave himself away.'

'I was frightened for you, all the time.'

The fire fell softly.

'I won't go,' David Grant said, 'not just because of this. I love you.' He felt his bloodless legs knotted under him; the poison still had the power to freeze movement sometimes. 'But he violated everything.'

'He changed everything.'

'I hope to God he's dead.'

Marisia said: 'You'll never exorcise him if he's dead. You know that. There will always be the memory.'

'You're very remote,' David said. 'Why don't you look at me and really talk to me?'

'I want to,' Marisia said. 'But it's hard to concentrate on your pain now. I'm supposed to speak for the bank – be the bank in public. While Koolhoven beavers away and tries to sort things out, I'm the one who goes out like a public-relations flak and strokes people.'

'They said in the papers that you were much more than that.'

'Not really. I don't understand banking, not much, and there's no time to learn. It's a question of putting on a brave face.'

'You did very well on television.'

'I'm good with cameras. It's my job.'

'If things are so bad, why don't you just walk away?'

'It's family and friends now,' Marisia said. 'And it's still what I wanted. If I could save it, it would all still be mine.'

'But it belongs to all the other shareholders – to those people in California, to all the people who put money in.'

'They need a Van Helding. They need the glamour. It's

only glamour that gives them a central place for the money markets and the stock exchanges and the rest. Glamour they can buy, for ready cash. Old-established names, with old-established ways, they can't – at least, not often. Glamour is new, it's vulnerable, it needs what they can offer.'

'You're taking up Pieter's crusade.'

'No,' Marisia said. 'My own. It happens to look like Pieter's.'

The telephone rang. Marisia heard Katherine say she had found some papers and some keys – should she tell Koolhoven? Marisia said yes. Katherine said she was lonely and awkward in the house, and the servants were gone, and Marisia tried to check with David that she could invite Katherine, but David was not looking. She took a chance and told Katherine to come. It would clear the air, perhaps, and it would be a diversion. Also, it might salvage Katherine.

She arrived within fifteen minutes, as though she had called a car before calling Marisia.

'I'm very grateful,' she said to them both. 'I needed to be somewhere else.'

David shrugged.

'And I wanted you to have these, Marisia. I don't know what they are. There are keys, they might be a safety deposit box, and there's a sort of lease on a storage room, somewhere by the river. And there's a list of numbers. They were in his desk.'

'Thank you,' Marisia said. 'I'll show them to Koolhoven.'

Katherine shivered. 'It's like waiting for winter, isn't it? We know what's going to happen. Nobody else does.'

'We're still trying to stop it.'

'If Pieter went away, it must have been too late.'

'You believe that, too? I think that's what Koolhoven

believes – that he went to the bush just to run away from the Mob and the bank inspectors and the rest.'

'He hasn't even died, officially,' Katherine said. 'That's the awful part.'

Marisia held her. 'Only a few more weeks – then we'll know if the banks can survive. If they can, we all go back to normal. If they don't then from what Koolhoven says, it's the end of the world.'

David Grant said: 'Not quite, surely?'

'I don't know,' Marisia said. 'He seems terrified. I can't imagine Koolhoven having emotions, let alone fears, but he does. I've learned that. It's one of the reasons I stayed to help.'

'And tomorrow?'

'We get through the day,' Marisia said. 'If we do, we're doing well.'

'I have to explain assets,' Koolhoven said. 'Give me a minute of your time.'

Marisia nodded.

'Banks keep the money deposited with them on their books. Overnight money, where they're not yet officially told to pay out, goes in the assets column. It used to be a big part of the big banks in New York. Then the game started to change. After years when there were a few minor problems, and one very big one, they worked out the risk they were running. All day you could run up obligations in the dollar market in New York that you didn't have to settle until ten the next morning. That was fine, usually. But Europe is on a different time from New York, and Hong Kong on a different one still. A European bank could trade billions in a day, leave itself with millions to settle next morning, and at two in the afternoon their time, which is not yet nine o'clock in the morning here, that bank might go bust. Result: every transaction that bank had done collapsed. At ten in the morning, nobody got paid. The system fell apart.'

Koolhoven sighed. 'They tolerated that for years – almost ten years after it happened for the first time. That was a small German bank called Herstatt in 1974, and they didn't change the system until the eighties. Instead of being able to kill deals at ten in the morning, everything had to be settled the same day – five in the afternoon. That meant all the nice overnight money couldn't sit in a bank's books any more – it was off where it was meant to go by the close of business.'

'You mean we could have looked a much richer bank in New York if the system hadn't changed?'

'That's true,' Koolhoven said. 'I also mean that if we have a really terrible day, we might need to ask the clearing house to change the system back just for a few days – to give us a breathing space overnight. They'll take some persuading.'

'Do we need that soon?'

'Yes,' Koolhoven said. 'I was hoping that you might make the presentation.'

Marisia said: 'I don't understand it all.'

Koolhoven said: 'You're good at politics, even if you don't know everything about the technicalities. Our case would be pretty simple. There's a hundred billion dollars a day going through the New York Clearing House. On most days, the banks pay over a billion, they get a billion; it's all paper transactions and it balances out at the end of the afternoon. But if you break the chain, all those deals become real money – maybe a billion Chase bought for clients and now it won't get its money, or millions other banks were expecting from us, and we can't pay. And of course, think of the people we deal for. It's banks more than anything else – banks throughout the Western world. If they send money and it disappears into a bank collapse they're in terrible trouble. And it could be even worse. Those billions of dollars pretty much represent the currency in which the world does trading. You don't buy Colombia coffee for your Paris teahouse with francs. That's the scale of what's at stake – the big banks, world trade, and the whole New York Clearing House.'

Marisia said: 'It's terrifying.' She went to the office window and looked out across the matching towers of midtown, all secure and self-important. They seemed less safe now. 'Pieter knew exactly how to make himself central, didn't he? Even now he's gone. It's as though you take Van Helding away and you take away the keystone of the system.'

'It needn't be like that,' Koolhoven said. 'The point is that from the books, we are in grave difficulty keeping Kellerman Unger and Security National afloat all the time. But it can be done, unless there's some hidden horror we don't yet know about. What frightens me is that we could trigger that domino effect among banks very simply. Say the Grunwalds finally did declare bankruptcy. Say Providencia defaulted so spectacularly that we couldn't find a polite way to hide it any more. And say it all happened on a single day while the banks were still weak . . .'

'That's what you've been telling me will happen,' Marisia said.

'Exactly,' Koolhoven said. 'It's a little like knowing the end of the world is near.'

'People have been wrong about that before.'

Koolhoven shrugged. 'Perhaps. I don't think that should make us happy, though.'

'So our argument is – give us more time on any day when we have a crisis, or the whole system comes tumbling down. Is that it?'

'The clearing house doesn't like it known when it has

problems. When Herstatt went down, almost the only sign was a dip in the stock markets round the world. I think they'll want to be discreet.'

'But it'll be obvious if they suspend same-day clearance, won't it?'

'Not to customers,' Koolhoven said. 'We'd just need a meeting when they do the domestic clearing at ten in the morning. That could be almost invisible. And then customers would get their money next day, as they do normally. There might be a few who wondered why there had been a hiccup in the system, but only a few. It takes seven weeks to clear a foreign cheque through New York as it is.'

'It would just be the clearing house giving us more time – to save the world.'

'If we can. And if we can't, to do the sums.'

'We couldn't just tell the truth now?'

'And shut the bank doors? There'd be panic.'

'But it would be a different sort of panic – controllable.'

'I can't do that. This is Pieter Van Helding's bank and I will keep it going until the very last.'

'I don't feel that loyalty,' Marisia said. 'You know that. All I want is to save the family bank.'

'And to prove you're a Van Helding, too? To do what Pieter did?'

'To undo what Pieter did,' Marisia said.

When she had left, Koolhoven's brightest and most thuglike assistant came charging into his office. Koolhoven was feeling particularly fragile and old, unsure of why he troubled to make things work. The assistant took no notice of all that.

'I found the room,' he said. 'Van Helding's leased it for six and a half years. It's a store-it-yourself room, in one of those blocks by the river, south of Christopher.'

'Why would a banker want a room in a warehouse?'

Koolhoven said. 'He could keep anything he wanted in a safety deposit box or the vaults – anywhere.'

'Maybe it was something private,' the assistant said. 'Something he didn't want anyone to know about. Then everybody would think like you're thinking. We wouldn't have looked for a storage room if Mrs Van Helding hadn't found those keys.'

'True,' Koolhoven said. He puzzled what Van Helding would have concealed so carelessly, since a warehouse is not a bank vault, and yet so privately, since he never wanted its hiding place to be known. 'We'll go down there tomorrow,' he said. 'I'd like to be there.'

The assistant was impatient.

'I thought I'd better get down there fast. I checked the building and I talked to the manager – but I did a damn fool thing. I tried the wrong key in the room lock, and he got suspicious.'

'He won't be suspicious of me,' Koolhoven said.

'You cannot do this,' Edouard de Grunwald said, his usually dull, flat voice rising to a shrill plateau of alarm. 'This is unthinkable. This is impossible.'

'I have my own loyalties,' the Baron Gilles said. 'Family. Name. And my race. I can't help any of them if I stay in the bank.'

'But if you remove your money, we're finished.'

'We're finished in any case. It's simply the *coup de grâce*.'

'The Grunwalds are not finished until the last moment. We can still hope to regain our place.'

'Wind,' Gilles said. 'Piss and wind. We're like the bull with the swords through him. We're waiting for the mercy of death.'

'I don't know why you came here. You were never wholeheartedly a Grunwald. You never cared about the bank.'

'Protected myself, that's all. Protected myself against you and Hugh and your ideas, not against family. Now it's my judgement it is over, and I want the end to be quick.'

'We'll sue.'

'Perhaps.'

'I never thought a member of the family would do this.'

Gilles pushed himself to the door. 'I don't lecture people,' he said. 'But I never did feel part of this family. You never were Jews. You were frightened to be. You tried to hide yourselves in your Christian clothing and your châteaux. Me, I cared about two things.'

And he was gone.

In the car, Noam Gregory said: 'It was a hell of a choice.' Empathy and sympathy were not muscles that Gregory often used.

'Choice?' Gilles said. 'My family is an investment that went wrong. I did everything I could. Now there isn't anything to do. I want to save the money – there's work to be done, your work, and other work. I want that to continue. So I shall go to my vineyard and write cheques.'

'God bless you,' Gregory said.

'I hope,' said the Baron Gilles de Grunwald.

At ten in the morning, the messengers came down from every bank in New York with sacks of cheques and orders. They left off those that had been paid into their own branches the day before, and collected the ones their branches would have to pay out. They pushed and they scrimmaged, and they moved the sacks in and out within minutes. That morning, a surprising number of senior bank officers were with them, and when the clearance had been done, those officers climbed to the second-floor boardroom with its Victorian pictures and Victorian furniture. They competed discreetly for the chairs, too few for the more than fifty banks in the clearing house. They huddled, and they waited.

At five past ten, the chairman of CHIPS introduced Marisia Van Helding.

She looked severe, a woman who had at last come into power when there was nothing left to savour. All she wanted was to put the brakes on a disaster.

'Gentlemen.'

They looked at her quizzically. In a time of crisis, a familiar man might have pleased them more. Yet she had undeniable authority, and she had Van Helding's name, and because she was not known to them as a banker, they credited her with more strength than the Security National men they knew too well. They would listen.

'I have been told by telex from Paris that the Grunwald Frères bank has been placed in receivership at ten minutes of ten our time. I had wanted to come here to argue about a principle and to ask a favour. Now I have to ask for action today.'

The bankers shifted on their seats, as though a cold breeze passed among them.

'Security National and its parent company Kellerman Unger are facing difficult times. The chairman is missing. We had a substantial commitment to Grunwald Frères. We were their New York correspondent, and we shall have to assess the scale of that damage – all their deals done during European bank hours this morning are of course on our books. And as you know, we have our own structural weaknesses, as do you, and we have our commitment to Providencia. This is not a happy time.'

She drew breath. The money men were not used to such directness. They always denied problems, or masked them. Mentally a dozen itched to place sell orders in the market, and a few more thought of cashing CDs.

'Our problems are made acute by the Grunwald collapse. At five this afternoon, we may or may not be able to settle. We are confident that with a little extra time, we can organize everything – including the problems caused to the rest of you by this collapse. But we need time. What is at stake is the future of this clearing house – all our futures. We promise action and we ask for your discretion – no statements about the collapse, a day to work out how bad things are, clearance of international deals overnight instead of this evening. We hope to be able to report at ten tomorrow morning that the worst of the crisis has been averted.'

The man from Citibank said: 'And if not? What happens then?'

Marisia said: 'We will have lost twenty-four hours, but the situation will not be worse.'

Koolhoven watched her with some pride.

'I don't have to tell you, gentlemen, that at stake is the future of banking and banks. We all know the scale of the underlying problems of which the Grunwald collapse is just a symptom. Those problems could overwhelm us unless we are flexible today. If one member of this clearing house were to go down in present circumstances, how many of you could be sure that you would be here the next day?'

Marisia let her words echo round the room. In corners, bankers were still scuffling for space and a view of her as she spoke. They had felt as though they were playing musical chairs. Given what Marisia Van Helding said, it started to seem more like Russian roulette.

Koolhoven left the office at two in the afternoon because he could no longer focus on the figures. They had their extra hours to settle business, but still the scale of the Grunwald catastrophe was not clear. One major bank had simply frozen all the Grunwald cash it held, a move of dubious legality which at least left a pool of funds to settle some Grunwald obligations. Whether the bank was entitled to make itself a favoured creditor by one quick grab was a question to worry the lawyers when this crisis was over.

Marisia joined him in the limousine, and they went south, along Seventh Avenue, down through Greenwich Village and past the warehouses and gay bars and truck stops and post-office depots by the river. They seemed incongruous and elegant in a rough zone.

'I don't know you,' the man at the warehouse said.

'Seven E,' Koolhoven said. 'I have the key.'

'Someone wanted Seven E yesterday. I didn't know him either. And he didn't have the right key. What's so hot about that room?'

'I thought you didn't ask what people wanted to store.'

'We'd ask fast enough if it was going to blow up or catch fire.'

'It isn't,' Koolhoven said. 'I promise you.'

Grudgingly the man took them up in the freight elevator to the fourth floor, and a long row of blank doors hung with various locks. He stopped at 7E.

'You Van Helding?' he asked.

Koolhoven nodded.

'I thought you was younger.'

'I was,' Koolhoven said, 'this morning.'

He took out the key. Since there had been three similar keys in the bunch Katherine had found, there was still a slight chance that this one was also the wrong one. It seemed to look the same as the locks on the door. Koolhoven tried it.

'If it ain't the right key, I call the cops.'

The warehouse man had backed off to the elevator, and was holding the doors – ready to move quickly to the phone if the key was wrong.

Koolhoven turned the key. It did not seem to move for a moment. He pushed the key more deeply into the hole, and it budged. The lock was stiff, but it was opening.

'Not,' said the warehouse man, 'that I ever had a moment's doubt.'

He still looked unsmiling and unsure.

Koolhoven pushed open the door. It was an airless, windowless room, perhaps 10 feet by 25 feet. He turned on the lights.

In the centre of the room was a desk and chair. They had not been stacked like furniture in store; they seemed to be for use. Around the walls were boxes – carboard, secured by old, brown sealing tape.

'Like another office,' Marisia said. 'For another business.'

She and Koolhoven launched themselves at the boxes, tearing at them. There was no point now in discretion. There was no Pieter Van Helding from whom to hide their knowledge of his secret room. The manager watched from the door of the room, puzzled by the fury with which the old man and the great-looking broad (his terms) were opening and checking.

There were books. There were files. Some were the old-fashioned Kellerman Unger files, tied with pink-red legal ribbon; some were computer print-outs from Security National, together with papers and forms and letters.

Koolhoven tore open a box of books. They were sea-stained and old, dusted with the fine black droppings of cockroaches. They could have been books Van Helding had at home on the Caribbean island where his father died.

Marisia checked the drawers of the desk, and then moved a cover from its top surface. There were more books, with the same stains, and there was the vellum concertina of a map Van Helding remembered, with a red dotted line that showed the path of Walter Raleigh when he looked for Eldorado. Van Helding had kept the special books together, in a kind of shrine, kept private and away from others.

In a desk drawer she found the stash of US Intelligence files which Noam Gregory had pushed on Pieter Van Helding. There was no time to read, only to see the headings and labels. Her heart stopped for a second. She wondered if she wanted to know what the files contained.

'Twenty-seven,' Koolhoven said, piling the bank files onto the desk. 'The twenty-seven files missing from Security National – the blips on the computer tapes. It's all here.'

'And a lot of dreams,' Marisia said.

Koolhoven set his reading glasses on the end of his nose and began to study one of those Security National files. It concerned a loan, $23 million, to a corporation in Cayman Islands, with no security. It was a no recourse note, so that nobody had to pay it back. It was one of the twenty-seven.

'I think I can tell you exactly how bad things are,' Koolhoven said. 'We're not going to last the night.'

'You can't be sure,' Marisia said.

'Yes,' Koolhoven said. 'I can.'

'Then should we ask them to go back to same-day clearing, after all? If we can't survive, then . . .'

'No,' Koolhoven said. 'I can't do that. You can't do that. And it wouldn't make any difference now.'

Marisia picked up the books, like a schoolgirl between classes, and said: 'We'd better go.'

Koolhoven, broken and tired, leafed through the pages of a file and set it down. He walked to the desk and sat there a moment, as though trying to occupy Van Helding's mind as well as his place. He opened a little drawer that

Marisia had not thought to check, and drew out a tiny child's train. Perhaps it had once belonged to Pieter Van Helding, or later to one of his sons. He looked up beseechingly at Marisia, his eyes full of tears, and he held the train in his hand so hard that he cracked it.

'There's a Chase night officer on the line,' the assistant said. 'Some rumour that we've got computer trouble.'

'No trouble,' Koolhoven said. He wondered if he should go to dinner. 'Tell him no trouble at all.'

10

Katherine de Grunwald Van Helding sat at a side table in Regine's, dress slipped off the shoulder, talking with three beautiful young Colombians. They were old money, before the Mercedes crowd of cocaine dealers came up to El Chico heights, and they chattered about parties and they tried little jokes to make Katherine listen. She always seemed interested. Nobody could tell if the talk ever touched her.

They ordered more champagne, putting it on Katherine's account.

It was her last appearance. She had performed so well, so long and so intently in the smoke and laser lights of places like this, and she could now be free. There was no more Grunwald Frères to salvage, and no more Pieter Van Helding to placate. The boys did not know, as she knew, how much she had felt like doll and whore to Van Helding in the last years.

She rose to dance. The air was cut with light beams, light stars, and music rushed to her head, brought grace to muscles made stiff by politeness. Light from behind caught her hair and made it a golden halo. She flung up her arms, chanted with the music, the least discreet of the middle-aged dancers and the stiff young preppies on the floor. A full-fat couple with skimmed-milk children stared at her from the ringside – the man mesmerized, the woman disapproving, the children, sceptical of life after thirty, faintly pitying.

The tune ended. Some mix of organ, railways, screams, and bass came up out of the speakers, and the light was suddenly wrong for her. She seemed blank. No more Grunwalds. No more Van Heldings. Only a woman starting life.

'I have to go home,' she said.

'We could go on,' the Colombians said. 'Somewhere less middle-aged.'

'Not me.'

'There's still Consuela's party at the Studio.'

'Get Jean to get me a taxi.'

'We could walk you home.'

'I'm going alone.'

The taxi driver kept saying, in almost his only English words, 'Pretty lady. Pretty lady.' Katherine was still full of music and she ignored him. She only asked him to wait for a minute while she undid the house door. She slipped the three locks, put on the light, and the light caught mirrors which showed back her perfect, painted face.

A doll, she thought, slamming the door. An alert, sensuous doll, the sum of her performances – nights at Xenon with models from Zoli, nights at Studio where Bob Colacello checked off your escort's name, nights at the old Danceteria when there was performance art, at Mudd in the first nights of punk when it surged in from the Rhode Island School of Design, nights at Interferon, but not many, nights with proper escorts at fund raisers or Regine's.

The trouble with organizing a house without live-in maids, she thought, is that from midnight to nine you are so much at the mercy of whatever they did wrong during the day.

She began to fix the three locks, set the chain. She reminded herself under her breath what she had to do. It was absurd, this prison atmosphere, where people with no names went out in the streets to rob. She checked the ground floor, room by room, pausing at each door, throwing the door open like a child looking for demons, then turning on the light and summoning courage to go in.

It was odd that the taxi had not gone away. The driver was staring out at the house, mouthing, perhaps shouting, 'Pre-tty la-dy.' She flicked the blinds shut. In the basement kitchen there was coffee ready for morning, and she wondered if that was what she needed. One in the morning, godless time. She pulled a bottle of Louis Roederer Crystal from the refrigerator and poured some into a mug.

Check the basement. If a cat crossed the floor, bells like a country wedding would toll out, and sirens go off in the police station. Turn on the burglar alarm. Retreat to the ground floor. She could build her safety for the night, floor by floor.

She sat on the stairs for a moment, looking at the grand Frank Stella which hung in the hall. She thought she heard a noise above her, and she turned her head; old houses settle and sigh, even New York brownstones on the Upper East Side. She climbed to the first floor, turned another switch for the burglar alarm, waited.

The taxi had not moved. Yellow and bulky, it sat by the roadside. She wondered if the man was still shouting. Why did he not go?

As she climbed the house, she moved away from her public self. She became something more than the sum of her column inches. There was a floor where there might have been a nursery, a ficus soft in the corner of a dark room. She checked again, she found everything calm.

The next floor was less comfortable. When Pieter had been in New York they had sometimes shared a grand bed, but uneasily; they were not contoured for each other. It was her territory now and Pieter was gone for ever. She finished setting the alarms, and she thought of the brownstone as her fortress, with electronic sentries on permanent go. She was quiet, she was safe, and flowers that lined the balcony behind her house glinted in moonlight.

She glanced out into the street. The taxi had still not moved. She thought she heard a rustling, like cloth moving in whispers, in the next room, and she flung open the dressing-room door. Nothing. Nobody. The windows were all sealed shut. She opened the bathroom door and she shone back at herself from a dozen mirrors. Perfume had spilled on the floor, and a heady, musky smell filled the room, a little like incense; the mirrors were her church.

And her ceremony was a kind of exorcism. She took the bottles from an upper shelf – Joy, Opium, Halston – and brought them crashing down to the tiled floor. The same heavy scents came up. She searched in the cabinet for pills – Tuinal, the doctor recommended, and Dalmane for the less bad nights, and the uppers, too, and she spilled them into a wild cocktail on the bathroom bench. She added Tylenol for headaches. Something in all that pile would cure her, once and for all.

She had the mug of champagne, and she took pills at random from the pile. She had made her decision and now she needed sleep and time to carry it out. She remembered something appalling about Tylenol – if you took too many, the liver damage was irreversible, even if they pumped your stomach. She wondered what she had taken. If only God would let her sleep.

She stared into the mirrors. Coughing from taking the pills had made her eyes red and moist. She suddenly looked tired, even haggard. She thought back to the château near Montpellier, to the grand wedding of Pieter Van Helding and Katherine de Grunwald, and the start of it all. She wondered how she could have let herself be so constricted by Pieter. She wondered if she could even mourn him.

And she asked herself what pills she had taken. She felt woozy, woollen-headed, and her senses were imprecise. She heard something, and told herself she was hearing things, imagining ghosts in the night. She thought she heard a few steps, a flourish from the burglar alarm that was quickly stifled, then more steps.

She propped herself against the bath, trying to make eyes and senses concentrate. She listened hard. She knew there was someone with her. They would know where she was by the lights. Someone wanted her jewels, or wanted to do her harm, or had come for her like an avenging angel. A thousand fancies from the New York nightmare hemmed her in. And if they could get into the house at all, and pass the alarms, there was nothing to stop them entering her sanctuary.

She pulled herself upright, scattering pills among the perfumes on the floor, leaving a treacherous, slick surface over which she had to pick her way. She took off her shoes, felt the sharp edges of tablets against her soles before they crumbled into the wet. She came into the master bedroom. Perhaps they knew where she was, already. Perhaps they wanted something tangible – money, a painting, silver. Or perhaps they wanted her. They meant her harm. After all she was alive and available, a target for revenge against Pieter.

She stumbled at the edge of a rug. She collected her wits, drug and drink tainted, and she peered out through the window blinds. She did not want to be seen, and someone might be watching. Down in the street, the yellow Checker cab was still there. She could see its off-duty light.

Now the house seemed alive to her. It seemed to shake with almost purposeful movement. Subways, she thought, but the nearest subway passed five blocks away. Perhaps she would be safer on the balcony. She could climb down the fire escape into the gardens and walk until someone took her in. But who would risk saving a woman walking alone in private gardens in the night? She knew that if she had heard trouble outside, she would have locked the windows, retreated to her safe place. You never knew what circled out there in New York – what desperate, what nothing-to-lose creature prowled just beyond your safety.

She wanted to be safe. She had thought so much about risk and new beginnings and now she wanted safety. Just let me live, she thought, this night, and keep me safe from the monsters.

Telephone. Dial emergency number. Dial – and listen to a recorded message. How could she ask for help in a voice that sounded like gin and Quaaludes? They would take hours to arrive. Out there a thousand patrol cars watched the shadows and waited for a call. But they were far away, and the soft, soft noises were only a floor below.

Why did the alarm keep quiet?

She thought she might hide on the balcony and she stepped through the windows. Along the boundaries of what she could see, leaves and geraniums and high, twisting stems of wisteria curled and threw confusing shadows. She found herself reading the shadows, finding demons there. Her senses were grazed by fear.

She swung round.

There was a man by the window, waiting for her, a man who seemed to think that he belonged there.

She made herself walk towards him. She would ask what he wanted. A real man was somehow less threatening than the imagined demons in the trunks of trees.

She wanted to sound calm and clear. Instead, the drink and fears and drugs made her slur. 'Who,' she managed, 'are you?'

She moved forward and found a light switch and made the room full of brightness. She blinked.

'Christ,' she said.

Pieter Van Helding stepped forward to break her fall.

It was late in the desolate evening before Koolhoven allowed himself to start the calculations. Amsterdam and London were primed to work through their early morning. It seemed clear that there was no solid centre left to either bank. They had been hollowed from within and eroded from outside, made to play great games that went wrong and to suffer the consequences, but also, quite simply, stripped of money, assets, and resources. The question was when the authorities would realize how bad things were.

He worked with his assistants until he saw one of the boys slump forward, asleep. He sent them all home, and he put on his coat and hat, leaving like an ordinary man and the end of an ordinary day. The lobster shift, the overnight telex and computer operators who would take in orders and buy and sell money when Hong Kong opened, when London opened at five in the morning New York time, were just arriving. Men and women scampered to their desks and took out coffee and sandwiches, Their job was to follow the green tracery of money on the video screens, to track the billions. It was, as far as they knew, a busy night, but not a terrible one.

Koolhoven paused for a moment outside the Security National tower. It was tall and bland, set about with a street-level mask of trees, An old man, swaddled in newspaper, a bare leg purple with raw rot, slept there. And above him, those sentinels of power persistently shouted all the money and authority they represented.

But not any more, Koolhoven thought. He hailed a taxi.

* * *

'I'm not going,' Katherine said. She was sitting on a sofa, quite assured, her sharpness of mind returned from the unfriendly fog that had blanketed her only minutes before. 'I don't want to know anything more about you.'

'You have to,' Pieter said.

'There isn't anything I have to do any more,' Katherine said.

'You don't even want to know what happened to me?'

'No,' Katherine said. 'It's obvious. You needed to run away from everything, so you staged your own disappearance and recorded it with a thousand photographs. They brought them back. You were sure everyone would think you were dead. And if you were dead, I suppose you thought nobody would come looking for you.'

Pieter grinned. 'You're exactly right.'

'As far as I'm concerned,' Katherine said, 'you're dead.'

Pieter stretched out a hand. 'Come on,' he said. 'Isn't that hand warm? Isn't it good?'

Katherine said, very coldly: 'That's enough.'

'Very well,' Pieter said. 'I'm offering you a ringside seat at the end of the world, but if you want to turn it down . . .'

'What's so special about tonight?'

'I'll tell you,' Pieter said. 'At two o'clock in the afternoon, Amsterdam time, the bank inspectors will walk into Kellerman Unger and declare them insolvent. That is seven in the morning here. When that happens, there will be a chain reaction that will be unstoppable.'

'How do you know about Kellerman Unger?'

'You know I know things.'

'You can't know what the bank inspectors are going to do.'

Pieter looked directly at her. 'It's all going to be over,' he said. 'I know.'

Katherine settled into the corner of the sofa, crumpled and wan. 'My God,' she said.

'Come with me,' Van Helding said. 'You wouldn't want to miss it. It'll be like the night a comet passes or the moon goes into eclipse. Everyone would like to see it.'

Katherine thought. If she went with Van Helding to the bank, she might be able to break away from him, and there would be other people, alert and helpful. If she followed him, she had a chance of escaping him.

She wanted to observe him, too. By every rational test, the man was defeated, running away from the end of his empire. Yet he was like a boy, wild-eyed and fascinated, who is making a scalpel ready to torment a frog or breaking a bird's wing. He wanted to see the worst he could do.

Guards with their pistols challened Van Helding at the door of the bank. It took minutes, and various passes, to prove his identity.

'Yeah,' said a guard. 'I know the face from the pictures.'

'I'm sorry for the inconvenience, sir. Just doing our job.'

'Quite right,' said Pieter. He rushed into the hallway, laughing that they should so assiduously guard a structure crumbling around them. He even laughed as they walked into the elevator. He was audience to a great show.

The elevator opened on a landing with locked, bullet-proof glass doors. Van Helding slipped his electronic pass into the slot and bundled Katherine through.

There was a busy, long room full of computer terminals, with a bank of telex machines against the wall. Years ago, such rooms might have been full of flustered clerks and paper. Now each man and woman was boxed away with a screen, a keyboard, and a set of files, alone in the middle of money. There were a couple of untidy desks, covered with a print-out. Katherine thought she also caught in the sterile air a faint, unmistakable whiff of marijuana.

'Can I help you?' asked a meticulous black man at the first desk. 'Unauthorized personnel are not allowed on this floor.'

'I'm Pieter Van Helding and I've come to watch.'

'Sir,' said the black man, smartly. 'Welcome back.'

'You're running?'

'Hong Kong's opening.'

Pieter steered Katherine by the elbow to some stark black office chairs, and she sat there, waiting for the moment she could get away. She couldn't remember what she had taken, not even why – if she'd only meant to sleep or if really she had meant to die. She felt sore. She noticed that the black man was on the telephone, and she also sensed that Van Helding wanted to know what he was saying, but the screens absorbed the noise. The room was protected as though against earthquake and fire, a secure place for the occasional chatter of the telex, the faint electronic blips of the computers.

The black man had called Koolhoven, who came blearily awake on the telephone. He reported that Van Helding had arrived, with a woman, his wife. There were no problems. He had not said what he wanted.

Koolhoven said he would be there, immediately.

The black man offered coffee. Katherine wondered if she could take him aside and explain. She also wondered which side he would be on; it was never simple.

Koolhoven woke up Marisia and told her the news.

'Poor Katherine,' she said, and then, 'where is he?'

'That's the curious part,' Koolhoven said. 'He's in the international room at Security National. He's come back for something particular.'

'Maybe,' Marisia said, 'he came back for the end.'

'I could pick you up in twenty minutes,' Koolhoven said.

The great car settled by the Security National tower a half-hour later.

'We don't know what state Van Helding is in,' Koolhoven said. 'I take it we don't have a bruised and bloody jungle victim on our hands – and I assume he's rational. If he wasn't, the staff would have called the guards by now.'

'If they dared,' Marisia said. 'He's the president, after all.'

'They did sound puzzled, though.'

'It's not often the dead take an interest in the money markets,' David Grant said. He meant to be jocular but he sounded grim.

'We should go up,' Koolhoven said.

The quiet of the elevator in the silent building was almost oppressive. Nobody came to the doors, got in or got out. The place was lonely.

Fairbairn had already arrived. He was pacing the empty corridor by the executive offices, waiting for the others, furious.

'I knew this would happen,' he said.

'What do you mean?' Koolhoven said. 'You knew Pieter Van Helding would return?'

Fairbairn stamped his feet. It looked as though he was trying to keep them warm. 'I was a damn fool to let this happen. I should have brought the bank down before I trusted it to you.'

Koolhoven said: 'We don't know that.'

'I know that,' Fairbairn said. 'I reran your calculations on the two banks. I know damn well where we stand.'

'You're not the only one who built a great bank from nothing,' Koolhoven said. 'Pieter Van Helding did that, too.'

'We never closed our doors, not even for a day, not

even in 1929,' Fairbairn said. 'And he's pulled the whole thing down.'

'And he'll survive, I suppose,' Marisia said. 'You can't sue or prosecute or kill a man who's already dead.'

They went down to the international room.

Yesterday's deals still lay waiting to be cleared, but on the screen the moving dot spelled out millions moving to pay for a steel mill in Indonesia, money to pay off one gasoline supplier's bills in Kowloon, money put briefly into Security National's care, until ten in the morning. If they lost it all, if the cheques simply bounced because the bank was no longer there, the money would disappear – millions, even billions.

'Welcome,' Pieter Van Helding said. 'I'm glad you all came to watch money die.'

It was Fairbairn who, bull-like, stepped up to menace Van Helding, and called him a bastard. 'You ruined the whole thing,' he said.

Van Helding took the comment like a kiss.

'What do you know?' Marisia asked. 'Why are you back this particular night?'

'You'll see,' Van Helding said.

'Something's going to happen?' Koolhoven said. 'Is that why you're here? Kellerman Unger is going down?'

Van Helding listened to the speculations, but as he did so, he moved like an athlete restless for the start of action, unable to keep his body still. He turned back to say only: 'I don't know anything.'

'He knows,' Katherine said. 'He always boasts about his information.'

The neat black man came over and said deferentially: 'I'm sorry to interrupt, but the staff are having difficulty concentrating.'

Van Helding smiled, an abstracted smile.

Fairbairn watched the big numbers coming up on the

computer screens. He wanted to tell himself the figures were smaller than usual, a lesser risk. Yet the numbers stayed mercilessly huge. All the world's trade done in dollars flowed nightly though these machines and the rest of the New York Clearing House.

In Fairbairn's office, Van Helding was still truculent. He was only interested in the steady erosion of money that was taking place five floors down from these overtasteful offices.

'If you know somethings,' Koolhoven said, 'we need to know it, too. Perhaps we could stop the worst from happening if we were forewarned.'

'We could suspend trading,' Marisia suggested. 'I mean, just stop. Say we had a computer malfunction or something. That way, things couldn't get worse in the next few hours.'

'I don't dare,' Koolhoven said. 'Everyone's watching us at the moment and everyone's worried. Anything unusual is going to start a panic – even the rumours did last night. I had bank officers calling me up to ask if we'd had a power failure, if our computers were down. And they were frightened. I can't risk starting the end of Kellerman Unger and Security National, not unless I can't do anything else.'

David Grant made himself speak. 'What,' he said, 'are you going to do, Van Helding?' There are times when Grant's Englishness came close to caricature; Marisia waited for him to suggest that Van Helding do the decent thing.

'I don't have to do anything.' Van Helding said, reasonably.

'Then why are you here? What did you come back for?'

Van Helding smiled.

For Fairbairn, that was the last straw. The old man had taken to the great chair behind his desk, and in the top drawer was his pearl-handled Colt. He drew it from the desk and lay it on a blotter before him. He, also, smiled.

'Put it away, Fairbairn,' Koolhoven said, and turned to the others. 'Perhaps we should deal with this as a family thing.'

Fairbairn said: 'Does that mean I have to leave?'

'We might be able to talk more freely. I don't know that we will get anywhere.'

'Talk,' said Fairbairn, 'is not what we need.'

'I want to talk to Pieter,' Marisia said.

'Don't think you can shame him,' Fairbairn said. 'He's beyond shame. Just look at him and you can see that. The rest of us are scared and angry and confused, and for him it's just another scheme. It doesn't even stir him.'

He slammed the office door, sending a great wind through scattered papers.

Marisia looked out to the Art Deco neon of the Chrysler building, white bars and triangles in the night. 'It's over for you, too, Pieter,' she said, very softly.

For the first time, she was conscious of her own power against him; his trick had always been to stop other people sensing their advantage, to make them think he must have the upper hand. 'You think you're going to come through, but you're not.' She settled before him, squatting, looking very carefully into his eyes. 'You can't live without all the deals and the machines and the banks. You need all that. When the whole thing collapses, there'll be nothing for you to run or manipulate. You think you can just disappear and come back – but you can't come back. There'll be none of your life left.'

Koolhoven listened intently and took his cue. 'Maybe you wouldn't want to go on,' he said. 'Maybe you'd be better if you did simply disappear. The banks can't help you any more and your name doesn't work any more. It's not magic. I'm sorry.'

Van Helding shrugged, but he had begun to seem nervous. He could stand off against the Fairbairn bluster and the gun. Kind talk and gentleness unnerved him.

'No more friends,' Marisia said. 'That's the sad part. Nobody left who will do what you want. No more family or contacts or rich men in Palm Springs. They'll be after you, all of them, for revenge, and they will not give you anything else. You had your chance.'

'You failed,' David Grant said.

Marisia's idea was not to shock Van Helding or attack him. It was to use that same relentless, gentle pressure, that sweet but venomous reason, that he had used on brother Willem.

'You really did disappear, Pieter,' she said. 'You went out of people's minds when you vanished in the forest. You don't exist for them any more. If you did, they'd hate you.'

She came close to Van Helding, carefully not touching him.

'You remember what you told Willem. Bad blood. You remember how you told him the blood never changed.'

'He believed it,' Van Helding said, 'because he was very young.'

'I think you believed it, too.'

Van Helding got up, troubled but unshaken. Along the corridor there was the jangle of an alarm bell and the faint sound of men running. The telephone rang; a bass voice reported a false alarm. Nobody should worry. 'Systems malfunction,' he said.

'I shall survive,' Pieter said. 'Better than the rest of you, I think.'

'Willem thought that,' Marisia said. 'He was certain he could find out anything, be told anything.'

'I don't have Willem's sense of guilt.'

'Do you think you could know the whole truth about your father's death and still not have that sense of guilt?'

'There is no truth,' Van Helding said. 'Only information.'

Koolhoven shifted in his seat. He wondered what Van Helding would say and what its consequences would be. He wondered if Marisia had troubled to read the file they had found in the storeroom.

'You didn't really think I would fall for all this, did you?' Pieter said. 'I know how to persuade people, better than any of you.'

'If you had any sense of honour,' Marisia said, 'you'd go down with your empire.'

'I have already killed myself, officially,' Van Helding said. 'My name doesn't exist any more. I left all that on the riverbanks.'

'You can't hope to survive,' Marisia said. 'Too many people saw you here.'

'You don't understand yet, do you?' Pieter said. He had a trace of pity in his voice. 'This is the night money dies. This is a night when everything falls apart. There won't be a world tomorrow where I can be chased and caught.' He had glinting eyes, like a cat in the dusk. 'I found my limits and I brought everything down. I want to see that. I walk out of here without my name and that makes me safe. I walk away because there's nothing any more that I could run or control. The banks are dying tonight, don't you see that? Banks and money and trade and credit. Your world is dying. Why should it matter to me if people see me, when they won't catch me again once I've left this building? And why should I care if I can return or not? There is nothing to return to. Nothing.'

'That's theatre,' David Grant said. 'Just a speech.'

Van Helding looked offended. 'Theatre works,' he said. 'I got friends from Venezuela to send in a helicopter – a perfectly ordinary helicopter, with a few hired hands – and you believed I'd been slaughtered by guerrillas. It took one helicopter and four men. We hired them from one of the big savannah ranches. The rest you all imagined – and you can hardly stop yourselves believing it even now.'

'He doesn't listen,' Grant said. 'Don't you realize that? We speak and we think that he must be affected by what we say. But he knows exactly how to keep the sound and the sense out of his mind.'

'I just wish I knew what was happening in Amsterdam,' Koolhoven said. 'I wish I knew why he came back tonight.'

Out in the international room, Fairbairn sat before a computer terminal and watched the green spot move across the screen, leaving a line of luminous figures behind it like a trace of a snail. Seven million nine hundred thousand dollars traded, due to Hong Kong; another three and a half million due from Singapore, from a correspondent bank; a few moments of silence when the operators got up from their desks and stretched, and then the sharp, demanding blip that meant another transmission was playing itself out on the cathode-ray tube.

It was like a dance of money in its regular course and Fairbairn thought of a roundabout at some autumn fair suddenly stopping, and how the children and revellers would come tumbling down, and how the machine would sit wrecked in the middle of its red and gilt remains and the children would cry. The image would not leave him, a kind of childhood horror. Each green line on the screen, each new amount and new command, would once have satisfied him deeply – the proper workings of the great bank he had built. Now, the same lines were a reproach and they very efficiently brought nightmare closer.

Soon, they would stop, short. There would be an electronic silence. There would be no sounds or symptoms, as with a human drama, but only the blank screens. The operators would be puzzled. The phones would sound. And all the lovely, elegant, gaudy roundabout, with all its proud wonders, would lie broken.

'Busy night, Mr Fairbairn,' the shift foreman said. 'Nothing wrong, is there?'

'Just wanted to show people how things work.'

'I hope you're satisfied, Mr Fairbairn.'

'You're doing well. Keep it up.'

Too well, Fairbairn thought, too well. He took water from the cooler, thought briefly of the roundabout stopping, and found he had crushed the little paper cup and spilled the water. He dropped the cup; it was evidence. He climbed very slowly, feeling his age, up the back stairs of the building. They were half-lit and wintry, bare concrete and great, red EXIT signs. He felt for the gun in his pocket and what had long been a symbol of his eccentricity now seemed a test of will. He should kill Van Helding. Van Helding had taken everything from Fairbairn; Fairbairn could at least take life from Van Helding.

He dawdled on the stairs, breathing heavily with fear and exertion. He heard voices.

'I don't think any of you will want to stop me,' Pieter Van Helding was saying. 'And I really think it is time for me to go.'

Koolhoven's voice sounded as though feeling had been blotted out of it. 'Is there anywhere – anywhere we can reach you?' He knew the line was absurd, but he needed to know.

'Does it matter?' Van Helding asked.

Fairbairn was at the fire door. He could push it open and he would be at Van Helding's side. He could shoot and they would all be grateful.

Or would they? Van Helding was now officially dead, a man missing in the rain forest who could not hope to survive. That gave the others a chance to live through this night and the scandal that would follow; they had done their best. But if there was an inconvenient corpse, their story would be ruined. They would seem like accomplices with Van Helding.

Fairbairn held the gun firmly. He let off the safety catch.

'Adieu,' said Pieter Van Helding, elaborately. 'We may meet again.'

Fairbairn heard his footsteps pass.

And he turned the gun on himself, and fired. Heavy doors muffled the sound; it might have been a car backfiring on the street far below, the sound borne freakishly up the emergency stairs in the draught. Fairbairn fell, and Van Helding walked past his body hidden behind the walls.

The others were in a cluster, watching him walk away, making no move to follow. He walked like a man who is leaving the office for the evening, a little jaunty, perhaps anticipating an early evening tryst, happy with what he had done that day. He came to a stretch of corridor where the lights were out, and he vanished. The others heard the faint sound of the lift, saw the lights as the doors opened, and Pieter Van Helding stepped out of their lives.

In the elevator, he passed the first ten floors and went into the limbo marked 'X' on the floor guide. He decided to go back to the townhouse for a drink. There was no sense in waiting for the worst to happen, since he knew precisely what it was. He could have breakfast before the staff arrived at home, and then set out for JFK. The worst, he knew, was happening inexorably now on the hooded computer screens in the international room.

The elevator doors opened silently. He went briskly into the hallway, heels clattering on marble.

'Good night, sir,' the security guards said. He did not recognize their faces, but he assumed the shift had changed. He did not do more than mechanically acknowledge their politeness. He went to push at the revolving door.

The guards took him from behind, They pushed at the door, rushed him through, and bundled him into a waiting limousine. They left the door of the great bank tower propped open. The old man with the leg full of ripe sores pulled himself gratefully across the sidewalk to the prospect of warmth and shelter.

'What is this?' Van Helding said, out of breath.

He fixed on one seemingly kind and generous face, and placed the man with difficulty. 'Did I know you,' he said, 'in Palm Springs?'

The man grinned delightedly.

'I demand . . .'

Van Helding got no further. The man had kind eyes and a sawn-off shotgun, held to Van Helding's face.

'You don't demand,' he said. 'Mr Klein and the others didn't want you to miss nothing. And they didn't want you to skip.'

It was incongruous and sinister, a limousine of guards in peaked caps around a man in Cardin slacks and sweater. The car went down around the Helmsley building gilt and into Fifth Avenue, down the line of Victorian palaces and shops, past the lions of the Public Library and cold, dark, empty streets, past paper tousled in little winds and occasional great trucks roaring and churning through the night. It might have been dawn, but the sky was hidden.

They passed the Flatiron building, Barnes & Noble's bookstore, and then swung west on 14th Street. There were drunks to dazzle as they screamed round a corner, and one small theatrical scene in a pool of streetlight – a tiny, furious man screaming in Spanish, beating with a baseball bat on the head of what might have been a woman on the ground.

The locked shops and the Salvation Army citadel and

the funeral homes and Teamsters offices gave way to the less comforting West of Manhattan. There was a scatter of gay clubs among the blood and suet of the meat markets, The streets were narrow and slick and grim, without peace or hope, with great metal façades that hung with rails on which the carcasses would be swung off the trucks and into the warehouses. In the distance, there were the pale waters of the Hudson. There was a smell of dead animals.

The limousine stopped by a line of warehouses. Four men came downstairs from an anonymous doorway, cased in black leather, laughing. A handful of taxis cruised for the four-in-the-morning stragglers from the clubs. As they saw the limousine, they peeled away from the sidewalks as though they scented trouble.

The guards shoved Van Helding from the car, up onto the raised sidewalk. He did not try to escape; he seemed to be dazed. They rang a bell by a corrugated steel door, and a Judas door opened. They pushed Van Helding through.

The room was long and vaulted. A great elevated track ran around with killing hooks hanging down. The track would carry the animals whose fat and sinew and bone were muddled with sawdust on the floor and tamped down by workmen's boots. The place seemed to be deserted.

The guards said nothing. The smiling man kept the shotgun trained on Van Helding. They left him suspended awkwardly, feet barely touching the ground, hands slung from rope around one of the hooks. He shifted with difficulty, trying to take the weight off rope-burned wrists. He hung there dumbly as they went away, and when the Judas door closed again, he thought to shout.

'Is anybody there?

'Please help me.

'Help me.'

He wondered if sound could pass the great steel doors.

He wondered if anyone would listen, or if passers-by would think he was crying as part of some psychodrama at the outer fringes of eroticism. Nobody could help him unless he could help himself.

Someone slipped into the room. Van Helding knew it. There was movement behind him. There was the sound of heavy feet, of some kind of avenger coming towards Van Helding as he struggled on the hook. He tried to look over his shoulder.

In the shadows, advancing, was a man in a leather mask, an executioner. The fetishistic walk, the sense of swagger, told Van Helding he was the victim now.

The executioner stood before him.

'Pieter Van Helding,' the man said. He took his glove and struck Van Helding across the face, and the metal buckle drew blood above the eye. The warm, slow trickle worked down until Van Helding was blinking, struggling to see, terrified that in his vulnerable state he would lose the use of his eyes.

And the executioner unmasked.

Henry Klein had left his quiet, suburban retreat in Westchester County that night, to amuse himself. He had not expected the message from the guards; he had believed that Pieter Van Helding was dead. But now the man who had disappointed him, made him look bad, was at his mercy, and it suited Henry Klein to have a victim. He could revenge himself and amuse himself, all at once.

Klein thought he should congratulate the guards in the morning. They had shown great initiative. They earned their pay.

'I did warn you,' Klein said. 'We will not be disappointed.'

He paced away for a moment and swung back.

'You will bring down banks, and maybe you will bring

down money, but you won't bring us down. We remain. We remember.'

Klein circled Van Helding, who hated most the moments when the voice, echoing from the iron rafters, seemed to come from behind him.

'You broke contract,' Klein said. He jerked the rope so that the banker's body became taut, and he began to tear away Van Helding's clothes until he was naked. He reached up to the rope and released it.

'It's the last game,' Klein said. 'Run. You can run wherever you like.'

Van Helding shuffled from foot to foot, instinctive responses gone. He realized he had pissed himself. He was unsure for the first time in his life of what he should do for the best.

'Run,' Klein said. 'Or I'll kill you here.'

Van Helding felt no hope. He made himself tense his muscles and sprint off across bone and rails upon the floor, terrified that in the dark he would collide with a fine knife or a great hooked engine of the meat trade. Bare like a carcass, skin grey when he came to an area lighted by the first dawn sun, he put back his head as he ran and he screamed.

At seven o'clock, the telex outside Fairbairn's office began to hammer out a message. 'Urgent Confidential,' it read. It seemed to have been written by someone unfamiliar with the tricky shifts of the machine. It was interspersed with occasional lines of figures, randomly typed.

'OFFICE BANK INSPECTORATE ENTERED KELLERMAN UNGER TWO REPEAT TWO TODAY DECLARED INSOLVENT SHUT DOORS REPEAT INSOLVENT PLEASE ACKNOWLEDGE.'

Koolhoven was hollow-eyed, and Marisia asleep on the sofa in his office. David Grant said he would send the answer when Koolhoven had prepared it. It was something to do, something familiar from days in sweaty tropical telex offices. He hit the unyielding, awkward keys mechanically. He hardly registered, through shock and tiredness, the message he was sending.

'CONFIRM RECEIPT INSOLVENCY MESSAGE KELLERMAN UNGER AMSTERDAM PLEASE SAY EXTENT PROBLEMS PLEASE SAY LIKELY EFFECT SECURITY NATIONAL.'

The machine spewed out white punched tape, the tape ran swiftly through its gates to send the message, and the machine went quiet. They could only wait.

In eleven minutes the telex machine spoke again.

'ANTICIPATE INSOLVENCY SECURITY NATIONAL BASED OBLIGATIONS CALLS KELLERMAN UNGER,' it said.

Koolhoven took the strip of paper and stared at it. The Dutch authorities would already have told the New York authorities. Their message would lie in the Federal Reserve, and perhaps also in the New York Clearing House, through the morning hours, like an omen.

Marisia stirred and rubbed her eyes. The night had been hot and oppressive. The air still seemed close. She wanted to leave the building and walk in some fresh, green park, but she knew that was impossible. She held David Grant's hand. She had lived so much with him that she had almost forgotten that he was central to her life, and his touch, after arid weeks of suspicion, was welcome. She saw Koolhoven's exhaustion, and Katherine curled in a corner, her furs sprawled over her like a friendly pack of warm animals. She wanted at least to prowl the corridors for a while.

She noticed the side door marked EXIT and she tried to see where it would lead. Push as she would, the door would not budge, as though something were lying against it, something heavy. She pushed again, and it gave a little. She slipped through. She saw Fairbairn lying there, saw blood and the little pearl-handled gun. Her first thought was how such a fine toy of a gun could lie in such a ham of a fist, and make such a terrible explosion inside the old man's head.

She retched, but she pulled herself back. If she could wait out a night like this, she could cope with death. She went to call the guards, but they did not answer. She thought of the guards on the front door. She took the elevator down and walked through the echoes of the marble hallway.

The avenue door was open. The first of the day shifts were arriving, and the cleaners were just leaving. The ordinary ebb and flow of the building had begun for the day. Out of their changing room the new shift of guards came smartly, in almost military formation.

Marisia said: 'We have some problems.'

They barricaded the doors of the building, notified the police, set up a cordon to keep the public away from the entrance. For once the public park around the tower was useful. As the managers came in, they were deputed to shut down the central retail computer which managed the kerbside electronic banks. The branches were all sealed off, with managers instructed to call their staff to stop them coming to work; then the managers installed themselves in glass cages, with extra guards and a supply of food.

At seven forty, Security National told its correspondent banks worldwide that it had ceased to conduct business. The Federal Reserve was officially informed. The process seemed to have taken only minutes, and Koolhoven summoned in senior vice presidents to audit the books as thoroughly as possible.

'The sooner we know how bad things are,' he said, 'the sooner we know if we have a chance of reopening.'

Koolhoven looked at his watch. They had until ten, but not a minute longer, to decide if Security National could reopen its doors. The Federal Reserve, of course, might order them shut, but it would be unusual for it to do so with such speed. It was unusual enough for a bank to shut voluntarily. But the decision hour was ten, when the clearing process for domestic cheques began. Either Security National could accept and pay, or it couldn't.

At eight thirty-five, the computer systems went into overload, blinking 'GARBAGE, GARBAGE, GARBAGE' at the anxious vice presidents.

At nine, the men from the Federal Reserve arrived and Koolhoven tried to explain just how serious things were.

'You've been very honest,' the men from the Fed said.

'We're past the point of hiding anything.'

'Maybe you should have passed that point some time ago.'

On the central CHIPS computer, in its grand home on Church Street, operators under the Fed's watchful eye began to rerun transactions of the night and the previous day to see what harm had been done by the sudden closures. The sums were horrific. There were billions in the system which were frozen now until the final accounting for both banks, and the final accounting would take weeks. Until then, other banks would suffer and fall, and the market in dollars had suspended itself – like a suicide.

The CHIPS computer operators were grim-faced at first, but then fascinated by the data-pig's challenge that faced them. Fingers bounced over keys, conjuring up the basic equation: take two great banks from the world's economy, and what's left?

Seventeen senior bank officials from outside the failed banks called to see what was happening. Of these, eight asked for Fairbairn in person, and would not be satisfied with any account of where or how he was. Koolhoven had no desire to report a suicide; he had ordered the guards to leave the body where it had fallen, and to block the stairs so that nobody should find it by accident.

By ten minutes to ten, the senior men from New York's banks were clamouring for the too few chairs in the mahogany room which served as the clearing house boardroom. They squabbled over where to sit; there was one fist fight.

The Federal Reserve men had concentrated on using their diplomatic privileges to check with other central banks on the impact of the failures. Rome was desolate, convinced a dozen weak banks would go down. London reported that one of the high street clearing banks, already in big trouble on its Third World loans, would be badly hurt, and might open late the next day. Businesses with close links to the Grunwalds had already gone down for, as Koolhoven found it easy to forget, there were three banks that had collapsed. The Grunwalds were not just a trigger; they were a disaster in their own right.

The Fed reported, inexactly, that in their opinion the whole thing was catastrophic.

And it was only beginning. Commuters on their way to work stopped at banks, and found every Security National branch was sealed. The kerbside banks, where they were accessible, showed TEMPORARILY OUT OF SERVICE. The telephone for complaints did not answer. Doors to the main bank buildings were guarded and a handful of tellers milled inside with junior bank officers. At five past nine, it was obvious the closing was not coincidence. Twenty furious depositors rushed the 57th Street branch in Manhattan, hurling stones from the next-door building site.

And it was only beginning. Telephone lines into the bank were all constantly busy. Firms dependent on drafts for payment on orders – money stuck in the sealed Security National computer – began to puzzle over when they would be paid, if ever. Big department stores stopped taking credit cards with Security National on them. One Security National executive landed at JFK from Denver and knew the bank was down when he tried to hire a car with a VISA card on Security National. It was a gold card and he was refused.

The street word spread like wildfire. People seemed to have expected some terrible news to focus all their fury about money and jobs and rents and survival. Now they had it, their reactions were sharp and ready.

At ten past ten Marisia tried to talk to the assembled CHIPS bankers. She was shouted down at first, but she stood against the bellowing, very calm. She reported what had happened, flatly, and then said:

'At this moment, gentlemen, we are not able to honour any documents drawn on the bank, nor can we process any transactions involving the bank.'

That line brought a brief silence and then uproar.

'We are trying to calculate the exact scale of the default. We are trying to minimize the damage.'

A tall, grey, distinguished man in the front row rose and he shouted with all his force: 'You idiotic bastards. You bloody murdered money.'

The city turned sour in morning heat that was heavy with humidity. It curdled tempers, stoked panic. On Wall Street the rumours took the Dow Jones down by 200 points in twenty minutes – a drop accounted for by specialists' alarm. Some men watched all their substance go in the arbitrary dealing – nobody was buying to set a price – and they ran into narrow, dark streets of the financial district crying out loud. They felt something unjust, vindictive, unreasonable had happened, and they wanted to blame God.

Crowds jostled on the streets around the bank's

branches, and where the crowds assembled, the traffic backed up and let loose with its horns. On 14th Street, a wagon loaded with kebabs and the fire to cook them was rammed repeatedly into the glass doors of the bank. A furious lady in her sixties, white-masked and armoured in powder and lacquer, drew a gun on a guard and shot around her wildly.

The dealers in cocaine in the churchyard of Trinity, near Wall Street, had their worst morning in years, until twelve thirty, when suddenly everyone wanted an escape.

Downtown, by Washington Square, a policeman was tumbled from his horse by the crowds, and trampled.

Nobody stayed in their office that morning. They came outside to the oppressive streets, to find out what was happening, to see. The anger in the crowds was something to be touched and felt. The people who innocently went out to early lunches found themselves in the middle of a city gone mad.

The National Guard was called, on Governor Cuomo's orders.

At eleven thirty, Koolhoven was called from the CHIPS boardroom to take papers from a messenger who had struggled downtown with them on subway trains which were now a dance of riot.

Koolhoven reported the figures to the other bankers. Each had in front of him a quick calculation, done in his head office, of how bad the problems would be before each particular bank failed.

Koolhoven sat down. Men ticked or crossed on papers before them. One put his head in his hands.

'Holy shit,' said the man from Citibank. 'It's the goddamn end.'

Through the morning, the trucks came to the meat market, full of cold, stiff flesh. Great railways took the carcasses from the roadside to the deep freeze – pale, bloody beasts, without heads, gutted, open, great ribs splayed. Faint, soft, excremental smells still hung around them.

As the carcasses passed, an old man counted them in. There was something different among the bruised, hanging flesh. He saw a body that was smaller, headless and open, but with weakling ribs and a narrow pelvis and legs that were much too thin to yield meat.

The old man stopped the line.

11

The rain came at midday, violent rain that hammered at the sidewalks and turned the air smoky. Saturated crowds huddled in doorways, or else stood out in the street with their anger for shield against the weather. Water cascaded down into one subway line and left it flooded out, adding to the chaos of a city that had already lost its temper and was close to losing its mind. It was not so much the fact of one bank shutting, but the terrible rumours, the lack of news, and the sudden caution of banks and businesses alike.

At one, Koolhoven decided there was nothing else to do. In time, they would have to calculate the last balance sheet of two great banks, but neither could be salvaged. With Katherine, Marisia and David, he went to the East Side heliport and took the flight to JFK in time for the afternoon Concorde. They were among the few who made a clear, early exit from the city.

The place was sodden and wretched now, as miserable as angry. Crowds milled around for their money and fights broke out and the police had no more control. They could see the wide tracks of tanks on Fifth Avenue from the air, and that white middle-class uprising did nothing for the summer tinder in Harlem. As the helicopter pulled away from Manhattan, the first belches of chemical fire were lighting up the storm-dark buildings. They were starting to torch the city.

'I never thought of this,' Marisia said. She stared at the colours in the billowing fire.

'Very simple,' David Grant said. 'This morning, they lost hope. It's made them mad.'

'We could have done something else. We could have . . .'

'Nothing,' Koolhoven said. 'Too late.'

Early the next morning they were in Amsterdam, and Koolhoven gave them virtual orders to find what haven they could. The sights of New York burning were on the front pages, and the impact of the Kellerman Unger closing was sudden and horrid. There had been an overnight lull; nobody had thought the closing of some merchant bank whose name they hardly knew could touch their lives. Instead, it broke them.

Koolhoven, in his office overlooking the fires and the canal, told his story to the small machine. He wondered who would hear it, whether it would burn up with some petrol-filled Coke bottle the kids were throwing in an access of anarchy or whether the army would bury it with the heavy artillery they were now wheeling into place.

For after a day, the panic in New York had taken Europe. It began with sophisticated, calculating men who realized the scaffolding of international business had suddenly folded on itself. Every piece of paper was in doubt. Trust broke, the dollar broke, and the bourses tumbled.

Koolhoven had been two days in the Kellerman Unger offices, but the war zone came too close to the doors and the canalside, and he knew it was more important to stay alive than to assess the damage.

It was time for them all to move out. It seemed necessary to make formal farewells, even in the middle of this confusion. There was risk in coming to the heart of Amsterdam, but there was risk on the unpoliced roads. The troubles in banks made perfect cover for assorted thieves and terrorists, with special ambitions. The city seemed no worse than the open plains.

David and Marisia came first. Koolhoven stood to

welcome them by the bank doors. Soft plumes of grey smoke tinted the sky, like a cloud tethered near the street. It looked friendly and smelled of sulphur.

'We have a plane at Haarlem,' Marisia said. 'Schiphol is almost empty. People just crashed the flights – to be anywhere else.'

'Where will you go?'

'Scotland,' Marisia said. 'We bought a house there years ago. Funny, we found out later it belonged to a Mrs Rogerson – the mother of Pieter's Sally. We met her once. She was drunk.'

'It seems secure,' David Grant said. 'If anywhere is secure.'

'There'll be refugees,' Koolhoven said.

'Yes,' Grant said, 'but no gas and no transport.'

'Is Katherine going with you?' Marisia asked Koolhoven.

'No,' he said. 'She wants to be with her family. I suppose they think it's like the revolution all over again and they want to be in a fortified house, together.'

'Things aren't so rational,' David Grant said. 'You can't tell what's safe.'

'I think of Pieter,' Marisia said. 'He ruined all those wonderful paper castles, and when they blew away there was nothing but fear.'

'The castles were rotten,' Koolhoven said. 'He did nothing other banks didn't do. It no longer had anything to do with real wealth. It was a huge, marvellous game to play, a way to divert attention from the world of things and obligations. Just that. But he was a brilliant man.'

'I don't want to hear,' David Grant said.

'But you should,' Koolhoven said. 'I sometimes wonder if this time he has really disappeared.'

'You hope, don't you?' Marisia said. 'I suppose you

love him. I suppose I did, at least until the end. It was love. It wasn't just fascination.'

A little boy came pelting out of shadows, scampering along the street. An adolescent ahead of him heard footsteps, seemed to panic, turned and fired an air pistol he had hidden under his coat. The boy fell down.

'No more talk,' David Grant said.

'David's friends in London,' Marisia said, 'seem to think the Soviets have massed along the border – Baltic to Trieste. They say the old men in the Kremlin are terrified of what's happening in Europe – they think they'll have to police it for themselves. And they say there is no way the Americans will put up with that.'

'I don't see the Russians saving us from ourselves,' Grant said. He still looked out of the window, into the city of nightmare. 'There's a car. It must be Katherine.'

She had an escort, the Baron Gilles de Grunwald, stiffly sitting in the front of the car with a shotgun. The driver was a man called Noam Gregory.

'I'm going back to the family,' Katherine said. 'If God is good.'

And they kissed, and the driver blew the horn impatiently, and they said goodbyes.

Katherine drove away along the canalside road. The Baron Gilles seemed to have won back his life, guarding a convoy, working his mind as he would have done in the Resistance days. His eyes shone.

The car disappeared behind a curtain of black, sour smoke that came from oil burning on water.

They checked Grant's car, in case some unseen saboteur had passed while they were talking, and Marisia embraced Koolhoven. As he stepped into his car, she said: 'I loved him too.'

'I know,' Koolhoven said. 'I wanted to be close to him and to make things work for him. You do know why, don't you?' His strong, old face was shattered now, broken by lines and sleeplessness. 'I was very close to your mother. I . . . I wanted your father dead. It didn't work like that. And I had to look after Pieter and cherish him.'

Koolhoven started the engine of his car.

'You'll find out in time,' he said. 'You always love your first-born son.'

The limousine window snapped into place, electrically, and Koolhoven was no more than a blur behind tinted glass.

David Grant said to Marisia: 'Let's get out of here.'